"The Moonstone Covenant is a many-layered feat of imagination, gathering the stories of four very different women who share a marriage—as difficult a feat in their world as it would be in ours—and spinning them through the traumas of a world on the edge of chaos, a place where magic is core to the lives of the women who wield it, but is loathed and feared by those who surround them. Each wife's viewpoint, her unique voice, opens up the weave of this world, leading us by the hand into a magical and spiritual system deeply embedded in the earth: trees speak here, and have opinions that can change the way the world works.

In lyrical and beautiful language, Jill Hammer lays bare the prejudices of an island landscape where the waterways are as important as highways. Through the tale of a four-way marriage, she carries us into the depths of relationships between women, the flows of feeling and passion, history and trust, treachery both imagined and real. Betrayal lies at the heart of this story, but its healing is a thread running through from the start. A genuinely engaging, enlivening, and inspiring read!"
—**Manda Scott**, author of *Any Human Power* and host of the *Accidental Gods* podcast

"Part murder mystery, part political thriller, part fantasy epic, *The Moonstone Covenant* celebrates the power and wisdom of books, the natural world, and queer love. This wondrous novel is a gift of imagination for readers everywhere."
—**Jonathan Vatner**, author of *Carnegie Hill* and *The Bridesmaids' Union*

"Like Tolkien and Le Guin, Jill Hammer has conjured up a richly detailed world, alive with magic, political intrigue, and a robust cast of fascinating characters. Readers of fantasy will love this book!"
—**Ellen Frankel**, author of *The Deadly Scrolls*

TURTLE'S CLUTCH
HUNDRED KEYS
HUNDRED QUAYS
SCATTERED PEARLS
Niniane's Spear
THE LID
SORCERER'S KETTLE
The Palace
Short Bridge
STRING OF COINS
The Library
OPAL ISLAND
Sand Market
Drake's Hoard Bath
Gilded Bridge
JUNIPER ISLAND
DRAKE'S HOARD
GOLDEN SANDS
Long Bridge
SEVEN LANTERNS
Sandwell
The Sanctum
Sandmaze
THE LANTERNELLES
HOLY IBIS
Undersong House
THE PERFUMERY
Bilha'a
MOON'S DAUGHTERS
VEXMERE
Cedara
VEXRIVER
LITTLE VEX
The Fortress
Vexenden

THE MOONSTONE COVENANT

THE MOONSTONE COVENANT

Jill Hammer

Ayin Press

This book was made possible through the generous support of the Opaline Fund, Anne Germanacos, and Lippman Kanfer Foundation for Living Torah. We are grateful for their commitment to the transformative power of creative work, and to amplifying a polyphony of voices from within and beyond the Jewish world.

Cover illustration by Federico Parolo
Moonstone map illustration by Melina Sonia Monteagudo
Cover and book design by Cem Eskinazi
Typesetting by Utkan Dora Öncül

Typeset in Fedra Serif, designed by Peter Biľak *with Bahman Eslami, Kristyan Sarkis, Khajag Apelian, Gayaneh Bagdasarya, Panagiotis Haratzopoulos, and Michal Saha.*
Released by the Netherlands-based foundry Typotheque in 2003.
Printed in the USA

First Edition
First Printing

Ayin Press
Brooklyn, New York
www.ayinpress.org
info@ayinpress.org

Distributed by Publishers Group West, an Ingram brand

ISBN (paperback): 978-1-961814-15-8
ISBN (e-book): 978-1-961814-16-5

Library of Congress Control Number: 2024931835

THE DISTRICTS AND CHARACTERS OF MOONSTONE

THE THIRTEEN DISTRICTS OF MOONSTONE

Golden Sands
Holy Ibis
Hundred Quays
Juniper Island
Moon's Daughters
Opal Island (The Library)
The Perfumery
Scattered Pearls
Seven Lanterns
Sorcerer's Kettle
String of Coins
Turtle's Clutch
Vexriver

THE RESIDENTS OF UNDERSONG HOUSE

Olloise Mazall
Apothecary, daughter of *Zevid* and *Nidaba Mazall*
Istehar Sha'an
Illuminatrix of the Sha'an people
Annlynn Jissakhar
Warrior Librarian of the Moonstone Library, daughter of *Sterven Jissakhar,* Lord Censor of the Library
Vasmine Kinora
Ink-merchant,
daughter of *Taurelanthe Kinora*
Bastina Rhuga
Housekeeper

THE HOUSE OF MAI

Rulers of Moonstone, Keepers of the Library, Rulers of the District of Opal Island
Archprince Jalian Mai
Archprincess Tilgana Mai
Daughter of *Hanae of Mor* and sister of *Lord Griseus of Mor*
Prince Vilya Mai
Son of *Jalian* and *Tilgana*
Princess Kalicent Mai
Daughter of *Jalian* and *Tilgana*
Archprince Surian Mai ☿
Founder of the dynasty of Mai

LADIES-IN-WAITING OF PRINCESS KALICENT

Zelibet Fosca
Memmiam Yurenai
The archdeacon's daughter

THE HOUSE OF DHAGURA

Rulers of the District of Seven Lanterns
Prince Hoel Dhagura
Chief Interrogator of the Moonstone Council of Princes
Princess Angelissa Dhagura
Wife of *Prince Hoel*
Prince Aske
Heir to *Prince Hoel*

THE HOUSE OF LUTEI

Rulers of the District of String of Coins
Prince Giya Lutei
Prince Symiel Lutei ☿
Father of *Prince Giya Lutei*
Princess Praxinia Lutei ☿
Great-grandmother of *Prince Giya*
Prince Karel Lutei ☿
Founder of the dynasty of Lutei

THE HOUSE OF ZUZIERRE

Rulers of the District of Golden Sands
Prince Egno Zuzierre
Princess Talva Zuzierre
Sister of *Prince Egno*

THE HOUSE OF NETHRE
Rulers of the District of Scattered Pearls
Prince Hallan Nethre

THE HOUSE OF CHEI
Rulers of the District of Sorcerer's Kettle
Princess Sajine Chei
Lady Onyxe Chei
Wife of *Princess Sajine*
Tesper Chei
Husband of *Princess Sajine*

THE HOUSE OF QUAREEN
Rulers of the District of Holy Ibis
Prince Ebel Quareen

THE HOUSE OF BERDUIN
Rulers of the District of the Moon's Daughters
Princess Sylte Berduin

WARRIOR LIBRARIAN CLAN OF THE JISSAKHAR
Sterven Jissakhar
Lord Censor of the Library
Elibet Jissakhar
Wife of *Sterven Jissakhar*
Valenten Jissakhar
Supervisor, Night Bookwardens
Farrick Jissakhar
Director of Acquisitions, Art Division
Lieta Jissakhar
Wife of *Farrick Jissakhar*
Julis Jissakhar
Coordinator of Fire Safety
Melgret Jissakhar
Archivist, Legal Division
Dunekin Jissakhar
Chief Supervisor of Loading Docks
Jada Jissakhar
Surgeon

OTHER STAFF OF THE GREAT LIBRARY
Oskin Feathe
Assistant to the Director of Client Oversight
Galter Heyn
Assistant Director of the Maps Division
Tommas Penthenos
Archivist, Controlled Section
Kirin Spong
Librarian-in-Chief
Renice en Frone
Catalogue Hall Technician

CLERGY OF THE ABBATINE CHURCH
Fausten Yurenai
Archdeacon (father of *Memmiam*)
Beldrus Leathe
High Deacon of the Shrine of Holy Ibis
Ursel Kyze
Deaconess and tutress of *Tilgana Mai*

PEOPLE OF THE SHA'AN
Nizhar Sha'an
Healer and tribal leader of the Sha'an
Tiarath Sha'an
Gardener and friend to *Istehar*
Dozya Sha'an
Tiarath's husband and caretaker of Undersong House
Hanael Sha'an
Boatman
Eyra Sha'an
Warrior
Maliki Sha'an
Flower seller
Ketiya Sha'an
Chief teacher of the Sha'an school for children
Lalvah Sha'an
Nurse
Salomir Sha'an
Elder
Yilshik Sha'an
Silk house supervisor
Lufriki and Eferel Sha'an
Silkworkers
A'ariya Sha'an
Their daughter
Mereb Sha'an
Elder
Zilfa Sha'an ☿
Illuminatrix
Nurifir Sha'an ☿
Healer
Leona'ar Sha'an and Tiarath Sha'an the elder ☿☿
Istehar's parents

TEACHERS AND STUDENTS OF THE RIVER SCHOOL
Abigella Shorn
Rectoress
Othe Azhuin
Healer, a man of the Zhinj
Joeve
Student

Selba
Student
Chessa
Student
Pirrip
Student
Ursario
Student

RESIDENTS AT YAN'S

Moa Nhakbir
Bartender at Yan's
Fimias
Bookkeeper at Yan's
Thalweg
Fortuneteller

OTHERS

Cattiette Salbera
Captain of the Skyboat
Darda'a
Zhinj houndskeeper
Fyfe
Palace boatman
Lerreg
Bookseller
Ngin
Pawnbroker
Saroi and Horgance
Lacemakers
Shem and Yora
Flour-millers
Tamsyr
Laundress, cousin of *Tommas Penthenos*
Taurelanthe Kinora
Retired concubine of the lord provost of the College of Scattered Pearls and *Vasmine*'s mother
Trip
Innkeeper at the Leaning Inn
Uhela
Zhinj milkwife
Zevid Mazall ☿
Apothecary
Nidaba Mazall ☿
Benefactress and assassin

☿ The person is deceased.

For Raya Leela
of whom I am so proud

THE MOONSTONE COVENANT

CHAPTER 1
Istehar Sha'an, Illuminatrix
Juniper Island
Anteceday, 11:00 a.m.

At the foot of the stairs to the Juniper Island bookmarket, a dozen bookboats huddle close to the shore—crowded, overburdened, shambling creatures of slats, spines, and pages. The goods are second-rate—scribbled-in textbooks, castoffs from estate sales, bestsellers from decades ago, crude children's stories painted on wood, pamphlets printed by ranting fanatics. These things are what the poor can afford, and the bookboats recycle them over and over again, buying an item back at a quarter what someone paid for it. Bookboats are floating piles of junk—beneath any Librarian's notice, Annlynn says, and she's a Librarian, so she should know. But now and then something unusual surfaces from the maelstrom, like a spout from a whale's blowhole. And that is what I'm looking for.

I wince as a portly bookwife leans across a gap, her boat tilting, to upbraid a colleague who's blocked the lane. I've seen one of those boats go over—or worse, catch fire. When it happens, the whole neighborhood jumps into the water to help save the merchandise—those books are someone's livelihood, after all. And it's Moonstone. Books are sacred.

But I've also seen the Library censors come and burn a boat to the waterline for having some book it's not supposed to have. To a censor, a book is only sacred if it's legal. The booksellers take risks anyway, with pillow books and strange religious tracts and works of arcane magic and tell-all tales about government officials. Romance, heresy, and sedition sell, no matter what city or century. Humans are what they are.

I pull off my shoes and shove them into my bag, then hop up onto a bookboat close to shore. I scan the shelves and boxes and listen for a moment. The bookseller, in the stern, scrambles toward the prow, sales pitch on his lips, and pauses, confused by my stillness. I don't hear what I'm looking for, so before he recovers and reaches me, I hop onto the next bookboat.

This one is anchored under a little willow with yellow branches bending down to the water's surface. Yes, there's something here. Mixed with the hum of the tree is a harsher buzzing sound—the books. One yowls out its maudlin romance, another spews political rage, a third officiously gives advice about canal-dredging. My head starts to ache, but the humble, gentle song of the willow steadies me. I remember when I was a child in the Sha'an forest, and I'd put my hand to a tall cypress or an overhanging cherry, and it would tell me which animals or people had passed that way, how much rainfall there had been that winter, which leaf would cure a plague. My pregnant mother lived inside a giant hollow syssyrup tree for months, in the hope that I'd become a tree-speaker and one day be the tribe's illuminatrix. I remember that tree, too, its hollow fragrant with sap. I visited it often as a child. You could sing inside it and your voice would be magnified, deepened, as if you had become a tree yourself.

"Oi, Snowhair," the grizzled proprietor calls from mid-boat. Some of the booksellers call me Madam Sha'an, and some call me "Reverence"—which in Moonstone is the proper term for a religious functionary (though by law, as a foreign clergyperson, I'm not entitled to the title). Some of them don't talk to me at all, and think I might be a madwoman, witch, or bookthief. Those booksellers stare to make sure I don't pocket anything. But the ones who know me from when I was younger and climbing around these canals know me as Snowhair. Years ago, when I wrote my first Book of the Tree in my twelfth year, I spent all night among the roots of a gnarled old apple tree, listening and transcribing, the book's cover of soft bark smooth in my hands.

In the morning, the book was finished, the tree had bloomed, and the fine, wavy hair that fell in a mass down my back was white as snow. Olloise calls that story my "fairy tale," but it's true.

"Afternoon, Lerreg," I respond, using my staff to balance on the rocking boat. "Anything good today?"

"Sure," he grins. "In the mood for a pillow book? I always got bunches of those. The housewives sell 'em when they're done reading 'em."

To be friendly, I return the grin. "Maybe one day." There's something here, something that wants to be found. Bracing myself with the staff, I squat by a box that looks like a fruit crate and search through pamphlets, tolerating their mewling voices. One of them comes easily to my hand, but when I touch it, it gives off an awful, hateful chitter. When I look more closely, I drop it in disgust.

"Oi, don't harm the merchandise," Lerreg complains.

"How can you have this here?" I demand. Lerreg hangs his head a bit. I pick the thing back up. It's a screed published by Vilya, crown prince of Moonstone. On the cover is an image of a gaunt sun-browned man in a tattered robe, with eerie green eyes, dipping his knotted fingers into the purse of a well-dressed, well-coiffed lady. The man looks something like a tree, and a great deal like my uncles and cousins—men of the Sha'an forests.

It's an outrage that Vilya should paint my people this way. Sha'an fighters fought off Lord Griseus of Mor and his soldiers long enough for many of us to escape. Sha'an healers helped us survive on the long journey downriver to Moonstone. I would surely have been killed if kind villagers had not taken me to safety after my parents' death, when I hid inside the hollow tree and sobbed, and would gladly have died there defending the place of my birth.

"It's written by the crown prince himself," Lerreg points out.

"More's the pity," I mutter.

"They was handing them out at a canal bridge," Lerreg adds. "I thought I'd just take a few. As a curiosity. They're legal!"

"The archprince shouldn't permit this to go on," I say.

"Well, that could be true, Reverence," Lerreg says, becoming distant, and likely angry with me. "But there's plenty of people think there's too much foreign magic in Moonstone."

"Foreign magic cured the archprince," I reply coldly.

"Mm," Lerreg half-agrees, and looks away. But I'm on thin ice. I shouldn't admit to magic, or even speak of it.

The archprince, Jalian Mai, is a tolerant man—one might say, a placid one. His people benefit, and sometimes suffer, from his benign neglect. He was ill much of his early life. When we Sha'an came here, bedraggled and wounded, we brought rare healing mosses with us. Using those medicines, the healer Nurifir Sha'an cured the archprince of his illness. Jalian Mai has favored us ever since, helping us tend our poor and our orphans these last ten years.

But Jalian's only legitimate son, Vilya, surrounds himself with fools and charlatans peddling hatred of my people. Savages, he calls us—beggars feeding off Moonstone's riches and infesting the city with impure magics. Maybe Vilya hates us because by saving his father, we deprived him of the throne he craves and is so ill-suited to occupy. Or maybe his reclusive mother, the archprincess Tilgana, has poisoned his mind against us. She is, after all, from the House of Mor, and sister to the man who exiled us and burned our forests for farmland.

"Anyway," I say, "we're not foreign anymore. We live here."

I shove the detestable thing in my bag to show Annlynn. "Don't you dare charge me for it," I growl at Lerreg, who glowers at me uneasily. He may have known me since I was fourteen, but like many Moonstone folk, he's superstitious about my people, and my hair. I prepare to jump onto the next bookboat, but something stops me. There's something here, among the voices of the books murmuring their little tales. Something for Olloise. A birthday present.

I prowl the rows of sacks and boxes and find a sturdy leather envelope, much finer than the type I normally see on such a boat. "Where'd you come upon this?" I ask, carefully squeezing it open. Lerreg says nothing and I don't expect him to.

What I find in the envelope is old. I'm not Annlynn, but we've all learned a smattering of one another's trades over the years. I can see a number of very small linen-bound books, carefully sewn at the spine. When I take one out and page through it, traces of gold illumination sparkle on the pages. As I leaf carefully through the tiny volumes, one seems to grasp at my fingers.

The title on the cover reads: *The Poisoner's Guide to Moonstone: A History of Murders by Elixir*. When I open the book, I find a variety of tales, from the boastings of an alchemist to the plottings of a courtesan, all ending with the story of a fatal venom. Some of the pages reveal recipes for the poisons they describe.

"Cheerful," I comment to myself. And it might be illegal, if anyone could actually understand it. The language is from so long ago it's hard to decipher, like an ancient play staged at the Library theater. It might upset Olloise, remind her of her parents' murder. But it's speaking to me, and I have to trust that.

In the same way I can listen to trees, I can listen to books, so long as they're made of plant matter. But unlike the dense, slow songs of the trees, the voices of books are tree-consciousness mixed with human intentions: brighter and louder. Neither trees nor books tend to use the kind of speech one gets in a conversation: usually, it's more like a jumble of feelings and images. But still, I can size up an author's intention without even touching the cover. It's unfair, Annlynn says, that I can read books without opening them. A Librarian could use such a gift, she says. But this talent appears only rarely even among my people, who lived among the great trees of the Sha'an forest for generations—until a despot drove us out so he could own the trees himself, and cut them down at will.

"This one I'll pay you for," I say to Lerreg, and drop a silver coin into his hand, more than he's seen in a month, I would guess.

"Likely worth more'n that," he objects halfheartedly.

"Maybe," I say politely. I wish I hadn't gotten angry with him. The city is steeped in hatred; it's not his fault. "Thanks, Lerreg. Drop the rest of the prince's pamphlets in the river, will you?" I wrap the small book in the extra shawl I keep in my bag. I nod farewell to the little gentle willow drowsing in its sunlit dream. Then I clamber back across several bookboats toward the shore, noticing the earthy smell of the river and the leathery scents wafting from the boat decks. I look back to catch the view of the Library dome towering like a mountain in the distance across the water. I'll need to catch a gondola to Seven Lanterns, get off at Inkstone Point, and then walk across the bridge to Undersong House. I hope the shortbreads I put in my bag a while ago are still intact. And that Olloise, who is so particular, doesn't hate my present.

The weight in my bag reminds me of the day we came down the river to Moonstone, hungry and wounded. The sentinels searched our fleet of small coracles and confiscated our sacred books, suspecting us of sorcery. They let us into the city only because we knew how to grow moss-silk, and because our healer promised to cure the archprince. The Council commanded me, as leader of the Sha'an, to attend the River School, where the city trains its princelings, warriors, Librarians, and scholars. So I would come to see this place as my home, they said. So I would become like them, they meant. Inside myself, I swore Moonstone would never be my home.

The Sha'an are in danger here. If I gave the order, my people could pack their belongings within a few days. None of us has much. We are forest folk; we know how to find what we need. We could travel elsewhere without much more difficulty than moss-silk seeds on the breeze. But how can I leave my wives? Annlynn could never abandon her post at the Library. I cannot even imagine the fair Vasmine, who has the ear of princes, making her way through a forest.

And Olloise—this city is all she has left of her dead parents. The Council was far cannier than I thought, when they demanded I attend their River School and learn the things their princelings and scholars learn. I met my wives there, and they are of this place, to the bone. Now, how can I ever go?

As I climb up from the shoreline, a pebble strikes me in the shoulder. I turn to see an urchin staring. "Witch!" he calls before running off into the maze of alleyways and stairs.

So it begins.

CHAPTER 2

Annlynn Jissakhar, Warrior Librarian
The Library
Anteceday, 1:00 p.m.

When my aide finishes speaking, I place a stick of incense in the incense-holder and light it. Smoke wreathes my head as if I were a dragon breathing out smoke. I always light incense when I'm irritated. I claim it calms me. The truth is that it gives me something to do with my hands besides throttle someone. I lean forward over my desk, flick my topaz-colored braid over my shoulder, and enunciate my words carefully.

"I am a warrior librarian. I provide security for ambassadors bearing ancient scrolls. I extract rare tomes from pirate ships. Interrogate forgers. Thwart thieves and saboteurs. I do not deal with overdue books."

My aide wrings his hands. "I understand, Your Vigilance. But this is a prince with an overdue book."

The long-suffering aide spreads his hands as if to imply that surely I must see the delicacy of the situation. I snort. I know exactly which prince it is. Giya Lutei, ruler of the String of Coins district, is forever checking out documents that praise his less-than-illustrious family. He has them copied by scribes so he can show his children what a proud heritage they have. This is all well and good, except he has kept one rare volume out for months. This is unacceptable to the Library, even for a prince. Rules are rules.

"Where is he?" I ask.

"In the Reading Room," my aide offers, backing away.

Long ensconced in his post, this graybeard knows when not to get underfoot.

I rise from my desk and stride down the hall, scratching a scab on my thigh—a wound from a fight with an armed bookthief in the Catalogue Hall. Down a short hall is the entrance to the Reading Room. That chamber is larger even than the Council Chamber, with red marble walls streaked with gray and a bronze-figured dome at the center of the ceiling. Its three-story glass windows are framed in gold; its long legendary wooden tables are of ebony. The Reading Room of the Library is one of the wonders of the known world, but I do not, at this moment, care.

I scan the room. There are perhaps two hundred visitors in the space: a slow day. I pick out a few regulars—a court reporter who reads rare Tamirlian mysteries on her day off. A researcher who is currently investigating the origin of the names of days of the week—Anteceday, Deceday, and so forth—in ancient Taradian ancestor veneration. An architect with spread-out blueprints who comes to examine every building in the city so that he will not run the risk of duplicating anything in his famous designs. There is a small tear in one of the onionskin blueprints. I frown my famous frown and gesture to a bookwarden to discipline the offender. Ignoring the sounds of protest from the architect's table, I continue my scan until I find my prey.

Prince Giya Lutei, his pale blue velvet beret at a rakish angle, is lounging in one of the soft maroon chairs arranged near the windows, examining several antique maps spread out on the table before him. Two thickly built cloaksmen, the un-uniformed spies and protectors who accompany all the princes, slouch nearby, trying to appear inconspicuous. I head toward the trio, my boots clicking loudly on the marble floor. Giya Lutei is an attractive man, if one is attracted to wolves. His face is long, with a prominent nose, heavy jaw, and sensual mouth. His thick sandy hair is cut long in the front, and hangs in his eyes. His coat is the same pale blue as his beret and impeccably cut. He is perhaps thirty years old, young for a prince—his father died of some unknown disease around the time I left for school. Some of the Library's other readers are sneaking surreptitious looks at him. Others, regulars, are too sophisticated for that.

The prince looks up when he sees me coming toward him. He nods in greeting but does not rise. "Your Vigilance," he drawls.

"Your Eminence," I counter. I don't drawl. I stand quietly in front of the prince for several seconds, studying the bag made of fine red leather on the seat beside him. The two heavyset bodyguards stand straighter, square their shoulders. I rest my gaze upon them, leave it there. They begin to look uncomfortable under my scrutiny; I know how to use my tall, athletic build to intimidate. One of the cloaksmen risks a sidelong glance at the sword on my hip.

"Your Eminence, you have not returned the volume you borrowed," I say evenly.

"Renew it for me, please." The prince waves a hand negligently.

Do I look like a desk clerk? I take a breath. "As Your Eminence surely knows, that is not possible. Overdue books from the Controlled Section cannot be renewed."

"In that case, my apologies. I do not have the item with me. I will bring it the next time I come." The prince's face and voice now display annoyance. "I came today to look at these maps. They relate to my father's historical research. He was honored by the city years ago." Other patrons are shifting in their seats, uncomfortable.

I know which book is overdue. It's the one he always checks out, holding on to it months longer than he should. I know about it because each time he's required to sign a special contract holding him responsible for its care. The text belongs to a set of second-century volumes, all obvious forgeries of the Moonstone Covenant. Each forgery claims a different prince from a different district as the archprince and ruler of the Council—though the ruling family, the Mai, has been stable for hundreds of years, since the Founding itself. The books used to be read at parties as a joke, or perhaps as an elaborate satire. They're two hundred years old now. Prince Giya likes to check out the one in which the archprince is a Lutei. Naturally. Pompous idiot. He stokes his delusions of grandeur, instead of caring for the hungry people in his crowded district. And the wear and tear he wreaks on the book is criminal.

I swiftly lean forward, snap up the red leather bag, and extract a volume bound in moonstone-studded, embroidered silk. "Your Eminence must have brought it by accident. How fortunate; you will be spared any further fine."

Prince Giya stands, furious, his face even more wolflike with his teeth bared. "I am still using that book," he insists. "It is an urgent state matter."

If it is a state matter, my umbrella is a state matter. I put the book back in the bag and the bag under my arm. Furious, Prince Giya raises his hand and sweeps the maps from the table onto the floor.

"That's vandalism," I snap. "It incurs a fine." Prince Giya rises. I set my hand on the pommel of my sword as his cloaksmen begin to step forward.

"Assaulting a Librarian of Moonstone is a crime punishable by exile," I remind them icily. "And the consequence of refusing to return a book, particularly a rare one, is immediate revocation of Library privileges."

Prince Giya stares me down. I stare back. He too wears a sword, an elegant rapier that reminds me of my father's. "You insult my honor," he growls. "I am a prince of Moonstone, a guardian of the Library. I don't steal books."

The man looks as if he might challenge me to a duel. I scowl. "Then don't start now."

Prince Giya glances at one of his cloaksmen. The man snatches at the bag under my arm. I jab my elbow into his nose so quickly almost no one sees what happens—though the sudden spurt of blood gives it away. A few patrons hastily leave the room. I don't blame them.

"I don't mind dirtying this floor with your people, Prince Giya," I say. "We do have cleaning staff here."

The guard with the bloody nose glares at me. Prince Giya looks away. To Moonstone folk the Library is sacred, watched over by the saints as a repository of sacred wisdom. It's literal sacrilege to disobey the Library's rules. Plus he could lose his borrowing privileges. I can't imagine what possessed him to carry our conflict even this far. After a tense moment, Prince Giya waves his hand loosely and his bodyguards stand down. I set the red leather bag on the table. The volume stays in my hands.

"I'm going to have you demoted to floor-washer," Prince Giya threatens, his voice cold and quiet. "You'll never touch a book again. They'll give you a scrub-brush instead of a sword, and then your Sha'an wife won't have your protection anymore, will she?"

"Princes of this city do not supervise Library staff," I retort. "The archprince does, and I understand he doesn't like you."

"We'll see," Prince Giya says. "Your father is the censor here, and I understand *he* doesn't like *you*."

"Your Eminence thinks he can relieve me of my duty?" I say evenly. "Try it."

"I won't forget about this," Prince Giya murmurs.

"Neither will I," I reply.

After we stare one another down for a moment, the prince saunters off. One of the thick-necked men snaps up the bag and follows him. The other glares at me before turning to follow as well. A few seconds later, a beveled glass door slams shut. Patrons stare, then go back to their mystery novels, folktales, knitting patterns, and so forth. A bookwarden comes to clean up the maps, glaring at me for disrupting the peace.

This is my life. Every day, thieves, spies, collectors, forgers, and entitled aristocrats enter the Library and attempt to copy or steal rare novels, engineering manuals, medical textbooks, and all manner of valuable tomes. They threaten, cajole, whine, and sneak. No matter how many scoundrels we keep out, there are always more. The temptation is so great that we have to search clients, and even our own staff, as they enter and exit. There is a reason the Librarians of the Great Library are warriors.

Members of my family have served as warrior librarians of Moonstone since the city was founded. Ours is a time-honored and noble profession, one my family never expected me to take on once they disowned me. I enjoy my work, and I confess I still enjoy shattering my family's presuppositions (though I don't enjoy running into my father in the hallway). But Prince Giya's arrogance has infuriated me, and right now, I feel like marching up to chaos, demanding it return the operating manual for the cosmos, and fining it five gold coins a day for every day since creation, excepting weekends.

I walk back into the restricted area and head back to my office. "File this," I say to my aide, as I stomp past his cubicle. I shove the forged Covenant at him. "The Controlled Section. Give it straight to Tommas; he'll know what to do with it."

I close the door to my office. My narrow slit of a window looks out on Festival Square and the spire-laden mansions and chapels that surround the heart of the city. My office is one of the few rooms with windows in the dim Library, and the light pouring in is blinding. As I look away, my eye falls on the surface of my broad carven desk, where I keep the rare gift Vasmine gave me four years ago on the morning of our wedding day, her heart-shaped face tilted up toward me, the waves of her crow-black hair coiled into a knot suggesting infinity, her eyes of dark amber…A far more pleasant thought than Giya Lutei and his overdue book.

I take the gift carefully in my hands. It's an ink-castle—a tiny silver castle with many turrets, crafted on the Isle of Belakkos, where the silverwork is so good, the Belakkosi say that fairies taught them how to do it. Each of the turrets is hollow and contains a different type of rare ink; you can uncap any of the towers and dip a brush in. "So you will understand me better," Vasmine said when she placed it in my hand. The little castle indeed is just like her: so many secret compartments inside. I smile, remembering a few nights ago, when I found a few more of them. I'm glad she and I had our own small wedding, before formally taking on those other two!

The clock gongs noon. It's a lovely spring day; a long lunch would not be unheard of, and I'd rather avoid my father. If he's going to expel me from the Library, I'd rather it isn't today. If I hurry, I'll be able to catch Vasmine before the boat arrives to take her to the palace.

In a few minutes, I'm making my way through the winding, slanting streets of Opal Island, avoiding beggars, pushcarts, and processions. I cross the Long Bridge with shops and shrines tucked into its arches. I stroll through the shady walled lanes of Seven Lanterns, cross the Lanterners' Canal, make the turn at the corner where Vasmine has her ink shop. My belly grumbles as I jog over our small bridge and walk around the back of Undersong House. Its roofs are steep and layered in the Yanuilti way, its little towers impossibly peaked, as if someone had pinched them in two fingers and pulled them up toward the sky.

A brightly painted gondola is dropping Istehar off at our little dock. The boatman, a young man of the Sha'an called Hanael, thanks her profusely as she hands him a small square item. He has tears in his eyes. She's likely found one of those Sha'an family treasures the Librarians impounded and carelessly sold to secondhand dealers. Sometimes my colleagues are disgraceful.

Vasmine is coming out of the house in full court attire, black hair piled in her signature knot. She's magnificent. She's on her way to the engagement of the archprince's daughter, no doubt the social event of the season.

"You've got muddy feet, wife," she points out, laughing a little, as Istehar steps onto the dock. "Don't stain my dress!

What a little mess you are. Hold that gondola; I'm getting in."

I heave a loud sigh as her subtly floral perfume wafts by. Vasmine looks back at me and blows a kiss. "Wait on dinner for me, dearling," she commands, grinning wickedly. "I wouldn't want to miss anything."

The boatman poles off into the current. Istehar smiles and squeezes my hand, then wanders off to the well to wash her feet, clearly preoccupied. I don't have the heart to tell her about my encounter with Giya Lutei. I think I'll take the rest of the day off and work out some of my frustrations with a rolling pin instead of a rapier. Tonight, after Vasmine returns, we'll have Olloise's birthday dinner. The four of us at one table is an unusual occurrence these days, one worth celebrating.

CHAPTER 3
Olloise Mazall, Apothecary
Prince Hoel's Barge
Anteceday, 2:00 p.m.

When I left the house to meet the prince's barge, I should have told someone where I was going. I was so excited to finally show Prince Hoel what I've been working on all these years, and maybe I was afraid the others would tell me not to go. If Istehar notices I'm gone, she'll worry. But there's no help for it now.

I gaze up at the pale blue stream of sky flowing high above the river. On spring afternoons like this one, on our balcony that overlooked the water, my father would tell me legends of the city. Demon innkeepers on the Isle of Sorcerer's Kettle. Winged books flying in the gardens of Seven Lanterns. Ancestor-spirits dueling in the crypts of the Sanctum on Holy Ibis. Ghost-cats that swallowed people into the morning mist off the shore of Drake's Hoard. A mirror that you could step into and go back a hundred years in time, hung on the wall of a spice market in Hundred Quays. The city has a soul, my father would say. Its thirteen founders conjured it out of the river—a living, breathing thing—to guard the treasures of civilization. They named their new creature after the jewel-toned river that flows around its islands: Moonstone.

Then I would command: "No more fairy tales, Papa. Magic is against the law!" He'd laugh and wrap me in his blue quilted coat with silver buttons. I'd snuggle into his lap and he'd tell me a story about how he met my mother, another story that turned out not to be true. Years later, reading through papers I'd found hidden in my old bedroom, I learned that my mother and father had met at a meeting of the Council: he was the chief forensic apothecary, a solver of crimes, and she was their most skilled assassin. I grew up knowing what he did; I never knew what she did until after they were both killed.

He would bring me into his laboratory from the time I was small—I loved the beakers, vials, and double boilers, and the colorful potions inside them. The mad scientists, my mother would call us, and we were of a kind: same stocky build, same dark gold skin, same roundish face, same intense black eyes, same jet-black hair cut short so it wouldn't dip into the flasks.

I saw her so little. Sadly, my most vivid memory of her is her body half-spilled off the wide bed she shared with my father—all that blood on the apricot satin. Strangely, I cannot remember finding my father's body at all, only the books and papers from his desk, strewn on the floor and dotted with scarlet.

I remember, too, my first meeting with Prince Hoel Dhagura, the Council's chief interrogator and ruler of the district of Seven Lanterns. When he appeared, I thought I was a suspect, but he kindly offered his condolences, and said he remembered me from his hours working with my father. He explained that the Council had arranged for me to attend the River School, as my parents would have wanted. My parents had both attended, each in their own time, and had excelled—even though my father was a Silvilline, a long-distrusted religious minority descended from long-ago Sha'an refugees, and my mother had been orphaned by a plague and raised in an orphanage. I too would excel, the prince told me. It was only a matter of time.

Without Prince Hoel, I don't know what would have happened to me. For years, I spent summers with him and his wife, when other students had family to visit. When I would hole up in my improvised laboratory in his attic, he'd coax me to go on excursions to markets, visit beaches, ride in hot-air balloons, meet my friends at the city theaters. He often walked with me in the gardens of the Lanternhouse. He even discussed his cases with me. "Your mind is just like your father's," he would sometimes say. "You should come and work for me one day."

I have not seen him in a long while. As the barge sweeps on over the water, the ornate lamps and great houses of the Lanterners' Canal slide past. A butler gestures for me to step into the black lacquered box of the barge's riding compartment. Silk pillows line low benches. I bow deeply and wait as Prince Hoel puts down his cordial and comes to embrace me.

"No more little Loli," he jests, standing back to look at me. "You are grown now, Olloise. Your parents would be proud."

His princely blue beret covers much of his bald head. He is a short man, but his shoulders are broad, and his two-pointed white beard is thick. His nose is bulbous like a dwarf's in a story, and his eyes are a piercing gray-blue like water at evening. He has a grave air, as if the world has shared with him its most painful secrets. I have always liked that about him.

At the shrine in the corner, his portly wife kneels in a modest lavender dress, beating notes on a xylophone with a soft hammer, her hair confined in a blond-gray knot on the top of her head. By this ritual, she remembers the saints and ancestors. Princess Angelissa prays frequently and makes generous donations to Abbatine chapels. She is a strikingly conventional woman.

"Do you wish to ring for your parents?" the prince asks politely.

"I am Silvilline, Eminence," I reply reluctantly. "We have other customs regarding the dead." The princess stiffens. Her prejudices are well-known. During the time I lived with her, she never once alluded to my religion, and when I slipped away to a Silvilline gathering on a full moon night, I often found the door locked when I came home.

"Of course," says the prince quietly. "I had forgotten."

He strokes the two points of his beard.

I make a half-bow. "Thank you for being willing to see me, Eminence. I hope you know how much your kindness has meant in the years since my parents' murder."

"I only wish I could have found the one who killed them," Prince Hoel replies. "Your father is much missed. And I know it was painful for you to find yourself alone at fifteen."

"Your Eminence was kind enough to assist me," I reply. "And I was fortunate to have the River School as a refuge. My friends there became my family, as you know."

I sit down on one of the cushioned benches, spreading my sensible trouser-skirts around me. From one of my deep pockets I draw a small wooden box and open it. "Your Eminence may remember that the night my parents were murdered, I found something among the papers in my father's desk: what seemed to be a chemical formula, written in an indecipherable language."

"I remember," the prince replies. "You took it from his desk and showed it to me after the murders. It was the only item we could not account for. The investigators could make no sense of it."

I present him with a stoppered vial from the velvet-lined box. "I brewed this from that formula," I say. "I spent six years seeking out and learning the language, deciphering the abbreviations, tracking down the ingredients, and creating the finished product."

"Did you? Remarkable." Prince Hoel soberly examines the amber fluid, glowing in the room's light. Until now, I hadn't realized how much I was hoping for his praise. "What is it?"

"As it turns out, it's a poison," I say. "A rare recipe. Some of the ingredients don't exist here; I had to obtain them from abroad."

"Why would your father create such a thing?" the prince asks, staring into the liquid. "Do you have any idea for whom he intended it? If he needed a poison, there are far easier poisons to brew."

“I don’t know,” I admit. “I was hoping you might have some thoughts on the subject.”

“Nothing in my investigation suggested that your father planned to kill anyone,” says the prince. “And there was no poison in the house at the time of the murders.”

“I wondered if my father might have planned to compound it for my mother,” I suggest reluctantly. “If she might have had some use for a rare poison in her…work. Or perhaps someone had found out who her next target was to be, and wanted to stop her from proceeding with her…assignment?”

“She was not on assignment at that time, to my knowledge,” the prince murmurs. “Though as you remember, we did think it likely some foreign agent had a grievance against your mother. There were so many who had reason, as you know.”

I lower my eyes. Before her murder, I’d always thought my mother was a benefactress who raised funds for the poor of Moonstone. That was true, it turns out, but not the whole truth. Now I think about the times she was away for work; I wonder who died while I was wishing for her to come home.

“How extraordinary that you were able to produce this potion, all these years later,” the prince remarks gently. “Well, your filial devotion is legendary. I will examine this, and look through our files and the items recovered from the murder scene. Perhaps something will surface.”

“Thank you, Your Eminence,” I say. “That is all I ask. And be most careful with it; it kills on contact.” I hand him the box. He deposits the vial into its depths and shuts the lid.

The princess has ended her prayer and rises to join us on the benches, her stiff skirts rustling. “And how are your wives?” the princess asks, in a courteous tone I know is insincere. Group marriage is legal in Moonstone—there are a hundred varied wedding customs here—but the Abbatines frown on it. “The Librarian and the…deaconess?”

“Much like a deaconess,” I agree, although it’s a bad comparison. Deaconesses pray, teach children, and keep shrines; they don’t prowl the city singing to trees and talking with books. Of course, Princess Angelissa wouldn't bother to learn the word *illuminatrix*.

I suppose I should count it as a blessing that at least she didn't say sorceress.

The princess doesn't mention Vasmine so I don't either. Perhaps she finds the subject awkward. Prince Hoel and Princess Angelissa knew Vasmine when she was Prince Hallan's treasured concubine. Back then, Vasmine would entertain the city's royalty and throw famous parties where underwater dancers performed in glass tanks, or trapeze artists in lace veils impersonated snowflakes. She'd invite ambassadors from the thirteen founding nations and beyond, and recite poetry in all of their languages. She'd hang on Hallan's arm and make the whole city jealous. Vasmine's an ink-merchant now, very successful, and still a court favorite, though no one can understand why she would have left the handsome, wealthy, and powerful Prince Hallan. She is, of course, still beautiful. The rest of us are widely regarded as unreasonably lucky women.

Later, after Prince Hoel dismisses me, I climb out of the lacquered box and into the daylight. The sky is full of clouds. Princess Angelissa emerges onto the deck after me and puts her hand on my arm, a rare gesture of tenderness that surprises me. She was always cold, even as I put my mother and father in the ground.

"Olloise," she says kindly, "we all know how difficult the death of your parents was for you. But I must tell you, it's time to set aside your obsession with an unsolvable crime! Look at you: decoding languages, concocting potions. Think of all you could do with that time and energy! You're just as brilliant an apothecary as your father. The Council would gladly hire you to take your father's place, if you would stop spending all your energies on a quest for revenge that only steals more years of your life."

I stare at her, trying to keep the anger out of my face. I can smell her sweet-musty hair oil, feel the strangely intense pressure of her fingers.

"Consider this an offer," says the princess. "The arch-prince is old. His son, as we all know, is not well-disposed toward Silvillines. Why not obtain a favorable position for yourself while you still can? Just think of all the people you could help!"

I lower my eyes and bow deeply. The princess does not seem to expect another answer. She only nods, stepping back into the lush darkness of the compartment.

We are passing the western edge of the isle of Seven Lanterns. A rounded stone looms over the docks: Inkstone Point. Across a bridge is a very small island, just big enough for a house and garden. In the garden, a gnarled tree leans out over the river. In the branches of the tree, a slight figure sits in long skirts, swinging bare feet over the water. Her hair is as white as the tree's blossoms. Istehar.

"If you'll dock for just a moment," I say to the boatman, "I will get off. I am home."

CHAPTER 4
Vasmine Kinora, Ink-Merchant
Palace of Innumerable Pearls
Anteceday, 6:00 p.m.

Laughter comes to us from over the water. The last streaks of sunset are fading from the sky. From the bench where I sit, I look out at dozens of small dome-roofed pavilions that seem to float on the water's surface. Some are one story high, and some are two stories or even three. Hundreds of tiny lanterns light the little structures and the intricate bridges connecting them. The Maze of Fireflies. One of the famous glories of the Mai palace.

Another of those glories sits here beside me, in a layered gown of scarlet and smoke-purple and burnt gold, jet-black hair braided and scented and netted with a silver mesh dotted with pearls and moonstones. Her bronze skin is very like her father's. Kalicent Mai is the archprince's only daughter. Around her sit princesses, noblewomen, and ambassadresses in silks and brocades, here to celebrate Princess Kalicent's engagement to Prince Egno Zuzierre, heir to the Golden Sands district. She's invited me because I excel at enlivening a party.

In my lap sits a red velvet box with a number of fine paper notes inside. I pull one out with grave ceremony, flourishing emerald satin bell sleeves slit to reveal the flesh underneath. Dramatic sleeves are of crucial importance when playing a game like this one.

"Let me see." I ponder the handwriting carefully and then close my eyes for a moment. When I open them again, I announce: "This handwriting belongs to Zelibet Fosca. See the rightward slant and strong verticals?"

A squeal comes from tall Zelibet, a lady-in-waiting in a sky-blue dress made of intricately crossed ribbons. The ribbons enlace her arms, hands, and fingers. She claps her beribboned hands to her mouth.

"What can you discern about our Zelya from her writing?" Kalicent asks playfully.

I lean forward intimately. "She is ferocious in bed." Peals of giggles.

Smiling, I pull out another note. "Ah, and this one shows shyness and a poet's heart. It clearly comes from the hand of our dear Memmiam." Memmiam, slight with elfin features, turns paler than her ivory brocade dress.

Kalicent looks over my shoulder and her eyes twinkle. "You're wrong this time. That note is from my bridegroom's sister, Talva. Isn't that so, dear sister?" A lovely, dark-skinned woman at the edge of the bench, draped in pearl-studded cream-colored silk with a pomander hanging from her waist, is blushing and shaking her head. But Kalicent doesn't notice, and continues: "I put it in the box for her. She wrote my beloved a note to tell him how much she loves him. Isn't that sweet? I found it in his room this morning."

I lower my eyes. The note isn't from Egno's sister. It is, in fact, from Memmiam, who looks ready to fall into a dead faint. "Ah yes, Your Eminence has fooled me," I answer casually. "The handwriting is Princess Talva's."

But Kalicent is no fool. She stares at me, her flashing eyes demanding. I glance back at her furtively, shaking my head as if to say that Memmiam is innocent. Kalicent assesses my expression. Then she rises, strides across the small round space, and unceremoniously pushes little Memmiam over the low railing of the pavilion and into the river.

Memmiam shrieks and flails as several friends rush to pull her from the water, calling for help from the blue-clad servants who move invisibly about the maze of pavilions. River water is cold and not as clean as one would wish.

Kalicent stalks off to find the man I suspect will soon

be her former fiancé. Other women might have to put up with such goings-on, but she is the archprince's favorite child. Her brother Vilya, while more empowered, is far less loved.

Women wrap the drenched and wailing Memmiam in a shawl and hurry her away, likely never to be seen in the palace again. She may even be dead before nightfall. Memmiam is the archdeacon's daughter, so now I've made a powerful enemy, which is unfortunate, although to be fair, the archdeacon never liked me to begin with.

I pack up the red velvet box, put it into a pocket in my robes, and discreetly depart the pavilion. On the way, I stop and pat Talva on the shoulder sympathetically. She looks at me sadly. She won't be Kalicent's sister-in-law after all. Still, her family owns the largest beach in Moonstone, so this won't ruin them.

"If she doesn't marry a prince, her children will be commoners," Talva says softly. "She should forgive my brother."

"Alas, she's not inclined to compromise," I reply. "Nor is she easily intimidated."

But Talva's right; Kalicent's children will only be royalty if she marries a reigning prince. Moonstone, perhaps because it is so top-heavy with thirteen kinds of royalty, has no hereditary nobility. I was called Lady Vasmine once, when I was Prince Hallan's concubine, but only as a courtesy. In Moonstone, the division between royalty and ordinary folk is precipitous.

"There's always the possibility of a foreign alliance," I say. "Or a shipping magnate. Or perhaps an archdeacon?" We both laugh. Kalicent marrying into the Abbatine clergy is about as likely as a seagull squatting and laying another Library dome.

I make my way through the webwork of lanterns, over the filigree bridges, through various small pavilions, farther out on the river. In one of them, the jovial and dashing Prince Egno holds court in his scarlet vest and cloak. Surrounded by well-wishers, he has no idea he's about to be jilted. He's chatting with Sajine Chei, the ruling princess of the district of

Sorcerer's Kettle, and her spouses: Tesper, great-grandson of a previous archprince, and Onyxe, a radical philosopher-dancer with, some whisper, a criminal record. Via these two liaisons, she manages to appeal to traditional and forward-thinking classes at the same time. Most impressive.

"Settle something for us, Vasmine," Prince Egno calls. "Has Sajine married these two fine people because she's Errantine, or because she's a sailor?"

I laugh. Sajine Chei is indeed Errantine, of a religion that dissented against the great Abbatine empires and inspired a revolution or two, back before Moonstone's founding. The laws of this city grudgingly accommodate such folk—but even among Errantines, polygamy is controversial. It is more common, as Prince Egno notes, among the sailing peoples of the Gengrassian coast, who have a spouse in every port, and have spread their marriage customs throughout the world. And Sajine does love her sailboat.

"All I can say," I reply, "is that I'm grateful to her for giving my own scandalous marriage considerable cover." Sajine chuckles.

Edging around the eager crowd, I proceed toward a three-story pavilion with drapes over the windows to conceal what lies within. The guards at the entrance admit me. Or more accurately, they pretend not to see me. Inside, a butleress with long coattails guides me up the spiral stairs to the third story, where I pass through a beaded curtain.

The archprince sits close to a window, his beard regal as the beards of ancient kings, his olive skin hinting at his family's roots in ancient Uluria, his thickset form filling out his cloth-of-gold. A telescope rests on a stand nearby but he isn't using it; he looks out unaided at the patterns of light dancing on the water. He glances my way. I make a deep obeisance, all the way to the floor, and wait.

"My son is waiting for me to die," Jalian says. He never greets me; he begins, as always, as if I had never left.

"Don't oblige him, my love," I reply, rising. "He's far too

spoiled already." I lean down and put my lips to the back of his neck. The dark curls at his nape have more gray in them than they did when our affair began. "Has he troubled you tonight?"

The archprince shakes his head. "He cracks this city apart island by island, the way an ice storm cracks branches from the trees. If it's not the Sha'an he's after, it's someone else." Jalian Mai's placid, lined features have a lasting strength, like a building that's survived centuries of flooding. "The day he succeeds me, canals will run red. But no matter, girl. I have burdened you enough with affairs of state."

I take his hand and squeeze it. "Will it ease your heart if I play for you?"

He nods gratefully and closes his eyes. Jalian Mai, scion of generations of archprinces from the Mai clan, has his servants cart a harp around wherever he goes—just in case I make an appearance. He'll let other musicians play it, but only until I arrive. He no doubt knows that my affection for him is somewhat impersonal; he is a powerful connection for me and my wives, no more. But he favors me nevertheless. He courted me years ago when I came to the Palace of Innumerable Pearls to play the harp and visit his daughter, clearly having no concern that I was (more than sufficiently) married. Not long afterward, he bent to kiss me behind a silk screen at the ceremony to bless the waters, one summer by the Gilded Bridge. It seemed prudent to accept his attentions. It still does.

I find the harp of blond wood, carved with an ancient love poem of the Fenge, in the corner, sit on the stool placed by its side, tuck up my sleeves, touch the strings, and coax out a melody that rings like pure crystal. After a few moments, I add a serene lyric. The archprince listens, slouched in his carven chair. The misery seeps out of him.

Before three verses have passed, my melody is interrupted by footsteps on the stairs. It might be Kalicent coming to let her father know the match with her fiancé has been emphatically dissolved, but the footfalls are unexpectedly heavy and quick. In fact, the footfalls are bootfalls and I am about to be in a room with Vilya Mai. As the beaded curtain rattles, I reach up and pull a hairpin from my signature figure-eight coiffure. A dark forest of hair tumbles around my shoulders, hiding a good bit of my face and dress. I bow my head, shrink into the shadows with a servant's posture, and continue to play.

Vilya is loud, fair-skinned like his reclusive mother, and of middling height—folk might even say scrawny if they saw him beneath his armorish garb, though some find his rattish looks attractive. The fuzz of hair beneath his royal beret is yellow, like a chick. He snaps his fingers at me to stop playing, paying no attention to the figure he assumes to be a court musician crouching in the corner.

"Father," Vilya complains, "they've gone too far." Rage coarsens the otherwise cultured voice. "The Sha'an are founding a school for their children!"

"Why shouldn't they have a school?" the archprince asks wearily. "The Abbatines have their own schools. The Errantines have theirs. The other Silvillines have had separate schools for years; a Sha'an school would be no different."

Vilya laughs bitterly. "No different! Everyone says you were a soft child; now you've become a soft old man. Don't you see? The Sha'an have been stealing from us since they came here! Claiming to be refugees! Thieves and poisoners, more like. And now they're teaching their demon spawn all their evil ways. That bitch sorceress of theirs goes around the city cursing trees, hexing the books people read, the very stones in the street, making our citizens sick and weak. If we do nothing, the Sha'an will rule us soon. The Library of which you are guardian will fall into their hands! How long will it take for them to put their sorceress on your throne?"

"Mind how you speak of the Sha'an," Jalian Mai warns. "Their healer saved my life."

"Saved your life so they could slowly poison the rest of us!"

Vilya shouts.

"I have said it before, and I say it again," roars Jalian. "I forbid you to conduct hunting expeditions against my citizens! It is beneath your dignity as prince. The Sha'an are a small minority in the city and they mind their own business. You have a grudge, not evidence!"

Vilya slams his fist on the table that holds the archprince's iced drink. A splash from the glass beads the hem of the archprince's robe. "Oh, I'll get evidence. Let me arrest their leaders and turn their possessions out on the street. I promise you there'll be evidence!"

Jalian pauses, weighing his response, and glances at me for a moment. In that pause, Vilya's eyes shift. The harp, of course, is a giveaway, even if one he previously missed. Vilya knows the rumors about me and his father. He is about to realize who I am. When he does, the affront of my presence will outrage him. *My father is sleeping with Istehar's slut*, he will call to his followers below. *Look, here she is in the living flesh, whispering in his ear. Time to depose my weak, corrupt father and kill the witches and foreigners.*

There is almost not time to do anything. My fingers find the harp strings, play a note that hovers in the air like starlight. Both men look toward me sharply as I play another note and then another, improvising a melody. The scowling Vilya falls silent, listening to the notes unfurl. This will go one of two ways, and if it is the wrong one, these men will know me for what I am, and I may not be home for Olloise's birthday dinner, or possibly ever again.

Vilya turns back to his father. The two stand for a while before the gap in the curtains, looking out at the lanterns and the night, as I spool my lacy melody out into the spangled dark. They pay me no attention.

"Do nothing," says Jalian quietly to his son. "I warn you."

"I'll be back," mutters Vilya, and he turns to leave the room. The bootfalls are audible for a full minute.

Jalian Mai and I find ourselves staring at each other. He likely does not remember my melody at all. "Shall I disrobe,

Your Eminence?" I ask, mustering a smile. He nods, slightly disoriented still from the music, and attempts one of his own.

As the dress falls from my shoulders, he rises, approaches, places his arms around my waist. He reaches up, pushing my loose hair behind my ears. Then we both hear the still-furious Kalicent tearing into the pavilion, scattering guards and handmaids on the ground floor. Her shrill voice gets louder as she makes for the stairs below us. Jalian and I both heave a sigh.

"Go on, girl," the archprince says to me. "Go back to your wives and your ink shop. No need for you to worry; I won't let my son off his leash, I promise you."

He pauses. "And don't tell Istehar Sha'an or anyone else what you heard here. That's an order. I don't want a panic in the city."

I nod, pull my dress back on, and make a quick obeisance. Descending the stairs to the pavilion's second level, I dart behind a curtain so Kalicent doesn't see me on her way up. Only then do I allow myself the deep breath I have been fantasizing about all evening. Only then do I think of my mother.

She was the concubine of a provost at a minor college. Technically, he was my father, though I prefer not to think of him that way. He liked to lord it over her, but she had a way to pacify him—she called it her "trick." Her mother taught it to her; it has been passed down the motherline for generations, part of a "concubines' religion" that, at least in Moonstone, doesn't even have the dignity of a name. The way it worked was this: My mother would play the zither, visualizing the notes as drops of water floating in the air. Into each drop she would infuse her wish that my father would lose consciousness. The notes would travel to him as he fumed at his desk, and usually, he'd amble over to his armchair and quickly fall asleep.

When I was younger, I doubted her. I thought it was just her lovely playing, or wishful thinking, that gave her these secret "powers." Then one night when I was fourteen and had stayed out all night with a professor's son, my father called me "damaged goods," demanding I be contracted to a house of public concubines that very morning. My mother played, her hands shaking, and he forgot everything he'd said. Not long afterward, he sent me to the House of Blossoms to train to serve princely families. Before I left home, my mother gifted me my first harp.

I haven't used my mother's trick very often. If I were caught charming my overlord, I'd be executed straightaway for sorcery. But the gift I learned in secret from my mother has helped me in desperate moments. It is enough to make one wonder, if one were not so cynical, about fate.

Istehar says that we all live in a Library much vaster than the one Annlynn tends. The books of that vast Library are the things of this world, she says, each written in a hidden language. If we learn to read those words, their grammar and intonation, we can commune with the spirits of trees, of water, even of music.

No matter. I need to leave the palace before the Mai clan—father, son, or daughter—take any further notice of me. Once Kalicent and her retinue have finally passed, I descend the last of the stairs.

As I make my way down the colonnade to the palace dock, I catch a glimpse of the archdeacon's dark belly-length beard, his hawkish nose, and his pale blue and silver vestments. His frail weeping daughter, Memmiam, sobs on his chest in the shadow of a pillar. The girl, exposed as Prince Egno's lover, is wearing a cloak; she's likely been exiled, or is simply fleeing Kalicent's wrath. A little maidservant waits nearby, hugging herself as if eager to be gone. The archdeacon peers at me as I hastily pass. His eyes track me as if he were a bird of prey preparing to lunge.

CHAPTER 5
Istehar Sha'an and Olloise Mazall, Students
River School, Vexmere
Eight years ago

Outside the bedroom, the floor creaks. A few hours ago, a girl on the stairs—Joeve—had yanked at Istehar's long hair, fine as tassels of a silversilk tree, and threatened to cut it off. Istehar wonders if that girl has come to finish the job.

Istehar's somber, owlish roommate is restlessly asleep, and Istehar does not want to wake her. She silently gets out of bed, lifts her staff from where it leans against the wall, and takes a few steps toward the door. Any farther, and the floorboards will give her away.

The door opens and a boy is there. A much older boy in white school clothes, thin and just above Istehar's height. Joeve is with him. Moonlight spills in through the window, illuminating them just well enough. Leaning on her staff, Istehar waits.

"I wanted to see what my enemy looked like." The boy's voice is cold.

"Am I your enemy?" she asks.

"Not mine personally. But I know of you. The Sha'an sorceress."

Istehar has been warned not to answer to that term. "I am the illuminatrix of the Sha'an."

The boy smiles to himself, still cold, and almost bows. "I am Vilya Mai, the crown prince of Moonstone. My mother is the sister of Griseus of Mor."

Istehar thinks she is supposed to bow. She finds she

cannot bring herself to do it. The boy frowns, and now it is Joeve who smiles to herself.

"I happen to know you bowed before my father not long ago," Vilya accuses. "You were right to show him deference! The fool gave you a home here."

"We are grateful to His Eminence the Archprince," Istehar whispers. She does not know what else to say. She has reached the limit of her political acumen.

"They say a healer of your people cured him, but I have no doubt you made him sick to begin with," the boy snaps. "You are beggars, witches, and thieves. The Sha'an forest belongs to the lord of Mor. You were squatters there, and a nuisance."

"We belonged to the Sha'an forest," Istehar flares. "Until Griseus of Mor burned it. He is not the forest's lord—he is its executioner!"

"He burned trees so he could grow crops to feed his people," the boy retorts. "There is nothing wrong in that; the trees were his to burn. And you, little maggot, are still squatting on Mor land. Do you even know that long ago the Mor settled this very island of Vexmere?"

"And murdered its people," Istehar fires back. "The Mor have stolen everything they claim to own!"

"You see, Your Eminence, it's just as I said: she's insolent," Joeve tells the boy triumphantly, tossing her frizzy, tawny hair.

"My father has made a grave mistake," Vilya snarls. "And one day soon I will correct it."

He walks up to Istehar, stares into her eyes, wrests her staff away with his pale spidery fingers. He wields it, ready to hit her. Istehar feels frozen. If she harms a prince, her people will surely be expelled from the city. Yet the staff belonged to the last illuminatrix and the one before that. It is carved with images of the leaves and blossoms of the oldest and most revered trees of the Sha'an. It is a sacred thing, a gift from the trees to her people. It should not bear the touch of his hands.

Vilya gloats, seeing her face. He chooses not to beat her, thinks of something better, more powerful. He holds the carven staff to his knee, applies pressure. Istehar cries out, and he laughs. The sound buries itself back in Istehar's throat. She watches quietly then, with a grief that unfolds like a suffocating cloth, filling the room.

With a terrible crack, the wood snaps. Istehar lets out a wail as Vilya triumphantly raises the pieces, crowing in victory. She thinks she sees something curl out from the ragged pieces of the staff—a near-invisible smoke, perhaps. She's not sure she is seeing anything at all, yet it seems the smoke branches and twists and forks, its farthest tendrils reaching the ceiling—a massive tree spreading through the entire room. Wisps of the smoke-tree graze her face; spirals of it waft into the prince's flaring nostrils. Vilya coughs, gives a sharp cry, and drops the pieces of the staff clattering to the floor. He clasps his chest as if something inside burns him.

"What is it?" Joeve asks. Vilya does not answer. The pieces of the staff lie quiet. The smoke is gone now, but scattered across the dark floorboards, Istehar sees a handful of dark-bright specks, like tiny coals. One by one, they wink out. The last one vanishes, like the final spark of a doused fire. Istehar shivers. Vilya sucks in a breath. Joeve, her ice-colored eyes wide, shrinks back toward the doorway.

Istehar's roommate, Olloise, snores on. Perhaps she has taken a sleeping draught; she does not sleep well, Istehar has learned. Her helmet of dark hair lies on the pillow like a bowl of night itself.

The prince stares at Istehar, thinking. Then he strides over to Istehar's night-table and opens its drawer. He snatches up her Book of the Tree with its cover of soft bark, the first she ever made. It was her parents' treasure; they kept it in the little ark in the main room of their underground home, and took it out only when the illuminatrix came to visit, when there was a birth or death or marriage to remember. They revered it, though it was the work of her clumsy hands. She remembers pleading for a clump of escaping villagers to wait while she ran to fetch it. Now it reminds her of the tender skin of the willow and silversilk trees she knew as a child.

"I'll teach you what happens when you use magic on a prince," Vilya hisses.

The boy begins to tear out the thick, textured pages, one by one. He shreds them, letting fragments fall onto the floor. Tears run down Istehar's face. She is an orphan, alone; she has no one to ask for help. She has very little left of her parents: a wooden cup, an embroidered moss-silk blanket, and this book. She can hear its pages, whispering, remembering, as each precious voice is cast out into the air. Each page is a memory of her loved ones, of the forest itself, that can never be recovered. She prays for the book to defend itself—Sha'an legend says it's happened before—but the pages just fall like leaves in autumn. The broken staff lies on the floor in pieces, useless.

"Your magic is worth nothing. Go shroud yourself in your freakish hair and die," Joeve taunts Istehar, cackling at her distress.

Olloise sits bolt upright in bed, staring sightlessly like a sleepwalker. "Don't die!" Olloise yells. "Mama! Papa! Be alive, please be alive!" The surface of Olloise's night-table is a jumble of bottles: tinctures, salves, infusions. She lobs the largest bottle into the center of the room, where it smashes and spills vile-smelling fluid everywhere. The prince coughs and gags.

"Crazy bitch, keep your nightmares to yourself!" Joeve shouts.

Olloise hurls a vial against the doorframe and it shatters, scattering glass and something pungent. Joeve shrieks, shields her nose and mouth, and flees. Istehar snatches the book from Vilya and crouches on the floor, protecting it with her body. Olloise throws a squat jar that hits Vilya squarely in the mouth. He gags and spits, his lip cut and bleeding. Reluctantly, he flees too. There are voices in the hall. Everyone in their wing must be awake now.

Within moments, the rectoress appears in the doorway with a lantern. She is a fearsome woman, so tall she has to stoop to enter. Thin-lipped, she surveys the shredded pages, pools of liquid, and broken glass.

"Olloise had a nightmare," Istehar explains meekly.

The rectoress looks threateningly at the shaking Olloise, who now seems more awake. "Have another nightmare like that and you'll be living in an asylum, not a school!" She picks up a salve-soaked page and a fragment of perfume jar. "None of these objects are allowed in this dormitory, as you well know. You're both on crypt duty for a week. This room had better be spotless by morning, and you had better not be late for class."

They hear her ordering everyone back to bed. After the light fades, Istehar takes the pieces of her staff from the floor. Tears run down her face as she strokes the pieces and speaks to them, gently fits them together, lays them in her bed, and covers them with a blanket. Then she fills a pail with water from the washroom. Olloise finds rags in the laundry closet in the hall. The two of them sweep, blot, and scrub together in the moonlight. Istehar picks up all the torn fragments of the book and smooths them out, then places each one in her drawer, gently and solemnly.

"Can you fix the book?" Olloise asks.

"The torn pages can't be mended," Istehar says sadly. "They must be buried. But much of the book is all right. I'll hide it somewhere so no one can harm it again." She wraps the little volume in a scarf and puts it under her pillow. "I'm sorry about your potions."

"I'll make new ones. It will just take time," Olloise says. "But the staff—"

"I can't hear its voice anymore," Istehar whispers. "I'll bury it, too. Tomorrow."

Olloise nods gravely. "I'll go with you," she says. Istehar gives a little nod of gratitude.

The two continue cleaning, the rags staining with the greens and golds and purples of Olloise's potions. "Was your nightmare very frightening?" Istehar asks after a while.

"Not as frightening as waking life," Olloise snorts. Istehar nods in agreement, and flashes a brief smile. She suspects there was no nightmare, that Olloise acted to save her from the prince. They work in silence a while more.

"He'll graduate in a few years," Olloise offers after a while. "You won't see him after that; he'll be at court. And Joeve's a coward. Her mother's a customs official; that's why she knows how to bully people so well."

"So you knew who was here?" Istehar asks. "While you were having your nightmare?"

"I heard them in the hall afterward," Olloise says. She pauses. "We choose concentrations tomorrow, you know."

Istehar nods. Of the four possible concentrations at the River School—Sword, Coin, Book, and Candle—it's clear Olloise will pick the one focused on all kinds of public health, from medicine to water welfare. "You'll choose Candle, I guess."

"And you'll choose Book," Olloise returns. Book is the concentration for those who want to work in the Library, or become scholars of history, literature, philosophy, or theology.

"Yes," Istehar says. She smiles ruefully. "Though I have a confusing relationship with books."

"I know what you mean," replies Olloise. "I have a confusing relationship with healing."

They laugh together, quietly so the rectoress doesn't come back.

When the floor is clean and the trash put down the chute, they are shivering; there's no heat in the River School at night. They climb into Olloise's bed for the remaining minutes before the rising hour. Round-faced Olloise is stocky and big-breasted; Istehar relaxes into her arms, her ample body and warm gold skin. The shock of white hair pouring down from Istehar's scalp feels lovely on Olloise's cheeks and arms, though it does get everywhere. Istehar tells about how she was born inside a syssyrup tree. Olloise tells the story of her parents' deaths.

"I don't think I know who my parents really were," Olloise says, looking into Istehar's pale green eyes, the color of new leaves. She does not know why she says this; she's sure she hasn't said it before, hasn't even thought it before. "So I'm not sure who I am."

"I think I might have some idea who you are," Istehar replies, warmth in her voice.

"And you? You know who you are?"

"I do. But here in Moonstone, I have no idea where I am," Istehar replies. "So maybe we're even."

Later that afternoon, after classes, the two girls return to bury the staff. With her delicate, agile hands, Istehar pulls back the blanket. The staff is in one piece. At the place where it was broken, a rough callus rings the wood, as with a living tree that healed itself. Olloise gasps in amazement. Istehar tilts her head, listening, then takes the mended staff in her hand, her face full of joy.

Prince Vilya ignores the two of them from that night on. The only people they ever tell about what happened, later, are Annlynn and Vasmine—who don't entirely believe them. Istehar's staff never does anything unusual again. And even Olloise sometimes wonders if Prince Vilya ever came to their room or if the whole thing was a dream, though Joeve's persistent nastiness to them suggests otherwise. But Istehar—whose Book of the Tree is missing pages, and whose fingers often brush against a lumpy ring on her staff she can't otherwise explain—has no doubts at all.

CHAPTER 6

The Wives

Undersong House

Anteceday, 8:00 p.m.

All the rooms have a view of the water. The back room's windows look out on the little apple orchard and the dock, and its high hearth is built of sea stones. The Sha'an bought this house for Istehar. Later, she moved her wives into it.

Annlynn has put Istehar's bag on a broad stone counter and is rummaging through it. "You crushed the shortbreads," Annlynn complains.

"I'm sorry, Anya," Istehar replies, hanging her cloak on one of the pegs by the front door. "I put a book on top of them."

"Even worse, Istya," Annlynn mutters. "You might have ruined the book!"

"Spoken like a true Librarian." An unusually cheerful Olloise kisses Annlynn on the cheek and deposits a fragrant tray of hot spiral-shaped onion pastries on the counter. "A wonder that the great warrior returned before midnight for my dinner."

"That's what family does," says Annlynn. "Not that I would know."

"They still haven't written, have they?" Istehar offers sympathetically. She almost puts a hand on Annlynn's shoulder but doesn't. Strong and straight-backed Annlynn doesn't take well to sympathy. She has inherited this trait from a long line of stern and resolute people.

"Not even when I was appointed Director of Public Oversight," Annlynn mutters, setting out the crumbling shortbreads on a plate. “Not even one of my siblings. Becoming the youngest warrior librarian in generations is not enough to inspire my family to forgive me for marrying you three disreputable women.” She smiles a bit and hands Istehar an onion pastry.

“Maybe it was worth it?” Olloise asks playfully, and tugs gently on Annlynn’s long braid before heading back toward the hearth to snatch a sugarfish pie from the oven.

“Not on the days when we all need the upstairs washroom at the same time,” Annlynn replies, a quick smile showing on her face. She flips her braid to the front and goes on arranging the celebratory plate of little desserts. Each small pastry has a little edible scroll of good wishes wrapped around it or baked inside. An old Moonstone custom.

Outside, a gondola, lit by a single lamp hanging from its steeply curved prow, stops briefly at the little dock near the apple trees. They all watch through the window as a woman in a rich satin cloak gracefully disembarks. Bunching her gown in one hand to keep it out of the dirt, she makes her way down the stone path. She pauses, the way she always does, waiting for one of them to open the door for her. Istehar rushes forward and flings the door wide.

“You’re here!” Istehar announces, as if they don’t all already know. Vasmine enters, her long, wavy black hair shockingly tumbled about her shoulders, her emerald-green satin dress the brightest thing in the room.

“Vasmine, you’re late for my birthday—we were about to eat without you,” scolds Olloise.

“Apologies, sweetest,” says Vasmine. “It took time to hail a gondola. The line of guests fleeing the engagement party was endless.”

“Is she engaged to the prince, at least?” asks Istehar.

“Far from it,” Vasmine snorts, undoing the fastening of her magnificent amber cloak, and hanging it up on a hook. “She likely had him chased from the palace.”

“Might you have had anything to do with that?” Annlynn asks suspiciously, eyeing Vasmine’s tousled hair.

"More than I would have liked," admits Vasmine. "But that's not the real story of the evening. I overheard a conversation between the archprince and his son. Vilya means you harm, Istya—you and all the Sha'an. He threatened to bring his thugs here tonight to collect 'evidence' of your crimes."

Istehar suddenly looks much older than her usual wood-nymph self. "How long do we have?" she asks briskly. Once in the past, she hailed a gondola and floated down the canals yelling to the various Sha'an houses. She would do it again if she had to.

"It won't be tonight," Vasmine explains gently. "Jalian stopped him. But I have to say, I don't know if the father can contain the son much longer."

Istehar sighs and nods. "I saw one of the prince's pamphlets today on a bookboat by Juniper Island. There was so much hatred in it, it burned my hands."

Olloise looks uneasy. "It's just talk."

"Maybe," says Istehar, "but we need to plan for more than talk. If a mob attacks the Sha'an neighborhoods in Seven Lanterns, folk will come to Undersong House to hide."

"They may hide here, but this house will stay visible enough," Annlynn says. "The mob will know where to come."

A silence falls on the room. Olloise rummages among the vessels on the counter—which include a cluster of freshly washed vials from her apothecary's business; she sells medicines to local healers and hospitals and the occasional unwell neighbor—and produces a glass. She fills it with water from a pitcher on the counter and hands it to Vasmine, who gratefully downs it. Then she hands around the carefully arranged tray of pastries, to try to lighten the mood.

"What were you doing on Juniper Island?" Vasmine asks Istehar, deftly removing a blessing scroll from a pastry before devouring it.

Istehar smiles a little. "Shopping for Loli's present."

"On a bookboat?" Annlynn looks incredulous. "They sell junk."

"Not this time," Istehar crows triumphantly.

"Let's see this alleged birthday present," Olloise says. "Maybe it will take our minds off the rest of it."

"Before dinner?" teases Annlynn.

"Yes," says Olloise, laughing. "Is that a problem? Cut yourself some sugarfish pie if you're hungry."

They gather in the pillow-nests by the hearth, Annlynn with a large piece of pie on a plate. Istehar has wrapped the book messily with a scrap of silk and a ribbon. Olloise settles on a pillow, pulls off the ribbon, and unwraps the silk. There is a long pause as everyone stares at the cover.

"Istehar, how could you?" Annlynn demands angrily, the fork clattering onto her plate. "That's morbid! Not to mention cruel."

"I like morbid," says Olloise, but she says it quietly.

"Loli, I hope you're not angry," says Istehar humbly. "It called to me. I thought it might help with your investigation."

"*The Poisoner's Guide to Moonstone* called to you?" Annlynn continues to scowl. "It's her birthday! We should be trying to take her mind off her parents' murder, not remind her of it!"

There is an appalled silence. Olloise stares at the hearthfire. Istehar looks too upset to speak.

"Well, I think it's splendid," says Vasmine. She takes the book from Olloise's unresisting hands and flips through it. "Look! It's wonderfully old and wicked. Some of Moonstone's best scandals are in here. Look, my very favorite murder: Avrilla, concubine of Meren Mai, did him in with a poisoned hairpin during a chamber concert in the Library parlor. No one noticed until the encore. And by then she was long gone with her lover, the archprince's zither tuner..."

"Give me that," Annlynn snaps, putting her plate down roughly. She takes the volume from Vasmine and wrenches it open to a middle page. Her face changes.

"What is it?" asks Olloise, trying to see over Annlynn's shoulder.

"Buying this was insensitive," says Annlynn briskly, "but Istya wasn't wrong that this book is valuable. It's old. I can tell by the stitching and the print type. And the archaic grammar makes me think it's a copy of an even older book. I bet the bookseller got it from an estate sale. Or else it's stolen."

Olloise reaches out her hand. "Well, let me see it."

Everyone is quiet while Olloise turns the book's pages. "If I wanted to train to be an assassin, this would be the perfect gift. How can this book even be legal?"

"It isn't," Annlynn says. "The Library forbids books that teach murder. We could be arrested for owning it."

"How exciting!" says Vasmine. "Let's read it aloud at parties."

"Let's throw it in a canal," suggests Annlynn. "I only just made warrior librarian; I don't want to disgrace my profession! And with a mob on the way, the last thing we need is for them to find a poisoner's manual here. It would give people all the evidence they need that the Sha'an are up to no good!"

"It would certainly start rumors about our marriage." Vasmine smiles mischievously.

Istehar, who's been anxiously watching Olloise's face as Olloise reads the book, cries: "Loli, what is it?"

Olloise hesitates. "This is the recipe I've been decoding for six years," she says. She looks stunned.

"How could that be?" demands Annlynn.

Olloise points to a page. "This is the formula of the poison I just bottled for Prince Hoel! The one I made from the coded recipe left on my father's desk the night of his murder. Only this one's not in code or in a foreign language. The ingredients are all right here, written plainly. This alchemist who wrote the book claims he used that exact poison to assassinate a prince, the year Moonstone was founded."

Vasmine looks shocked. "That can't be right," she protests. "How could the recipe be exactly the same, four hundred years apart? You must have made a mistake, Loli!"

Annlynn peers over Olloise's shoulder. "The Cloakroom Murder. That's what he's talking about."

"What's the Cloakroom Murder?" Istehar asks.

Annlynn sighs. "You're a barbarian, Istya. Four hundred years ago, Moonstone was a city with districts governed by different countries: an international city, founded to house the Library and share the world's wisdom equally. But after multiple catastrophic conflicts among the city's parent nations, thirteen envoys from Moonstone's different ethnic districts named themselves princes—one was a princess, actually—and agreed to form an independent city. They elected the first archprince, Surian Mai, and signed a Covenant to govern all the districts."

"Very good, Professor," Vasmine smiles. Back at school, she loved to sit back and listen to Annlynn lecture about history.

"Six-year-olds know this," Annlynn scoffs, and goes on. "But before the princes went into the Council Room to sign the Moonstone Covenant, Prince Karel Lutei of the String of Coins district was poisoned in a Library cloakroom. He took a glass of wine from a tray there, and it killed him. A few hours later, his thirteen-year-old son, Erius, signed the Covenant in his place."

"Why was he murdered?" Istehar asks.

"No one is exactly sure, but it's thought that one or more of his victims killed him," Annlynn says. "Possibly even his wife and son played a role. Historians say he was poisoned by lordsbane, a common poison wives would mix into the drinks of cruel husbands."

"So he was a cruel person?" Istehar wonders.

Annlynn nods. "That's putting it mildly. Historians claim he was a known sadist when he was the envoy from Nordynor, and would have done much worse as prince of String of Coins. Someone decided not to give him the opportunity. Lutei's descendants are still rather off, ethically speaking; today Giya Lutei tried to steal a Library book!"

"And this alchemist who wrote the book confesses publicly to the most famous murder in Moonstone history?" Vasmine asks. "That seems unlikely. Perhaps he's making the whole thing up to get attention."

Vasmine gets up from her pillow-nest. "Who wants another piece of sugarfish pie?" She goes to the counter, takes a second sugared scroll-pastry from the tray, and delicately munches it. She shows everyone that the scroll reads "peace and serenity"—then tosses it into the fire so it will come true.

Olloise frowns, still turning pages in the old tome. "This alchemist calls himself the Deacon, and claims he's an old man nearly on his deathbed, telling the true version of the story to preserve the memory of his role in history. He doesn't give his real name or many details of the crime, but he claims he conspired with the Council to kill 'one cruelle prince,' and ultimately saved the whole city from tyranny."

"At the very least, the Deacon exaggerates," Annlynn says. "String of Coins is hardly the whole city. And the poison you concocted isn't made from lordsbane! Vasmine's right; this Deacon may be telling a false tale."

"False tale or not, I know the reason I couldn't easily obtain the ingredients for the formula on my father's desk." Olloise shakes her head in wonder. "They were from a poison used hundreds of years ago! I wondered why so many of them were hard to get."

"So that's why the book spoke to me," Istehar whispers, looking into the flames on the hearth. "But I still don't understand: Why would your father need an antique poison? And what did it have to do with his death?"

"He was the Council's forensic apothecary," Olloise replies, closing the book for a moment to consider. "He investigated murders. Maybe he was investigating Karel Lutei's murder."

"A four-hundred-year-old murder?" Vasmine looks skeptical as she serves Annlynn another piece of pie. "Sounds like more of a task for an archaeologist than an apothecary."

"Or the recipe might have had something to do with my mother's work," Olloise muses. "She did kill people for a living. Maybe he was making something for her to use. Maybe there was a reason she needed a poison from hundreds of years ago."

Olloise looks off into a corner of the room, and the rest of them all know she is thinking of her parents: how much she loved them, and how they died. Vasmine offers her a birthday scroll, but she demurs.

"How did your father even come across this formula?"

Istehar asks. "Copies of this book can't be common, if it's so old. And none of you were aware of the Deacon's story, so it's not like it's widely known."

Olloise thinks. Her thinking process is so intense it tends to stop conversations. They all wait in silence. The fire crackles.

"Does the Library have a copy of this book?" Olloise asks Annlynn.

"I have no idea," Annlynn replies. "I've never seen it, but there are thousands of books I haven't seen."

"Can you find out?" Olloise presses. "If it's there, and someone checked it out five years ago, or even requested to see it, maybe we'd learn who gave my father the formula."

Annlynn's eyes shift nervously to the sword hanging on the northern wall. "Library records are sealed for everyone except law enforcement. I'm not supposed to read them without a warrant."

Vasmine throws back her head and laughs. "Live a little, dearest. What's becoming a warrior librarian for?"

Annlynn frowns mightily. "Well, first we have a potential massacre of the Sha'an to cope with." Istehar shivers and looks toward the window, where a torchlit barge is lumbering past the dock and the apple trees.

Olloise snorts. "It sounds like you'd rather deal with a massacre than upset the Library."

An unsmiling Annlynn counters: "Wouldn't anyone?"

CHAPTER 7

Olloise Mazall, Apothecary
Undersong House
Ancilliday, 2:00 a.m.

In the wee hours, after taking pages of notes on the Deacon's story, and breaking open cookies to read my almost-forgotten birthday blessings, I stumble up the stairs toward my room. Years ago, when I moved in, I asked for the balcony room on the third floor so I could aim a telescope at the sky. Istehar's room and study are on the same floor, just opposite mine—she has a view of Inkstone Point and a spiral staircase down into the silvirium. Sometimes I think about the ways I prefer to look beyond the world and she's always trying to dive farther into it.

It's late enough that the river has gone quiet—a sleeping serpent, quick to rouse at the first hint of light. The faint traffic across the footbridge has died down. Istehar went to bed long ago, as did our housekeeper Bastina. Annlynn is dozing in a chair by the back door, her sword in her lap. Dozya, the Sha'an caretaker who sometimes watches over the public rooms of the house, is asleep by the front door. As my footfalls creak on the aged stairs, I try not to scare myself by thinking of what happened to my parents.

I jump and nearly scream when Vasmine, still wearing her alluring gown, waylays me at the landing. She laughs a little and pulls me into her bedroom. I can smell the heady perfume wafting from an open bottle on Vasmine's delicate seafoam-painted vanity.

"*My* birthday present will be much better than a book," she purrs as she closes the door. There's a breeze from the half-open balcony window, and my shivering becomes more pronounced. "Poor orphan, you're shaking with cold. Let me warm you up."

"Istya might be upset," I say nervously as Vasmine takes hold of my dark blue velvet coat and strips it from me. "We're always together on my birthday."

"Let the elf child sleep," Vasmine scoffs, shrugging her gown from her shoulders and extracting her arms from the ornate sleeves. "You know how she loves to dream."

I nod warily. Naked, standing in a pool of emerald satin, Vasmine strips off my gray sweater and trouser-skirts. Fixing me with her eyes of dark amber, she reaches up to slip her hand behind my neck. Her lips find mine. I feel, as I always do when I am with her, as if I am falling into water—into another world, more fluid and mysterious, where one breathes some other way. We somehow find our way past the elaborately knotted bed curtains and onto the soft coverlets. Our lovemaking wakes the fish Vasmine keeps in a bowl near her bed; they swim round and round as I cry out my birdsong.

At the River School, for a long time, it was Vasmine and Annlynn, and Istehar and me. It made sense. Vasmine was a beauty from a prince's household, and Annlynn was an aristocrat from an important family. Istehar and I were Silvilline orphans; most of our fellow students thought us odd and maybe dangerous. The four of us were friends mainly because Annlynn had a soft spot for misfits, and wanted someone to discuss poetry with—or at least, that's what she claimed.

In those years, it was hard for me to be close to anyone. I was often cold to Istehar, who, after my parents died, was the first person to fiercely love me. The frequent hurt in her eyes seemed inevitable: the cost she had to bear because of my grief. Then one night Vasmine invited herself into my bed. "You aren't well, Loli," she told me. "You need medicine." Then she smiled encouragingly and delivered her medicine expertly, as if I were some princess entitled to such perfections.

Vasmine became my tutor, my physician, and the thorn in my side, always drawing me out of myself. Istehar, wrapped in the strange confident magic of her gifts, didn't seem to mind that she had a rival. In fact, as my heart softened, Istehar and I became closer, and I could be gentler with her. The hard part of our foursome, for me, was Istehar and Annlynn. Once given permission, they met one another with an uncivilized fierceness. Their love often stayed beneath the surface, but when it rose, I found it untranslatable, unsettling. When I would lie with Annlynn, I think it was partly to interrupt the hidden world she and Istehar seemed to share.

And yet we were not truly a foursome, for Istehar would never lie with Vasmine; she would hide behind her ridiculous long white hair and shyly stare at the ground. *You are too beautiful for me*, Istehar would say. *One day, elf child*, Vasmine would tease. *One day*, Istehar would whisper, and go off climbing the trees or wading in the river.

Later, lying under furs in the dark mahogany bed, I turn to Vasmine and ask what else happened at the palace. Vasmine regales me with tales of Princess Kalicent's fury at learning how her beau betrayed her with an archdeacon's daughter. Then she frightens me with an imitation of Vilya's accusations against Istehar and her people. Chilled, I ask her not to go on.

"What exactly did you tell Prince Hoel this morning?" she asks me then.

"I gave him a vial of the poison I compounded from the formula on my father's desk," I explain. "I told him how hard I'd worked to translate the language and locate the ingredients. I asked if perhaps my father was planning to make the poison for my mother's use."

"And what did the prince say to your theory?"

"He said he'd look through the items they found that night. I think he doesn't plan to reopen the case; he seems to feel the murders were revenge for some foreign killing my mother carried out long ago."

"Don't press it with him, Loli," Vasmine advises me with an odd intensity. "I know you care for him, but don't forget he's the chief interrogator. It's best not to arouse his interest."

I stare at her. "Prince Hoel was my guardian. If he hadn't sent me to the River School, I might never have met Istehar. Or you."

"Such great good fortune Prince Hoel provided us," Vasmine admits playfully as she takes her comb from her night-table and pulls it through my hair. "But, Loli, you never told me you were going to speak with him. You didn't even tell me the poison was finished."

I think for a moment. "I'm sorry, Mina. You haven't been home much."

"Please tell me things like this, sweetling," Vasmine says. "You know how I hate not being let in on secrets."

I stroke her cheek. "It won't happen again. I promise." I still haven't told her how Princess Angelissa asked me to give up my search for the murderer and take a job as Council apothecary. But now is not the time.

Vasmine nods and subsides into the blankets. I could wait for her to fall asleep, then go up to Istehar's bed and pretend to have been there all along. But Vasmine never falls asleep first.

Warm under the furs, I let sleep steal over me.

In the night, I awaken from the dream I've dreamed on and off for years—my mother in a white nightgown on our balcony overlooking the water, holding a letter out to me, while my dead father lies at her feet. I try to read the letter but all I can make out are signatures scrawled at the bottom—some of them seem familiar but I can't place them. My mother reaches out with the letter, but it's slick with blood and when I try to take it, I drop it to the floor. I grasp at her nightgown, leaving bloody fingerprints; I can see the whorls and swirls.

I bolt upright in bed, heart pounding. Istehar is in the doorway, her nightgown as white as the one my mother wore in the dream.

"The house said to come," she says, matter-of-fact and inexplicable as always.

I nod wordlessly. Vasmine slumbers on. Istehar takes my hand and pulls me up to the third floor.

CHAPTER 8

Annlynn Jissakhar, Warrior Librarian

The Library

Ancilliday, 7:00 a.m.

Bookwardens in black kilts stand at nervous attention as I pass through their ranks. The marble steps are worn to smooth scallops by the boots of my ancestors, and the columns on either side of the door are carved with images of the destroyed libraries of old. Every morning for hundreds of years, we Librarians have begun the day armed, prepared for savage hordes to descend and wipe out all knowledge back to the invention of the wheel. We remember the War of the Libraries, before Moonstone was founded, when the great empires of Uluria and Taradia burned one another's troves of knowledge and impossibly precious tomes were lost forever. We are here to beat back the tides of history—though most days, we only have to deal with thieves, forgers, and arrogant princes.

"Your father just went in," one of the door-sentinels ventures timidly as he diligently searches my bag and pats down my person.

"He's left his mistress's bed early," I mutter. My father's attitude that rules are rules apparently doesn't extend to his (allegedly monogamous) marriage. My mother, like the genteel lady she is, pretends not to notice. Of course, my father's hypocrisy doesn't prevent him from criticizing my marital choices.

I leave thoughts of my father aside. Early morning is my favorite time in the Library. There are no patrons to deal with, and the whole staff is in motion—reshelving returns, balancing accounts, filing new books, preparing rare tomes for viewings. It's as busy and dark as an anthill. The Library was designed with wafer-thin marble walls so that sunshine would filter through just enough to light the halls with a dim reddish light. Some genius thought of that so lamplight wouldn't damage the books.

I can hear the distant rumbling of wheels. Underneath the ground floor of the Library is a network of channels cut into the stone, so unmanned carts can be hauled by pulley from one place to another, carting books where they need to go. I pass by one such station, where an underlibrarian, standing in a waist-deep round opening in the floor, hauls books wrapped in oilcloth out of a little square cart. When he finishes, he reaches down and pushes the wheeled cart into the tunnel and back the mysterious way it came. Then he climbs out and struggles to pull a wooden cover over the opening.

As I stride through the halls, smells of paper, leather, silk, ink, dust, wood, thread, glue, and water pervade the air. Tall bookcases face each other, slightly curving toward one another at their tops, so that one has the sense of passing through a tunnel or a thick forest. Many Librarians claim they can make their way through this labyrinth blindfolded. I haven't tried it. The truth is, I should be back at Undersong House keeping an eye in case the mob shows up. But Olloise wants the answer to her question, and if I don't get it for her, she'll likely sneak in here herself.

What I need is the archived records for the Controlled Section. Tommas is in charge of that section, and he keeps offering to sire a baby on me, so likely he'll do as I ask. But to get to his hidey-hole, I have to go past the Censor's Office—and that's where my father will be right now. I'd say he and I make a game of avoiding one another, except it's not a game—it's in deadly earnest.

I descend a flight of stairs and pass the Censor's Office in a stride, without even a sidelong glance at the sour staff within. Then my luck runs out. My father turns a corner, escorted by a brace of bookwardens. He has some vast tome in his arms, no doubt some heresy destined for a locked undercellar. He loves to forbid people to read things.

We come nose to nose. His entourage skids to a stop.

"Are you lost, Your Vigilance?" he snaps at me.

"I have business in the Controlled Section, Your Vigilance," I reply coldly.

"I imagine you do," he mutters. "After all, your… companion keeps requesting books on poison. Her requests of the Censor's Office have been quite shocking as of late."

"She's trying to solve a double murder," I say.

He laughs. "If you ask me, she's got a guilty conscience. Or else she's planning to strike again."

I half-close my eyes and pretend I'm in my office lighting incense, to avoid taking a swing at him. His attendants lean in a little. They don't want to miss anything.

Every time I see the man, he goes after one of the four of us. The only question is which of us he's going to target. He's called Istehar a charlatan and Vasmine a whore. I, of course, am an undisciplined, perverted, spoiled brat. But this is the first time he's called Olloise a murderer. He's fortunate Moonstone law prohibits duels between blood relatives.

"What possible motivation could a young girl have to kill her beloved parents?" I ask fiercely.

My father laughs. "She got an inheritance, didn't she?"

"Unlike some daughters I could mention," I snap. "Keep your slanderous accusations to yourself, before someone hauls you in front of a magistrate. And let me pass; I have work to do."

"Really, madam? What work do you have down here, aside from doing your paramour's bidding? Shouldn't you be chasing down some overdue book?"

I have, in fact, prepared a response for this very question. "She's my wife, not my paramour. And an overdue book is why I'm here. I need the Lutei forgery of the Moonstone Covenant. Prince Giya Lutei had it out for months and held it past due.

If he's damaged it in any way, he's barred from checking it out again."

"Well, well, well," my father chuckles. "Power over princes. That must make you feel big. I understand you had quite a run-in with Prince Giya. Surely you're aware incidents like that could endanger your position here."

"I was upholding the family motto," I say. "'Protect the books.'"

"You're hardly a paragon of family loyalty," my father accuses. "And you know perfectly well the motto is 'Guard Wisdom.'"

"Same thing," I shrug. "Excuse me."

Leaving my father and his people, I stride quickly down the dark hall before he thinks of another of my wives to insult. The door of the Office of Records for Controlled Books gapes slightly ajar. I knock on the marble doorframe.

Tommas looks up, smiling as usual. He has reason to smile; after all, his curly-haired, chocolate-skinned good looks are the talk of all the young bookshelvers of any gender. I grew up with Tommas; we played canal-ball together. His parents are import/export folk, and they wanted him to go into the business, but instead he worked hard to prepare himself to be Library staff—and he's been buried in tomes ever since. My parents would have been thrilled for me to marry him. I suppose we might have found things to like about it too.

His dark eyes widen a little in surprise as he sees I've come to his den of indices and miscellanies.

Best not to waste time. "I need a favor."

"Excellent. I've been wanting to reproduce myself," he replies cheerfully.

"I'll have a scribe make a copy of you," I say. "Listen, there's a book I suspect is here in the Controlled Section. It's called *The Poisoner's Guide to Moonstone* and it's at least two hundred years old. If we have it, can you pull the book?"

Tommas raises an eyebrow. "Planning to kill your father?"

I snort. "I wish. It's for Loli."

"Who's *she* planning to kill?"

"Don't start with me. I'm in a terrible mood. I ran into my father in the hall."

"Enough said." Tommas goes to a massive tome bound with metal rings and pages through it for a while.

"We do have it," he says. "It's marked both Rare and Controlled. We have an even older copy than the one you saw, I think."

"Great," I say. "Can you pull it for me?"

He nods and goes back to his desk for a heavy ring of keys.

I add casually: "Oh, and while you're opening vaults, bring me one of the forgeries of the Covenant. The Lutei forgery. You know, that weird antique party favor that claims the first archprince was a Lutei."

"Why?" Tommas looks at me quizzically.

I shrug. "I'm curious why Giya Lutei kept the thing out for months, and threatened me when I made him give it back. Can he really be that full of himself?"

"I think you know the answer to that." Tommas brushes past me and into the hall. "I'll be right back."

It actually takes quite some time. I finger a few ivory carvings on his desk—balls inside of balls, intricately linked. It reminds me of my ink-castle. Actually, it reminds me of my wives and me. The way we intersect, and don't, and sometimes don't quite fit and sometimes can't be separated. At different moments, any one of us might be the linchpin that holds us together.

As I turn one of the little sculptures in my hand, I remember back to that first year at the River School, Vasmine sidling up to me on the lawn by the riverbank, daring me to kiss her. I had not, up to that point, met anyone braver than I was. I remember, too, my father finding out, and the "talk" we had in his office where he told me I wasn't even sincere enough to be a degenerate, I was just out to embarrass him. He chided me for disgracing our ancestors, who guarded Moonstone's Library when it was built, and before that guarded the Librarium of Taradia. The warrior librarians of that great Abbatine empire, he said, were there when the Librarium burned during the War of the Libraries, and they perished in the flames rather than abandon their charge, while I was clearly too occupied in corruption of the flesh to live up to their example. He demanded my sword, the one he'd had made for me, saying I wasn't worthy of it. I told him if he wanted it back I'd be glad to stick it in him. At my graduation, not one of my clan came, except my little brother Dunekin, youngest of six, who sneaked out and stowed away on a barge so he could be there.

I hear a step in the hall. Tommas is back with both volumes—an imposing but thin one bound in moonstone-encrusted violet silk, and a small thicker one bound in simple linen, looking even more worn than the one Istehar brought home from the junk heap. I carefully take the little linen one from Tommas and expertly turn its delicate illuminated pages without damaging them. It's the same book as the contraband currently located in my house. It's remarkable no one's censored it yet.

"I need to see who's checked out this book," I say, almost casually.

Tommas looks a little shocked. "You know it's against the rules to share that with anyone outside my division," he points out, not entirely playfully. "Right to privacy. I could lose my position."

I nod solemnly. "I understand. But I need to know, Tommas, really. It matters. On my honor as a Librarian." I'd tell him it might solve a murder, but that would involve him far more than is good for him.

He glances uneasily toward the door and strides over to another large three-ringed tome, fatter and more unruly than the first. "Is there a name you're looking for?" he asks in a low voice.

"Nidaba Mazall. Or Zevid Mazall."

He nods and flips pages. Now he likely has a better idea of why I'm asking. I've shared with him often over the years about Loli's tragedy and her determined (one might say obsessive) quest for justice for her mother and father. I suppose I've always been a little jealous of her devotion to them. If someone killed my parents, I'm pretty sure the only thing I'd feel driven to would be a drink and a long walk.

He turns pages for an eternity. The close air hangs around us as if it's eavesdropping.

"No Mazalls checked out the book," he says at last. "Not then or ever. Giya Lutei did, though."

"What?" I lean in. "No. You looked up the wrong one."

"Not at all," he contradicts me. "Giya Lutei checked out *The Poisoner's Guide to Moonstone* a few years ago." He peers into the record. "In fact, he checked out that book just a few months before Olloise's parents were killed. It looks like it was returned just prior to their death."

My head is swimming. "This doesn't make any sense," I say. "How would he even know about it? Has anyone else checked it out?"

Tommas looks again and shakes his head. "No one else in the last decade. A few scholars, in the decades before that. The book is Controlled, so it would be hard for anyone to even know we have it."

I feel like a thunderclap has sounded between my ears. I keep shaking my head to get rid of it. Tommas is flipping through pages; I can't think why.

"Nidaba Mazall did check out a Controlled book a few days before her death," he says to me.

The hair on the back of my neck stands up. "What are you talking about? Which one?"

"The Lutei forgery," he says. "She checked it out for three days. It was returned the night of the murder." He looks at the tome again. "Actually, she seems to have checked out all six of the Covenant forgeries during the same time period. She must have gotten special permission."

"What could Loli's mother possibly want with six elaborate hoaxes from two hundred years ago?" I ask in frustration. "Those books were meant to create a stir at parties. All they did was stroke princes' egos by inviting them to imagine themselves as archprince!"

"I don't know, but she died right after reading them," Tommas says. "And, looking at the time of return, I'm not at all sure who returned them. Maybe her, or maybe someone who found them after her death."

"Or the murderer," I say.

I put my hand on the hilt of my sword because it helps me think. So Nidaba Mazall checked out the Moonstone Covenant forgeries. Prince Giya Lutei checked out *The Poisoner's Guide to Moonstone*. And *The Poisoner's Guide to Moonstone* contains the formula on Zevid Mazall's desk. This all seems to mean that Prince Giya trying to make off with the Lutei forgery yesterday has something to do with the murder of Olloise's parents six years ago, and maybe something to do with the murder of Giya Lutei's distant ancestor. I have clearly uncovered something much bigger than a breadbox.

I take my bag and dump its contents—snacks, handkerchiefs, and the like—into Tommas's trash can. "I need to take both books," I say. "Istehar has to see them."

Now Tommas really does look shocked. "Annlynn, I can't help you steal books!"

"I'm not stealing them! Check them out in my name. I have a Library account!"

Tommas looks worried. "Look, if you check them out, I have to make a record of it. And you know an application to check out a Controlled book has to go through your father's office before it can be approved. You know how likely it is your father will say yes, especially after what happened with Prince Giya."

He's afraid. I can feel it. "What do you suggest?" I say.

"How about you bring Istehar here to look at them? I think I can authorize that without your father." He doesn't quite believe me that Istehar can speak to trees and books, but he humors me.

I shake my head. "There are too many books here. She can handle a small bookshop, but this place makes her literally insane."

Tommas stands firm. "If she can do what you say she can do, she'll only need a few minutes."

I stare at him, then make a decision. "I'll be back in an hour," I say. And this time when I pass my father's office, I'm moving too fast for anyone to get in my way.

CHAPTER 9
Istehar Sha'an, Illuminatrix
Silvirium, Undersong House
Ancilliday, 9:30 a.m.

When we fled, we took the air in our lungs. We took herbs, roots, and flowers in our medicine boxes. We took staffs and bows made from branches gifted us by wind and rain. We took cups and bowls carved from burls. We took children on our backs, with wilted wreaths on their heads and seeds in their pockets. In a sack, I carried our Books of the Tree. The forest came with us; it shelters us still. But this city will never understand that.

I will never forget the first time a Librarian opened a Book of the Tree to see what was in it. It was not long after our miserable arrival, when we were all penned at a checkpoint in the Vexriver Fortress south of the city. Such a shiver passed through the man when he opened the cover of rough, ridged, and furrowed bark, and saw the thousand carefully handmade pages were blank. He turned page after page but could make out no writing, no language at all. I think the city's hatred of the Sha'an was born in that moment.

"If you produce books like this, you'll be begging on the streets in no time," he said.

"Books like this are how we survived this long," I told him.

Morning prayers are finished. I have sent everyone out of the silvirium, even my friend Tiarath with whom I often sit after prayers, and closed the door. Surrounded by potted trees and sunlight pouring through glass walls, I open the Book of the Tree that lies on a moss-silk pillow, the heavy one with a cover of thickly furrowed bark and yellowed pages, the one my teacher's teachers made, that has held our memories for generations. A young apple tree, planted in a hole in the floor, pokes its branches up through apertures in the ceiling, its foaming blossoms and pale green leaves sheltering me and the book. Other Books of the Tree, even older, with pages fraying at the edges, hum to themselves in an ark in the corner. Once we prayed in a towering grove; now we must fit into this little room.

I speak to my ancestors, human and arboreal. I ask how to protect my little tribe in this vast heartless city. There is no ill archprince now for us to cure. And where can we go if we leave here? The Sha'an forests are smoke now, and evil folk rule the treeless fields that are left.

I press my hand to a page and close my eyes. Forest floor rises up, fungus and damp soil. A circle of houses half-buried in the earth. My parents, alive. I climb down a ladder into a deep roofed pit. Zilfa, the illuminatrix who came before me, takes my index finger, holds it to the earth, then to a page of the book open before her. She is showing me how to imprint the page with feelings and sensations and memories, how to fill it with the light of the day. In this deep place, webs of roothair poking from the walls, I feel safe, sheltered by trees and earth.

My foolish brain interrupts my vision. Why has the book shown me this moment? We should not have to hide underground. We are allowed to live here. That was what the Council promised us, the day they sent me to the River School. The Moonstone princes wanted me to become one of them, to lead my people like a lady of Moonstone and not like an illuminatrix of the Sha'an. I knew I would never do that, but I went to the school, to buy goodwill for my people. And there I found what I did not expect: a family to replace the one I lost. A family as diverse and raucous as this city. A family I will soon lose, if the Sha'an are driven from this place—or else my wives will have to come into exile with me, and I do not want that for them.

Guided by the all-seeing trees, I feel her before I see her: a fierce beast of a person, raging into the house. She is urgent, intent on her hunting. I hear her steps in the hall. She opens the door into the silvirium, then stops, shame-faced to be barging into a sacred place. I turn to look at her, jolted as the vision of the book and my eyes' vision align. Annlynn bows a little and makes that funny two-handed Abbatine gesture—pinching the first three fingers on both hands to make saints' candles. I carefully close the book. The vision fades.

"I might know who killed Loli's parents," she says urgently. "But I need your help. I need you to do something very hard."

"Yes," I say.

There is, apparently, no time for boats. I leave behind my staff, thinking the Librarians may find it worrisome, but I feel unsteady without it. Annlynn herds me over the little bridge to Inkstone Point, and then through a maze of bridges and alleys, boardwalks and catwalks. I hurry after her as if we are fleeing for our lives. The damp air is chilly on my skin; I have forgotten my shawl. The great hive hums at the edge of my consciousness, as it always has ever since I came to this city. We pass carts of jewel-like fruit from the micro-orchards of Seven Lanterns, pots of pickled fish being sold at market, ancillas begging for alms for their sisters in the ancillary, and weavers hawking cloaks of sea-sheep wool. All of it makes no sound to me, compared to the Library.

As we cross the Long Bridge onto Opal Island, the buzz of thousands of voices grows louder and louder, like a landslide starting. We wind up narrow slanting streets and under high arches, passing haughty-looking deacons, stern sentinels, schoolchildren, poor folk seeking day labor, and the palanquins of ladies. As we come around a sharp corner, the great white dome appears. The voices in my head are like hornets, stinging me with hopes and fears, with stories, laws, and dreams. As we make our way across Festival Square, I have to stop to get my breath. When Annlynn speaks to me, I cannot hear what she is saying.

The voices of a forest are calming, but the voices of books—the consciousness of trees bonded with human words and will—are far more demanding. I have been in this building only once before, to meet with the archprince and the Council, and I was in bed for days afterward with what felt like an iron stake in my brain. The first time I really spoke with Annlynn, back at the River School, I told her I could not come even so far as the market in Festival Square. She liked that about me. But now she wants me to go into the Library itself.

She rushes me up smooth marble steps guarded by black-clad warriors. As they search our bags, I notice some of these folk looking at one another—what is Annlynn's snow-haired witch doing here? But Annlynn pays them no attention, and in moments we are in the red, dark halls of this ancient anthill, with little noisy books lining shelves and shelves and shelves as if they will go out as an army and overrun the world.

We go down steps and around corners. People stare as we pass. I clutch my head. "Just a little farther," urges Annlynn. A friendly face looks out from a doorway and through that doorway we go. There is a cluttered office with cabinets and a table, and on the table are two books I know. One looks like the book I brought to Loli as a birthday present. The other looks like the one I saw on the table when I met with the Council: the Moonstone Covenant. But it is not the same book; I can feel that in the ripples it leaks into the room.

Annlynn solemnly hands me the smaller book: *The Poisoner's Guide*. I hold it and try to concentrate, to shut out the myriad books clamoring at me like babies wanting to be fed. Annlynn and Tommas watch me intently and anxiously, as if I may explode.

A little girl with dark hair is playing with vials and stoppers at my feet. Then she is older, taller, expertly pouring from one beaker to another. Then she is gone—my hands, covered in blood, reach out for her as I fall. The smell grows stronger as the light fades. "Loli's father held this book," I whisper, trembling so hard the book shakes. "It was near him when he died."

"But he never checked it out," says Annlynn's friend—Tommas is his name.

"Prince Giya did," Annlynn says grimly. "And now we know something we did not."

"You think Giya Lutei is the murderer?" Tommas asks. "He's a prince of Moonstone. What could be his motive for killing the Council's forensic apothecary along with their most skilled assassin?"

"Maybe to thwart an investigation. I don't know, but I intend to find out, and give Loli some peace at long last." Annlynn's hand is on the hilt of her sword. She thinks better that way, or so she says.

Her hand is still there when bookwardens come into the room, followed by a fearsome, straight-backed, sour-looking, gray-haired man in a black robe.

"Father," Annlynn greets him with a face like winter. Then I know who the man is.

"Your Vigilance." Tommas makes a little bow. Annlynn shoots Tommas a cold glare that spells *traitor*. Her hand stays on her sword.

"May I ask why a Sha'an witch is perusing a book on poisons?" asks Sterven Jissakhar, Lord Censor of the Library. The question hangs in the air and I realize that if I am arrested, Prince Vilya will take the book as evidence that I have conspired to poison the whole city. I will be killed, and the Sha'an people will likely be expelled. What has Annlynn done, bringing me here? I can barely think. I feel thousands of books clamoring at me, demanding I surrender to their pinprick voices.

"Well?" Lord Jissakhar barks. "Why is this diabolical book club occurring under my very nose?"

Tommas swallows and stares straight ahead. "Madam Sha'an is here with permission, sir," he says.

"Is that so?" Lord Jissakhar looks impressively dubious. "And who exactly gave her permission to bypass my office?"

Tommas hesitates. "His Eminence the Archprince," Annlynn interjects. Annlynn sometimes gambles in the floating casinos; she knows not to let her face give anything away. But the tension in her is palpable.

"Paperwork," Lord Jissakhar demands. He stares at his daughter with a rage I find shocking.

"I will obtain it for you at once, Your Vigilance," says Annlynn, very correctly.

"Madam Sha'an stays here," says Lord Jissakhar. "If you're not back in an hour with something legitimate, I will put her in a cell and send for the sentinels."

Annlynn bows and leaves the room. Perhaps Archprince Jalian will sign a letter on my behalf. Perhaps he will not. It is true my people saved his life, but I am only a foreign witch, and I am becoming unpopular.

"May I offer you a chair, Madam Sha'an?" says Tommas. It is bravery, of a sort. I nod gratefully and sink into the seat he slides toward me.

Sterven Jissakhar stares at me as he picks up the forged Covenant and puts it under his arm. He has never met me. The day the four of us went to the Magistery and signed a marriage certificate, he sent Annlynn a letter repudiating her as his offspring. No doubt I am the one he blames. The marriage was my idea.

I shiver. My shawl is back at Undersong House. So is my staff. The books roar like an ocean in my ears. I fantasize for a moment that I am drowning in them. One of the guards whispers a curse under his breath. Then other words. *Witch. Poisoner. Demoness.* But his is not the voice I am worried about. The voices of the books are loud enough to drive me mad, I think, in not too long a time. And I did not even get to hold the second book Annlynn wanted me to hold.

"Stand guard," the censor says to his bookwardens. "I'll be back."

I close my eyes, trying to escape the pounding in my head. A smell rises into my nostrils. It is not the smell of dust and mold but the smell of soil and roots, the smell of the home of my teacher Zilfa: the smell of my vision not long ago. And then I remember another art I saw Zilfa perform in her pit of earth, different from the making of Books of the Tree. It is a rare and dangerous magic, she told me, only for moments of dire need. But it seems I have run out of options. I will need paper, or a book. Ironic that there are so many just out of reach.

"I wonder," I say to Tommas humbly, "if I might have a prayerbook. To pass the time."

"A Silvilline prayerbook?" Tommas inquires.

"Yes, if possible."

"Of course, Madam Sha'an," he says, and goes off into the stacks. The bookwardens chuckle nastily, but don't object.

"She may as well pray now," one of them nudges the other. "In an hour, she'll have something to pray about." He leers at me.

Tommas returns with the prayerbook, simply bound in blue linen, printed in large letters. The same kind one would see in a silvirium anywhere in the city. Not a Book of the Tree. An ordinary book, albeit with holy words inside.

Long before the Sha'an were driven here, folk sometimes left the forests and went to dwell in Moonstone, where there was ample food and work. Those people called themselves Silvillines—people of the woods. They brought their reverence for the Great Tree with them, but they tamed that reverence, and became like any of the many sects of Moonstone. They wore ordinary clothes and took last names, so as to be like the others in the city. Now we, their wilder cousins, are here, and no doubt causing trouble for them. I consider them my people, but not all of them return the favor. Still, the city Silvillines make lovely prayerbooks and I am grateful for this one. In my mind, it has a cozy, pleasant droning, like a lullaby one has heard many times.

I open to the first page, bend my head over it, and begin to move my lips. Tommas and the bookwardens pay me no mind; who pays attention to a woman praying? The words are a hymn to the Great Tree—so odd for me to see the Tree depicted in words and not in images within my mind. I picture the ritual Zilfa taught me: she took a book, opened to the first page, and used an awl to make a hole through the pages, all the way from top to bottom.

But I have no awl, and unlike Vasmine, I do not have a hairpin always at hand. I use my thumbnail to make a little, scalloped hole in the middle of the first page. I manage to tear the page slightly, but to tear through all the pages will take time and I will run the risk of making a tearing sound. One of the bookwardens will see. The voices in my head buzz louder and louder and I feel faint. I close my eyes and in desperation begin to murmur the words I heard Zilfa say: "Loam, return to leaf. Leaf, return to limb. Limb, return to life."

I murmur this over and over again, almost succeeding in banishing the stinging bookminds from my head. Minutes later, I dare to open my eyes. The tiny hole is still a tiny hole. My heart sinks.

But as I stare at the little gash, I begin to see the faintest hint of blackened edges, as if I had made the hole with a match instead of my fingernail. As I watch, the hole deepens, and its edges glow and turn to ash, as if I am slowly pressing an invisible poker through the pages. The book is now hot to the touch. Afraid of being burned, I close the book abruptly and nearly drop it. Tommas and the bookwardens look up.

I compose my face, bend my head, and very carefully open the book again, angling it so the men cannot see. The hole through the pages is now coin-sized and perfectly round, and extends to the very last page. Without warning, voices burst through this hole at me, angry voices, like treetops lashing in a storm. Worse, almost, than the books of the Library. The sentinels laze by the door; Tommas sits at his desk, tapping his foot nervously. I cannot believe they cannot hear this awful sound.

The voices grow calm. They greet me. They make me a promise. And then they are gone.

CHAPTER 10
Vasmine Kinora, Ink-Merchant
Inkstone Point
Ancilliday, 10:30 a.m.

"Do let me wrap those for you," I say to Prince Hoel. "Fragile things benefit from delicate handling."

"Indeed," he replies. For just a moment, his eyes meet mine. Outside the shop, the usual dock-loiterers have made themselves scarce—the prince of Seven Lanterns is not known for his forbearance. Hoel's boatmen, tending the barge anchored outside, are silent as the Library Reading Room. I can hear wavelets slapping against the dock.

The prince has laid a set of horsehair calligraphy brushes with jade handles on the counter, along with a box of inksticks from Gengrassia. For his wife, he says. It all costs a fortune, but of course he has one to spend. From a niche in my ornate desk, I produce a green satin sack, the same fabric as the curtains hanging in the window that faces the river. A nice touch, I think. The prince waits politely but impatiently as I gently swaddle each of the brushes in a swatch of fabric before putting them all in the sack. Outside my open door, Hoel's cloaksmen, swords visible, lounge in the late-morning sun.

An ink shop proprietor always knows who is writing and what is being written. The printing presses of Hundred Quays are busy with penny journals and religious tracts, novels and political manifestos, but the poets and composers, the playwrights and literary masters of the city still write their drafts by hand. They all come into my shop and discuss with me the best tools for their work. I enjoy what I do. It makes me independent, and it allows me to know things.

"It is always a delight to see you, Your Eminence," I say, handing Prince Hoel his purchase.

"Is it?" replies the sturdy old man, stroking his two-pointed beard with his thick fingers. "I think it possible you are a liar, Vasmine."

"I am always honest with *you*, my prince," I counter, smiling. He gives me a dubious glance and strides out the door, across the pier, and onto his barge. The cloaksmen follow. The boatmen push off.

As soon as Hoel's barge is out of sight, Annlynn slinks across my threshold. She has the face she has when she's been fighting. Annlynn after a fight makes me hot. I used to jump her in the washroom after fencing class.

"You look exercised. Are you here for medical attention?" I ask. "Or another kind of attention?"

She wordlessly shakes her head. I open a cabinet and take out a porcelain decanter and two matching glasses. "You clearly need a drink."

"I need help," she says. Which may be a sentence I have never before heard her say. "My father's detained Istya at the Library. I took her there to show her their copy of the *Poisoner's Guide*. He caught her with it."

I suck in my breath. All my work to get peace for this little tribe, and she ruins it all in one morning. "River take you, you fool," I snap with deliberate force. "Why would you take Istehar to the Library?"

She shrugs and won't meet my eyes. "Tommas wouldn't let me take the book to her, so I brought her to the book. I thought we'd be in and out in a moment. We may have learned who killed Loli's parents." She shakes her head. "But that doesn't matter now. I need you to ask the archprince to write a letter giving Istehar permission to be in the Library reading that book. I need you to go to the palace right now and do this, Mina. Please. I have very little time."

She looks at me expectantly, with her infinite hope that all evils can be resisted. I shake my head. "I can't, Annlynn."

Annlynn recoils as if I've struck her. "What do you mean, you can't?" she demands. "Saints' teeth, Mina, she's your wife! And the archprince cares about the Sha'an, you know he does! He'll help!"

Annlynn's brain is a bit of a blunt instrument. "Anya, he does care, but think how this looks! A witch with a book of poisons? They'll think she planned to poison the river! If Prince Vilya finds out, and he shortly will, there'll be a mob out with torches by nightfall. If the archprince doesn't want to be deposed himself, he'll have no choice but to throw Istehar to the wolves." I take a deep breath. "Once she's in prison, we can try a bribe. But there's nothing we can do right now. And there's a danger she may confess, thinking they might take her and leave the Sha'an alone."

Annlynn's pale eyes burn into me. "Vasmine. Please do this. You're his lover."

"You've just made me a liability," I snap. "If this goes very wrong, you and me and Loli will need to get out of the city. This damned revenge quest of Loli's may have ruined us."

"I'll ask him if you won't!" Annlynn barks.

I laugh. "They'll never let you into the palace! And don't go home right now, either, because the Sha'an will think you turned her in. I can't imagine what they'll do to you."

I've always tortured myself with the idea that Annlynn secretly loves Istehar more than me. Maybe I'm about to find out it's true.

I go over to the hidden drawer where I keep my earnings and empty the drawer's contents into my purse. Just in case. I suddenly, guiltily, wonder, if we do have to run, if we should bring Loli to some safe place and leave her there. Anya and I might be better on our own.

Then there are noises outside: loud voices and the familiar knocking of a boat against the pier. I wonder if the city watch has come to arrest us, but I hear the jangle of bells, which is odd, and then through the window I see four strong men walking a lavish palanquin off a barge and up to my front door.

The door of the palanquin opens. All the tiny silver bells embroidered on its roof jangle melodiously. One of the men helps Kalicent Mai, Princess of Moonstone, directly into my shop. Annlynn bows and steps back into the shop's shadows. I make a courtly obeisance. The princess sheds her cloak of crimson lace into the hands of one of her servitors.

Kalicent's skin is flawless as usual, her height commanding, her ink-black hair perfectly coiffed in towers on either side of her head. But her belly is swollen. I can see that under her splendid scarlet gown, her breasts are enlarged. She looks for all the world as if she is with child. I can make no sense of her condition. She had no such belly-swelling last night at the engagement party.

"Your Eminence," I greet her. It is not politic to imply any indelicate state could exist in the archprince's daughter, so I have no idea what to say next.

"That witch whore Memmiam has cursed me," Kalicent rages. "Look at me! I am under a spell. The little chit is angry that I ended her fling with my ex-fiancé and exiled her from court! I am certain it is she who has used this foul sorcery against me! She has made me suddenly pregnant! If my father sees me like this, he will think I have been loose! He'll exile me to some island somewhere. I will lose my chance to marry! This is a catastrophe, Vasmine. You must do something!"

I do not even dare to look at Annlynn. "I do know someone who could help Your Eminence," I say with as much confidence as I can muster. "As you know, Istehar Sha'an, one of my wives, is a powerful healer. She could surely counter the spell you are under." I pause. "Unfortunately, she is currently detained at the Library. There has been a misunderstanding about a Controlled book she read without permission—"

The princess interrupts me: "This is easily taken care of." She turns. "Bring me my father's seal," she snaps at a servitor waiting in the doorway. She waves her hand at the contents of my ink shop; the brushes and inksticks and fancy papers. "I assume you have something to write with?"

"Indeed, Your Eminence," I reply. And in short order Annlynn has the document she needs and makes an unseemly rush out the door. She runs like her soul is in peril, which maybe it is; I would not venture to say.

"When will the healer come to see me?" Kalicent demands. "This must be over with before my father hears!"

"She must gather the needed items," I say. "At midnight tonight she will come to you. Until then, rest and prepare yourself. The process may be arduous." I do hope Istehar has the powers I have claimed for her. If she doesn't, as they say on the docks, we've climbed out of the canal only to fall in the river.

The princess climbs back into her palanquin and is borne away. I pick up my heavy purse and wonder if I should go home, or if it would be safer to hire a boatman and abscond to parts unknown. I shrug, lock up the shop, and head for the bridge. This life has always been dangerous. And, there are people I chose to face it with.

Who chose me to face it with. I don't forget that.

CHAPTER 11

Annlynn Jissakhar, Vasmine Kinora, Olloise Mazall, and Istehar Sha'an, Students
River School, Vexmere
Seven years ago

The rectoress has been droning on for close to two hours about the districts of Moonstone: the original dwellers, the arrival of settlers, the claiming of islands by different nations, the ethnic origin of each population of the thirteen districts, the micro-cultures that still exist within the city. The dismissal gong sounds. Olloise and Istehar have been at the front of the classroom, which means that they will have to wait for the crowd to thin before they can head for the garden to eat lunch. No one else in the class says anything to them. Everyone knows Istehar is a sorceress, and Olloise only talks about death.

There's an anteroom outside the classroom with a door to the front lawn. Stairs go up to the girls' bedrooms. The popular girls, who are good at running, sword fighting, and canal-ball, lean back against the wall of the anteroom watching the boys file out toward their dormitory. "Oi, Pirrip," freckled Selba calls, "don't you know the archprince is coming tomorrow to pick who's going to be running his fine city five years from now? Get a haircut!"

"Don't bother," Annlynn adds. "My brothers and sisters have all the good jobs already."

Pirrip laughs. "Don't worry, Annlynn, you'll make Junior Secretary for the Recovery of Books that Fell into Canals and Floated Out to Sea." He jumps up to tap the lintel on his way out. "Or maybe Overseer of Tax Collection on Islands Too Small to Notice..." he calls behind him.

"Or maybe Chief Investigatrix of Cadets with Excessively Long Hair," Annlynn jibes back.

Olloise and Istehar keep close to the wall as they make their way toward the back stairs. They prefer no one notice them. Annlynn nods to the two as they pass. She likes weird brilliant girls, even if she can't show it much in the hallway. Sometimes she even meets them in the study garden outside the school library and they read ancient poetry to each other. It helps with languages class, or at least that's what they tell people.

The between-class chaos stops dead when the front door of the cadettes' dormitory opens and a long-fingered, heart-faced girl walks in, followed by three men with large valises. Her gaze is distant yet intensely engaged, her flared silk coat clearly comes from the fashion district in Scattered Pearls, and her dark hair is piled on her head in a complex twist that would stump the geometry teacher. She is gorgeous in the way princesses are supposed to be gorgeous but usually aren't. A cloud of hatred and lust rises up from the crowd like spores from an injured puffball.

"That's her," Selba says, nudging Annlynn. "Prince Hallan's concubine. I heard she was coming." Selba's father is the school registrar; she always knows the news before everyone else.

"What's a concubine?" Istehar asks Olloise.

Joeve, slouching at the edge of the in-crowd knot, collapses against the wall, wheezing with laughter. "You don't need to know, freak! You're not eligible for the job." Selba chuckles meanly. Annlynn frowns.

The tall rectoress, with a tome the size of a loaf of bread under her arm, strides through the crowd to greet the new arrival. The girl—or lady—bows in an understated way that somehow makes everyone stare at her even harder.

Istehar opens her mouth to ask another question. Olloise takes Istehar's arm and explains very, very quietly: "Concubines are like wives, only they don't share their spouse's name or title. Their children belong to them, not to the person they're contracted to. They're trained specially to entertain high-class folk."

Istehar frowns. "So, artists? Or sex workers?"

Olloise chuckles. "Some of both, I guess."

"Why does anyone want to send a high-class whore to boarding school?" Joeve asks loudly. "Isn't she good enough at sex already? Why would she need to learn fencing and library skills?"

"Leave off," Big Chessa chides, annoyed. Big Chessa can always be counted upon for fairness. "It's not her fault she's a concubine. It's hereditary. Mothers pass it down to daughters."

"It's not hereditary," Annlynn sighs. "It's not a disease. It's a Moonstone tradition. There are concubine genealogies going back hundreds of years."

"Hasn't your father got one?" Selba asks her slyly.

Annlynn rolls her eyes. "He has a mistress, Selba. That's different."

"I can't keep track of this," Istehar murmurs from the back wall. Annlynn smiles a little.

"You'd best be nice to her," Ursario, one of the remaining boys, says without taking his eyes off the new girl. "She's not just any concubine. She's hitched to Prince Hallan of Scattered Pearls. If she was his wife, she'd be royalty."

"Well, she isn't, is she?" Joeve snaps.

The rectoress bows, says a few words, and leaves through the front door. The three men take the large suitcases up the stairs. And the new girl, left alone in the center of the room, reaches into her coat pocket and draws out a wicked little silver-handled knife, polished and beautiful. She wields it as if she intends to use it. A few of the boys laugh in a startled way. Joeve stiffens.

The girl grins. "Anyone know where I can sharpen this?"

Joeve lets out a furious breath. Olloise turns her face aside; she doesn't like knives.

"There's a whetstone in the armory," Annlynn says before anyone else can answer.

"If you'll be so kind as to show me, I'll take the opportunity to hone my instrument." Another wicked grin. "I'm Vasmine." With her other hand, she takes the knife's scabbard out of her pocket and sheaths the blade. She's playing to a rapt crowd; there's silence in the anteroom. "Vasmine Kinora."

Annlynn makes a courtly bow; she knows how to act. "Annlynn Jissakhar."

"A Jissakhar? From the clan of Librarians? Is that so? Then we have the two oldest professions."

Annlynn barks a startled laugh. "Oh, she's outrageous," Olloise murmurs. Selba whispers to Big Chessa, and Big Chessa laughs heartily. The boys start to slink away.

Annlynn and Vasmine exit down the back stairs. Joeve melts away, disgusted, into the crowd. "It's bad enough she talks to those two freakish fiendspawn," she mutters. "Does she have to collect every low-class waste of time at the school?"

The logjam in the anteroom clears, and now there's a path to the front door. As they step out into the morning light on the lawn facing the river, Istehar says to Olloise: "If that's a concubine, I think her skill set may be broader than the one you described."

Annlynn proudly squires Vasmine around campus. They view the little harbor, the firepit, and the wisteria arbor. Annlynn explains the dormitories, the departments, the fencing-hall and the infirmary, the chapel and the meeting-hall. A few hangers-on follow them halfheartedly, then trail off when no one pays them any attention.

As they walk along the back river, Vasmine takes Annlynn's arm. She asks questions about the rectoress, about the other students, about Annlynn's family. She pays careful attention to the answers. Annlynn finds herself telling about her childhood: how she and her siblings would visit the Library before hours, running on the marble floors when her father wasn't looking, peering into musty books and rolled-up scrolls.

"It's my favorite place," Annlynn confesses.

Vasmine looks up into Annlynn's face and smiles magnificently. "Do you want to see it from above?"

In an hour, Annlynn has rowed them over to Vexriver Fortress, where the sentinels are experimenting with hot-air balloons to watch over the city and the port. Vasmine has what she calls "contacts" among the officers, and soon the two of them climb into a massive woven basket. The balloon is striped sky-blue and sea-blue, the city's colors.

The balloon-tenders light the flame. Annlynn and Vasmine cling to the basket's edge as the balloon rises up. The River School, with its orderly arrangement of rectangular buildings, passes beneath them. Vasmine points out the ribboned barge ferrying Prince Hallan back to Scattered Pearls.

"Do you like him?" Annlynn dares.

Vasmine shrugs. "I appreciate his good taste, and he appreciates mine. I've increased his social capital considerably."

"And now you're training to be his cloakswoman?"

"Hallan and I travel together a great deal. It makes sense for me to serve as his bodyguard when necessary." Spread out below them are the patchwork fields of the Perfumery, the rounded isles of the Moon's Daughters, the Narrow Forests on either side of the river. Annlynn feels she can almost touch the soaring cliffs that frame the city. She restrains herself from whooping. She doesn't want Vasmine to think her coarse.

"I've met Prince Hallan when my family and I go to the Sanctum," Annlynn says instead. "He's handsome."

"He bought my first contract," Vasmine says. "He whisked me away from my small-minded father, so I'm grateful. But he *is* one of Prince Vilya's partisans." Vasmine frowns. "He and Ebel Quareen from Holy Ibis. They're tired of the old archprince." She shrugs. "I rather like the archprince, myself."

"He's been good to the Library," Annlynn says. She pauses. "And the Sha'an."

Vasmine raises an eyebrow but says nothing, so Annlynn judges her not too prejudiced. Annlynn is relieved; she plans to spend more time with Vasmine, and it would have been awkward with Istehar. "So you've been at parties with Prince Vilya."

"Not voluntarily," Vasmine confides in a whisper. "Vilya's father hates him, so the boy dotes on his mother, who stays locked in a palace tower brooding about the dangers of magic. She's terrified of being ensorcelled. Once, a seamstress finished a gown for her overnight. Archprincess Tilgana judged the feat impossible. She had the girl sentenced to death."

"The archprincess writes letters to my father asking him to censor books," Annlynn notes. "Lots of letters. The books locked in the Library cellar are piled to the ceiling."

"When Vilya is archprince," Vasmine warns, "the Library will need a bigger cellar."

Below them now are the squares, bridges, canals, and alleyways of the three main islands: Opal Island, Seven Lanterns, and Drake's Hoard. Off to the east, Holy Ibis and the Sanctum, and beyond them, the crowded docks and stepped streets of Juniper Island. To the west, the two small isles of the Lanternelles, and the beaches of Golden Sands. The Library, with its round domes, dominates the scene. It is wondrous to see it from above. As a strong wind pushes them east, Vasmine stumbles into Annlynn, and Annlynn steadies her with an arm around her shoulders. Vasmine's scent, some rare perfume Annlynn can't identify, is intoxicating.

As the balloon-tenders lower the flame, they drift lower. The bulbous towers of the archprince's palace are below them, and the tall Seaspire, then the many tiny isles of Scattered Pearls. "There's City-of-Bridges!" Vasmine exclaims. Annlynn sees dainty round buildings built on micro-islands, connected by a lacy network of arches.

"That's where you live?" Annlynn asks.

Vasmine smiles. "I live at the River School. With you."

Annlynn blushes a little. She points out the haze over the island of Sorcerer's Kettle. "Because of the factories," she says. Vasmine proposes they try to count the uncountable ships docked at Hundred Quays. The balloon-tenders bring them down in a field on a minor island in the district of

Turtle's Clutch. Annlynn doesn't know which one it is: it's not Bellbillow, Sesserina, Kestrelery, or Saintsfish. She doesn't know Turtle's Clutch at all; it was settled by insular farmers and fishermen from Upper Phantos who still speak Phantosi and never go anywhere. The tenders have been a little reckless; not far beyond the folds of the deflated balloon, the river meets the sea.

The balloon-tenders stay to wait for the military boat that will return the balloon to Vexriver. Annlynn and Vasmine hire a private barge for the long ride home. As soon as they set out, Vasmine closes the curtains of the felze, and the two of them have their first kiss. It turns out they need every minute of the journey.

CHAPTER 12

The Wives

Undersong House

Ancilliday, 12:00 p.m.

When Annlynn and Istehar come in the back door, Olloise and Vasmine are waiting for them. There is a full glass of something blue-green on the stone counter. Istehar is shivering uncontrollably and her eyes are half-closed. Vasmine drapes a thick wool shawl around her.

"Thank the Great Tree you're all right," Olloise fusses, embracing Istehar. "And Annlynn, you could have lost your position!" Annlynn's strong, squarish face looks crestfallen. Istehar's oval one looks worried and exhausted. She goes to her staff in the corner of the room and touches it, as if to make sure it is still there.

"I did something, Loli," Istehar whispers. "Something I maybe shouldn't have done."

"All right," Olloise replies. "We'll discuss it. Drink what's in the glass. It may help with the headache. A pity it won't help your good sense!"

"It was my fault," Annlynn interjects as Istehar takes the glass in two shaking hands and dutifully takes a sip of the foaming concoction.

"I have to concur," Vasmine notes, settling into a chair. "Istya doesn't know Moonstone, Anya. You do. You should have known better."

"I've lived here for ten years, Vasmine," Istehar corrects wearily, sinking onto a stool. "I know the city well enough."

"I was upstairs in the laboratory the whole time,"

Olloise says, her fury starting to show. "All either of you had to do was come up and ask me what I thought about this plan of action!"

"You did ask me to find out about the book, Loli," Annlynn murmurs resentfully. "I did exactly what you wanted." She takes a crystal decanter from a shelf and pours herself a few finger-widths of the amber contents.

Olloise sighs. "I said, 'Find out if someone checked out the book.' I didn't say, 'Take Istya to a building that may cause her serious injury, and then get her nearly executed as a witch.' Be sensible, Anya!"

Annlynn slams her fist on the counter, nearly spilling her drink. The rest of them flinch. "Did you think there was no risk involved in solving your parents' murder? Your mother was an assassin, Loli! Do you think the person who killed her and your father was an amateur? Did you think there would be anything safe about this? This is only the beginning of the danger we're going to be in from now on!"

The four of them are silent. "You're right," Olloise says quietly. "I need to know why my life was derailed. But I don't have to involve the rest of you any further."

"You've already involved us," Annlynn points out. "My father put a demerit in my file and barred me from the Library for three days for 'filing late paperwork.' So you may as well hear what we've found out."

"All right," Olloise agrees. She sits down on a stool next to Istehar, looking worried. Istehar takes her hand.

"I did get to hold the Library's copy of the *Poisoner's Guide*, Loli," Istehar explains. "When I did, I saw your father, and I…saw blood on his hands. That means he was holding that book not long before he died."

"So the recipe from the book *was* what he was working on," Olloise concludes softly. "At least now I feel sure about that."

"But Loli," Annlynn adds, "I learned your father never checked out the book from the Library. Giya Lutei did, which was a surprise to me. Even more of a surprise was that around the same time, your mother checked out all six copies of the Moonstone Covenant forgeries, including the Lutei version."

Olloise gasps. "So maybe my parents were working for him," she offers. "Trying to solve the murder of Karel Lutei hundreds of years ago."

"And maybe he killed them to keep them quiet about it," Vasmine finishes.

"Or maybe someone else killed them, to stop what they were doing," Istehar suggests.

"Well," says Olloise slowly, "this is much more than I knew before. Maybe this is enough to convince Prince Hoel to reopen the investigation."

"I don't think so, Loli," Vasmine contradicts gently.

"Why not?" Olloise demands. "He's the chief interrogator; it's his obligation to pursue this! He should interview Prince Giya! The timing of the book's return is suspicious at the very least!"

Vasmine looks troubled. "Yes, sweetling, but it's Istehar who claims the book was in your father's hands the night of the murder. I know Prince Hoel has been kind to you, but that doesn't mean he'll accept one of Istehar's visions as evidence."

"Mina's right," Annlynn adds. "Istya's word isn't going to be good enough. We need more proof."

"No. I don't want you to pursue this any further," Olloise says with finality. "You're right, I've put everyone in danger. It's time for me to stop this selfishness."

"But we may *have* to pursue it," Annlynn replies heavily.

Vasmine looks startled. "Why attract the attention of princes? If the murderer *is* Prince Giya, he's beyond our reach in any case!"

Annlynn nods thoughtfully. "I hear you, Mina. But if Prince Giya learns about the scene at the Library today, and he *is* the killer, he might decide he'd breathe easier without us around. Would anyone know or care if he made four unconventional women disappear? I think we have to learn what happened. For our own safety." Annlynn pauses and takes a pull from her tumbler. "I should figure out how to get the Lutei forgery into Istehar's hands."

"No more Istya in the Library!" Olloise warns.

Istehar runs over to a bucket in the corner of the room, grabs it, and noisily vomits. Olloise rushes over and smooths Istehar's hair back. "Are you sick because of the books?"

"My guess would be no," Vasmine says. "My guess would be this dysregulation has to do with Princess Kalicent's sudden pregnancy."

Istehar wipes her mouth, breathes heavily, retches again. When she is finished, she makes her way back to her stool. "Did you make Kalicent pregnant?" Vasmine asks. "And more importantly, can you relieve her of her condition? Because if you can't, we have a problem."

"I don't know," Istehar says. "I made a Book of the Loam."

Vasmine throws up her hands. "Eight years with you and I still cannot understand you when you speak!"

"Be quiet and listen, Mina!" snaps Olloise.

"How could you have made anything at all?" Annlynn asks. "The bookwardens were watching you the whole time!"

"I asked for a prayerbook."

"That shouldn't make someone pregnant," Vasmine points out. "Explain yourself."

Istehar leans on the counter. Olloise hands her a tumbler of water. She drinks, then speaks. "A Book of the Loam is a container for the spirit of a tree that died wrongfully. A wronged tree doesn't want to return to the earth; it craves a new body so it can avenge itself. If the tree-spirit is given a book as a home, it offers its help to the maker. A Book of the Loam is transactional magic; a bargain with the spirit world. An illuminatrix shouldn't use it, except in the direst emergency. But I was desperate."

Annlynn, out of reflexive piety, makes the sign of the saints. "Which tree did you summon?" Olloise asks, looking troubled.

"There are so many trees who died wrongly during the war. I invited all the tree-spirits of the Sha'an forest," Istehar replies.

"All of them?" Olloise asks weakly.

Istehar nods. "I invited all the murdered trees who wanted to come. And they did come; the book's voice became so angry and strange…"

"More witchcraft." Annlynn shakes her head. "If they'd caught you…"

"No one was looking at me much," Istehar insists. "They thought I was just praying."

"What happened next?" Olloise pleads.

"The tree-spirits agreed to help me. They didn't tell me how they would do it. One of them must have entered Princess Kalicent."

"She's pregnant with a tree?" Annlynn asks. Then she blanches. "Where is the book now?"

"Tommas took it. It's back on the shelf."

Annlynn smacks her forehead. "With an angry forest inside it. Saints' toenails! We have to get hold of it before some unsuspecting Librarian opens it."

"Is this spirit going to be willing to leave Kalicent's womb now that it has aided you so kindly?" Vasmine asks. "I'm sure Loli can mix us up an abortifacient, but I don't know if it will work on aggrieved trees. And if we fail to help the princess, our failure will have consequences."

"I'll ask the spirit inside Kalicent to leave," Istehar says. "I will do my best to fix this, Mina. But first I need to lie down. Making that book took all my strength, and then I had to memorize the book-number so we could find it again. Annlynn is right; it can't be left for someone else to open." She shakes her head. "When Annlynn finally came with the sealed letter, I thought I might not be able to get up from the chair."

"Seeing my father's disappointed face must have been bracing," Annlynn chuckles.

"For *you*, yes," Olloise murmurs. "The rest of us could do without annoying Lord Jissakhar." Then her tone softens. "Thank you, all of you. You took so many risks for me today."

"Perhaps a little harp music for the heroes, to restore our

spirits?" Vasmine offers, getting up from her chair and making a sweeping bow the way she would at court.

Istehar winces. "My head, Mina. Maybe a little later."

CHAPTER 13

Olloise Mazall, Apothecary
Undersong House
Ancilliday, 12:30 p.m.

She is pulling me toward the silvirium. I don't want to go. When she opens the Book of the Tree, I'm not sure she stays sane.

"We should go upstairs," I say desperately. "You need to sleep. You said so."

"I have to do this first," she insists, gripping my hand. She has enlisted me to accompany her, rather than Annlynn or Vasmine, because I am Silvilline and she thinks I understand. But she's wrong. The arched door of the silvirium appears and we enter. Somehow it seems more momentous that what it is: a room of pillows, bookshelves, and potted trees.

"The Book of the Tree can wait a few hours for you," I plead.

She shakes her head. "The tree-spirits saved my life. If they think I'm ungrateful, they'll be angry. When one receives a gift, one must offer a gift in return." She intones this last sentence in a singsong voice as if she learned it as a child. She opens a drawer in the beautifully carved book-ark in the corner and takes out a knife, a sharp one, like the kind I use for chopping herbs.

"You're not going to cut yourself!" I shriek, aghast, as she takes the knife over to the massive bark-sheathed book on a pillow at the center of the room. It looks like a living thing, as if it might sprout branches and grow up toward the ceiling, or burst into bloom. "Istehar, what kind of deity needs your blood?" But at the River School we studied all the countries in the known world, and I know exactly how many gods ask for blood.

She kneels on the floor, parts the pages of the book, picks up the knife, and takes a fistful of her white hair. She holds the hair so that it dangles over the book, touching the page and looking weirdly like entwined roots. Istehar without her hair...I squeeze my eyes shut.

And then, I hear something like sound underwater, like voices two rooms away yet also very close. *We ask more of you than this.*

Heart pounding, I try to breathe normally. When I summon the courage to open my eyes, Istehar's hair is untouched. The knife is still in her hand. "Did you hear that?" I ask. "The voices?"

She nods. "Did you see the syssyrup tree?" she whispers. "My mother was curled up inside the hollow, pregnant. Her belly was so big—it was maybe a few days before I was born."

I shake my head no. I did not see the vision. But I did hear the trees speak. I cannot believe it. Now I too have touched sorcery. Or Istehar's madness, if that is what it is, is catching. "What did they mean, *more than this*?" I demand, my voice high and brittle.

She shakes her head. "I don't know. Maybe they showed me my life's beginning because now my life must end."

"Why would they want your death, after they saved you?" I stammer. "That doesn't make any sense."

"I wonder if maybe they saved me so I could sacrifice my life for the Sha'an," she says quietly. "If Prince Vilya kills me, he might be satisfied and leave my people alone."

The room is bright and lovely, but my skin is crawling. "Please," I say. "We'll figure it out later. The spirits can't ask any more of you right now. Please put the knife down. Come upstairs and rest."

"All right," she says obediently. "I *am* very tired."

She puts away the book and the knife. I hurry to the door and wait for her there. When I was young, my parents and I went, every month or so, to a little room rented from a local gardening association, with a potted walnut tree at its center. We sang there, or sometimes we sat in silence. I knew we were different because a few children at my school made fun of me for being Silvilline. But I never saw a sacrifice, or heard the voice of a book possessed by tree-spirits. I do not recognize these occult rituals as my religion. Right now, I do not recognize Istehar at all.

When we exit the silvirium, there is someone in the little tiled foyer, waiting for us to emerge: Nizhar, elder and healer of the Sha'an. A dignified, jowly, short-bearded man with a long graying braid of the kind worn by men of the Sha'an, and a round belly that makes him seem kindlier than the man actually is, Nizhar is the disciple of the now-dead healer Nurifir Sha'an, who cured Archprince Jalian. He walks with a sturdy cane, because of an injury he sustained on the long flight out of the forest. He opposed Istehar's marriage and she has never forgiven him.

"I am deeply sorry to trouble you, *ihan-tanon*, but there is news," he says to her in his gravelly voice, using the Sha'an term for illuminatrix; it means "inscriber of light." He ignores me as usual, even though he and I have more or less the same profession. I try not to take offense. I know he wishes I hadn't spoiled the illuminatrix for one of the men of the Sha'an.

"I am listening, Nizhar Sha'an," she says, slipping into a Sha'an dialect I can only partly understand.

"It is not good news. Dozya and Tiarath Sha'an were out on the Lanterners' Walk this morning to scatter petals, to call a soul for their first child. Men passed by and accused them of poisoning the water. A mob gathered, shoved them into the canal, and threw stones at them. Some of our people saw and pulled Dozya out, but Tiarath was hit in the head with a stone, and could not be found in time. We recovered her body and have laid her out in the Chamber of Roots." He bows. "I grieve with you, *ihan-tanon*. I know she was your friend. May the Great Tree shelter our dead!"

Istehar leans on the wall, weeps, wails, murmurs words of prayer. She and Tiarath came from the same village, traveled downriver together, gardened the orchard together. Tiarath was three months pregnant. Istehar was looking forward to playing with the baby. I put my hand on her shoulder, but she seems not to notice. "Tiarath," she whispers to the wall. "I should have taken you home."

"Forgive me for disturbing your grief," Nizhar Sha'an continues relentlessly. "We heard from Bastina that you were detained at the Library this morning. Now Tiarath has been killed. You led us here ten years ago with all good intention, but this is no safe home for us. The Sha'an should leave this place. I have gathered the elders to reason with you."

She led them here? She was a child then; they might have followed her visions, but they did so of their own will. And now he is presenting her with an impossible dilemma. Leave Moonstone, where she has made her home and family, and return to the Sha'an forest—or leave her people and stay here with me, Anya, and Mina. Either way, this choice is going to break her heart.

Istehar composes herself and nods. "One moment, Nizhar Sha'an," she says. She walks to the door that leads into the back room, opens it, and goes in, leaving me and the Sha'an healer to avoid one another's eyes awkwardly. She comes back with her staff. And instead of going up the stairs to rest, she walks with Nizhar toward the Chamber of Elders.

The way the Sha'an govern themselves has always confused me. Istehar has a say over many things, and receives great deference, but the elders also have the power to decide communal matters. She meets with them for many hours, sometimes, until they come to a consensus. I've never been sure what would happen if the illuminatrix and the elders truly disagreed. Maybe I'm about to find out.

I wonder if Istehar will reveal to her people that she has unleashed a vengeful ghost forest on the city, and what they will think if she does. Maybe they won't believe her, or maybe they will be glad their beloved trees have come to defend them. Maybe they will summon the ghost-trees and ride them all the way back to their lost villages. Maybe they will decide they don't need to go home after all, because the Sha'an forest is already here and invisibly taking over the city. Maybe I am letting my imagination run wild because the thought of Istehar leaving is terrifying.

Istehar looks back at me over her shoulder with exhausted eyes. "Loli, please gather the items for the ritual I must perform later," she says. "Salt. Cedar. Tinctures of vervain, rosemary, apple, and lavender. A few clean bowls. And that river-drake's eye of Vasmine's, if she'll lend it." Nizhar glances at her uneasily.

I've been a healer long enough to know the plants Istehar has asked for aren't for ending a pregnancy. They're used, by some folk, for easing contact with spirits. This appointment with Princess Kalicent makes me nervous. And the Great Tree alone knows what Istehar wants that drake's eye for. It may have come from some impossible ancient beast, but it's never performed any wonders, as far as I can see.

The two Sha'an disappear down the hall. Istehar's step is weary; Nizhar's step is slow and uneven. I hear Nizhar say to Istehar: "Your parents would have wanted you to raise a family. You should marry properly and have a child, *ihan-tanon*. It would convince the people there is a next generation to hope for."

I leave the hall and gallop up the two flights of stairs as if I am being chased by Istehar's disappointed parents. Arriving in my laboratory, I resist the urge to fling flasks against the wall. All of this is my fault. If I hadn't sent Annlynn after that book, there would be no tree-spirits, no detention in the Library, no Princess Kalicent demanding magic, no Sha'an fleeing the city. I have poisoned the life we've built as surely as the Deacon poisoned Prince Karel Lutei. Sterven Jissakhar is right. I *am* a murderer.

I look around at the neat shelves of vials and beakers, mortars and pestles, thermoscopes and magnifying glasses, tinctures and essences. Bunches of herbs harvested from the garden hang from the ceiling. My workbench of sand-colored wood is clean and empty. I roll up my sleeves and start gathering the items Istehar named. I take down bottles and ampules, and get out a knife for chopping. I don't like knives, ever since finding my parents. But I work, steadily.

I've finished the cedar bark and vervain flowers and started on the apple when Vasmine comes in. "Istehar should be sleeping," she complains. "The theater performance for Princess Kalicent this evening will be spoiled if the sorceress is yawning."

"Let's hope it's not only theater," I grumble. "Istya needs your river-drake's eye." Vasmine never lends out that jewel—it was a gift from Prince Hallan when she was still his concubine, and is the most rare and precious thing she owns. She pawned it once to buy the ink shop, and bought it back later when the business was successful.

But Vasmine goes down to her room, fetches the velvet-lined box with the eye, and brings it to me. I place it in a larger wooden box along with other items that will go to the palace tonight. I can tell from Vasmine's unusually quiet manner that Bastina has told her about the death of young Tiarath Sha'an, but I don't want to talk about it.

"I read a little further in the *Poisoner's Guide*," I say by way of conversation as I start the next pour. "I've been wondering why the Council would have Karel Lutei murdered. Lutei was only one of the thirteen princes. The others could outvote him if he was being obstreperous. Why would they need to kill him?"

Vasmine spies a bottle of hyacinth extract on the shelf, uncorks it, sniffs its intense fragrance, and sighs with pleasure. "Who knows? It's Moonstone, sweetling. After all, the Council hired your mother to kill people. It's how they do business. Some rivers only flow one way."

I sigh. "That's disturbing, since they've offered me a job."

"A job? What do you mean?" Vasmine looks up from the bottle.

"Angelissa Dhagura told me the Council wants to employ me as the city's forensic apothecary," I say, stoppering the vial of apple tincture I've just poured. "Like my father. I do think I'd be good at it."

"You *would* be good at it," Vasmine agrees. "But they'd own you, and you might find yourself doing more harm than good. If I were you, I'd turn that offer down." She recorks the perfume bottle. "Unless they've given you a reason you can't refuse?"

"No, Princess Angelissa didn't try to force me. She just made me feel guilty for wasting my life on vengeance." I nestle the little bottle of green-gold elixir inside the velvet-lined box.

"Keep your head down, Loli," Vasmine advises. "Halls of power have unsteady floors. It's easy to fall."

Later, when the box is fully packed and Vasmine has gone to make her own elaborate preparations, I hear Istehar come upstairs, slowly and carefully, as if she is old, with tracks of tears on her face. She doesn't want to talk about the meeting, or the future of the Sha'an. "I wish I could wash Nizhar and the elders off," she says to me. "And Vilya Mai, and the Library, and the whole city."

We go into her room together. I turn down the covers of the old-fashioned four-poster bed. Istehar strips out of the shawl Vasmine put over her when she came home. Off comes her long vest, then her dress, then her shift, until she is as naked as the moon. Suddenly I remember her pulling off her shift for the first time—a woods into which I had blessedly strayed, a language of leaves and water I had somehow learned to speak.

CHAPTER 14
Annlynn Jissakhar, Warrior Librarian
Library Docks
Ancilliday, 4:00 p.m.

The oval mound of Opal Island juts up out of the river, flaunting its creased iridescent cliffs, its climbing, winding streets, and its ornate buildings crowded with domes and arches. It is the largest and most central island of Moonstone's archipelago. The Long Bridge reaches it from Seven Lanterns in the south. The Short Bridge connects it to the sprawl of Sorcerer's Kettle in the north. The Gilded Bridge comes to its western shore from Drake's Hoard, the main island of the String of Coins district. Opal Island's busy streets and squares, and even the palace courtyards, all seem to lead to the domed Library that looms at the island's highest point. The Library was built on that height to avoid, as much as possible, the damp air close to the river.

On the east, just beneath the Library, is a loading dock set into the cliffs. Caves in the cliff lead to passages set with metal tracks so that books and supplies can be loaded into the Library's basement via wooden carts. Boats put in at the Library dock many times a day, freight boats as well as merchant ships from foreign lands, bringing goods, visitors, and diplomats. There are always jugglers and snack-mongers and singers and storytellers to entertain tourists. And, there is always Yan's.

Yan's is an inn and liquor parlor, built of sandstone brick, facing the south side of the docks. It's frequented by loaders, sailors, Library workers, merchants, performers, and those just passing through. Sitting-pillows surround long, low tables. On the walls are candelabras, mirrors, flower vases set in bronze brackets, and all manner of odd decorations set on tiny shelves, including a silver-green leviathan's egg the size of my head, and an antique nautical lamp said to come from one of the original settler ships. The liquor selection is vast, fed by the kegs in the liquor-cellars dug into the rocks below. The crepes and pancakes are excellent. And more to the point, Thalweg is usually here.

I walk fast across the docks to avoid any sightings of my father or siblings, who often drink here. As I duck through the low round-arched door, Moa, the knowledgeable and fastidious bartender, nods to me, rolls up his sleeves, and starts fixing a moonwater. Moonwater, made from the local white-fleshed moon-plum, is sold all over the city, but it's different in each district. The kind I prefer is crystal-clear and brewed on Juniper Island just behind the bookstores. Moa hands me my glass before I've finished striding past the bar.

Thalweg, who has a nearly shaved head, hoop earrings with giant pink pearls, and no gender of record, is a palm reader. They live in a room upstairs and often set up shop in the corner of the parlor at a nice secluded table. Any number of locals and foreign visitors line up for a reading. Thalweg is known for ruthless accuracy; many a hopeful young lover has run away crying after receiving bad news. But palm reading, no matter how accurate, doesn't earn enough to pay the monthly rent for a room at Yan's, and so Thalweg also works as a bookmender, mending spine-seams and page tears. They have been employed at the Library for years and are highly respected for their craft, which is why I want to talk to them.

Fortunately, the line isn't very long. I nurse my drink and wait through Thalweg's financial predictions for a Fengen entrepreneur, then through a discussion with a middle-aged pastry chef from Hundred Quays about the possible outcomes of her leaving her husband. At least the woman doesn't leave crying.

When it's my turn, I slide onto the pillow opposite Thalweg and set my almost-empty glass on the table.

"I'm pretty sure you already know your fortune," Thalweg complains.

"I know it up until right now," I say.

"Hmm," Thalweg murmurs. "Calling in a favor, are you?"

Sometimes an arrogant shipping magnate or a temperamental sentinel doesn't like what Thalweg tells them. Such folk tend to blame the messenger. Once in a while, after a reading, someone pulls a knife on Thalweg. Other times the assault comes a few days later, when things have had time to sink in. It's not uncommon for me to draw my sword to defend Thalweg from such attacks. I have even corralled bookwardens to guard Yan's, after particularly bloody threats. So Thalweg owes me a favor or two.

"I need you to find an antique Silvilline prayerbook in the Controlled Section and borrow it for a day," I say.

"Can't steal books from the Library."

"Why?"

"Getting caught."

"You won't get caught. You're going to claim it's damaged, which it is. And you're going to return it once it's repaired, which it will be. It's not censored or valuable, so they'll let you have it with the usual bond payment. No problem."

"Still can't do it."

I nod. "Why?"

"Sacrilege."

"Stealing this book is the opposite of sacrilege."

Thalweg stares. "Why?"

"It has demons inside it that need to be expelled."

"Uh-huh." Thalweg looks skeptical. "Since when do you believe in demons?"

"Since this morning."

Thalweg's eyes widen. "That sounds like a story."

"It is, but you're better off not knowing."

Thalweg nods, frowns, and pauses.

"This is not a thing that I do, Annlynn."

"Which is why no one will suspect you."

"And this is not a thing that you do."

I find myself unable to argue with that.

"So if it's not a thing that I do, and it's not a thing that you do, why would we be doing it? Considering that we would offend every saint there is, not to mention the government and the Library. And considering the demons you just mentioned."

I lean in so close I am almost touching the giant pink pearl hanging from Thalweg's earring. "Look, Thalweg, I can't do this myself—I've been barred from the Library for three days. I know Tommas won't do it—not after what happened this morning. And I can't ask anyone else. I don't dare, not with sorcery involved."

"And it can't wait three days?"

"I don't think it can. Look, I've watched sentinels threaten to arrest you for sorcery, even though you keep telling them you're just a con artist. You *are* the real deal. I know you believe in this stuff. And I am telling you that if someone finds this book on the shelf and opens it, that person will be in for a terrible time. Maybe even the whole city will be in for a terrible time."

Thalweg fixes me with a knowing eye. "This has to do with Snowhair, doesn't it? I warned you what your life would be like if you married that girl."

I sigh again. "Look, I don't tell *you* which people to marry." Thalweg is also in a group arrangement, though their spouses are off on a ship somewhere and not likely to come home for a month or so. "If you can't do it, you can't do it. I respect that. But it matters, Thalweg, and you're the only one I can ask."

"Fine," Thalweg says after a long moment, and looks over at an ornate porcelain clock set on one of the little wall shelves. "My book run starts in half an hour. Give me the shelf number, and I'll see if I can find it."

I reach into my jacket pocket and hand Thalweg a little piece of paper with the number Istehar memorized indicating the book's location. Thalweg tucks it into a colorful waist pouch and rises from the table.

"Listen, Thalweg," I warn, "don't open the book. Really. I don't know what will happen if you do."

Thalweg runs a hand over their scalp and chuckles. "You work in the Library as long as I have, you learn to mind your own business. But this better not get me into trouble. I don't want to lose my room with the river view."

"You're the one who tells fortunes," I say. "If you were going to get in trouble, you wouldn't do it in the first place."

Thalweg snorts and gets up. I wait a few minutes after they leave, sipping the dregs in my glass. Then I put a few coins on the table and stand up to leave. It's not good for Moa to remember me idly hanging around, if sentinels should come asking.

The side door of Yan's opens into Hourglass Alley, the narrow street that runs between the docks and the Sand Market. People say the Sand Market is called that because the merchants there are so good they could sell you a handful of sand. But probably there was a beach there once. Now there's wall-to-wall shops, tents, food stands, gambling dens, and pearl-trading floors.

I head past the glassblowers' forge opposite Yan's, and make a left off Hourglass into the even narrower alley that runs behind Yan's and meets the river. That little back lane barely has a name, but on maps it's called something fancy: Skyward Close. I'm planning to walk to the shore, circle around to the Library docks, and either walk home through the streets or, if the ferry's there, catch a ride to Seven Lanterns, since it's already been a long day and I'm exhausted.

I don't see it coming at all, which is rare for me. Something heavy hits me in the back, and I stumble face-first into a rough stone wall to my left. I feel wetness, realize I've scraped my nose and forehead. At first I think it's an accident, or someone's thrown something from a window. But then someone has hold of my hair. I feel my head bang against the wall, which is sickening. I know I need to avoid a repeat of that awful thud, or whatever this is will be over before I've found out what's happening. Ignoring the pain, I manage to turn and drive my knee into the gonads of whatever cutthroat is trying to kill me. Then, still without looking much, I land a punch. A tall, unshaven, square-jawed man groans and flails into the opposite wall. Somehow he doesn't look like a pickpocket. That worries me.

I have just enough time to pull my sword from its scabbard before he's recovered and come at me again, drawing his own blade. Two other men saunter toward us from the right, and I realize this is an ambush, and that someone has followed me to Yan's. One of the two new thugs is about my height, red-faced, bald, stocky as a barrel, with a quilted cloth coat that looks foreign in origin. A sailor, maybe. The other is young, dark, and wiry and carries himself like a Moonstone native. They all have identical rapiers, I notice—which means they're working for someone. Thieves don't use their hard-gotten cash to buy matching weapons.

"What do you fiendspawn want?" I demand, pitching my voice so people will hear. "I'm a Librarian! It's a sin to attack me!"

The tall one sneers. "Sure, it's a sin. You fornicate with a witch and a whore and a murderer; you're not so holy!"

"The saints ain't going to miss you," the young one adds, smirking.

So they know who I am. I try to think as they circle me. Possibility one: Giya Lutei sent them to stop me from finding out he killed my in-laws. Possibility two: Vilya Mai sent them to get rid of me to make his attack on Undersong House easier. Possibility three: my father's clan is tired of being embarrassed and wants me gone.

The tall, unshaven one lunges toward me. I parry his rapier. The young one circles around and makes a try from the other side, so I slash at him backhand, just barely fending off his blade. It feels like an exercise in fencing class.

"Three against one ain't fair, huh?" The young villain grins at me. I can tell he's had River School training, and that's not good news.

There are people passing in Hourglass Alley. I call out again, but they hurry away, not wanting to get involved in a robbery. If I'm lucky, someone might tell the sentinels stationed at the entrance to the Sand Market. My opponents seem to think of this too, and the bald one takes a swipe at the backs of my knees, wanting this to be over already.

I glance riverward, hoping for escape that way, and see a nondescript little boat with a cabin, anchored at the dock at the end of the alley. That boat might be their getaway after they kill me—or maybe they plan to take me with them. Either way, I don't care for their plan.

The young one's blade flashes at the edge of my sight. I've been careless. I block it with the flat of my sword, but the blade's edge slips off and nicks my arm, which bleeds profusely. The tall one tries to take advantage, but I push him off toward the opposite wall with a few vicious slashes.

Not knowing how much longer I can keep this up, I back down the alley in the direction of the river. The stocky one chases me in a leisurely way, as if he's not worried. I lash out with my sword and cut his fine quilted coat. I glance behind me and now there's a fourth thug, a woman, thick-bodied and implacable, carrying a heavy quarterstaff, stepping off the boat and casually blocking the alley. The tall one and the young one close in with their rapiers, smiling.

If these people take me down, it'll look like a robbery gone wrong. The investigation will be shallow and over by morning. I risk one glance at the thin ribbon of blue sky above me, wanting to make sure I see it one more time. I did the same thing the day my older brothers dragged me into the icehouse after I kissed the dovekeeper's daughter over the back fence. The young one, who seems to particularly have it in for me, lashes out with his rapier and nearly connects with my throat. He laughs, knowing how close he is to winning.

And then, the stocky woman backs off, jumps into her boat, and poles away. I can't understand why, but then, as if a single-file flock of birds has landed, six blue-clad sentinels rush into the alley from the river side. The three other thugs race away in the other direction, taking a left at Hourglass Alley, no doubt intending to disappear into the chaos of the Sand Market.

I lean against the wall and catch my breath. Three of the sentinels pass me and head for the market, an expedition unlikely to yield fruit. The other three head back toward the river and turn left toward the Library docks. Neither set says anything to me or seems to notice that I'm bleeding from arm and scalp. I see my father, in the black velvet coat of the censor, observing from the corner of Hourglass Alley.

"I ought to cite you for disturbing the peace," he barks, and turns back toward the Library.

Reluctantly, I tear a strip from the short black skirt of my Librarian's uniform and wrap my forearm to stop the bleeding. I'll need Loli to tend the wound properly. As I cross Opal Island, I choose a route of back alleys and little makeshift bridges, and watch for pursuers. I think about my father, and what he was doing in Skyward Close, and what on the saints' good earth could have made him want to help me—or whether he was the one who organized the whole thing.

When I get to the Long Bridge, there are cloaksfolk at the ramp onto the bridge, clearly looking for someone. They're wearing Lutei colors: crimson and hyacinth sashes that couldn't mark any other house. No other house could afford dyes like that. This could be another attempt on my life. I pause in the shadows, trying to figure out how to get around them, or whether I need to go back to the Sand Market and catch the ferry, which I'm reluctant to do because my wounds will be so noticeable that someone may call a sentinel, or a hospital-boat.

As I lean against the wall of an inn, Prince Giya Lutei gets up from the inn's outdoor tea-garden and walks up to me, looking just as wolfish as he did the last time we met. He stands next to me as if idly perusing the crowd, teacup in hand, watching folk go by. He's older than I am by a decade, but the gaze that roams the passersby is as intense as a teenage poet's. His hair is in his eyes, of course. Some people stare, recognizing him, and give little bows.

"I understand Madam Sha'an was nearly arrested in the Library today," he comments to me, as if to a passerby he's just happened to stand next to. "By your father, no less. For handling a book you confiscated from me just yesterday. I wonder what could have compelled her to enter a building she is rumored to find distasteful, and what interested her about that book?"

He glances at me once, casually, and brushes a fleck of the city's dust off his velvet coat. "And further, I wonder what might have compelled Princess Kalicent to intervene on her behalf when she was discovered."

"And I wonder, Eminence, what compelled you to check out a poisoner's manual a number of years ago," I retort. I'm worried that he knows all this, but since he's clearly onto us, I may as well go on the offensive. "Was the art of poisoning a person part of your research?"

"Just as I told you yesterday," he says, seeming unruffled. He leans back, bracing himself with one foot on the plaster wall of the inn. "I am pursuing an urgent state matter." He glances pointedly at my still-oozing wounds and the bloodstains on my clothes. "You don't look well, Your Vigilance. Have you had an argument with someone?"

"I think you know perfectly well with whom I've had an argument," I seethe, hoping I don't bleed onto my shoes.

"What I know is that you are running out of time before your adversaries catch up with you," says Giya Lutei, and now he does look at me fully. "I want that book back, Annlynn Jissakhar. If you bring it to me, I may decide to save your life and your family's lives. Bear my offer in mind. Your friends in high places won't be able to protect you for long."

If this arrogant, obsessive man puts himself on Moonstone's throne, that'll be an urgent state matter, all right. And he might be Olloise's parents' killer.

"Nothing on earth could make me trust you," I say. "You don't even return your Library books on time."

He crooks a smile and shakes out his lace cuffs. "You may be sorry you rejected my offer," he replies.

"Are you threatening me?" I ask.

"I have no need to threaten you. You well know what this city does to its 'friends,' never mind its enemies," says Giya Lutei. "If you ever have more you wish to share, you know where to find me."

And he stalks off toward the Gilded Bridge as if he owns it, which he basically does.

CHAPTER 15

Istehar Sha'an, Illuminatrix

Moonstone River

Ancilliday, 11:00 p.m.

As the Lanternhouse chimes sound across the isle of Seven Lanterns, striking eleven in the evening, a palace gondola comes to our dock by the apple trees. The boatman is early. The princess must be in a hurry.

I don my hooded cloak, take up my staff and the box of ritual tools, and hurry out to the river, feeling as secretive as I must look. Vasmine comes behind me with a courtly gait. We settle next to one another in the little felze. As the gondola shoves off, I close my eyes and listen to the singing of our apple tree. The box is on my lap. Marsh-frogs peep nearby. Boatfolk call to one another on the water. The dinner Annlynn insisted on cooking in spite of her injuries is warm in my belly: duck-egg stew, a Moonstone delicacy I came to love in my early days in the city, and orange-bread with slices of citrus preserved in honey.

Across from me, Vasmine draws back the curtain. The cold bright light of the moon pours like milk into the felze, and catches her white lace dress so that it blazes. Across the water, a collection of rooftops glitters. When the people of Gengrassia settled the isles of the Moon's Daughters, they brought with them their pointed roofs, silver-scaled like fish.

We pass Inkstone Point and the Lanternelles, and travel north toward the Gilded Bridge, where every year the arch-prince comes to bless the waters. As we sail under it, I make a wish—a superstition Annlynn taught me years ago.

She grew up on Drake's Hoard, and played in the shallows near the bridge. I wish for success tonight, whatever that means.

"You know not to call whatever you do to her magic, or sorcery," Vasmine reminds me. I nod. Yes, I understand that. I think how rare it is that Vasmine and I are alone together. It feels as if we are going to a ball. I have a sudden desire to hold her hand, but I worry she will think I am frightened. I *am* frightened.

The boat veers to the right, around the curve of Opal Island, and sooner than I expect, we come to the palace complex. The steep-roofed palace buildings, with their steeples and towers, sit partly on land and partly on massive stone piers built out into the water. The thick towers are carved with images of winding waterways. The river laps against riverweed-flecked marble walls as if water and wall are equally ancient. I have been past the Mai stronghold, of course, out on the water, but I've never been inside it.

In the shallows between the jutting fingers of the palace are tiny island pavilions and water gardens teeming with flowers. On massive green saucer-like pads, water lilies of a dozen colors are in full bloom. Cheerful, garden-loving Tiarath would have loved this and set about admiring each plant. Instead, the man responsible for her death, Vilya Mai, who spreads vicious lies about the Sha'an, enjoys all the glories of this place.

At the broad docks with their wide bronze roofs and wrought-iron banisters, marble steps extend downward into the water. Assisted by the boatman, we hop up onto the first dry step and make our way up into the covered passage. Before long, we are hurrying up broad steps into the golden light of a palace chamber. I lift my skirts so as not to brush the royal marble. Vasmine goes confidently; she no doubt knows the way.

We are surely in one of the minor halls, but its splendor is still blinding. The walls are adorned with silver brocade and inlaid with painted scenes of snowcapped mountains. Delicate crystal chandeliers dangle like icicle formations. I become chilled looking at them. A pert-looking, round-cheeked butleress in a long-tailed pale blue coat greets us and leads us down the hall, through a door that is invisible until she opens it. We go up a spiral staircase, and through a foyer paneled in painted silk. A sentinel asks me to leave my staff against the wall. I do so, reluctantly. The butleress ushers us through a carven door depicting an ocean scene with seabirds, and into the rooms of the princess. I imagine servants and spies moving behind the walls, like mice.

"The healer has arrived," the butleress says to Princess Kalicent. The princess is a rounded lump beneath pure white sheets and blankets, in a four-poster bed draped with a canopy of intricately woven cloth-of-gold ribbons. Her dark hair spreads out on the pillow like a river delta; her face barely shows. Keyhole-shaped windows let in the fragrance of water lilies and jasmine.

I look around. A silver tray with a covered tureen and silverware sits on a table, looking abandoned. A statue of a pink-cheeked singing-maid with a lute stands in a corner. The ceiling and walls are covered in what seem to be thousands of white feathers, as if we are nestled on the back of a massive bird. I hope the feathers are artificial and that hundreds of seabirds weren't murdered to decorate this chamber, but my hopes may be in vain.

Seeing us, the princess pushes off her covers and sits up at the edge of the bed, her crimson dressing-gown on the white coverlet like blood spreading on snow. She waves for the butleress to depart. The butleress discreetly takes the tureen as she goes. "I'll be just outside," the butleress promises before she closes the door.

Vasmine gracefully kneels and makes an obeisance with her forehead to the floor. I feel intensely awkward. But this woman holds our lives in her hands, so I set my things down, lift the edges of my cloak and dress, kneel on the ground, and put my face to the white-blue-and-orange patterned rug, which has images of ibises woven into it. I like the ibises and wish I could stay on the floor with them. I can feel the palace whispering to itself, a house so big it has many different selves that only sometimes speak to one another.

"Your Eminence, I have brought the healer Istehar Sha'an," Vasmine announces as she rises. As I rise far less gracefully, her eyes flicker to me in warning, lest I say anything untoward.

Kalicent gazes at me in silence. I notice the chain of moonstones around her neck. "My father was healed by a Sha'an healer," she says then. "How appropriate that this should also be my fate. It is right that a daughter should follow in her father's footsteps!"

Vasmine has told me not to thank the princess for her intervention in my arrest this morning—such matters are beneath a royal lady's notice. "How do you fare, Your Eminence?" I inquire.

"I wish you had come earlier! I am even bigger than I was this morning." Kalicent opens her robe and displays her swollen belly and enlarged, blue-veined breasts. "I have been told, of course, what it is like to be pregnant, but having it happen all at once is overwhelming, not to mention inconvenient. What malicious magic that mewling Memmiam was hiding behind her pieties! She bewitched my beloved Egno and forced him to lie with her, and now she has given me the form of a pregnant woman so that my father will disown me! What manner of child is inside me, healer? What can be done?"

"It will be my honor to assist Your Eminence," I murmur, avoiding the questions. "If I may proceed?" The princess nods.

On the table where the tureen stood a few moments ago, I set pouches of salt and cedar, bottles of tinctures, the silver bowls, and the river-drake's eye. When Kalicent sees the mottled red-purple sphere, she turns pale and glances at me questioningly. "To see within you," I explain. She nods, but her frightened look remains.

"I wonder what it will find," she murmurs.

I give two small bowls to Vasmine, one with the salt and one with the cedar, and instruct her to scatter these materials in the corners of the magnificent room. As Vasmine does so, I uncork the elixir bottles, and pour tinctures of vervain, rosemary, apple, and lavender into a larger bowl. I add a little water and honey. With a small whisk, I stir the ingredients together. I sing as I do this: Sha'an songs, songs I once sang to the forest.

Limb and leaf and root and stone,
we belong to you alone.
Leaf and stone and limb and root,
you the seed and we the fruit.
Stone and root and limb and leaf,
you are the roof we lie beneath.
Root and leaf and stone and limb,
we will return to you again.

I have never known spirits to come when called. The substances I have brought are mostly to placate the princess, and to let the tree-spirits know how desperate I am. At the Library, when I called the wronged trees, I thought only to save myself. I did not consider how they might go about saving me, or what it might cost. If I cannot cure the princess, the Sha'an may well suffer, just as they would have if I had been arrested. It is an unpredictable business, trying to avoid one's fate.

And then, as I am mid-thought, the forest comes: unfathomable roots twining underground, interlocking branches veiling the sky. It is all around me: the green effusion of the leaves, the guardianship of bark, the murmur of communities of branches. They are here, as if they never burned at all. Vasmine and Princess Kalicent have vanished behind tree trunks. The great trees lean toward me, and I feel myself dissolving, as if I am a fallen log about to be swallowed up by moss and mushrooms and little saplings.

After several long blinks, the room comes back, with its four-poster bed and feathered walls. The forest disappears. My hands shaking, I try to pour some of the mixture I've concocted into a cup, so I may hand it to the princess. But to my dismay, when I look into the bowl, the mixture has something wrong with it. The liquid should have an amber color, but the fluid I am looking at is clear, like water. Astonished, I dip in a finger and taste it. The taste is unmistakable: tree sap, from a syssyrup tree. The kind of tree in which my mother lived while she was pregnant. I catch my breath.

And then a voice speaks from inside me, somewhere below my heart. *We followed you to this city, my kind and I. We were ghosts dwelling in smoke and ash; we had nowhere else to go. We crowded into the little toy forest you built for us. We slept in the petals of your book-creatures. We would have stayed like that forever. But then you asked us for help. We considered. I chose to take form to save you, I, who held you when you were no more than a seed.*

The room has vanished again. The forest is all around me. I feel as if I am falling to the ground. Dimly aware that Vasmine has rushed to my side, I stammer inside myself: *I honor you. I greatly honor you. You watched over me as if I were your own child.*

You grew within me, daughter of the forest. I was a mother-tree to you. So it was I who came into this body to compel it to aid you. This body I am within is more powerful than other humans, and can make things happen that others cannot—the elders explained this to me though I do not completely understand.

Yes, I say. *She is powerful. But she is also only human. You must leave her body now. She is not able to carry a being like you within her. She may not live.*

The silver cup has fallen from my hand. My feet are wet, though I barely feel the chill. If the tree-spirit stays inside Kalicent and is born as a human infant, the child will be known as a bastard child. Jalian Mai will exile his daughter. Kalicent Mai will surely take revenge on me and the Sha'an. I can see that as well as I can see the ibises woven into the carpet.

Come back into the Book of the Tree, I coax the syssyrup spirit. *It is a better home for you than the form of a city-dweller. We will honor you as a beloved. We will tell your story.*

I do not want to be shut up inside a book. I want to live in a body. I hear your wish, but I have done enough for you, child of the Sha'an. After all, you did not save me when the fire came, when even the sap within me burned.

I remember then the message of the Book of the Tree: *We ask more of you than this.* I know now what they meant, and I know what I must say. *You cared for me when I was in my mother's womb,* I whisper to the tree-spirit. *It is only right that I care for you. Leave the body of the city-dweller, and enter mine. Be born through me.*

Treespeaker, the tree-spirit sings in its low rumble. *Illuminatrix. You offer much.* I feel a small tendril touch my mind—body?—gingerly, as if testing the texture or temperature.

If I leave this room pregnant, none of my wives will understand, not even Loli. And what will I say to the Sha'an? To Nizhar and the elders who are already disappointed in me? They will think I have broken my marriage vows. Or worse, they will think I am possessed.

There will be consequences later. But this is the only way.

Come, honored one, I whisper. *Come the way a child comes. Come as a little seed.*

My uterus cramps, and I feel a discharge from my vulva I know must be blood. I collapse to the carpet, nauseous. The liquid in the dregs of the glass on the carpet is not clear; it is amber. When I put my finger in to taste it, it tastes like Loli's tinctures. I have a strange desire to sink into the carpet-weave and sit in the water among the ibises.

Kalicent has thrown off her dressing-gown. She sits on the edge of the bed, her stomach and breasts deflating like emptying waterskins. Her skin hangs as if she is an old woman. She grabs at the flaps of herself, shrieking: "What have you done to me? What sorcery have you performed?" The butleress cracks open the door and peers in. Surely the sentinels will come at any moment.

Vasmine rises, grabs the forgotten bowl on the table and brings it to the princess. "Drink this," she commands. "It will restore you to your normal state." It likely won't do anything of the kind, but Kalicent steadies herself, tips the bowl, and drinks every drop of its contents.

As she drinks, the wrinkles in her skin shrink little by little. The skin tightens. The breasts become firm. By the time Kalicent wipes her mouth, her body has returned nearly to its normal state. She breathes out slowly, her eyes dilated. I cannot tell if she is traumatized or exhilarated. I am searching inside me for the little voice that will indicate the conversation I just had was real, but I don't hear anything. I only see a few drops of blood on the carpet beneath me.

"The spirit that inhabited you has fled, Your Eminence," Vasmine announces to Princess Kalicent. "The healer has been successful. The pregnancy has left your body."

Kalicent nods, satisfied. She turns to me, without any trace of sentimental gratitude. "You have done as you promised," she says. "I will not forget it. Now find me the witch Memmiam."

I knew she would ask, and it is for this that I brought the river-drake's eye. There is an old Moonstone legend Olloise told me long ago, about how a river-drake's eye can see far and wide and even into the past and future. I do not know if it is true, but I am counting on Princess Kalicent knowing this legend.

Vasmine told me of the unfortunate Memmiam, the archdeacon's daughter who dallied with Kalicent's intended. I don't know her and I don't know where she is, but I cannot let her be assassinated for something that I did.

"The river-drake's eye will search out where your enemy has gone," I tell the princess.

I take the jewel in both hands, hold it at arm's length, and stare into it for long moments. "I see deep waters," I intone distantly, as if I have gone back into trance. "The archdeacon's daughter Memmiam, fearing reprisal, threw herself off the Watchers' Heights, and washed out to sea. She is drowned. I see her cold body in the deep."

As I speak, the purple-red jewel grows icy in my hand, as if it knows I am lying and resents it. I shiver.

"The harlot has deprived me of vengeance," complains Kalicent. "Just as she deprived me of a husband. But I thank you, Istehar Sha'an." In her now-loose crimson dressing-gown, she begins to pace the floor.

"I wish I could plead your case with my brother," she says, "but he is dead set against the Sha'an remaining in the city. When my father dies, my brother will expel you all. He will be archprince then, and the Council likely will not stand in his way." She gazes at me solemnly. "I will pay you well for tonight. My advice to you, Madam Illuminatrix, is that you store away what I pay you. It may be enough to buy ship's passage for your people."

Exile, again, for us. It is not a surprise, but it is hard to keep the tears from coming. I bow to hide my face, and reply: "Your Eminence is most kind to be concerned for us."

"Eminence, your exalted father is still strong," adds Vasmine smoothly.

"I suppose you would know," Kalicent counters with a small smile.

I realize she has dismissed us. I step to the table. Vasmine helps me put away the vials. Before I can wrap the river-drake's eye in its cushioning fabric, Kalicent steps close and takes the smooth stone of the petrified eye in her hand. "It's beautiful," she comments, as if she is surprised. She hands it to Vasmine.

Vasmine and I finish packing. The princess rings the golden bell that rests on a nearby table. The butleress opens the door, guides us into the foyer, allows me to take back my staff, and hands me a purse of coins. Then she shows us out through the great hall of brocade and icicles. She is young, round-faced, alert, and clearly in Kalicent's confidence. I wonder if she is going to tell anyone about what happened in the princess's bedroom.

As we walk down the covered passage to the docks, Vasmine whispers to me: "You've never divined using a river-drake's eye in your life." We both giggle. I wonder if something might happen between us in the gondola. If I should at last say yes to Vasmine. Before exile happens, or arrest, or something else that separates us. Before it is too late.

I have stared at her, often, when she tries on new dresses, or lounges in the garden gossiping with a friend, or tests drops of ink on silk-paper in her ink shop. I have held her hand in the dark when she was ill. I have even married her. But I have always been too shy about my body, too unsure I could ever measure up to brave Annlynn or brilliant Olloise. Maybe I have felt I am too foreign for her, or she is too foreign for me; she is always calling me an elf-child or some such thing. Maybe it is the magic hiding within her that disturbs me. Maybe I am afraid—I do not know of what.

When we arrive at the roofed marble docks, two men in palace livery are there waiting for us.

"The archprince wishes to see you, Madam Kinora," one of them says.

"You may return home, Madam Sha'an," the other says to me. "May" clearly means "must." I steel myself to protest, but Vasmine shakes her head.

"Go, Istya," she says to me. "Rest. I'll be fine."

And so I find myself alone on the river in the quiet hours, gliding under the Gilded Bridge and trying to sense the seed growing somewhere within me. I look up at the glinting arches and make three wishes: for the tree-child, for the Sha'an, and for Vasmine. Three wishes is far more than my fair share of the wishes in this city, but I hope they all come true.

CHAPTER 16
Vasmine Kinora, Ink-Merchant
Seaspire, Palace of Innumerable Pearls
Daemoniday, 2:00 a.m.

The sentinels shepherd me along the covered walk as if I don't know the way. Ahead, the Seaspire at the prow of the palace faces the Bay of Scattered Pearls. The Seaspire is so tall that it is the first sign of the city ships see, even before the towers of Hundred Keys, the fortress that guards the seaward approach to Hundred Quays. Jalian is up there, brooding, no doubt.

I dawdle on the way, stopping several times to retie my sash and rearrange my skirts, because there's a lamp burning out in the Maze of Fireflies. I can hear a voice, and I recognize it. It's Prince Ebel Quareen, the pious, punctilious, and covertly libidinous tyrant of Holy Ibis. Ebel used to hold forth at Hallan while they drank, and Hallan would listen good-naturedly. During those late-night conversations about law, theology, and politics, Ebel was often uncomfortable having me in the room, because he desired me, or despised me, or both. He used to oscillate between trying to get my attention and complaining that I was compromising the prince's privacy and should leave.

Out in the pavilion, I hear Ebel ranting. "The Errantines preaching on street corners! The Sha'an building schools! Librarians cataloguing Zhinj books! Fortunetellers scamming the tourists right outside the Library! My cloaksfolk are telling me terrible things, Vilya. Your father's hand has slipped off the city—the place is like a horse with no rider!"

As if anyone in Moonstone rides a horse. It would have to be a seahorse to be useful.

Probably, given his choice of metaphors, Ebel's been reading accounts of the ancient Taradian saints again. *They* had horses.

Someone spits into the water. And then Prince Vilya speaks, more quietly than usual, which likely means he's up to no good.

"You can't expect anything like strength from my father," Vilya says. "When I was six, some fishmonger wormed her way next to us while we were going to chapel, and spit on us. Her little son was a sorcerer, so the deacons had given him spikerose to tamp down his sorcerous powers, and sent him to be raised at an ancillary, and the scrawny thing had died of overdose or grief or what-have-you. The city was better off, of course, but his fiendshit mother blamed my father and the saints and me, and stood there and cursed us all, as if any of it was my fault. You know what she yelled at me as they dragged her off? 'Bastard—you're no better than my son! You don't even look like your father!'"

"She was probably a witch herself!" Ebel says scornfully.

Vilya chuckles. "You know what the great Jalian Mai did! Forgave her! Let her go! Gave her a little coin, even, so she could live to curse us another day! After she called me a bastard and cast aspersions on my mother!" Vilya barks a laugh. "My mother nearly died from shame. She wouldn't speak to him for weeks. She went off into her tower after that and more or less never came out." Vilya's voice becomes more bitter. "If it had been Kalicent on the barge and not me, he'd have defended her!"

"You don't need to follow in his footsteps," says Ebel Quareen. "Your uncle's a better man."

"I intend to follow Jalian Mai in only one way," Vilya says vehemently. "I intend to be archprince after him."

Ebel guffaws. "Saints hasten the day!"

It's treason, but the palace-dwellers here and there along the colonnade are resolutely not paying attention. The sentinels pretend they haven't heard and hurry me along. I think about what I've learned.

We continue onward till we reach the Seaspire. A perfect marble staircase spirals up and up toward the tower's top, but I won't be walking. At the center of the spiral is a lifting-chamber, hoisted using counterweights. I leave the sentinels in the entrance hall and step into that octagonal, uneasy room of wood and glass. It carries me, alone, up to the highest level of the Spire, rocking slightly back and forth as it ascends. When the chamber finally stops, I open the door and step out. If it were morning, the windows in a circle all around would reveal a breathtaking vista of the city, the river, and the sea.

But it is the dead of night. To the east, there are thickly spread lights where Sorcerer's Kettle lies. To the west, where lie the islands of Scattered Pearls, the lights gather in gay clusters like fireflies. Out on the river, the lights are sparse, like stars. If I listen carefully, I can hear the waves throwing themselves against the cliffs, out beyond the fishing villages of Turtle's Clutch. Above it all, the regal and generous moon, archprincess of the sky, limns the outlines of the islands and bridges, guiding boats to harbor. How I have loved this view. I have enjoyed it many times from Jalian's bed. Sometimes we've looked at it together and recited poetry. Sometimes, by moonlight, Jalian has regaled me with secrets of arch-princes past. It's a gift, now and then, to be with someone who knows this corrupt and complicated city as well as I do, and loves it, in spite of itself.

I draw my attention back to my immediate surroundings. To my right is a door to a discreet room where a few cloaksmen and servants lounge. Nearby is the door to a fine washroom with a round marble tub set into the floor. To my left is a sumptuous bed and wardrobe and writing desk. Directly ahead is a regal chair facing out toward the bay, with a harp and stool nearby.

In the chair, Jalian sits waiting for me. I approach him and make my usual gestures of greeting. We both like the ceremony of it, the way it allows us to draw out the moment. When I raise my head, he says: "I would have bought your contract at any price."

"I know." I lower my eyes and smile. "I know, Jalian, and it means a great deal, but I no longer govern myself by contracts."

He shakes his head. "You would be safer now."

"Safer from what?"

He snorts. "As if you didn't know. From my saintsforsaken son! He'll be archprince soon. At his back will be the ignorant mob he has been cultivating for years now. His mother, curse her, will egg him on. The Council may try to rein him in, but they will fail. I fear for the city, girl. I fear for my Kalicent; he may get rid of her outright. He will not want to share a drop of his power."

I am not as all-seeing as I think I am. This is a bitter way to learn it.

"You are not well," I say.

He laughs a disgusted laugh and shows me his bloated fingers. "My kidneys are failing. The doctors say I have days left. It makes no sense; I drink wine, it's true, but not enough to kill myself! I have been poisoned; I am sure of it. The doctors say no, but how can I trust them to tell me the truth? Already my courtiers leak away to my son. I am a sinking ship. The rats are fleeing."

Now I understand why Vilya sounded so triumphant in the Maze of Fireflies. I think of Karel Lutei in the Library cloakroom all those years ago. If Jalian Mai has been poisoned, he isn't the first prince of Moonstone to die that way, nor, likely, will he be the last.

"Eminence, I can bring healers…" I venture.

Jalian laughs a full-throated laugh. "Such talented wives you have. But no, your women cannot save me. The Sha'an preserved my life ten years ago; I'm grateful, but there won't be a second reprieve. I trust my doctors that far, at least. And I may not be able to save *you*. But I can warn you, at least."

"Your daughter already warned me," I say. "Vilya plans to exile the Sha'an."

"He has told her so, yes, but it's worse than that. He intends to use his thugs to herd them back upriver, to the Sha'an forest, where Lord Griseus of Mor will be waiting to do them in. Vilya has always wanted Griseus's favor, more than he ever wanted mine. He will have it, if he delivers the Sha'an." Jalian shakes his head.

"Is he so eager to eliminate his playthings? Once the Sha'an are gone, whom will Vilya have to dangle before the mob?" I ask.

Jalian's voice is sorrowful. "There are sorcerers and such, if he needs someone to persecute. Or he can always start in on those who read banned books. Or those who read, period. Wisdom is his enemy, and he knows it. My historians tell me all great Libraries have burned eventually."

Jalian is the archprince of Moonstone, but he is first and foremost Protector of the Library. It must be bitter to be leaving his charge in the hands of a barbarian he himself engendered. I bow before him, honoring not his power, this time, but his grief.

Jalian takes off one of his rings and hands it to me. "There is little I can do for Moonstone, but for you, at least, I can do something. I have designated a ship in Hundred Quays for you, the *Windswift*, the captain of which will know you by this ring. If you wish, take your wives and however many of your friends you can save. Go to Belakkos or Tamirlia or the Fenge. Only do one thing for me. Play the harp for me, this last time."

Tears sting my eyes as I tuck up my sleeves, sit on the stool, and put my fingers to the harp strings. His eyelids close in anticipation. I have it in my power to numb his pain, to bring him peaceful sleep. I might even have the power to end it all for him now—who knows? I have never tested my sorcery so far. But I cannot bring myself to try, even if he desires me to do so—even if he means to ask me to. Jalian knows more than he says, always.

And so I play, not magic, but music. A song of old Moonstone. Music that floods the palaces of the soul. After a while, I sing, and then he sings, and we duet, passionately, cherishing the song as if it is a life.

The river embraces a thousand shores
as I embrace your thousand shores.
The river witnesses a thousand seasons
as I witness your thousand seasons.
But the river's great love is the sea,
as our love is the sea, the endless sea.

The flood of music ebbs away and leaves a clean quiet behind it. I close my eyes, transported by the power of the song.

Then I feel a hand on my shoulder. Jalian is not in his chair but standing near me. I rise, knocking the stool over. It may be the first time I have been awkward in his presence.

Then he bends and kisses me the way he kissed me that first time, near the Gilded Bridge, that summer at the blessing of the waters. I can see that this causes him pain, but I can also see it is important to him. He pulls me to him with what must be the last of his strength, and then we are so entwined that the bed seems too far away for us to reach it. We make the effort, for comfort's sake. He blows out the lamp, and the moonlight wraps us around like a silver veil. Whatever pain we both know, that pain does not deprive us—yet—of the joy we take in one another.

I put on the ring and leave in the light of early dawn. Jalian sleeps heavily, without stirring. I do not look back, not even to catch a glimpse of the bay.

Being with Jalian has never felt like betraying Annlynn, or Olloise, or Istehar. It has always felt like service I render to the soul of the city, a way I can keep the river flowing in the right direction. Tonight's events suggest that might have been true, once. And yet the covered passage to the docks, which I again traverse escorted by sentinels, feels like a walk for the condemned. The boatman hands me into the felze, his hands rough, his gaze appraising. As I settle in my seat, I reach into my pocket and find the river-drake's eye.

CHAPTER 17

Annlynn Jissakhar, Vasmine Kinora,
Olloise Mazall, Istehar Sha'an, Students
River School, Vexmere
Seven years ago

Clouds are gathering upriver. It's late afternoon on Daemoniday and the students are off classes. Just across the strait, on Vexriver, loggers are taking the seven-year pines. The fall of each tree is loud enough for everyone on the back shore of the River School to hear. Istehar has been squatting on the riverbank all day, watching. Joeve walks by and shoves her so that she falls into the mud. Joeve has just gotten home from a visit to her parents in Turtle's Clutch and is in a particularly bad mood. Joeve's friends laugh, but from a distance; they know Istehar is unpredictable.

But Istehar isn't paying attention to them. As a particularly beautiful pine tree crashes to the ground, Istehar pushes herself to her feet, strips off half her muddy clothes, wades into the water, and starts to swim toward Vexriver.

Vasmine has been near the firepit to nab some charcoal for eyebrow-drawing; she's been running a class of sorts, teaching younger students the art of self-creation. One of her trainees sees and points. Vasmine runs across the field, her fashionable wide sleeves flying. "Stop!" she calls. "The current's too strong. You'll drown, you idiot."

"They're killing the trees!" Istehar calls back, still fighting toward Vexriver. "They're too little to die! I have to stop this."

"Those are the archprince's loggers," Vasmine shouts. "They won't stop because you say so. Come back, Istehar, be sensible!

They'll expel you. Annlynn! Annlynn, she's gone mad again. Do something!"

Big Chessa, lounging in the sun, laughs hysterically, but she does get to her feet, knock on the fencing-house window, and yell, "Anya! You're needed outside. Your little savage is getting in the way of civilization. Don't put on your shoes, you'll just have to take them off again."

Annlynn comes out the door, sweating and irritated. Still laughing, Big Chessa points. "Saints' piss," Annlynn curses, and takes off toward the shore, where Istehar is a quarter of the way across the strait. Vasmine points, unnecessarily. Annlynn strips off her tunic and trousers and dives in. She's a fast swimmer; in moments, she's overtaken Istehar. After a few seconds they both start back. Istehar is ahead, Annlynn behind, sweeping the water with her eyes in case of debris or snakes. Vasmine, watching them, frowns a little.

When they reach the bank, Istehar pushes herself up on shore and huddles with her knees up to her chest. Annlynn heaves herself out of the water, shivering and complaining. Vasmine strolls up to them. Big Chessa is already telling the story to a trio walking past.

"What possessed you?" Vasmine asks Istehar. "I'm afraid I mean that literally."

"The trees are screaming," Istehar whispers. "Just like when the soldiers of Mor burned the trees in my village. I could hear them until we were downriver almost to Moonstone. I hate hearing that sound again."

"I don't mean to be insensitive, but do vegetables scream on your plate?" Vasmine asks. "You were gobbling up the peas last night."

Istehar casts her what, for Istehar, passes for a dirty look. "I do feel something around plants, but it's not the same. Trees are…" She shrugs. "They have more self. I don't know how to say it in your language."

"If you stop the loggers, there'll be no more books," Annlynn points out. "Or bookcases or houses or boats.

The Sha'an make things from trees too, don't they? I understand trees are like people to you, but this is a big city, Istya. People need things. We can't just wait around for trees to fall by themselves."

"But so many trees!" Istehar shudders. "It's like draining the water out of the river and letting all the fish die."

"They'll plant new trees, sweetling," Vasmine says kindly. "In the spring. You'll see. There will be gurgling baby trees for you to listen to."

Tears begin to run down Istehar's cheeks. "How long is this going to go on?"

Annlynn shrugs. "A few weeks, likely."

"Weeks?" Istehar looks around at the dormitory, where their room hides near the roof. "I can't stay here. I have to pack."

Vasmine sighs. "Istya, if you run away from the River School, the Council will be offended, and they might expel your whole tribe from the city. You're a leader of the Sha'an; you can't just do as you like. You must think of your people." Istehar stares at her miserably.

Behind them, there is a step. Vilya is there, with his coterie. Joeve is hanging on his arm. "Does the logging remind you of home?" he asks Istehar. "What's left of your home, that is." He grins as Joeve guffaws.

Annlynn's fists ball. "If you kill all the trees," Istehar replies, "you'll be king of a sandbar."

"Better a sandbar than an ash heap," Vilya retorts. "Witch." His friends laugh, but uneasily.

"Anyone would think you cared about trees more than people," Joeve adds, tossing her hair. "There's something wrong with you. The Department for Interrogation of Sorcery should get involved."

Annlynn gets to her feet. "Speaking of interrogations, I wonder how the archdeacon would feel about your father's loggers taking trees on Daemoniday," she says to Vilya. "Seems to me that's not customary."

Vilya glares back. "Seeing as my father pays the archdeacon, I don't think it will be a problem."

"The prince hardly needs some commoner's advice," Joeve snipes.

"Curious that you don't apply the same principle to yourself," Vasmine comments quietly. Joeve sniffs, offended, and turns to go.

"I'll leave you to enjoy the view," Vilya mocks, sweeping his arm to indicate the falling trees on the far shore. "A preview of your own fates, no doubt."

When the pack leaves, Annlynn curses. "Those fiends-begotten hellhounds would burn down the city if anyone gave them a match." She looks at Istehar. "You want the logging stopped?"

Istehar nods, wiping her eyes with her soaking-wet, filthy sleeve. Vasmine glances Annlynn's way, curious.

That night, on Vexriver, there are ghost-howls all through the pine tree stands. In one old tree close to the loggers' camp, the team captain finds notches torn in the trees, seeping with sap—twenty-three notches, exactly the number of loggers in the team. In the morning, the loggers all mill about, too frightened to enter the pine stands. There are demons in the woods, the loggers say. The project supervisor comes and threatens the men. They log for much of the day. The next night, there are howls again, and notches in a tree even closer to the camp. In the morning, a third of the men have crept away.

After three nights of howls and notches, closer and closer, the logger captains give up and order boats of loggers sent farther upriver, to a stand of dying trees, hoping the tree-spirits will be less offended. The school gossips that Vasmine's prince bought off the loggers so that his concubine's studies wouldn't be disturbed. Vasmine encourages this rumor by inviting Prince Hallan to attend a concert she gives in the conservatory.

Annlynn has a horrible cold and fevers for two weeks. Each night, Olloise makes Annlynn herbal tea and brandy. Olloise says she doesn't mind the superstitions of her fellow citizens being used against them, as long as it's for a good cause. When Annlynn can't sleep, Istehar tells stories of the long-ago illuminatrix Esthama'ar, who married the forest and thereby obtained permission for human folk to settle there and become the Sha'an. She tells of the hero Ilinith, who scaled a cliff, averted an avalanche, and saved the forest-dwellers, human and tree alike. Meanwhile, Vasmine sings to Annlynn and strokes her head.

Some nights, while Annlynn sleeps, Istehar goes outside to sit on the grassy bank under the moon, gaze across the channel, and watch the stands of baby pines getting bigger. Vasmine and Olloise find they have time to get further acquainted. The downstairs parlor is empty at night and has a divan meant for guests, with very soft pillows. Olloise particularly likes to play with the long iridescent bird feathers in a vase by the parlor door.

One night, Istehar goes out to the riverbank. She notices a misty spot of light in the little woods nearby and investigates. Under an old tree with a full canopy of leafy branches, Annlynn has draped a gauze curtain over a branch to make a little tent. She has laid out a lantern, a few down quilts, and a bottle of moonwater that Istehar at first refuses. Later on, Annlynn presses her fiercely against the tree, as if the tree too is their lover. Istehar, who refuses to use coarse Moonstone terms for sex, teaches Annlynn the Sha'an word *ehar*—the interweaving of bodies, of things and events. It is part of Istehar's own name, which means "the stars' entwining."

In a dormitory room, Vasmine curls up with Olloise and teaches her to sketch her brows with charcoal. The two of them brew enough invisible ink to prank the next incoming class, then proceed to things that are less mentionable. The next morning, the whole school knows what happened last night between Annlynn and Istehar on the back shore, and marvels that Vasmine and Olloise don't seem troubled at all.

CHAPTER 18
Istehar Sha'an, Illuminatrix
Undersong House
Daemoniday, 4:30 a.m.

In the Bay of Scattered Pearls, late-night casino-boats and floating liquor parlors are having their last calls in the wee hours. Barges and gondolas crowd the area, looking for fares. The ride home is long, and I'm impossibly tired and wondering what's happening to the tree-spirit in my belly. I breathe a sigh of relief when I see Undersong House off to port, but even in the dark I can see a strange thickening in the air. The royal boatman stabs his long pole into the river floor and jolts the whole boat. "River-fire," he calls to me, and ties up near the bridge to avoid running into the wreck that seems to be smoking up ahead.

A strange sweet stench reaches me over the water, and a voice: Maliki Sha'an, the flower seller, calling for help. Every day, he comes past Undersong House in the pre-dawn on his way to the Lanterners' Canal, the wide canal that cuts the island of Seven Lanterns in half. Housewives, shopkeepers, and servants are often up early to buy fresh flowers, herbs, milk, eggs, and other such things. They're happy to buy fresh flowers for their entrance hall vases and their ancestor altars, and for corsages when they go to dances and plays. It's his boat that's burning.

Summoning energy from some unlikely reserve inside me, I leap off the gondola and run over the bridge. Skirting the house, I can see Olloise briskly filling buckets from the well. Annlynn is hip-deep near the shore, throwing water onto the flaming vessel. The wreck is in full view now, an awful sight even in the dark. Maliki takes another bucket from Olloise.

Dozya Sha'an is coming from next door with a pot to use for dipping up river water. Fire on the river means everyone helps.

"What happened?" I gasp, running up to the well.

"Men were hiding in your garden," Maliki says to me as he takes another bucket from Olloise. "They threw lit torches at me when I passed. The boat caught fire."

"But why?" I ask, leaning my staff against a tree and setting down my box. I'm dizzy from fatigue and nearly fall over when I bend down.

"No time to ask that now! Get a pail!" Olloise dips another bucket and runs to the fire. I take a third pail from the garden shed and join the bucket brigade, but the question of why is worrying me.

Annlynn is dipping up river water to pour on the hot embers and charred wood. "No shortage of trouble in this fiend-infested city," she complains. Smoke and steam rise into the pre-dawn sky. Dozya Sha'an joins her in the river. The fire is nearly out now. Maliki sobs as he throws water on a pile of what once were lush flowers.

"Such an act of hate," I say to Maliki. "It must be folk who despise the Sha'an, who wanted to harm you."

"A sad but plausible theory," Olloise agrees.

"Oi," the palace boatman yells from around the curving bank of the little island. "Madam Sha'an! People went into your house!"

"Saints' piss!" Annlynn swears with percussive force as we all realize this isn't over. Her sword is just inside the back door. She runs for it.

"They'll burn down the house!" I shout, filling a bucket and imagining, with horror, the Books of the Tree going up in smoke.

"They've come for me!" Olloise cries, frozen to the spot where she is standing. She begins to tremble violently. "Don't go in, please, Istya, please don't go in!"

What does she mean? I think. *Who's come*? And then I realize that, whoever murdered her parents, Olloise believes those people are now here for her. That her investigation has led to this. It's all happening for her again. I squeeze her hand, but she's staring in front of her, not looking at me.

The truth is, I'm remembering the smell of burning forest, myself.

"Loli, I have to go in," I insist in a shaking voice. "Annlynn and Bastina are in there. We have to do something! You can stay here if you need to." I pick up my staff, and take it and the bucket toward the house, hoping all this labor isn't harmful to the tree-spirit inside me. It's a good thing I drank Olloise's potion yesterday; it's likely giving me more energy than I ought to have right now. Dozya, wielding his iron pot, comes with me.

Behind me, I hear Maliki comforting Olloise. "I will come with you to the house, *ihante*," he says to her. "Don't be afraid." He uses the traditional Sha'an title for the spouse of an illuminatrix. I think I haven't heard anyone call one of my wives that before.

As I get close, there is the sound of breaking glass. It goes on far longer than it takes to break a window. "The laboratory," Olloise gasps, and, overcoming her fear, breaks into a run toward the house. Maliki follows.

I've gotten to the back door now. "Bastina!" I call. "Annlynn!"

Bastina answers me; she hid in the laundry closet on the first floor when she heard men come into the house. I open the closet door. Her usually animated face is still and white as a sheet. I hug her. "It will be all right," I say to her. *At least it's not a fire*, I think. *Not yet.*

"Stop in the name of the archprince!" I hear the royal boatman bellow, somewhere by the front stairs. I hear rumbling above me, maybe from one of the many small roof-ledges of the house. Someone is definitely climbing on our roof. I move toward the stairs, but Maliki stops me.

"*Ihan-tanon*, you don't know who they are or what they are willing to do!" he counsels, using the Sha'an term for illuminatrix.

Annlynn clatters downstairs. "They climbed out the windows!" she tells us, breathing hard. "They smashed the laboratory!"

Olloise, behind me in the hearth-room, gives a strangled gasp. "My potions!" And no one can dissuade her from running upstairs to see what has happened. Her miserable cry tells everyone what she's found. *Someone knows about her little experiments,* I think. *Someone who wants to bring all that to an end. Olloise told Prince Hoel Dhagura what she was doing in that laboratory. Whom else might he have told? Giya Lutei? Vilya Mai?*

Was this a warning? If we keep pursuing the murderers, what might they do next?

Or was this malice against the Sha'an? Were the vandals just happy they found something to break?

The tree-spirit says nothing. I feel it dreaming in a packed, tight core somewhere inside me, uninterested in matters beyond its seed-self.

Annlynn rushes outside to try to pursue the vandals, and some of the local Sha'an who have awoken at the sound of the cries come out to join in the search. The miscreants are nowhere to be found. The whole neighborhood is awake and talking about what happened. If Maliki's boat can be burned, if the house of the illuminatrix can be invaded, none of them are safe.

When we regather on the front steps, the boatman and Dozya describe how they saw several persons with veiled faces climb down the vines at the side of the house and vanish into the night. The local searchers return home. The boatman, who gives his name as Fyfe, walks with Maliki, Dozya, and Annlynn around the premises to make sure the intruders have gone.

A grieving Olloise shuts herself into her smashed laboratory, railing at unknown murderers, vandals, and bigots. Bastina calms herself by doing for others: she goes upstairs and knocks, offering to help clean up. Bastina is youngish, with short dark hair and a ring in her nose. She generally puts up a fierce front, but now her hands are shaking. Bastina knew Olloise when they were children and has worked for us since we left school; she is used to a fractious household, but this is more, perhaps, than she bargained for.

"Shall I bring the sentinels?" the boatman asks me as he prepares to return to the palace. Tellingly, no one else in the neighborhood has suggested this.

"You have done far more than your duty," I tell him, knowing that if princes are angry with us, the sentinels might do more harm than good. "The vandals might have burned our house along with Maliki's boat if not for you. We're grateful."

Dozya Sha'an goes to tell the various elders what has happened. It's possible, he says, that this was directed not at us but at the whole Sha'an community. Maliki has a cup of tea and a pastry of rolled-up dough, nuts, and cinnamon. He has to get home to the Moon's Daughters and tell his family the bad news.

The startlement of events is wearing off and I'm exhausted, but I make myself walk to the dock with him. Annlynn hails a milk-boat coming from the Moon's Daughters and explains the situation. The milkwife, Uhela, is a bustling, queenly Zhinj woman, from the tribe indigenous to the city. She manages a large dairy of sea-sheep and has been delivering our milk for years. Admirably, the Zhinj do not eat meat, but milk, yogurt, and cheese are a large part of their diet and therefore of their expertise. Exclaiming over the wreck, Uhela ties up at our dock and agrees to tow Maliki's ruined boat back to his home.

"High tide in the city right now," she says, using the Zhinj euphemism for troubled times. That sounds about right to me.

It's light by now and the damage to the little flower-boat is shocking. The day's flowers are all burnt up. The housewives won't get their corsages today or for many days to come. A weary and grief-stricken Maliki tells me he doesn't want the sentinels involved.

"I am Sha'an," he says. "Maybe they will find something wrong with my permit." Annlynn nods unhappily and sees him into the milk-boat. I wave sadly as the boat pulls away into the current.

CHAPTER 19
The Wives
Undersong House
Daemoniday, 6:30 a.m.

"It's all my fault," Olloise mumbles as she comes down into the back room. "All of it is my fault." She sits down at the table and cradles her head in her arms. Bastina, still in a busy mood, has stayed upstairs to see what she can do about boarding the broken windows.

"We don't know that," says Istehar, just awoken from a nap, setting out plum rolls, sweet-sour jam made of rare flying-fruit from a neighbor's tree, and fresh cheese on the counter. If they all have to flee Moonstone, their stomachs may as well be full.

"But someone's after us, all right," Annlynn adds grimly, cradling her wounded, wrapped arm, which has just done far too much work. Her forehead is bruised and her fingers are swollen. "What did they take, Loli?"

"With all the smashed bottles, I'm not sure," Olloise says, raising her head. "But the vials of poison I brewed are gone. That much I know."

"It's that Lutei," Annlynn growls. "He must have heard about your investigation and ordered the attack on me. I should have cut him down in the Reading Room two days ago!"

"Istya, you shouldn't have left Vasmine at the palace by herself," Olloise scolds. "Prince Vilya is there. It could be *him* who did all this!"

They consume small amounts of the breakfast, barely noticing the excellent jam. They're all too uneasy to sit, and wander around the room while chewing. When the gondola bearing Vasmine in her white lace finally glides to the little dock, they all rush out.

"Where were you?" Olloise demands.

"What did the archprince say?" Istehar pleads.

"Vilya plans to sell the Sha'an to Griseus of Mor," says Vasmine once she has stepped up onto the dock. Her makeup is smeared and her eyes are exhausted. She lifts up her finger to show an ornate ring. "Jalian's dying, and there's nothing he can do. There's a ship waiting in the harbor for the four of us, so we can flee Moonstone." Stunned, they all follow her into the house.

"Flee Moonstone!" Annlynn repeats heavily, sitting down at the counter. She fumbles one-handed for the decanter. Olloise helps her. Vasmine goes to the pitcher and bowl at one side of the room to wash her hands and face, and then moves to stand by the fire.

"I can't leave here without my people," Istehar insists, sitting down hard in one of the pillow-nests by the hearth. "One ship won't hold them all."

"You could take *some* of them," Vasmine points out, turning to her.

"Some is not enough, Mina!" Istehar looks at Vasmine in shock. "How could you not know that?"

"Idiot, some is better than none!" Vasmine retorts furiously.

"Stop it, both of you!" Olloise cries, setting down the decanter. "We don't have time to argue. They're watching the house, whoever they are—the Lutei, the Mai, I don't care anymore. If the boatman hadn't seen them, they might have lain in wait upstairs and ended us all! I've put you in danger. If we don't leave this house at once, they'll come back and murder us, like they did my parents!"

"That's just a theory, Loli," Annlynn points out. She's quickly swallowed her drink.

"Do you have one that fits the data better?" Olloise

retorts. "Weren't you nearly killed yesterday in the alley behind Yan's? It's a wonder Vasmine made it home alive!"

Incongruously, Bastina opens the back door and comes into the kitchen carrying a stack of folded moss-silk vests and dresses, woolen sweaters, satin slips, and black Library uniforms. "The laundry-boat just stopped," she explains in answer to their stares. "I saw it signaling us and ran out the side door to catch it." And indeed, when they look out the window, the laundry barge is lumbering past the dock, its spotless white flag flying. The smell of musk and lavender wafts in through the window.

"At least we'll have clean laundry in exile," Annlynn mutters.

"I hope our clothes aren't poisoned," Olloise grumbles.

"Oh, the laundress gave me this to give to you," Bastina says, and hands a coarse cloth bag, the kind that would normally hold a pile of towels, to Annlynn. But the shape and weight of the sack indicate that what is in the bag is not towels.

Annlynn feels the sack.

"Books," she says, surprised.

Olloise eyes the bag, suspicious. But Istehar's face tells them it is *definitely* books.

"Maybe Thalweg sent the prayerbook," Istehar exclaims.

"This is way heavier than a prayerbook," says Annlynn, wincing as she lifts the bag to the table. Bastina hurries out of the room, as if this act of smuggling has convinced her the household is skating too close to high crimes for her liking.

Olloise opens the bag's drawstring and pulls out the contents. There are three volumes, large but thin, bound in violet silk studded with moonstones. She lays them out carefully on the counter and opens each one. They all appear identical. Each one is a carefully calligraphed version of the Moonstone Covenant. The rest of them gather around. Nobody breathes.

Istehar reaches out a hand, then pulls it back as if she's been burned. "Oh, they're very loud!" she complains, shrinking back. "It's like they're fighting with each other."

A paper protrudes from one of the tomes. Annlynn carefully removes the paper and reads: "'Istehar didn't get the chance to hold this. I included two others for comparison. When I see you, I'll tell you how I got them out of the Library. P.S. Give the laundress the books when she stops by tomorrow morning.'"

She puts down the paper. "It's from Tommas," she says. "I recognize the handwriting."

"These are three of the six Moonstone forgeries," Olloise says slowly, putting the picture together. "The books my mother checked out before she died."

"Your friend the Librarian sent these?" Vasmine asks Annlynn. She looks, for a moment, as frightened as Bastina.

Annlynn, oblivious to all else, picks up the book in which the note was hidden and starts to read it. "This one is the Lutei forgery," she tells them. "See, here it says that Karel Lutei will be the archprince, and his heirs after him, and that the Covenant can never be abrogated while the city stands. It should, of course, name Surian Mai instead." She opens a different one. "This is the Dhagura forgery, where Draugar Dhagura is said to be the archprince." She opens the third. "This is the Quareen forgery, where Nesnessa Quareen is supposed to be the archprincess."

Annlynn shakes her head. "I can't believe he sent these on a laundry-boat. Tommas could be arrested."

Istehar edges closer to the three elegant books and looks down at them. "You say these are elaborate, expensive party favors." She shakes her head. "How could someone even have afforded to have them made? And just for the vanity of a few princes? No wonder this city is about to sink under the weight of its own corruption. Maybe we'll be lucky if we have to leave it."

"Maybe they're not party favors," Olloise says, bending down and taking a close look at the pages before her. "Vasmine, you're an ink expert. Come and see this."

Vasmine comes over slowly. She stares at the three books, then looks up at Olloise.

"Don't you see it?" Olloise says. "The ink in the Lutei forgery is very slightly reddish, just like the ink in the original Moonstone Covenant on display in the Council Room. It must have been black when the book was inscribed, but that old ink made from syssyrup trees and wine goes a little red over long periods of time." She points to the printing in the other two books. "These were written later, when ink contained soot. They're still perfectly black after two hundred years, see? The Lutei forgery is older than the others."

"Why would that be?" Annlynn asks.

Vasmine still says nothing. Her face has that stillness concubines of Fengen lineage are famous for. "Can I hold one?" Istehar asks.

"Turn around and close your eyes," Olloise orders. "I don't want you to know which one I'm giving you." Istehar does as Olloise asks. Olloise hands her one of the books.

Istehar takes the book back to her pillow-nest and, holding it in both hands, is silent for a while. Her hair twines wildly around her shoulders. Her face is pale and she's so still that Annlynn leans over to make sure she's still conscious.

"I smell ink," Istehar says at last, her eyes still closed. "A scribe's writing by candlelight. He's tired and sweating; it's hot. It must be late at night: there's a vast empty square outside with fancy buildings. Like the square outside the Library."

Olloise goes over, takes the book Istehar is holding and gives Istehar another book. "I see a room with marble walls and a high dome," Istehar says immediately.

"Go on," Annlynn urges.

Istehar's eyes remain closed. "There are banners all around. People in rich clothes are writing in the book, one by one. There are lots of people watching. There's a man in a grand chair, a tall man with auburn curls under a purple beret. He's smiling. I don't like the look of his smile..." Istehar shivers.

"Saints preserve us," Annlynn gasps. "It's the original."

"What?" Istehar comes out of her trance and, dizzied, leans back on the pillows.

Annlynn gently, almost reverently, takes the book from Istehar. "The Lutei forgery. It's the original. The original Covenant. That's the only thing that makes sense. The room you saw was the Council Room. Karel Lutei, the sadist with the cruel smile, was the first archprince. That's the man you saw. Surian Mai was black-haired; the Lutei were auburn-haired. This Covenant isn't a forgery; it's the first Covenant that was ever written."

"How could that be?" Olloise breathes. "How could Karel Lutei have been the archprince? Everyone knows it was Surian Mai!"

"The other forgeries were made to cover up the authenticity of this one," Annlynn goes on, as if she too is in a trance. "They must have been made in a hurry. That's why, when I gave her the Quareen forgery, Istehar saw a scribe working late at night!"

"Annlynn, that's impossible," Vasmine says. "Surian Mai was the first archprince, not Karel Lutei. That's what's written in the Moonstone Covenant in the Council Room, and that's what all the history books say."

"But maybe," Annlynn says, waving her hand in the air, "maybe there was an original Covenant that named the Lutei. Maybe Surian Mai was made archprince only after Karel Lutei was murdered. The Covenant that's in the Council Room could be the *second* covenant the Council crafted."

"Maybe they killed the Lutei so they *could* make another Covenant," Olloise says. "Maybe Giya Lutei hired my parents to investigate Karel Lutei's murder and uncover the first Covenant. Maybe he thinks *he* should be archprince."

"That would explain Lutei's interest in the so-called forged Covenant," Annlynn says. "It would explain why he kept checking it out of the Library. He suspected it was the real one." She opens it again and looks inside it, as if she can't believe what she's seeing.

"But the second Covenant would have abrogated the first," Vasmine argues from her place by the hearth. "Karel Lutei's son Erius signed the Covenant that made Surian Mai the archprince. All the princes did. What happened beforehand wouldn't matter."

"No," says Istehar firmly, sitting up. "The first Covenant included the statement that it could never be abrogated." She rises, takes the Lutei version back from Annlynn, and finds the passage. "That's the one that should stand, especially if the second one was written to hide a crime."

"So you're saying this one should determine how Moonstone is governed?" Olloise asks. "Not the one in the Council Chamber?"

Istehar nods. Olloise sinks onto a stool. "This is why my parents died," she says.

All four of them take an unsteady breath. In the stillness, there are cries from seagulls out on the river. The smell of blossoms from the orchard wafts in the window. The bells from a tiny onion-domed chapel over the water, on the easternmost shore of East Lanternelle, summon the faithful to prayer. Nothing in the land or air around them has changed, and yet the city itself seems to totter at the edge of an abyss, or to float unmoored from its foundations. Words create worlds, and the red-black words in the book Istehar holds could unmake everything they know about Moonstone.

"We have to tell Prince Hoel," Olloise says. "He'll know what to do about the multiple Covenants. Let's all go to the Lanternhouse. We'll be safe there from whoever is trying to kill us." She takes the volume from Istehar and starts to pack up the books.

"You cannot bring these to Prince Hoel," Vasmine contradicts her vehemently.

"I have to say I agree," Annlynn says. "He works for the Council, and the Council won't like this news at all."

"If it's true there are two Covenants, which Covenant is valid is for the Council to decide," Olloise insists. "Not for us. We have to turn this over to the authorities."

"The same authorities who sent your mother to kill people?" Vasmine asks incredulously, going over to face Olloise. "Those are people you trust?"

Olloise recoils as if slapped. “Prince Hoel cared for me after my parents were murdered,” she retorts. “He supported our marriage when your families didn’t.” She begins to pull on a sweater she’s found in the laundry pile. “I don’t care who is archprince. I don’t care which Covenant is the real one. I don’t even care who the murderer is anymore. I want us to be safe, and for the Sha’an to be safe. If Prince Hoel wants to suppress this discovery, fine. I’ll promise to be the Council’s apothecary the way they want, if Prince Hoel will make all of this stop!”

“You can’t tell him, Loli,” Vasmine says.

“Why, Mina?” Istehar asks. “Prince Hoel doesn’t like Vilya Mai; everyone knows that. This information might give him an advantage against him. And Prince Hoel has been good to the Sha’an. Maybe he *would* help, if we turn over the books. Maybe we can trade.”

“I’m going there right now,” Olloise declares, picking up the rough package she’s made of the books. “You’d better come with me.”

“Prince Hoel hired me to spy on all of you,” Vasmine says.

There is a long silence. “What?” Annlynn almost laughs.

“When did he try to hire you?” Olloise demands. “After I brought him the poison?”

Vasmine shakes her head. “Long ago. When I was Prince Hallan’s concubine, before I came to the River School. He hired me to go to the school and learn everything about you.” More silence from everyone.

“Why?” Olloise asks flatly.

“He did care about you, Loli,” Vasmine tells her. “That much is true. He was worried you might learn how your parents were killed. That you might find out he ordered it.”

Olloise sinks into a chair, shaking her head from side to side. “It’s a lie,” she says. “You’re lying, Vasmine.” Istehar puts her hand to her mouth and leans against the counter. Annlynn clenches her fists.

Vasmine goes on. “He didn’t believe you could solve the crime, but you were Istehar’s lover, and there were rumors she had visions. He was worried about what you might find out. He didn't want to kill you. He didn't want to kill Istya because the Sha'an might get restive and they were producing moss-silk, making his district prosperous. So he hired me to report back about what you knew and didn't know. He promised to buy out my contract in return."

"But *we* bought out your contract," Istehar says in a small voice.

"You did," Vasmine says. "I used the money from Prince Hoel to buy out my mother's contract and set up the ink shop. I never pawned the river-drake's eye; I just hid it away for a while."

"So you *never* wanted me?" Annlynn asks bitterly. "Or Loli, or any of us? You just needed to get close to us, to earn some money? The thing I gave up my family for was a lie?" Annlynn is the closest to crying that they have ever seen her.

"I loved you, Anya," Vasmine replies passionately. "I came to love all of you. But if I'd stopped working for Hoel, he would have had me killed, and he might have had you killed too. I couldn't risk that. So over the years, I fed him bits of information. I convinced him Loli's research was going nowhere, that Istehar's visions were all in her mind, that we were just living ordinary lives. But when you brought him that poison, Loli, he must have realized you were close. He must have sent his cloaksmen to smash the laboratory and find out what else you were doing in there. If you tell him what you know, you won't live another five minutes!"

"Did Archprince Jalian know about all this?" Olloise asks in a toneless voice.

"I could never be sure of what he knew," Vasmine admits. "I think his relationship with me has sheltered us, to a point. But now I do wonder if it's possible Jalian might have ordered the assassination of the Mazalls himself, because they uncovered the truth about the Covenant. That must be why your mother checked out the books. Your parents were investigating, and they had learned what we just discovered."

Olloise is crying now. "You worked for my parents' murderers! You took money from them. You slept with them."

"She saved us," Istehar says. "She did, Loli. You have to see that."

"It's because of me you've lived in peace all these years!" Vasmine has drawn herself up to her full height as if appearing at court, but they can all hear the grief in her voice.

"You call this peace?" Olloise retorts, gesturing at everyone. "You deceived us, Mina! How can I possibly ever forgive you for that?"

"Get out!" Annlynn roars, at a volume that makes Bastina, in another wing of the house, run out the front door.

Vasmine is quiet a moment, and more than a few tears run down her face. Then she picks up her purse, turns, and walks out the back door and down to the docks. They watch through the broad window as she hails a passing gondola and steps into it. Annlynn smashes the decanter and then the glass she's been drinking from. She stalks out of the room, leaving puddles and shards on the floor.

Tears are rolling in a torrent down Istehar's cheeks. "Where will she go? Will we ever see her again?"

"You knew, didn't you?" Olloise accuses. "You wouldn't sleep with her, all these years. You knew!"

Istehar shakes her head. "I didn't know. We *still* don't know, Loli. We don't know all the things she did for us all this time, that she couldn't say."

"She could have told us," Olloise says. "Anytime in all those years, she could have told us that when Prince Hoel came to her shop, he wasn't buying ink."

But Istehar leaves the room, quietly goes into the silvirium, and closes the door.

CHAPTER 20

Annlynn Jissakhar, Warrior Librarian
Moonstone River
Daemoniday, 8:00 a.m.

Most mornings in Moonstone, there's a moment when you can run the boats. You have to catch it just right. The river gets thick with boats ferrying this and that, and if people will let you, you can run from one island to another by jumping from one boat deck to the next.

Looks like it's that hour.

I leap from a loading dock on the eastern side of Seven Lanterns onto an unsuspecting flat-bottomed peat-boat, and take off running, clambering on mounds of salt on a salt-boat, knocking over a plate of cakelets on a tea-barge, pushing through the crowds on a paddleboat ferry with a sentinel after me yelling that I haven't paid the fare. House-rafts. Bookboats. Floating liquor parlors. I run them all. Four times I leap into the river, and haul myself up on the next deck, cursing. Riverfolk are looking up, laughing, cheering me on. They think I'm a hero. Idiots.

The Sanctum of Holy Ibis looms in my vision, huge, round, and white as the mound of salt I just climbed. Like a tooth rising from the river. It's the last place she'd go, and the only place I can think of that I want to be. A few more annoyed boatwives, a few splashes in shallow water, and I'm there. Broad steps come down to the river's edge, packed with worshippers and tourists and folk enjoying the view. I'm sopping wet and drip puddles on the marble. The bandage on my wrist is soaked. My braid is dripping down my back. My bruised forehead must be hideous by now. At the entrance, I make the sacred gesture, pinching my fingers to make the sign of the two candles. The porter on duty frowns at me mightily but lets me in. After all, I'm not the first miserable, disheveled soul to pass these sacred doors.

Like a sleek river-drake, silence swallows me up. The halls are cool and white and have arched ceilings. The Sanctum of Holy Ibis was built at the founding of Moonstone, before any Covenant (real or false) was ever signed, and it's been embellished over the centuries. When I enter the sanctuary, three-story-high gold saints stare down at me with blank eyes from the immense circular wall that surrounds the worshippers. Each saint holds a different object: a seed cone, a lantern, a gondola pole. When I was little and feeling guilty, I entertained the notion they would come to life and pelt me with their sacred things. Now, I want to tear each saint from the wall and throw all their toys in the water.

What have the saints ever done for me? Only let a woman I passionately loved lie to me and then use my salary to buy pretty dresses. Only that. Plus, not only my life but this whole city is built on a lie. The Covenant they taught me about at school was a cover-up for Karel Lutei's murder, and the murders have gone on till this day. Look at what happened to the Mazalls. And the Sha'an are going to be murdered now, and it seems I can't do anything about it. Aren't the ancestors supposed to help? What were those statues glaring at *me* for, all those years?

I snatch a piece of black lace from the lace-box, drape it over my head and shoulders to hide how sopping wet I am and cover my bruises, and take a seat in a pew. My seat neighbors glare at me as I slowly drip a small pond onto the floor. The gold statue of a stern bearded elder holding a book and sword stares down at me. "That's our clan founder, Saint Briaron Jissakhar," my father told me once. "He vowed his descendants would guard the Library in perpetuity. That means you." And he gripped my shoulder as if wanting to leave his fingerprints in me.

River take Saint Briaron and his Library. Visions of throttling the beautiful Vasmine rise in my inner sight, interwoven with memories of my body entwined with hers. In the choir loft, a plump deacon signals the choir. Bell-like notes pour through the air: the music I loved as a child, wrapping me in its glory. I find myself weeping and hope no one here recognizes me. It would be embarrassing for a warrior librarian to be seen crying.

As the melodies of the morning service fill the air, I get up, take a lit taper from the candle-tray, and begin lighting incense, moving through the incense banks in front of all the statues. It's a way to turn my back on everyone, especially the tourists whispering and pointing at everything. Though since they're not from here, my misery is less their fault than anyone else's, I suppose.

I inch around the vast circular shrine, one incense stick at a time, leaving drops of water on the floor. My wrist aches. I have no idea what I should do when I finish lighting incense. I don't want to go home and figure out what to do next about the Covenants, the Sha'an, Olloise's parents, Prince Giya's claim to Moonstone. I hate all of my wives: Vasmine for never loving me, Olloise for making me find out the putrid truth, Istehar for bringing home that damn book in the first place. Why couldn't she have brought home a nice cookbook instead? Or a book of poems about gardens? When I complete the circle of saints, I think I'm going to lie down on the altar and die. It's that simple. I'm not fighting for this city anymore. Or for anything.

When I finish, I decide it would be humiliating to die on the altar, and walk back to where I was sitting. A bespectacled subdeaconess in a brown pinafore gives me a dirty look as she wipes up the puddles I made. I sink into a pew and sullenly turn my head as a procession sweeps in from a side chamber, with candles and velvet and bells tinkling. The choir abruptly stops singing. Pew denizens murmur and kneel. At the center of the procession marches a buxom, sloe-eyed, golden-haired, heart-faced woman in a sea-green gown, black lace draped artfully around her cheeks and chin and topped with a moonstone circlet. The circlet makes it clear who she is. Tilgana Mai.

So the archprincess has left her tower. Interesting. She passes pew after pew, implacable as the prow of an icebreaker ship. She looks younger than her husband Jalian, as if time runs differently in her rooms high above the city. They say she has genealogists check her ladies' pedigrees for four generations to make sure they are good, ordinary Abbatines with no hint of witchcraft. Many a maiden has broken down in the queen's tower when interrogated about her past. I find myself wondering if she can read my mind, if she's here to silence me before I tell what I know. A chill runs through me. Maybe it's a chill from the river water pooling in my shoes. Hard to say.

The entire congregation stares and whispers. The choir strikes up a new tune. The archprincess and her ladies pass, then deaconesses with candles. I see Ebel Quareen, scion of long-ago Taradian conquerors and prince of the district of Holy Ibis, surrounded by his bodyguards. After that, a lanky man in a white shirt and leather vest—well-trimmed beard, barbered brown hair, mild, frightened eyes—walks chained between two armed sentinels. So there is to be a trial here today, and if the trial is being held here and not in the Magistery, that means magic. I have seen such trials here before: they occur periodically and are clearly meant to terrify the public into repressing any latent sorcerous skill they might have.

Saints' piss. I know the man. It's Moa, the bartender and owner of Yan's; I just saw him yesterday. He's one of the most well-liked people on the Library docks. He mixes drinks and dispenses philosophy to sailors and tourists. What could he possibly have done to offend the archprincess?

I freeze, remembering yesterday. What if the tree-spirits escaped from the prayerbook in Thalweg's apartment at Yan's and made trouble? What if Moa's arrest is my fault?

As I writhe internally, the archprincess and her company take seats in the row of narrow thrones near the gold altar. The pudgy, scowling high deacon of Holy Ibis, majestic in sapphire blue and cloth-of-silver, climbs to his lily-shaped pulpit and leans over its petals, as if he's a stamen. He fixes the prisoner with a sanctimonious stare. Of all the deacons of the city, Beldrus is by far the worst. He's known for accusing the wealthy of heresy and confiscating their houses, all while preaching the righteousness of the saints. Even my father avoids him.

"Moa Nhakbir, we have brought you to trial in the Sanctum because you stand accused of hydromancy," the high deacon orates nasally, emphasizing the "hy" in an almost comical way. "Sorcery is a crime against the ancestors, against Archprince Jalian and the Council, and against the people of Moonstone. What is your plea?"

"I did nothing wrong," Moa asserts bravely, if not entirely calmly. From here, I can see the sweat on his forehead. "No one has cause to accuse me of a crime."

"We have heard your plea. I now present the evidence against you," Beldrus continues coldly. He almost sounds like someone who should be taken seriously. He must have rehearsed.

A few people are passing me, moving to the doors, quietly so as not to attract attention. Some are tourists, and some are city residents. Some even look like Abbatine clergy. The trickle of exiting folk turns into a little stream. Not everyone agrees with the anti-sorcery laws in the city, and not everyone enjoys watching people be sentenced to death. But of course many people do, so the pews stay mostly full. Some are leaning in eagerly to hear the high deacon's words. On cue, people are shaking their fists, calling Moa fiendspawn. I bet half of them bought a moonwater from him yesterday.

Then again, I was married to Vasmine yesterday.

The high deacon gestures to a tall, serious-looking, tiny-nosed deaconess seated by the archprincess. Her impressive crown of auburn hair is wrapped in black lace. "I call Ursel Kyze, tutress of the archprincess, as witness," says the high deacon.

Ursel the tutress rises and speaks in a quiet voice that somehow carries through the whole sanctum. Her I *have* seen before, delivering the archprincess's censure requests to my father in the Censor's Office. She's pretty. I might like her right now if she weren't about to get my friend killed.

"When did you encounter this man's sorcery?" the high deacon asks, abandoning all pretense of neutrality.

"It was yesterday evening, Your Reverence," Ursel relates confidently. "Her Eminence Archprincess Tilgana sent me to Yan's to buy libation wine. She wanted me to inspect the wines myself and choose the best one. It was immodest for me to stand in the bar, so while I was waiting for the bartender to serve me, I stepped into a stairwell. I heard some kind of crying or moaning coming from below, and I thought someone was hurt, so I went downstairs to see. I peered through a half-open door, and found the bartender in a cellar storeroom, singing to a liquor jug."

"Singing to a *jug*?" the high deacon prods. "This bartender you see here?" He points at Moa.

"Yes, Your Reverence. The jug was huge and almost empty, with only a small amount of wine at the bottom, and he was crooning, coaxing the wine in it like you call a cat or soothe a baby. As he called, the wine rose up from the bottom of the jug, poured out the spout, and filled the bottle in his hand."

Neat trick, Moa. Wineherding. Very useful talent for a bartender. No wonder you serve the fastest drinks in the city. Now that I think of it, you've always had an unnaturally elegant way of filling a glass.

"What happened then?" asked the high deacon.

Ursel blushes a little. "I screamed loudly, fearing the sorcery. Servants came running and saw the liquor unnaturally flowing upward before he was able to stop the spell."

"We have their testimony," says the high deacon, waving a paper at the congregation. "Did you know what liquor the jug held?"

"It looked and smelled like Taradian goldenwine, Your Reverence. The very same wine I'd come to buy. He was in a hurry to serve me and didn't want to call people to tip the jug, so he availed himself of his fiendish arts," Ursel speculates.

"You dare to taint libation wine with unholy magic!" the high deacon roars at poor Moa, who looks terrified. The archprincess frowns a disgusted little frown, like a schoolgirl who's seen frog guts. She's spent her life fearing sorcery, and seems nauseated that it almost got into her libation-glass. Imagine how tainted she'd feel if she knew Vasmine the harper-sorceress was sleeping with her husband.

I put aside that thought before I finish thinking it.

Moa says nothing. The high deacon frowns. "Let your silence speak for you," he tsks.

Then the archprincess's harsh Morish accent echoes through the vast sanctum. "This citizen would not have dared the depravity of sorcery without temptation. We have noted his business associates. Sha'an flower sellers bring him flowers for the making of liqueur. Sha'an fruit sellers bring him apples for the making of cider. Sha'an ice sellers bring him ice for the drinks he serves! These evil folk are constantly crossing his threshold, going down to meet with him in that secret cellar. The Sha'an have corrupted him!" Moa looks bewildered. The crowd hisses.

Everyone *brings him merchandise, you royal idiot. Everyone buys from him. Everyone meets with him. People from every part of the city, every corner of the world. He's the bartender at Yan's!* But I need to keep from shouting; I'll be arrested and charged along with Moa.

"The archprincess's staff has just delivered me evidence of these associations," the high deacon asserts. "Sentinels will be tracking down every single person who has spent time with this man in his storerooms!"

The timing of this encounter suits Vilya too well to be a coincidence. Maybe Ursel the fair has been shadowing Moa for years, and placed the order for a rare goldenwine when there was only a little left in the bottle, just to entrap him. Maybe Ursel and Vasmine have a lot in common.

Or, Moa's not a hydromancer at all, and Vilya and his paranoid mother just picked someone with lots of Sha'an contacts to persecute, so they can justify rounding up the whole tribe.

"We cannot allow the Sha'an to defile our city!" Prince Ebel calls from his place at Tilgana Mai's right. "We must act now before they corrupt anyone else!" Folk in the crowd roar in answer. Others look a little sick. It's a relief to know I'm not the only sane one here. But none of us sane folk is saying anything.

"Even the archprince does business with the Sha'an," Moa insists. He falls on his knees. "I beg for mercy from the archprince!"

The crowd chants: "Drown him!" The massive saints stare down, looking impressive but saying nothing. Useless.

"How dare you taint my husband by addressing words to him?" Tilgana Mai shouts at the accused, her careful lace face-wrappings becoming disarranged. She points at Moa with a beringed finger. "Fiend! Corrupted soul! You pollute this sacred city with your breath!" The crowd roars viciously. Deaconesses are fanning ladies who've nearly fainted, overcome with disgust.

Beldrus, who clearly thinks that as the high deacon he deserves the limelight back, proclaims hastily: "Moa Nhakbir, proprietor of Yan's, on the basis of testimony that you have committed hydromancy and conspired with sorcerers, you are condemned to death by drowning."

Moa, his head bleeding, shakes his head frantically as if trying to wake up from a nightmare. His eyes find mine, pleading. I hold his eyes for a few moments, trying to steady him, but I don't know what else to do. I don't dare look at him for long. Someone will notice. I break the gaze and melt into the crowd.

What would I want now, if I were Moa? Escape, but that's not likely. Safety for his employees and friends—Thalweg must be terrified, with that prayerbook lying around and Yan's swarming with sentinels. Moa's account books have the names of all his business associates. If Moa is declared a sorcerer, those books could be used to persecute half the city.

The high deacon cruelly begins to orate the details of Moa's execution. The crowd leans forward to listen. I rise, moving as quietly as I can in my squelching shoes, and exit out a side portal. In the foyer, there are four sentinels on guard. There's a nondescript door to one side that leads to the clerical offices. I've never been in there, but Librarians keep a set of skeleton keys. I'm hoping the city's public offices all have the same locks.

I double over, hiding my face and height, and gag as if I'm throwing up. "They're killing him," I wail, pitching my voice high. "O saints! They're killing him right in front of us. I can't look."

"An execution in the Sanctum?" one grizzled guard hmphs. "That's sacrilege!"

"Harsh times call for harsh measures," a younger one argues. "Make the fiendspawn an example!"

"Pull yourself together, madam," says a third, berating me. "Sympathy for heretics is a sin."

"It's the archprincess beheading him," I wail.

"Saints' piss!" the fourth guard exclaims. "That ain't ladylike. What will the archprince say?"

The guards crowd the door to see what I'm talking about. Later on, they'll conclude I was just some fainting flower who'd imagined things. Until they discover the theft, anyway.

The key fits. Quick as lightning, while the guards' backs are turned, I slip into a narrow hallway that connects a warren of poorly lit clerical spaces, and gently shut the door.

It's Daemoniday, so as I figured, the Sanctum office is empty. No one in the Sanctum wants to tempt the demons by trying to accomplish anything clerical on the fifth day of the week; most people throughout the city take off work lest the fiends unravel everything they do. I guess the archprincess picked today for the trial because she knew people would go to prayer today and the Sanctum would be crowded with worshippers. Or because she *is* a demon.

I'm fortunate no one's slipped in here to secretly catch up on their to-do list. Not everyone is equally pious around here. The Sanctum has a vast administration that oversees not only the daily prayers and physical needs of the second most important building in Moonstone, but also a seminary and theological college, a treasury of rare books it won't share with the Library, a graveyard for important persons, and its own printing press. Not far away from these marble halls are the affiliated ancillaries occupying excellent real estate on the banks of the island, full of holy ancillans and ancillas who pray day and night to the ancestors and to the future descendants who will one day be born—and the attached schools where, taught by deaconesses and deacons, young children learn. In many ways, the Sanctum of Holy Ibis is a city of its own—with its own agenda.

If I run into anyone here, I'm going to have a lot of explaining to do, and I'll likely end up arrested. At least the high deacon's desk isn't hard to find; it just requires opening one more locked door. In a little chamber with double-arched windows stands a massive wooden desk and chair. Carvings of various saints stand in the corners, particularly those of the Taradian sect the high deacon favors. A silver ink-castle stands in one of the niches, similar to the one Vasmine bought me as a wedding-present. The top drawer of the desk is locked. I kick it until it opens. I find Moa's leather account book, with names circled in red ink. I scan the names and suck in my breath.

I expected a list of Sha'an grocers and delivery-folk, but most of the names circled are old Moonstone names I know well. Librarians. Mine among them. My father's. My brothers' and sister's. Tommas's. Other experienced and noble colleagues. All of whom drink at Yan's.

I consider my visit to the Library yesterday. Hoel has spies everywhere. So does Vilya. Either of them might know that Istehar and I tried to get hold of the Covenants. Maybe one or both of them fear that Librarians are working against the Mai clan, planning to discredit them by revealing the forgery. Maybe this action of Tilgana's is a preemptive strike. My colleagues like to drink in that private room downstairs at Yan's. I've been there myself. They'll use that as evidence of our entanglement with Moa. We'll be accused of sorcery, and that will be it. We'll be drowned corpses in no time.

Or, it could be this event isn't about the Covenants, but rather is timed to coincide with Jalian's fatal illness. Now that our tolerant ruler is about to be irrelevant, the forces of ignorance may be planning to purge from power everyone who doesn't share their narrow-minded ways. If the Librarians were gone, Vilya could censor all knowledge, and all tolerance, in Moonstone.

Beldrus planned to turn this ledger over to the sentinels as soon as the trial ended. It may slow down the coming persecutions if I steal it. Moonstone folk do like to go by the rules, so they'll be stymied by the lack of evidence. Maybe they'll blame the theft on demons and be sorry they held the trial on Daemoniday.

As I pick up the ledger, I spot a sheet of paper on the high deacon's desk. It's a warrant issued by the archdeacon, and the name on it catches my eye: Vasmine Kinora. Apparently a lady-in-waiting turned Vasmine in for analyzing handwriting at Kalicent's party. Sorcery, the warrant accuses. Irony, more like. They could have turned her in for so much more.

Vasmine did get the archdeacon's sweet daughter Memmiam exiled with her little parlor trick. This must be payback. Unlike the odious high deacon, Archdeacon Fausten Yurenai is of the Ulurian sect of the Abbatines, the sect that honors the Blessed Initiatrix, the first ancestress of us all. That's why the archprince, who favors the Ulurian rite, appointed him as the archdeacon. Those folk can be particularly concerned with women's rectitude, so he's naturally dedicated to punishing the one who exposed his daughter to shame.

Vasmine is long gone, I'm sure. When we argued in the ink shop yesterday, I saw her take a small fortune out of her till and put it into her purse. She was eager to flee even then. Plus, the archprince gave her his ring. She could take her ship anywhere she wanted. If she's still in Moonstone now, she won't be by nightfall. But I can't help it. I take the warrant, fold it into the account book, and wrap the whole thing in an altar cloth from another drawer. I'm not turning anyone over to Vilya, not even people who have betrayed me.

There's got to be a door from the high deacon's office into the sanctuary. I find the door behind a curtain, just as voices from the choir swell. Hoping to time it just right, I make sure the veil is over my head and shoulders and slip out of the door; if anyone sees me, they might think I am a subdeaconess fetching something for His Reverence. Subdeaconesses are semi-clergy; they don't serve at altars or teach doctrine but they can serve the full clergy—and they're largely invisible.

Luck favors me, even if Vasmine doesn't. The archprincess is moving down the main aisle, exiting the Sanctum, her train trailing behind her like a demon's tail. All heads are turned toward her, and no one sees me re-enter the Sanctum. Sentinels are hauling Moa off. And then I see my mother in the crowd in her silk shawl and snood, whispering with a co-worshipper. I'm devastated to think she just witnessed Moa's trial; she'd never set foot in a liquor parlor, but she knows the rest of us make a second home of Yan's. This has to terrify her, even if she tends to idolize whatever the high deacon says.

My mother shifts her gaze for a moment, sees me—and turns away quickly, continuing to chat brightly. No doubt it embarrasses her that her estranged deviant daughter is at prayers looking like a canal-rat. Or maybe she's afraid that if she calls attention to me, I could be spotted and arrested. Tears start at the corners of my eyes as my mother leaves her pew and disappears into a herd of pious ladies. I miss my family so much. But that door is closed—even though everything I left them for is utterly wrecked.

Well, my clan might not be embarrassed by me much longer. Someone's already tried to kill me outside Yan's. What's to stop them from trying again?

I melt into the crowd and exit the Sanctum. I trudge to the landing to wait for the ferry, searching for a few wet, dirty coins from the sidewalk to pay the fare, the way I used to when I was a kid running around Drake's Hoard. But I don't see a single glint of silver or copper. What to do now? The boats on the river aren't thick enough anymore for me to run back home. Looking out at the green water, I laugh, realizing I now have another contraband book to add to the collection in our house. We're becoming a second Library.

Slowly I realize that the mood of the crowd is ugly. There are angry voices, sharp movements. I see clots of people pointing cross-river to the Sha'an neighborhoods, grumbling to one another. Then a few sentinels begin pushing through the crowd, searching folk with large packages and satchels. I look around nervously. If those searchers find me, I'm dead, but barging onto the ferry without having the fare is going to get me arrested even more quickly.

"Oi! Your Vigilance!" I hear from the water. It's old Lerreg with his dilapidated bookboat. I can barely see him amid the piles of bad novels. "The ferry looks full," he calls. "Do you want a ride?" I'm embarrassed to be seen on a floating pile of literary trash, but I haven't got much choice. I clamber aboard. He swiftly poles off toward Seven Lanterns. The murmurs of the crowd and the snarls of the sentinels fade behind me.

I'm not even sure how Lerreg knows who I am, but he does. "Us book-tenders got to stick together," he says gruffly. "I'll drop you at Lanterners' Canal, all right?"

"Yes," I say. "Thank you." So this is where Istehar found that saintsforsaken *Poisoner's Guide*. I wish I knew where he got it from—an estate sale, maybe? I look around and notice a number of empty crates and boxes, trying to think of something to talk about. "Good sales today?"

He shrugs. “Deacons came with a few thugs this morning and threw books overboard. Fairy stories. Zhinj legends. Pillow books. Sha’an song-poems. Things like that. They made a mess of the other bookboats too.”

“I’m sorry,” I say. “They shouldn’t harass you like that.” Clearly Vilya’s partisans are already shoving their way into power.

“Can’t you do something about those folk, Vigilance?” Lerreg asks me mournfully. “They’re awful for business.”

I can’t meet his eyes. “I’ll see who I can talk to,” I mumble.

We pass the lumbering ferry, larger than us and stuck in river traffic. Ladies with parasols are pressed against the railing, some of them (mainly the foreign ones) looking a bit green as the ferry rocks in a barge’s wake. Reflexively, I look for Vasmine. She isn’t there.

CHAPTER 21

Istehar Sha'an, Illuminatrix
Undersong House
Daemoniday, 11:00 a.m.

Tiarath lies on the long table, cold, dead, and lovely. With cloths and sponges, we wash her fingers and toes, her freckled face. We wash her breasts and belly, and clean out her navel. We wash the bloody wounds in her forehead and shoulder and calf, where the stones hit her. We scrub her soft skin. We wash her honey-colored hair, comb it, and braid it with herbs and blossoms—herbs and blossoms she planted and nurtured. I bring our Book of the Tree, heavy with the record of lives, and press her feet to an empty page—so she will always journey with us, wherever we go. Then we wrap her in a grass-green shroud, readying her to return to the Great Tree and be reborn, as child, tree, stone, water, or light itself.

I can feel in the air around me that the house is upset. Houses don't like change. Undersong House wants Tiarath to be alive and Vasmine to be in her bedroom, sleeping late.

So do I.

Who is that? the being in my belly asks suddenly. I have not heard its voice since it entered me.

Tiarath, I say. *My friend.*

A seedkeeper.

A gardener. Yes.

She was in full flower.

I nod and feel tears rolling down my cheeks as I scrub earth from Tiarath's fingernails. Soil from the garden where she planted flowers. Clay from the riverbank she scrabbled at as the river swept her away. As I scrub, Vasmine's hands somehow come into my mind—those pristine fingernails, elegantly shaped.

A knock at the door. I step into the hall, carefully closing the door behind me. Dozya has brought the Book of the Tree that I wrote for him and Tiarath on their wedding day. It has a beautiful green cover of moss-silk woven with dried flowers and just enough pages for a single family, smooth and even white pages since paper is so easy to get here in Moonstone. He sobs as he offers it to me. It is a little thing, just the right size for the two of them. "Are you sure you don't want to keep it?" I ask him. In its pages are the days of their marriage, their hope for a child.

"I want her to have it," he insists, wiping his tears with his sleeve. I nod, awkwardly pat his shoulder, bring the book into the room with me. The book's sorrow overwhelms me. Tears run down my face in rivers as we place the little tome in Tiarath's folded hands.

"Why did they kill her?" one of the women asks me plaintively. "They were only casting flowers on the water. What harm could anyone see in that?"

"They saw their own fears," I answer. "Nothing else."

The matron Lalvah mutters: "I wasn't born in this city and I don't want to die here. I want to go home. They tried to kill us there too but at least we belonged there."

"The Mor will get tired of fighting the forest," the crone Salomir advises. "They will leave eventually. We should go upriver and reclaim Sha'an land."

"Before it's too late," someone adds.

They are waiting for me to react, to offer wise words, but I don't say anything. I cannot say they are wrong about Moonstone. My father, who worked with wood, used to say that anything with a rotten heart will prove weak in the end. And what is the secret Covenant we have found, if not evidence of a rotten heart? I don't know how to blame Vasmine for lying to us. The city may be magnificent, but people must do terrible things to survive here.

I involuntarily glance toward the door. The Covenants real and false, along with the *Poisoner's Guide*, are hidden among the Books of the Tree in the silvirium. We should have buried them in the garden. May the Great Tree grant no one comes looking for them.

Another knock on the door, this one louder and less respectful. Bastina ought to be preventing people from coming in. I snatch my staff from its place against the wall and sweep open the door. It is the healer Nizhar Sha'an.

"The silk shops are on fire," he says. "People are burning. Come."

I run into the hallway and call up the stairs for Loli. She doesn't answer, and there's no time.

The elders stay behind to complete the wrapping of Tiarath's body, sing the Song of Returning to Earth, and sprinkle forest soil inside the shroud. The rest of us hurry with Nizhar over the little bridge from Undersong House to Seven Lanterns. Other Sha'an from the neighborhood join us. The silk shops are a few streets over from the bridge. We rush there in silence, too frightened to speak to one another.

No, I say to myself. *No, no, no.* As if such a little song could stop the river of what is.

Mossinger Lane, just off Lanterners' Walk, is the street of Sha'an silk houses. Archprince Jalian granted it to us. Each steep-roofed house has a little orchard of fruit or nut trees nearby, and each tree is draped in fibrous curtains of thick green moss. Several times a year, children climb the trees to cut the moss down, and then card it into filaments. Spinners spin the filaments into thread. Weavers string the thread onto looms, and weave light, soft, durable fabric, prized in Moonstone and beyond. We took a few threads of moss from our forest when we fled, and those threads have grown and grown, and never failed us.

We can see at once that five of the nine silk houses are on fire. The layered roofs are catching fire, one layer after another, until the houses blaze like the nighttime lamps on the Lanterners' Canal. Buckets won't be enough to put out these fires. We need the fire brigade, and who knows whether they'll come to a Sha'an street? There will be people trapped inside, many of whom fled the fires in the forest long ago. A cruel irony, fitting for a cruel city.

The mob has fled, but remnants of the crowd still clog the street, jeering at us, threatening us with firebrands that likely started these fires. There are no sentinels to be found. One of the vandals grabs at my robes; I whack him with my staff. The mood of the crowd grows even uglier. Someone throws a stone; the matron Lalvah has to be led away, her ear bleeding.

I eye the knots of looters and raise my staff again. "No magic," Nizhar whispers at me urgently, keeping his cane firmly on the ground. "They'll kill you!"

Magic. In the forest, we never used such a word. Magic was the undersong of life.

The Sha'an who have come divide into smaller groups and rush to each house. I want to join them, but voices howl in my brain. The trees are screaming. The houses are keening in shock. Birds are cawing and fleeing. People inside and around the burning silk houses are wailing. The stench is terrible; I recognize instantly the smell of the forest burning when the Mor attacked our villages years ago. It is all I can do to keep from screaming myself.

But I can't just stand here. I pick the closest house and go through the gate into the walled garden, then onto a porch and through a door into a workroom. A wild-eyed woman is beating flames out of her loom. I drag her toward the door, telling her she has to give it up. I push her out of the house and then turn back to help a graybeard overcome by smoke. I lead him also to the door. I call into the house but don't hear anything. I hope that's everyone, because flames are licking at the room's rafters.

Out in the courtyard, I take a pail of dishwater that's standing there and throw it on an old grandmother silverapple whose branches have caught. An adolescent girl, probably a silk picker, is sobbing from her burns. "Where are my parents?" she asks. I look back into the burning building, wondering. Trees, people—I do not know whom to help first.

I guide the injured girl out into the street and see that folk have formed a bucket brigade, bringing water from the river. There is still no help from the city. The water does help, and the many helping hands—it looks like a few of the smoking silk houses may still be standing tomorrow. Three of the houses are clearly going to burn to the ground.

I continue to find the wounded and bring them to the street where people can care for them. When the flames are mostly out, we wrap tree trunks with last year's dried moss, to try to save whatever trees we can. Some, perhaps, may heal. Some are whispering final words into the soil.

The children of this city are kin to lightning, says the being inside my womb suddenly. *They strike fiercely without reason. Like those who burned my people. Senseless.*

Defend us? I ask, knowing I shouldn't.

I spent all my strength to plant myself in you. Others might help, maybe.

But the spirits of the Sha'an forest are in the little prayer-book now, and the trees in these decimated moss-silk groves are too traumatized to fight. They call to one another, confused and fearful, asking: *Are you there? Are you there?* Their cries to their now-silent colleagues hurt me to the core. I want to cradle them in my arms, soothe their grieving souls.

The first fire-boat comes down the canal nearby only when the fires are out already. Sentinels spray water on the smoking, wrecked buildings and bark directions at the chaotically milling crowd around the ruined neighborhood. They want to prove they are keeping order, without seeming to help us. They do not want to be perceived as defending the Sha'an. Prince Hoel doesn't come. Seven Lanterns is his district, but we Sha'an are no longer his people.

We evaluate our wounded. The silk picker girl's parents are indeed no longer alive, having died of smoke inhalation while trying to evacuate a silk house's valuable stores. The girl—A'aliya is her name, and she plays the lute at morning prayers sometimes—screams and screams as an aunt pulls her away from the bodies that have been laid in the street, covered by a fabric. I hug myself, remembering how I found my mother face-down in her garden.

An elderly workroom supervisor, whom I know because he was one of the Sha'an who had a group marriage, has inhaled too much smoke and hasn't awoken. We don't want to send him to the hospital—we no longer trust our fellow citizens, even though a few brave Abbatine neighbors have kindly brought bowls of water and clean cloths for us. Nizhar Sha'an and I make the decision to bring the injured to Undersong House. Our people use singed bolts of moss-silk and charred roofbeams to make stretchers. The warriors among us take up staffs to guard our sad little procession as we make our way through the streets. People glare, or turn corners to avoid us.

At least Undersong House is on an island and easier to defend than the silk houses. We keep our staffs and bows out, unsure when the next attack may come. I fear the sentinels will come and arrest us for unauthorized use of weapons, but they don't. Maybe they are still afraid of the dying archprince, who once favored us. That might keep us safe for another day or two, maybe.

My thoughts turn to Tiarath, waiting patiently back at Undersong House for us to bury her. On our way back, when we have almost reached the bridge, I see smoke rising over Inkstone Point, from the delicate layered roofs of Vasmine's ink shop.

I break from our mournful group and run for the docks, which are weirdly deserted. The shop's roof is afire. *Not here too*, I think. When I open the green-painted door, I find flaming note-papers, burst ink jars, tarnished ink-castles, half-devoured wooden shelves, a blackened writing desk. "Vasmine!" I call frantically, thinking she might have gone to the shop after she left home this morning, but there is no answer.

After seeing the fires devour the silk houses, I'm terrified to go inside a burning building, but what if Vasmine is in there? I venture farther inside, calling again and again. I feel into the walls and floor but sense nothing, not even sorrow. The spirit of the place, like Vasmine, is gone.

Nizhar comes in behind me and grabs my shoulder. "What are you doing?" he shouts at me in the language of our home villages. "You ought to stop endangering yourself and attend to your duty! People are wounded and bereaved and they need you! Don't you realize harm has come to your people because of you?"

"What do you mean?" I ask him. "Vasmine is my wife; she *is* my duty."

"You are the *ihan-tanon*," Nizhar bellows, pointing his cane at me. "You should have married a tribesman and carried on the seed of your family. It was one thing for you to marry a woman, that would have been surmountable. But you tied yourself to not one but three foreigners and set a wretched example for the Sha'an! Your foreign wives have turned your heart away! You can't see that it is time for us to leave here and go home!"

I step back in shock, and almost step into flames. Smoke stings my eyes. The cries of the trees in the orchards of the silk houses are still echoing in my ears. Maybe Nizhar is right. Maybe this *is* all my doing. Maybe my stubbornness is causing my people great suffering.

Or maybe the hate in this place has entered Nizhar Sha'an more deeply than he would like to think.

Nizhar sees my hesitation. "You could repent by marrying Dozya," he ventures. My best friend's widower. I could not do that, not even if all of my wives leave, one by one.

I hear a low voice outside, and then flames lick up the curtains. "It's a trap," I shout at Nizhar. "They want to burn us alive!" Nizhar moves for the door but when he grasps the doorknob, he pulls back his hand, moaning—it is hot to the touch. We look at one another, ashen. If the Sha'an lose us both, it will be a blow from which they may not recover.

Was this the intention all along? To draw me here and kill me? So that there will be no one in this city who knows the thoughts of books?

I should never have come in here, not without knowing who started the fire. Vasmine is right. I *am* an idiot.

"Can't you do something?" Nizhar Sha'an asks plaintively. He's happy to yell at me when it's convenient, but he too relies on the illuminatrix in the end.

There are no trees here to call on, and the tree-spirit inside me is quiet. I want to use my staff to smash a window, but suddenly, weirdly, I find I can't lift it. It's as if I've gotten it stuck on something sticky, like honey or sap; the carven wood seems rooted to the ground. As if I'm holding a tree, not a staff.

And now I wonder if the tree-spirits have arranged all this. Perhaps I am not supposed to escape. Perhaps the spirits of the forest want revenge, because the Sha'an, their keepers, did not save them. I am the illuminatrix. The responsibility is mine.

What is happening? says the voice in my womb.

Fire, I say.

I do not want to burn again.

I know.

Mama, I do not want to burn.

It is the first time anyone has ever called me that.

Nizhar pulls at me, pleading that we have to find a way out. Choked by smoke, an arm shielding my belly, I decide to let go of my staff and make for the door. But as I begin to loosen my grip, something catches my eye.

At the base of the staff, thin silver lines are delicately branching out across the floor—unfurling tendrils, twisting and forking, like patterns of frost in soil. The lines glow a little, as if touched by moonlight. They are so beautiful that even in the midst of fire and smoke, I cannot look away. Wherever the lines reach, the fire leaps back.

I take Nizhar's hand. The silver lines braid and curl before us, making a path, as I lead him toward the door. The air is hot and smoky and I nearly collapse, but when we have crossed the room, Nizhar puts his palm against the door and pushes it open. We stumble out into the air. We take grateful, gasping breaths. Silver lace-lines branch out before us on the wooden planks, guiding us as we hurry down the curve of the dock. The marks almost seem like letters, as if a book is being written on the ground. I want to stop and read them but I don't dare. The fire is behind us now. As Annlynn meets us, with Dozya and Maliki and others behind her, the silver lines fade.

"We chased off vandals lurking outside the shop," Annlynn tells me. "They must have set the fire."

"More anti-Sha'an sentiment? Or something else?" I wonder. My right hand grips the staff, which is quiet, inert, and dusted with soot. Nizhar turns his gaze away from us and out across the water, as the ever-late fire-boat passes us on its way to spray the remains of Vasmine's tasteful ink shop.

"Are you all right?" Dozya asks urgently. "Was anyone else hurt?" I shake my head no, moved by his kindness. If only Tiarath were here to greet us too.

"Where are the injured?" I ask.

"We laid the wounded in the silvirium for now," says Maliki. "Some are badly burned. I can go to your house and bring your medicines, Nizhar Sha'an."

Nizhar nods his thanks. He will not look at me. He probably thinks I did not deserve a miracle. He's right. I didn't deserve this one any more than the one I received at the River School all those years ago. But it isn't up to me. As Zilfa used to say, the trees have their own thoughts.

"I'll organize Sha'an fighters into shifts, to guard Undersong House," Annlynn says. "The other Sha'an should stay inside the house, as much as possible. The city isn't safe anymore."

"Was it ever?" Nizhar replies bitterly. He pauses. "Thank you, Your Vigilance. *Ihante*."

Annlynn bows a little. She looks older and sadder than she did yesterday. Before he opens his mouth again to criticize my choices, Nizhar Sha'an had better take note of what my "foreign wife" does for us today.

I squeeze Annlynn's hand, still gripping in my other hand the staff of my ancestors. I don't understand why it shows up sometimes and not others. It's as if the universe can't make up its mind whether it's random or benevolent. Maybe it's both.

"Let's go home," I say.

Annlynn makes a face at the word *home*, but she comes.

CHAPTER 22
Olloise Mazall, Apothecary
Undersong House
Daemoniday, 1:00 p.m.

I have been on the floor of the washroom for hours, weeping and pounding the walls. Mourning my dead parents, my lost lover, my broken family, and every unwanted result of my foolish investigation. No one, not even Bastina, has knocked to ask me to come out. Which is what I deserve.

What was the point of trying to find out the truth? Everyone I love is a liar. My mother never told me she was a murderer. Prince Hoel never cared about me; he was just keeping track of me to protect himself and the Council. Vasmine never loved me; she was just doing her job as a spy. Istehar probably suspected about Vasmine all along and never said anything to me. Annlynn…hasn't lied, but sometimes I think Istehar might love her more than me, and in those moments I hate them both. I'm not sure it will work, the three of us without Vasmine.

I lie panting on the cool tiles. I can't stay in here forever. I reach up to the doorknob and crack the door, so I can stare at the floor full of broken glass in my laboratory across the hall. Vasmine has gone, the Great Tree alone knows where. Annlynn's gone—to get drunk, I bet. Istehar is gone to help with yet another ritual I don't understand. I am here alone, in this house that isn't mine, reminding myself this is all my fault. I wanted to know who killed my parents. Well, now I know, and the knowledge isn't doing me any good. It might even get all of us killed. Unless something else kills us first.

I should start sweeping glass. But then I notice there's a plume of smoke outside the laboratory window and I wonder why. Bastina calls from the second floor: "They're here!"

Who's here? I think but don't call. I get to my feet, cough, wash my face, and straighten my clothes. When I go out to the third-floor landing, Sha'an people are helping one another up the stairs, many of them clearly suffering from burns and smoke inhalation. When I look down the stairwell, I can see makeshift stretchers. Well, nothing like an instant war zone to clear the mind.

Most of my medicines have been smashed, but there are still rolls of bandages; there's honey in the kitchen, and healing plants are growing in the garden. I wish Tiarath were here; she was a good herbalist. I send some other woman out to harvest, hoping she knows what she's doing. Then I set to work in the silvirium, which is filling up with patients on pallets. Nizhar arrives, covered in soot, and takes charge of the injured who were brought to the Chamber of Elders. Maliki runs messages between the two of us.

Annlynn and Istehar arrive, soot-blackened, and ask me to step into the hall. They update me, in a few words, about the arson at the silk workshops. Annlynn explains Moa's fate, and shows the account book she stole, with the names of Librarians and the Sha'an.

"I haven't delayed the investigation for long. There'll be warrants soon," she concludes. "Maybe even for us."

"Why us?" I ask.

Annlynn sighs. "Think about it, Loli. This morning, Hoel, Vilya, and the Council didn't know that we have the original Covenant in our possession. They didn't know we know that Prince Giya may be the rightful ruler of Moonstone. And they didn't know we know that Prince Hoel ordered the deaths of your parents. But now Vasmine's gone and we have to assume she's told them everything. I saw a warrant for her arrest. She might turn us in to save herself."

"She wouldn't!" I say in spite of myself. Istehar is shaking her head.

"We can't be sure," says Annlynn resolutely.

"They'd be here already if she'd told them," Istehar insists, but she looks worried.

If sentinels search this house, they'll find what we've hidden and march us straight into the ocean. I can feel myself shutting down in shock. We truly may have to flee the city. I've never been anywhere but here, except for that one voyage to Uluria to research poisons. My mother traveled but never took me with her. I guess she was busy planning executions, or else she didn't want me to end up as collateral damage.

"Let's deal with the injured," I say. "We have to save the people we can save. Then we can decide what to do next."

Soon my life is full of blistered and charred flesh, moaning, herbs, honey, aloe, and linens. The truth is, it's a relief. Lalvah, even with her ear bandaged, is a competent nurse, and Nizhar is a good healer even if he's a bigot. We send the lightly wounded folk to the kitchen for food and drink. Others are badly hurt and in pain; a few are unconscious. I relieve pain where possible, and heal where I can. As I work, I have the weird feeling that the tomes on the silvirium shelves and the tree at the center of the room are all watching me.

Bastina comes to the door of the silvirium. "Now what?" I snap unkindly.

"You have a visitor, Madam Olloise," she announces, standing straight in her dark blue dress, white apron, and nose-ring. Bastina is the daughter of my parents' maid. Her mother died in a ferry accident not long after my parents died and I was sent to the River School. She spent a few years in an orphanage. I located her when I moved to Undersong House, and offered her a job. She never, ever calls me Madam Olloise.

"Who is it?" I ask warily, stepping out into the hall.

"Her Eminence Princess Angelissa Dhagura," Bastina replies, and gives a little curtsy, something else she never does. I nearly fall over in shock. Prince Hoel's wife is in my house.

The wife of my parents' murderer. And Bastina is trying to warn me of something.

I have to act as if I know nothing: as if I have no idea Prince Hoel ordered the deaths of my parents, as if I haven't seen the real Covenant, as if I don't know the princes of the first Council were killers. I look down at my bloody hands. I'd better wash. "Will you bring us something to drink?" I ask Bastina desperately. "And maybe some cookies?"

"The cookies are gone," Bastina says, clearly relieved that I have understood the situation. "There's a lot of foot traffic in the kitchen. But I'll find something."

After I wash up, I enter the small parlor off the front hall that Istehar uses for private meetings with her people. The princess, wearing a high-waisted apricot-colored dress with black lace trim, looks as she did when I saw her two days ago: past middle age, fleshy face and bulbous nose, blond-gray hair confined in a careful knot. Her matching parasol (could it be moss-silk from Sha'an workshops?) is folded in a corner. She likely has a footman and a lady-in-waiting outside, and cloaksmen too. I can't think what she might have made of Annlynn organizing Sha'an warriors in the courtyard.

I bow deeply. The princess nods graciously with just a hint of condescension. Given that it's my home, it's acceptable for me to take a seat in her presence, and I do. Bastina brings a tray: apple cider from the ice-room, and a few pastries that might be left over from my birthday.

"Prince Hoel and I are so sorry about the fires," Angelissa says, ignoring the cider, the pastries, and Bastina. "I hope there are not too many injured?"

"There are a number of them, Eminence. I can take you to visit the wounded, if you like," I say. "There are a few who may not survive. We rely on Prince Hoel to investigate the arsonists and the folk who stoned Tiarath and Dozya Sha'an yesterday. We have every confidence in the prince as Chief Interrogator."

Careful, Olloise. Sarcasm cannot creep into this conversation.

Angelissa nods and gives a small, tight smile. “I will convey that, certainly. The prince is, of course, very concerned about the situation.” She pauses. “The truth, Olloise, is that I came to remind you about the position.”

I have no idea what she is talking about. “The position, Eminence?”

“As the Council’s forensic apothecary. Your father’s position. Don’t you remember? I mentioned it to you on the barge.”

I cannot prevent myself from looking shocked. “That’s why you came? You...want me to work for the Council? To solve crimes for them?”

“Yes. Perhaps even these current crimes against the Sha’an.” Princess Angelissa fixes me with her intense gaze. “The Council desires you to begin right away.”

This has to be a trap. I gesture around me. “Your Eminence, as you can see, the neighborhood is in dire straits. I am needed here as a healer.”

The princess gives me an understanding look. “It must be hard to think about this now. But Olloise, you must consider your own future.”

“My future, Eminence?” I am definitely in over my head.

Princess Angelissa nods. “A position working for the Council would be a protection for you in case of ugly incidents like the one that unfolded today. You would not be tainted by association with undesirables. And such employment would provide you with a significant income of your own, should you choose not to live here anymore.”

She wants me to leave Undersong House. “This is my home, Your Eminence. My wives’ home.”

Princess Angelissa folds her hands in her lap. “Indeed. Your wives are quite a liability to you. The warrior librarian is, I observe, illegally organizing a Sha’an militia. That will come back to haunt her, I’m afraid. The ink-merchant is accused of graptomancy—divination by calligraphy. That’s a crime, as you know. And the *illuminatrix*—well, it should be obvious from recent events what shortly may happen to her. This is an Abbatine city. Scientists like yourself are appreciated, of course, provided you stay within the bounds of piety. But we don't tolerate sorceresses here."

So she does know the word *illuminatrix* after all, even though she pretended she didn't when I met her and Prince Hoel on their barge. She called Istehar a "deaconess." No doubt to make herself seem harmless. To make me not notice her hatred.

She pauses to let her words sink in. When I say nothing, she continues: "Prince Hoel and I feel strongly that you should start over. We have been your guardians since you were a child. We are concerned for you, in the current atmosphere. We hope you'll take our advice before it's too late."

The urge to leap up and strike her in the head with my cider glass rises within me. I look down.

The princess, sensing weakness, smiles encouragingly. "It may even be that if you come to work for the Council, you may be a moderating element when Prince Vilya comes to power. There are people you might be able to save, later on. But right now, the best thing would be for you to distance yourself from all this. You can stay at the Lanternhouse until we find you an appropriate establishment. You grew up in our home. We want to see you well-set-up in life."

I have to say something, or she'll know I see through her lies. "Your care means a great deal to me, Your Eminence. Do you truly believe it would be possible for me to save lives, if I take the position?"

Princess Angelissa fixes me with her sapphire-blue eyes. "I believe so. It would, of course, be necessary for you to stop obsessing about your parents' death. That kind of unbalanced attitude won't be welcome in Council offices."

Even when Vasmine told me about what Prince Hoel had done, I didn't blame his wife. I thought this officious, pious woman could not possibly know about my parents' murder. But now I see she does know. She is bribing me into silence, or luring me to my death, or both. She and Prince Hoel are gambling that I will want to save myself. And who knows? They might already have Vasmine on their side.

Or they might not, in which case they need me to tell them what I know, and who else knows it.

"Very well," I say, bowing a little. "I'll take the job."

Princess Angelissa beams. "Wonderful. Don't worry about your ruined laboratory, dear. Prince Hoel and I will replace it. Just pack a few things and we can leave at once."

"Thank you, Your Eminence." I pause. "But I hope you understand, I will need a little time to arrange things here. There are medical matters I must conclude. And I need to explain to my wives. I will come to you tomorrow morning."

"Now would be best, Olloise," she says firmly, raising a hand to smooth her oiled coiffure. "The situation in the city is spiraling out of control."

"I must find another healer to take my place," I tell her. "I will come tomorrow."

The princess hesitates, but seems to decide not to push further. "Do come early tomorrow morning, Olloise. We will expect you."

She takes up her parasol. I bow and accompany her to the door. She retrieves her cloaksmen, valet, and lady's maid from the front hall, exits the house, and boards a small barge docked on the other side of the bridge. As the barge turns into the current, a white bird flies up from the cabin window.

When I turn away from the door, Bastina is there, staring at me, wringing her strong, callused hands.

"Saints bless us, Loli, what will happen if you don't go with her tomorrow morning?" she asks, distressed.

"I don't know," I admit. "She and her husband might try to kill me." Then I remember Bastina knows little of this. "I'm sorry—this must be shocking."

"The ferry accident that killed my mum never seemed right," Bastina admits to me in a whisper. "I always thought the people who killed the Mazalls might have killed my mother too, just in case she knew anything. I don't think she did, though." She looks after the wake of the boat. "Was it those Dhagura folk who did it? The prince and princess?"

I nod, stricken. "It seems so." She has a right to know, as much as I do.

"They'll be after us, then," Bastina says. "Best say our prayers." She looks defeated, which is hard to see; she is usually so fiercely alive.

"You can leave Undersong House if you want to, Bastina," I tell her. "It's becoming dangerous here. You don't have to stay."

Bastina shakes her head. "This is my home," she tells me emphatically. We look at one another with understanding. Then, hearing a kettle hiss, Bastina rushes toward the kitchen. We're running out of time, I think. If we don't flee today, it may be too late. But I don't want to flee Moonstone. It feels like erasing my parents, to vanish from the city without a trace. And if we run, will we ever know what happened to Vasmine?

Something is niggling at my attention, something I saw out of the corner of my eye as I cleaned up broken glass. I run upstairs to the laboratory. Vials and beakers crunch beneath my feet. I don't know exactly what I'm looking for—until I find it. A final vial of the poison I made. And I know just what to do with it. I rush back downstairs.

"I need you to create a diversion." I say to Annlynn, who is sitting at the kitchen table wolfing down fish egg dumplings. "And ask Nizhar Sha'an to find someone to tend the folk in the silvirium for a few hours. Maybe Lalvah can do it. People are stable now and I won't be gone long."

"Do you need anything else?" Annlynn asks sarcastically.

I take a breath. "Yes. I need a boat."

CHAPTER 23
Vasmine Kinora, Ink-Merchant
Moonstone River
Daemoniday, 8:00 a.m.

"I almost didn't want to pick you up from their dock," says the boatman, "it being a house of witches and all. But you looked downright ill, if you don't mind my saying so, madam."

This one's a talker. And that's not good.

You'd think intelligent women might want to stay on good terms with someone who's been saving their lives since their school days. You'd think women who know that the city government is murdering its citizens, and has been since its inception, would understand there's more at stake than their hurt feelings. But no. Annlynn and Olloise had the luxury of being children once, and they've never kicked the habit. Istehar knows better, perhaps, but she doesn't want to offend those two idiots. River take them.

"The Sandmaze Hotel." I put in the effort to sound frail and a little foreign. My mother speaks Fengen, and her manner of speech comes easily to me. The boatman will engage his clearly active imagination and decide I've traveled a long way to get health advice from Moonstone sorceresses, and now I'm going back where I came from.

"I hope you got what you came for," the boatman probes.

I can't smell so good after a night with Jalian. I slump in my seat as if exhausted, wishing I had a parasol to hide under. I *am* exhausted, having had no sleep last night. I was looking forward to getting into my bed. "Is it a very long way to the hotel?" I murmur.

"Not far at all. Don't you worry, madam." He bows a bit, as if I'm a princess, and sets to work. Likely he's on Hoel's payroll. Or Vilya's. Or the Sanctum's. Or someone else's. No matter.

I never thought of it as lying to them. I thought of it as protecting them. I suppose it makes sense that Annlynn and Olloise don't see it that way. But if I'd turned on my heel and refused to spy for Hoel Dhagura, he'd just have found someone else even less scrupulous than I am, and that person might have learned about Olloise's little research project, and then all three of them would be dead.

We pass the isles of the Lanternelles, where sea-sheep graze peacefully on wide beaches and in the shallows, munching riverweed. The isles are a backwater where the local folk still leave offerings out for rock-elves the way they did back in Yanuilt hundreds of years ago. I have friends there I can visit in a pinch. I do wonder what will become of me now. I'm going to have to reckon with Hoel Dhagura, and then what? The guild of concubines likely won't let me back in. I could travel, I suppose. I have the coin for it.

I hate to think of never seeing those three again.

Of Istehar with no one to tell her how Moonstone works.

Of Olloise, imagining me with Jalian and thinking of her dead parents.

Of the hurt in Annlynn's eyes.

Boats ride the waters all around us; I watch to see if any come closer than they should, but it's hard to tell in the morning crush. Ahead of us is Moonstone's most ancient wonder: the Sandmaze. The boatman points to make sure I see it.

Long ago, the ancestors of the Zhinj shaped the massive sandstone walls of the Sandmaze. The passages within the maze wind toward a central place, where a spiral stone stair goes down to a deep well of dark water. The Zhinj say the Sandwell is a portal to the world of the spirits, where children came of age and where the old went to die. The Abbatine clergy say it is the spot where angels hunted demons back to the underworld.

These days, the city uses it as a tourist attraction—and sometimes as an execution ground. A calculated sacrilege.

I drowse. When I open my eyes, we are knocking against the beach stairs of the most famous hotel in Moonstone, hundreds of years old and owned by the princes of the district of Golden Sands. A porter with white gloves comes to help me out of the boat, discreetly looking about for my non-existent luggage. I tip him. I pay the nosy boatman and hurry up the steps, dizzy with fatigue. There are people watching me. I don't need to see them to know they're there.

I'm early. In my now-wilted white lace, I glide through the lobby with its tawny furniture, stop at the broad marble slab of the front desk, and put down coin to rent a "rest parlor." The lobby has little curtained cubicles by the back wall with a couch and table. Perfect for weary tourists waiting for a ferry to Hundred Quays, so they can catch a ship home to one of the thirteen nations. Also perfect for the genteel homeless like me.

It's noisy here. There are multiple celebrations happening in parlors just off the lobby: a young girl from the Moon's Daughters is having her hair braided by the matriarchs of her clan—an old Gengrassian coming-of-age custom, from the Bo tradition that folk say is thousands of years old. Nearby, Belakkosi youths in bright blouses are toasting each other on their name changes—the Belakkosi have a different name in summer than in winter and this lovely spring day must be the day to change. And I think I see what looks like a wedding, though I can't be sure. The heavily tattooed folk with silver head-jewelry seem like they might be from farther south, beyond the Thirteen Nations, from lands whose names I may not know.

I drink a cup of tea at the refreshment counter, then enter my little cubicle and lie down on the cushions of the provided divan. I won't be able to solve any of my problems if I don't sleep. I wish I could stop the conversation in my head, the one that has never happened. The one where I tell Olloise that if she doesn't give up digging up old graves, she'll end up digging new ones. The one where I say that no matter how ugly the images in her mind, it can always get uglier out here in the world. The one where I tell Annlynn and Istehar that books, blank or otherwise, can't solve everything. But it's too late now. None of them wants to hear anything I have to say.

I close my eyes, relying on the ornate bronze lobby clock, which contains tiny gongs of various sizes, to wake me. It does, right on time. I doze for another hour, am woken again. The hair-braiding party nearby is singing raucously in a Zhinj-Gengrassian hybrid language used only in certain districts of Moonstone. Some say Princess Sylte Berduin is running some kind of secret democracy in the Moon's Daughters and the Council hasn't put a stop to it because they pay no attention to anything said in Daughters' dialect.

I get up, douse myself with perfume from my purse, walk to the south of the lobby where a wide passageway leads directly to the Maze. I pay the fee to the bored clerk at the gate, and make my way down a flight of softly curving sandstone steps and into the Maze itself. A lad loiters at the foot of the steps, glances sidelong at me. Maybe he's waiting for someone. Maybe he finds me attractive. Or maybe he has been watching for me all day.

I can hear the faint sound of the river slapping against the thick outer walls of the Maze. Smooth, rounded walls rise up around me, impossibly high, so that I can only see a soap bar's worth of sky. It is like being in a giant's bathtub. Hoel is waiting for me in one of the maze's many hideaway nooks, on an ancient sandstone bench with river-drakes carved on either end. It shocks me how ordinary he looks: a bald old white-bearded man, not at all tall, with broad shoulders and a sizable belly from pastries, river snails, and goblets of moonwater. His prince's beret is nowhere to be seen, of course. It's best for him if people don't know who he is. He's paying me no attention, reading what seems to be a letter.

I sit down on the other end of the bench, take a fan out of my purse, and fan myself. It's hot; my underarms are wet and staining my dress. My mind summons the afternoon I first met Hoel at one of Hallan's parties. Hoel didn't speak to me then. He waited through many of those parties, watching me from the edge of the crowd as I engaged my guests with finesse, directing their attention where I wanted it to go. Finally, he invited himself to an intimate dinner with me and a somewhat disgruntled Hallan, and offered to buy out my contract if I became his spy. It was my—and Hallan's—patriotic duty, he said.

It wasn't just the money that made me say yes. It was the adventure, I claimed to Hallan and my mother. It was a break from serving Hallan, I eventually admitted to myself. And it was an opportunity to get closer to the halls of power. Perhaps I wanted that most of all.

"You slept in the lobby," Hoel notes.

"They threw me out," I say. "They think I belong to Jalian."

"Don't you?" Hoel doesn't look at me.

"I work for you, Your Eminence," I remind him.

"Indeed. Though your usefulness is now in question. Do you know the archdeacon put out a warrant for your arrest? Someone stole it off a desk in Holy Ibis, along with a trove of so-called evidence against Vilya's enemies at the Library."

"I didn't know," I say.

"I hardly believe that," he grumbles. "Vilya thinks I ordered the theft, and I'm not going to suggest that I didn't—how incompetent would I look? Now he and I are at odds."

"I see. That's unfortunate, given that he'll be archprince soon. Do you have instructions for me?"

He nods and takes out of his pocket a little vial. When I see it, I know without asking that it contains the poison Olloise so carefully concocted from the formula on her father's desk, and gave to him two days ago. For Hoel, the existence of that poison means Olloise has gotten much too close to the truth about her parents' murder. He might also know about Annlynn and Istehar seeking the *Poisoner's Guide*, back at the Library, in which case he must suspect they know about the murder of Karel Lutei. Hoel has people everywhere.

My heart sinks.

He glances over. "Worm your way back into your wives' affections tonight; that shouldn't be too hard. Olloise hasn't heeded the warning I sent via her smashed laboratory. The fiendsbegotten fool told Angelissa she'll come to us tomorrow, which means she won't come at all. Ah, well. I would have liked to speak to her before you killed her. But now I want her safely dead before mobs come to burn the house down. I'd like to spare her that, at least. She was the closest thing I had to a daughter, strangely enough."

He pauses. "Get rid of the Librarian, obviously, and the maid too. Food poisoning or some such thing. Istehar I'm not worried about; the mobs can have her. *That* will end this investigation of theirs."

"And the Mai dynasty will be safe," I conclude bitterly, wondering if Hoel decided Jalian was a threat and had him poisoned. "How *did* you end up as their fixer, anyway?"

He glances at me sharply. "Don't you dare protest, my dear. If you'd done your job, none of this would have been necessary. Once you're a widow, go seduce Vilya." He chuckles. "He may despise you, but he'll never pass up the chance to enjoy what his father once had. And I need eyes on him." Hoel's voice becomes a growl. "You seem to expect me to believe your wives didn't tell you about any of their escapades. Fiendshit. You'd better make yourself useful. This city is not safe for people who disappoint me."

I put out my hand and he places the vial in it. If I don't take it, he'll give it to someone else.

"I did hope it wouldn't come to this," he murmurs. "But their deaths shouldn't bother you overmuch. Clearly they're tired of you anyway." He folds up the letter he's pretending to read, nearly crumpling it. That's my signal to leave, and I rise from the bench and proceed deeper into the maze, walking at my ease, looking about, a tourist out for a stroll.

I need to get out of here before I start to cry. From where I am right now, the shortest way out of the Sandmaze is through the center, so I continue on. Making my way along the path, I hear voices. I shortly encounter a procession: sentinels, deacons, a mild-eyed man in chains. I've come upon an execution. How appropriate to the moment.

I dimly recognize the man—Moa from Yan's. I've sat at the bar with Annlynn. He had nice manners. An air of mystery. I enjoyed him.

There are lands where they burn witches. Not in Moonstone. Here, they use the once-sacred well at the center of the Sandmaze, to drown folk and send them to the underworld. I was here years ago when they drowned young Drucia, the archprincess's seamstress who mended gowns so quickly her work was judged sorcery. She wept bitterly as they led her down the spiral stairs. Folk do say the well is full of convicts' tears.

I edge to the front of the little crowd that has gathered to watch the killing, some cheering, others silent. "This hydromancer has refused to confess the names of his sorcerous accomplices," a herald reads out. "He is thus doubly guilty."

The death-deacons offer Moa a final drink of moonwater; I watch him register the irony. He shakes his head. "I had my last drink among friends," he tells them. They shrug and lead him down the spiral steps into the water, in his heavy chains. He doesn't plead. He's done that already, maybe.

Suddenly enraged, I wonder about what powers I could unleash. If I had my harp, could I play all these people to sleep? To death, even? And if the world is as full of magic as Istehar says, why doesn't the magic rise up and defend itself?

They shove Moa in with an awful splash. I lean over the edge and watch as Moa sinks under the water. Then his flailing ceases, and something under the water shimmers. The shimmering spreads, curves, and soon Moa seems to float in a bright soap-bubble. He's clearly breathing. Observers murmur, point, begin to panic. Some folk kneel and pray. The sentinels and deacons are shocked into silence, as if they had never truly believed in the existence of the thing they all condemn.

The soap-bubble, and the man within it, sink deeper and deeper, well beyond reach. The sentinels, magistrates, and death-deacons debate dropping a boulder into the well to finish the job, but are afraid of not being able to get it back out again. They will, after all, need the well for executions to come. No doubt there will be many more, when Vilya comes to power.

When Moa is almost out of sight down the seemingly bottomless Sandwell, the shining bubble bursts. Water rushes in. His body sinks and disappears. His own timing, his own element. Tears roll down my face. I watch helplessly as the sentinels dredge, judge the body unrecoverable.

If Annlynn were here, she'd have done something. But she isn't here. Likely she won't be here ever again. If she even survives a day now that Hoel Dhagura is tired of her presence on earth. What am I going to do? If I send a warning, it'll be noted—I'm sure the house is being watched—and the prince's wishes may be carried out even faster.

Locals leave the center of the Maze quickly and quietly, except for those who gather in knots to gloat. Tourists loiter in corners and debate the barbarity of this death, relative to their own nations' forms of capital punishment. I wriggle past the crowd and run through the winding paths, my skirt dragging in the dust.

Turn, then turn again, and again, and I am out. I rush down the river stairs, cut into the gondola line and, as people curse me, hire a gondola to the Lanternelles. It looks like I may indeed need my friends there. I step in, pay with shaking hands, step out without ever looking at the boatman. From the quiet dock where I have disembarked, I venture onto weathered cobblestone streets and duck into a lace shop that has rooms upstairs to rent. If there is anyone watching, they might think I've stopped to buy a clean dress, or hired a room for the night.

The elderly lacemakers Saroi and Horgance know me. They've made clothes for me for years. They take me into the back room, where I shed the white lace gown I bought from them a while back. Asking few questions, they fold it away for safekeeping. Saroi dresses me in a plain gray skirt and jacket, as if I am a schoolteacher or a shopkeeper. Horgance redoes my hair into two neat buns on either side of my head; they top the outfit off with an aging oilskin parasol so I can hide under it. I feel as if I'm leaving behind the life I created, the life that began in that little dormitory room.

I've pieced together their story over the years I've known them. Saroi and Horgance met one another while they were both apprentices in a lacemaker's workshop. One of them had a sibling who could speak to animals, who became agitated among sea-sheep led to slaughter, and who, after throwing a medicine cabinet full of spikerose into the river, fled to lands beyond the Thirteen Nations and was never seen again. The other—I sadly can never remember which is which—had a young lover who could shape stones with her hands, and who made irreplaceable sculptures before she was caught and drowned. I can see a nestling bird I know was made by that lost love, on a high shelf in this simple room.

It took them some time, I understand, to learn these things about one another—and when they did, they opened a shop together in this out-of-the way corner of Moonstone, a shop that had more purposes than one. When they were older, they made dresses for my mother, and sometimes, my feet swinging as I sat in a straight-backed chair too large for me, I'd hear them arranging for a "delivery to Cat." I thought Cat was the seamstress they'd hired. Only later did I learn Cat helped folk who'd been accused of sorcery "disappear," and that my mother, who had many social connections, was a key part of Cat's network. I formed my own friendship with Cat later on, and referred folk to her now and then—but I never expected to be one of her "deliveries."

Horgance, who has long white hair like Istehar's, strong arms, and a voice as steady as a mountain, takes me out back to their little dock that sits on an inlet. From here, she hands me into her rowboat and rows me upriver to the Moon's Daughters. When we are about halfway between

West Lanternelle and the island of Grace, Horgance points to a smoking ruin over on Seven Lanterns. It's my ink shop, smoldering, in ruins. The fire must have been visible from the hotel steps. I slept through it. Of course, of course the ink shop is gone too. The nameless goddess, the one my mother always spoke of, is erasing me.

Horgance looks at me, questioning whether she should divert us there. I shake my head vigorously. If there's a warrant out for my arrest, the fire could be a ruse to lure me into the open. Or, if a mob started it, who knows what they might do to me if I arrived on the scene?

"That was a lovely shop," Horgance comments placidly. I feel tears rise as I think of the jade-handled brushes and the green satin curtains. I genuinely loved that place; the first space in my whole life that was truly mine.

Likely the fire was a warning of what will happen to me if I don't do as Hoel asks. He loves to terrify people.

I hunch under my ugly parasol. More tears come as I think of the ink-castle I gave Annlynn, with all the hidden wells of colored ink. Likely she'll throw it away now. I feel in my purse, find the little jar of poison, the river-drake's eye, the prince's ring, and the pouch of coins. Taken as a whole, the four could make me a very wealthy woman.

"Maybe you will rebuild it," Horgance suggests quietly. I nod again, not trusting myself to speak. I suddenly wish I could help her row. But the person I hope to find won't want to see blisters on my hands.

We slip into a little cove, barely a crack, really, in the ragged shoreline of Grace, the smallest of the Moon's Daughters. A few round houses with glittering fishscale roofs cluster on the narrow shore. Above us, on a ledge above the cove, I see an older man meditating in the Bo tradition of Gengrassia, legs crossed.

"Will you be all right if the sentinels visit?" I ask. "Or Prince Hoel's cloaksfolk? Someone might have followed me." Horgance and Saroi are part of the quiet network aiding runaway magical folk in this city and I know they have practice in such matters, but I'm worried my visit has endangered them.

"Oh yes," Horgance says. "We'll say you rented a room and climbed out the window. We're just old seamstresses. Nobody minds us."

Horgance ties up the boat and I step out. She unmoors, nods to me, and pulls off into the channel.

Anchored in the same little cove is the Skyboat. Pink roses climb from pots and bloom against pale blue walls on which fluffy clouds are expertly painted. Silvery spires top the roof of the two-story houseboat, making it look like a fairy palace. Paddlewheels on either side of the craft are unmanned for the moment; the boatmen must have shore leave. Captain Cattiette Salbera, buxom and majestic with skin like dark-brewed tea and a halo of springy black hair like a dense thundercloud, hails me from the deck (or the front porch, depending on how one looks at it). I wave back and step on board.

"I have bad news, Cat," I say, placing my unsightly parasol in the provided receptacle and walking to her.

"Moa." Cat nods from her wheeled captain's chair. "I heard he'd been arrested. May the Fates receive him kindly." She makes a prayerful gesture at the sky. "That man had such a gift."

"All gifts are also curses," I say. That phrase is the password to the Skyboat, and it's also true.

"Are you here for a rest?" Cat asks me. A "rest" is a euphemism for relief from my magical gifts. Cat knows about my sorcerous talent, of course. After all, this houseboat is the oldest spikerose parlor in Moonstone. Cat inherited the boat and the trade from her mother, the renowned healer Ancilla Salbera. The Salberas are an old Errantine family, believing not in the saints but in the Fates and the Great Pattern. That must be how they cope with the capricious cruelty of this city.

"I'm here to see someone," I counter. Cat doesn't ask who; she never asks unnecessary questions. She hums a little, nods to herself, rolls her chair around, and leads me down the ramp into the first floor of the boat. There's what looks like a Sha'an teenager curled up on a couch, and some aristocrat's kid is laid out on a bench by the dining table, where what might be a dishwash-girl is devouring a bowl of something, wielding her spoon with rough hands. Cat's known for feeding those who need it.

A famous gondola singer is strumming his lyre in the corner, intoning some sad song: *I met a girl from Taradia, they couldn't get the witch out of her*. Through an oval door to a side room, I see a colleague of mine, a concubine to the prince of Hundred Quays, dreamily gazing into a mirror, a spikerose vial near her hand. I glide by so she won't turn her head and see me.

"You've got a full house, Cat," I say.

"People are frightened," she replies. "They're taking extra doses. They want to get rid of the evidence. The problem is, they *are* the evidence."

Spikerose puts people into a light trance for a few hours, but its real benefit is that it rids people of their magic, for weeks sometimes. Plenty of people want that, for plenty of reasons. Some people with a little sorcery in them, like Istehar, get ill from things like fire or babies or stone or birdsong, and are worried people will notice. Spikerose masks these symptoms. Others, like me, find themselves inexplicably itching to use their gift, and get themselves in trouble if they use it too often. If Cat can't help people escape from persecution, she helps them cope, as her mother did before her. Some say she also teaches magic, to those who are brave enough to learn.

What Cat does is illegal, but the Skyboat always eludes the sentinels, which makes me think the Skyboat's captain has some sorcery of her own—or that Princess Sylte Berduin of the Moon's Daughters, whose grandfather was a Salbera, protects the operation. Either way, Cat and her clients are beneficiaries of Jalian's reign of benign neglect, which will end literally at any moment.

"Vilya hasn't taken aim at you, has he?" I ask, concerned.

"Not aim, no," she agrees. "But with a weapon that big, it may not matter where he aims." She points to a narrow door. "Up the back stairs and to the left. Hallan's always here on Daemoniday, as you well know. And if you want something from him, Mina, stop at the mirror on the landing, fix your hair and straighten that awful dress. And approach with caution: he's in the bath, and I hear he's been telling bad jokes for the better part of an hour."

And indeed, Prince Hallan of Scattered Pearls, my ex-lover and ex-employer, is lounging in a claw-footed porcelain tub on a deck that looks out over the tiny cove and its village. He is handsome as ever: athletic, clean-shaven, devil-may-care, his golden curls wet with bathwater perfumed with oil of spikerose. Hallan always claims he's not trying to suppress anything—he just enjoys Cat's company. Demon turds, I say.

I curtsy. He stares. Then he spreads his hands and breaks into a smile.

"Vasmine! The only woman smart enough to leave me. Wonderful to see you. You look as luscious as ever! I thought you weren't speaking to me. How's the ink business?" Hallan leans back in the bath so that I can almost see the parts of his body I used to frequent. "What's your bestselling color these days?"

"Black," I say.

"I should have known." He gestures to the water strewn with rose petals. "Want to get in?"

"Alas, no, Your Eminence," I reply, splashing him. "I'm afraid I need a favor."

"A favor? Is *that* why you came?" Hallan squints at me. "Let me guess. You need me to get you out of Moonstone."

"Whatever makes you say that?" I inquire archly, though the observation is sound.

He shrugs. “One of your lovers is dying and about to be replaced by his criminally insane son. Your other lovers are about to be overrun by a foaming mob. Hoel’s furious with you. Oh, and for some reason the archdeacon wants you dead. It stands to reason.”

I pause, considering. Hallan used to be a partisan of Vilya’s. From the sound of it, he’s soured on the crown prince in the years since I left him. I didn’t know.

Soured on the crown prince. Which means he might be willing to help me make Vilya’s life more difficult.

Annlynn told me Giya Lutei approached her and asked if she had more to share. That must mean we, the wives of Undersong House, have something he wants. Knowledge, maybe. Evidence.

And, given that he seems the only alternative to Vilya Mai ruling this city, Giya Lutei may have exactly what we need.

I take a breath. “Wrong,” I say. “I need you to set up a meeting. I want to change sides.”

CHAPTER 24
Annlynn Jissakhar, Vasmine Kinora,
Olloise Mazall, and Istehar Sha'an, Students
River School, Vexmere
Six years ago

On an early autumn night, Vasmine is teasing Annlynn with a rose she has plucked from the garden—first the petals, then the thorns, then the petals again. Somewhere between thorn and petal, Annlynn rears up, takes Vasmine around the waist, and throws her flat on the bed. Vasmine laughs. They kiss passionately. And then, as if the world is conspiring against them, there is a violent knocking on their door.

"Don't answer it," Vasmine demands, annoyed, draping herself with the covers. "It's bound to be trouble. People are always killing each other out there." But Annlynn pulls on her trousers and shirt and opens the door.

It's Joeve, grinning and tossing her frizz of light brown hair, her ample bosom visible through her thin, damp nightgown. There are a few other girls loitering in the hall at a safe distance, watching to see what happens. Joeve pushes past Annlynn into the room, to where Vasmine sits up in the bed. "Sorry I'm wet. Vilya got drunk and fell into the river," she says, pausing to make clear she hasn't used the crown prince's title.

"What's that to us?" Annlynn snaps.

"He's cold. He wants girls to keep him warm. Come double-date with us, Vasmine." Joeve laughs wildly. "I mean, don't bring anyone else with you. Vilya said you should show him what you've got. He's heard how...talented you are."

"From whom might he have heard that?" Annlynn asks coldly.

"From whom?" Joeve mocks. "Oh, good evening, Madam Daughter-of-Librarians. I didn't notice you."

Vasmine rises, naked, from the bed. She takes her silk robe from a hook on the wall, shrugs it on, knots her hair into a figure eight, inserts a single hairpin, and faces Joeve. "Tell His Eminence I'm honored, but I have another engagement," Vasmine says.

"Oh, that's what you want me to tell him?" Joeve smirks. "You have another engagement? I bet you wouldn't like Prince Hallan to know how engaged you are with Annlynn this evening. I think you'd better come with me, Vasmine. Or else."

"Get out, Jo," Annlynn says quietly. "You're trouble. Vilya wouldn't have had the nerve to ask for Vasmine unless you suggested it."

"You're already sharing her," Joeve mocks. "What difference does it make if you share her a little more?"

Vasmine sighs. "You have no idea how to play the game at this level, Jo. Little girls belong in bed at this hour."

"And whores belong in whorehouses," Joeve retorts.

"You seem to have found your way to the royal whorehouse without help from me," Vasmine fires back. "I hope you realize he'll never marry you. You're not destined to be royalty, dear."

"You stuck-up slut, you think everyone wants you," Joeve shrills, stung.

"You're the one who wants her." Olloise has emerged from the curtained alcove where she sleeps with Istehar, her dark eyes wide and furious.

"What did you say?" Joeve snaps. Girls out in the hall are laughing.

"You heard me," Olloise says. "You've been drooling over Vasmine since she arrived. She doesn't want you, so get out."

Annlynn chuckles. Joeve's hands are on her hips. "Oh, she doesn't want me? Fine. But just so you know, nobody wants *you* either."

"I assure you that's not the case," Vasmine states quietly.

"Oh, that's not what I mean," Joeve sneers, facing Olloise. "Vilya told me your mother and father weren't murdered. They were a double suicide. That's what the chief interrogator found. He never told you. Your parents left you behind to fend for yourself. Now who's unwanted?"

Olloise is faster than one might think given her stocky build. "I need help here," Annlynn yells into the hall as Olloise lands a solid punch in Joeve's face. Blood spurts from Joeve's nose and she falls backward to the floor. Olloise gets on top of her, fists flailing, and Joeve reaches up and gashes Olloise's cheek with her fingernails. The two roll on the floorboards. Istehar flies out of the alcove, tries to pull Olloise off of Joeve, and receives a solid head-butt from Olloise in return. A few seconds later, Vasmine tries the same thing with Joeve, and Joeve claws her neck.

"Oi, leave off," Big Chessa shouts, arriving from the hall. "The rectoress will be here and none of us will get fed tomorrow!" Chessa takes hold of Joeve's arms while Annlynn grabs Olloise's.

"What're you staring at, witch?" Joeve screams at Olloise. "Did you see your mother's bloody ghost again?" Olloise struggles loose and gets hold of Joeve's hair, yanking it till Joeve screams.

"You've got witch blood, like the freak you sleep with," Joeve accuses, kicking Olloise in the chest.

"Everyone knows you failed genealogy. You have no idea what kind of blood I have," Olloise fires back as Chessa drags Joeve backward and Annlynn pulls Olloise in the opposite direction. The girls in the hall are cheering one or the other or both combatants.

There is a heavy step on the stairs, and immediately there is a general rush to get behind doors. Chessa pulls Joeve into the hall and slams the door. Annlynn, Olloise, Vasmine, and Istehar all breathe very quietly as the rectoress, outside their room, demands to know what happened.

"There was a soap bar on the floor," Big Chessa's voice is heard. "Joeve slipped."

"That explains her bleeding nose," the rectoress replies in icy tones. No one says anything further, certainly not Joeve, who can't afford to be a snitch. The rectoress rescinds breakfast and lunch for the entire floor, and orders everyone back to bed.

Olloise has closed her eyes and is breathing hard. Her fists are balled. Istehar, still half-stunned by the blow from Olloise's head, tries to embrace her but Olloise stiffens.

"The two of you go outside," Vasmine orders Annlynn and Istehar. "We'll meet you at the firepit."

Annlynn and Istehar open the door and silently move down the hall to the washroom, where they heave themselves out the dormer window. From there, they make their way from sloping roof to sloping roof. From the final roof, Annlynn helps Istehar jump to the ground. The firepit is on a little hill close to the back shore.

"It's not just Joeve. Your nose is bleeding," Annlynn says to Istehar when they settle on the ground.

"Is it?" Istehar takes a cloth from her pocket and wipes her nose, then examines the cloth. There is a dab of red. "The house feels bad," Istehar says.

"You mean it feels scary, after the fighting?" Annlynn asks with sympathy. Istehar didn't grow up with a pack of brothers.

"No, I mean the house feels sad." She closes her eyes and listens. "The trees are talking about sap." Istehar opens her eyes. "Oh! You're bleeding too!" she exclaims, pointing at Annlynn's collarbone.

Annlynn grins. "Not really. Just a prick from a rose." She takes Istehar's handkerchief and blots the scratch. The two of them hold hands for a while.

"Did you know," Annlynn says after a bit, "people claimed land here by shedding blood into the soil?"

"Which people? The Zhinj?"

"The settlers, I guess. It was an old custom from Taradia;

they used to do blood magic there, long ago. The princes did it, in all thirteen districts. According to the legends, anyway. That was before the law forbade magic."

Istehar protests: "But that doesn't make a person own anything. Everyone's blood ends up in the soil. You could call it magic, maybe, but that's just what is."

It is a long while before Vasmine and Olloise arrive. Vasmine is quiet. Olloise is bright-eyed and more like herself, even a little giddy as she points to the constellations, naming them: Leviathan's Tail. The Glassblower. The Twelve Princesses. The Drake's Egg.

"It's not true, what Joeve said," Olloise says finally. "I know it isn't, and I'm going to prove it."

Everyone else nods. There is nothing they dare say.

"Hoel never told me that suicide story because he knew I wouldn't believe it," she adds. "He must have told the archprince that so it would seem like he'd solved the case."

Istehar takes out her handkerchief, stained with her blood and a bit of Annlynn's. "We're behind you, Loli. Look, we bled for you." Olloise laughs and takes out a handkerchief equally bloodied.

"I used Loli's too," Vasmine says. "I saw no reason to soil mine, since Olloise chose this evening's entertainment." Olloise snorts and elbows her.

"Huh." Istehar looks up again at the stars.

"We could bury them," suggests Annlynn.

Istehar shakes her head. "No. We don't need to claim anything." She takes both handkerchiefs, walks down to the shore of the river, and washes them clean.

"Our blood's in the river now," Vasmine mutters to Annlynn. "That means it's everywhere."

CHAPTER 25

Annlynn Jissakhar, Olloise Mazall, and Istehar Sha'an
Undersong House
Daemoniday, 2:00 p.m.

The people of Moonstone love rules. Your neighbor will have no compunction about scolding you if you haven't returned a Library book on time. Of course, the citizens of Moonstone also love to get around the rules, and if you ask said neighbor how to return the Library book without paying a fine, the neighbor likely will know two or three ways to do it. At least one of those ways will involve a relative who works in just the right industry.

Sha'an folk are sitting in somber clusters all over the lawn, awaiting news of the wounded from the fires. On the dock near the little orchard, Bastina flags down her distant cousins, millers who live in the Perfumery. A husband and wife team, they pass by more or less every afternoon, wearing huge hats to avoid the sun. They usually don't do more than wave. The Perfumery, a low, wide peninsula on the river's western shore, settled long ago by Chaean farmers, supplies the city with grain, flowers, and vegetables. Bastina's cousins are ferrying sacks of flour to a bakery in Seven Lanterns for tomorrow's bread.

Bastina leans out from the dock, cups her hands to make her voice travel, and asks to buy a sack of flour. The kitchen is full of hungry people, she explains, and the baked goods have run out; she doesn't have time to run to the market. The boat comes to the little dock, the balding miller lifts out a sack, and Bastina goes into the house with the millwife, chatting a bit as they drag the sack behind them.

A few minutes later, a woman in a kerchief and a huge hat comes out of the house, waves to Bastina, walks briskly through the orchard, and gets into the rowboat. She and the miller row off toward the bakery.

Not long afterward, the miller drops Olloise off at a dock near the bakery. Olloise, wearing the hat and kerchief, bargains with a boatwife headed to Vexriver, hands over coin, and immediately sets out again. Meanwhile, the millwife, now hatless, kerchiefless, and dressless, puts on some clothes of Olloise's and chats with Bastina in the kitchen of Undersong House while Bastina bakes. When an hour is up, the millwife exits through the front door and walks to the bakery to meet her husband. She's made a significant amount of money for letting Olloise take her place. It's a risk for her, but then again, so is boating at rush hour.

From Vasmine's window on the second floor, Annlynn and Istehar have been watching to see if Olloise is able to leave the premises without being tailed by sentinels. To the best of their ability to tell, the ruse is successful.

"Is Loli coming back?" Istehar asks. "She didn't want to tell me where she was going, in case sentinels come and interrogate us. She thinks I'm not a good liar."

"You're not," Annlynn concedes absently, scanning the river.

"Did she tell *you?*"

"Maybe." Annlynn doesn't elaborate even when Istehar glares at her.

Istehar frowns. "I think the two of you are angry with me."

Annlynn yawns. "Of course we are. Because you feel sorry for Vasmine, that fiendish deceitful slut. And because you're strange all of a sudden. I mean stranger than usual. Ever since you went to the Library and summoned tree demons or whatever it was you did."

Istehar folds her arms over her belly. "*You* were the one who brought me to the Library."

"*You* were the one who brought home the *Poisoner's Guide*."

"I thought it would help. It *did* help. Now we know the truth!"

Annlynn snorts. "Turns out the truth is like a voyage at sea: more nauseating and dangerous than anyone thought."

Istehar smiles a little. "You're a Librarian. Aren't you supposed to defend the truth?"

"Absolutely," Annlynn agrees. "Or die trying. Which at this moment seems a likely outcome. I really could use a drink."

Istehar rises, goes over to Vasmine's vanity, takes a glass, and pours it half-full from a decanter of moonwater. She brings it to Annlynn. "I'm sorry," she says. "You must be frightened for your father and siblings and all the other Librarians."

"I'm frightened for you and your people too," Annlynn says.

Istehar gazes upriver. "Many of my people want to go back to the Sha'an forest. I'm afraid if we do that, Lord Griseus and the Morish troops might find us and finish what they started. But maybe we should try."

Annlynn is silent for a long moment. "Istehar, if the Sha'an decide to leave Moonstone, I'll get you back to the forest."

Tears begin to slide down Istehar's face. "No, Anya. You belong here. I know that."

"I'll get you there. In one piece. I promise. I'll take you home, Istya." Annlynn's expression is solemn.

"But you won't stay with me," Istehar's voice is quiet but the longing in it is clear.

Annlynn bows her head. "I don't know. I always thought my children would be Librarians."

Istehar wipes her wet face with her sleeve. She hesitates, about to say something else, and decides against it. "I love you," she says. "No matter what."

"Istya," Annlynn warns. "Don't get tragic. Please."

"I'm not being tragic," Istehar insists stubbornly.

"I'm just saying the truth." Offended, she pouts a little.

Annlynn kisses her, more fiercely than either of them expect. "Annlynn," Istehar protests. "There are dozens of wounded people downstairs."

"What about the two wounded people right here?" Annlynn counters.

Then Istehar smiles a little, an indulgent smile of a kind she only ever gives Annlynn. *Ehar*, she says, interlacing her fingers. Annlynn embraces her. The feeling that neither of them can explain rises between them, like sunrise.

CHAPTER 26

Olloise Mazall, Apothecary
River School, Vexmere
Daemoniday, 4:00 p.m.

The little flat-bottomed rowboat carefully navigates the channels that meander through floating fields of rice in the shallows between the Moon's Daughters. I'm in a hurry, but the boatwife doesn't care; if she harms the rice, the villagers won't let her pass here again. Once we make it through this watery labyrinth, Vexmere shouldn't be much farther.

The people of Moonstone say that all journeys upriver are slow. My mother often said so when I was a child and she made me leave the laboratory and fumble to learn things like dancing and sewing, which did not come naturally to me. Cooking came more easily, since it was not dissimilar to the arts practiced in my father's study. At Undersong House, I am often in the kitchen. Vasmine never cooks. Never cooked, that is.

Vasmine. I blame her bitterly. It's terrible to think of her sharing my secrets with the man I thought was my protector.

And yet, was not my mother, who went to foreign lands and wove her way into people's good graces so she could assassinate them, very much worse? But I remember my mother with love. And I remember Hoel being so kind—but the memories are all false. I cannot make sense of any of it. There is a maelstrom in my head, but there is also something real in my hand: the small vial of poison that had fallen at the back of a shelf, that the vandals did not find. The moment I saw it, I knew what I must do with it.

Ahead of us now are the looming forested ledges of the Isle of Vexriver. The Vexriver Fortress, much of it hidden in tunnels and caves within the island rock, protects Moonstone from attacks from Mor, upstream. To the east of Vexriver is the little island of Vexmere, often known simply as the River School, for the River School is the main thing there. From the rowboat, I can make out the stolid halls of peach-colored stone, the fencing courts, the smithy, the lighthouse, the library, the chapel, and the kitchens. I remember myself years ago, hunched in another little boat: a girl-woman in a mourning-cloak, curled around herself, wondering what would become of her. I remember returning here after a summer in Prince Hoel's house, older and more determined, standing up in the prow waving wildly to the three who waited for me on shore.

These memories no longer make sense, and yet they arise, like waves washing over me, leaving me drenched, eyes burning. I have come this far. I cannot turn back now.

The boatwife leaves me on the River School dock. There are students, as always, in the gardens and on the lawn and shore, clambering into boats or cooking fresh-caught fish in the firepit. Daemoniday is a day off from classes so folk are enjoying themselves. I take off the millwife's kerchief and hat, straighten my dress, and try to look official, reflexively fearing the wrath of a rectoress who, I'm told, retired last year. But Othe will be here, I am sure of it. He rarely leaves the school grounds.

A long-haired, lanky lad halfheartedly accosts me: "Do you have business here, madam? The school's closed to visitors."

"I'm here to see Othe Azhuin," I say. The boy nods and turns away. Othe has his own business, which is not to be interfered with. Everyone knows.

Othe is the school's healer. He is Zhinj, of the people who lived on the islands of the Moonstone River long before thirteen nations decided to build their grand international city here. To the Zhinj, the river is called *Copala*, the shining river-dragon, and the islands are called *Tuilarajn*, the moonstones—the scales of the dragon, some say.

When the first foreign settlers arrived, the Zhinj, out of generosity and a wish to avoid trouble, gave them the isle now known as Holy Ibis. Of course, that wasn't enough. Soon the settlers drove the Zhinj upstream into the caves of Vexriver, then into the Narrow Forests, and then into the Stone Waves atop the cliffs, where almost nothing grows. Many tribesfolk died. Those who survived re-entered the city as refugees: boatfolk and farm workers. Gradually, the remnant resettled some of the islands that had once belonged to them. Half of the slang of the Vexes and the Moon's Daughters is from the Zhinj.

There was a time, they say, when the River School hired Othe as a teacher and physician, but Othe has never shown any sign of having been anywhere but Vexmere. When he is asked where he is from, he says: "From here." As I walk through the courts of the River School to the infirmary, I close my hand over the precious, lethal vial I have placed within another vial, within an oilskin bag. When I reach the two-story infirmary, not far from the back shore, I knock on the low door near the corner of the building, and wait politely. Othe never answers right away.

When I first came to the River School, I missed my parents. At night after a nightmare, I'd walk across the courts to the infirmary and knock on the door, and Othe would let me in. He'd told me, one day in chemistry class, that he worked late and would be glad of a pair of extra hands. I'd sift ground herbs for him, or sort dried leaves of various kinds into leather bags or little jars. He called me Peeper, after the peeper-frogs with the big eyes that would hop up from the shore-pools and watch everything people did.

It was obvious I was looking for a father replacement. Othe didn't blame me for it, and neither did he try to meet my need; we just worked side by side, each for our own reasons. Later, when I had Istehar to comfort me at night, I visited Othe because I owed him for his kindness, and to learn what he could teach. He recognized me as someone who loved what he loved: the mixing of the powers of things to create new powers.

The door opens. Othe, about to turn me away brusquely, looks closer and then smiles. "Peeper," he greets me, smiling his broad smile as he towers over me. "How many seasons has it been? How grown you are. Come in."

He embraces me in his matter-of-fact way and I try not to bawl. I take my shoes off, to be polite in a Zhinj house. Inside, in the small kitchen, Othe pours mugs of hot tea from the kettle on the stove with his sure and agile hands. I help him carry them to the table. For a moment, it is as if nothing at all has changed. We sit down at his little table by the window that looks out on the herb garden.

"People tell me the Sha'an are having trouble," he says. "That means you too, these days, right?"

I nod. "We've been warned to flee the city."

"My people fled the city too," he notes. "We came back. People do. If they belong here."

"There's something I have to do, before we go," I say. "Something that has to do with my parents, but with Moonstone too. I was hoping you could help me."

Othe did help me, years ago, to decipher the formula that had been on my father's desk, and track down some of the listed plants. He stopped at actually brewing anything lethal; he was opposed to all that. But he understood I needed to do *something*.

Othe sets down his mug. I notice his leathery skin is more lined than a few years back, and his thick, curled black hair is turning white. "What have you learned?" he asks.

I tell him the whole story: how I finished brewing the poison formula and gave it to Hoel Dhagura, who turns out to have ordered my parents' death and bribed my lover to spy on me. How Istehar brought me the *Poisoner's Guide* that told of the murder of Karel Lutei and recorded the same deadly formula I'd just brewed. How Annlynn learned my mother had checked out the false Covenants right before she died, and how, through ink analysis and Istehar's visions, we discovered one of the "false" copies was actually the original Covenant.

Othe listens patiently. I explain that my parents might have been trying to solve Karel Lutei's murder, and Hoel might have killed them and their maid to cover up their investigation and preserve the second Covenant.

"And just this morning," I say, "people smashed my laboratory, probably as part of the same cover-up. Someone, at the city's founding, decided that Surian Mai should be archprince, and deposed Karel Lutei and the first Covenant. Powerful folk in present-day Moonstone are willing to kill to hide their secret. The Council says they want to hire me as their apothecary, but I think maybe they want to make me disappear. Like my parents. And to defend myself, I need proof of all this. I have one last vial of the poison I made, and I was hoping you could help."

Othe thinks for a while. "They say Karel Lutei was cruel," he says after a while. "Our people say he tormented the Zhinj who lived where he ruled."

"They do say that," I agree after a moment.

"So what you're saying is that back then, the Council stopped the reign of an evil man, and replaced him with a slightly less evil man," he says.

I think about his words. "You're saying it doesn't matter," I say bitterly. "Maybe you're right. What difference does it make that Karel Lutei died to make way for the Mai?"

He shrugs. "Killing was a thing they did without thought, those people who called themselves princes. They killed us, without hesitation. They took our most sacred place and made it into a killing ground. Why would you expect them not to murder one another? Why would you risk your life to prove which one of them is the true archprince? If you ask me, none of them should be ruling here."

We are silent together. Othe sips tea as I consider the wisdom of his words. "But Othe," I say, "my parents died trying to find out."

"Do you know *why* they wanted to know?" he asks.

"Not fully," I admit. "I think the Lutei family hired them. Maybe you're right that none of this matters, but my father and mother died to learn the truth. I don't want their deaths to be in vain."

We look at one another across the table. "I can't feel that what happened between princes back then matters, Peeper," Othe says after a while. "But I do think it matters who becomes archprince now. For my people, it matters a great deal."

I nod. "If Vilya Mai didn't take the throne, the city might not persecute the Sha'an, or magical folk."

"My thought is that Vilya Mai will turn toward the Zhinj when he's done with the Sha'an," Othe muses. He puts his cup aside. "So, I wonder why you came to *me*, Peeper."

"Eleven of the thirteen founding princes are buried on Holy Ibis near the Sanctum," I say. "But two founders of the River School are buried here, in the chapel. Ud Mingre, the first prince of Juniper Island. And Karel Lutei."

Othe nods slowly. "We need a bone or two," he agrees. "Though I'm not at all sure it will do any good, Olloise. I suppose we can only try." We rise from the well-used kitchen table, put on our shoes, go out the door, and stroll down the path to the chapel. To the side of the path are graves where lie the rectors and rectoresses of generations past. Othe stops at the gardeners' shed nearby to pick up a few things. It is a bright evening and the students and faculty are at dinner. There are, indeed, student sentinels on guard with weapons, but they don't look at us twice. Othe is beyond suspicion.

The ubiquitous Abbatine statues, of a saint with a lantern and a fiend with a sack, loom at the chapel door. Such images have been around ever since the Abbatine religion was founded in ancient Taradia and spread throughout the world. Around the side of the blond stone building is the low door to the crypt, where the sarcophagi of the two princes who founded this school have rested for hundreds of years. Istehar and I used to have to stand guard here if we got detention. I look back at the two young student guards with sympathy.

We descend into the ornate low-ceilinged halls of the crypt, and find Karel Lutei's marble casket. It takes only a well-applied crowbar, Othe's unusual strength, and my prying fingers to shift the antique lid. The dead have little defense against the living.

I reach in and unfold the golden shroud from around the ancient body. Linen and velvet and silk clothe the bones. The flesh is long gone. I push fabric aside from what once was a forearm. Othe carefully and gently locates a few finger-bones and removes them from the skeleton. He has brought a specimen-box, large enough for what we need to carry.

I feel a jolt of pain as one finger catches slightly while we settle the lid back in place. I pop my dusty, bloody finger into my mouth. It tastes of death. I wonder if Karel Lutei is exacting a tiny revenge for my disturbing his bones.

The Zhinj have a knowledge of chemistry and herbalism that most dwellers in the thirteen lands do not. As darkness falls, Othe lays the finger-bones on his workbench and goes rummaging in drawers. I take out the little double-wrapped vial I have brought. Othe nods and unrolls what looks like tanned leather on the workbench. Since the Zhinj don't kill animals, I know this leather must come from an animal that died on its own, or perhaps it was a gift—either way, Othe is granting me a huge favor.

"There was fiendsblossom in the formula on your father's paper," Othe says. "From Uluria. The most active ingredient in the poison. I mentioned it to you when you brought me the text years ago. Remember?"

I nod. Back then, Othe helped me locate the arcane ingredients my father had written down in an ancient dialect. Fiendsblossom was the hardest to locate; it grows only in the high mountains of Uluria and has been illegal to plant and to harvest for generations. These days, it is practically extinct. I had to take a ship to Upper Phantos, take a coach a long way down roads lined with fields, barns, cottages, hovels, and the occasional manor house, and contact a friend of my mother's, who took me across the border to a farmer in a reclusive commune on the slopes of Mount Endigonde. From that farmer, I bought a tiny packet of dried leaves and flowers.

"Fiendsblossom is so potent that even its residue in decaying organs, deposited on the bones, will blister the skin of one who comes into contact with it," he says. "Traces of the compound can last centuries."

Othe slices off a piece of the leather with a razor, places the scrap in a metal tray, and asks me to stand back. He carefully drips a small drop of poison from my vial onto that piece. The leather immediately blisters. He rolls up the contaminated piece of leather in a sheet of wax paper and puts it aside.

Then Othe uncorks a few jars on the shelf and mixes a potion in a battered kettle on the stove—much older and more dented than the teakettle we just used. From the kettle, he pours a dark fluid into the tray with the bones of Karel Lutei.

"It's an herbal bath that will activate any compounds that may still be there," Othe explains. He slices off another piece of leather and slides it into the bath. "Maybe it's been too long, but we might still get an effect."

He passes his hand through the air over the tray as if willing the liquid to do its work. I watch for long minutes. Nothing happens. I feel like pounding the table, but I don't want to distract Othe.

After ten minutes, he shakes his head. "I'm sorry, Peeper," he says.

But as he says it, I point: the red-brown leather has shallow and barely noticeable goose bumps. The blistering is much less than in the first tray, but still unmistakable. Othe examines the leather closely.

"You're right, Peeper," he concludes. "Karel Lutei was poisoned with a substance that included fiendsblossom, just as you said. It wasn't lordsbane as the history books claim. I can say that much." He pauses. "Remembering what I know of the formula, which included soporifics as well as fiendsblossom, I'd say the poison was intended to kill him instantly and quietly, so there would be no outcry."

Somehow, I can hear my father's voice in Othe's words—my father who was always investigating crimes in his laboratory.

See, Father, I want to tell him. *I am still with you, even now.*

"This gives credence to the Deacon's account that the Council hired him to poison a prince. The poison he claims he used matches the one in Karel Lutei's bones," I say.

Othe nods. "With this evidence, the Council might have to listen to you," he says. "If they don't kill you first."

I shake my head. "But it doesn't make sense. If Karel Lutei was too sadistic to rule, why did they pick him as archprince to begin with? They could have chosen someone else."

"He must have held something over them," Othe said. "Something he thought would work to keep him safe and in power. But in the end, it didn't."

As Othe rolls up the extra leather to put it away, I remember the rolled leather in the corner of my father's study. "My father must have been planning this very test," I say to Othe. "The Lutei did hire him to solve the murder." And then I realize what I must have missed.

Night has fallen by now. I rush back to the crypt, Othe cautiously following in my wake. Fortunately, there is a new set of bored sentinels at the chapel door and at the crypt. We descend underground and pry up the sarcophagus lid a second time, carefully this time so as not to pinch fingers. We unwrap the shroud. What we did not see before becomes apparent upon further inspection: there is a toe-bone missing.

"My father's been here," I say to Othe as we once again struggle to replace the lid so that it seems nothing has been touched. "Or someone has. But there was no toe-bone in my father's office when they catalogued his things. The murderer must have taken it. Or"—the thought occurs to me—"Prince Hoel found it but never told me." I must question everything, I realize. The feeling is unsettling. Who will I be, what will I have left, when all the secrets come out?

We walk back toward the infirmary, chatting about old times, to throw any suspicious watchers off the scent. We pass a former professor of mine who exclaims over me. I say I am visiting Othe to thank him for all he has taught me. In the distance, I notice the small village where Vexmere's few farmers and fisherfolk make their homes. Othe's family lives there, too; his wife is a Zhinj wisewoman. He's taking a huge risk. He's a leader of the Zhinj community, and the Council might secretly be glad to get rid of him if they had a reason, even though most of them have studied with him.

"You don't have to give me this evidence," I say to him. "It's not safe for you." I am once again risking the people I love, it seems.

"Vilya's my adversary as well as yours," he replies. "Like I said, we can only try."

Othe wraps up the bones and the poison-soaked leather and puts them away. He writes down his conclusions in a notebook. He has educated many princes; if I have to present this evidence to the Council, Othe's opinion will hold weight. But he doesn't give me the bones or leather; the poison is too dangerous, he says. He will keep them in case they are needed.

I try to thank him, awkwardly. Words don't suffice.

Othe walks me to the dock so I may wait for the public barge—the Tourmaline line, which serves the eastern side of the archipelago—to make a stop at the Vexmere dock. "Those folk of the Council all hold their offices falsely, as far as I'm concerned," he says to me, "but even by their own laws, the Covenant they uphold is a lie. There shouldn't be an archprince, but if there must be one, that person surely should not be from the clan of Mai."

Waiting with us on the dock are a few forlorn students with suitcases. Without asking, I know these are Sha'an children. Maybe the school has asked them to leave "for their own safety." Maybe their parents have called them home, in preparation for the anticipated journey. Either way, I'm running out of time.

CHAPTER 27

Annlynn Jissakhar, Warrior Librarian
Undersong House
Daemoniday, 6:00 p.m.

Sha'an have been pouring into the house all day. First, a few came to wash Tiarath's body. Then, after the fire at the silk houses, the Sha'an wouldn't trust the hospitals, so rooms filled up with the wounded. Now, people are climbing on the roof, boarding up the windows to Olloise's ruined laboratory, and organizing shifts of folk to stand watch. In the kitchen, Sha'an matriarchs are helping Bastina figure out how to feed everyone.

I'm not complaining. After all, the house belongs to them. But it's hard to take in the wreckage of my life with all this chaos boiling over in the hallways.

I'm taking a breath on the second-floor landing when Istehar comes down from the third floor, ready to re-engage the mess downstairs. "I've got to go," I say to her. "I don't even know what happened at Yan's when they arrested Moa, or if Thalweg was also arrested. I have to go find out. And I've left Thalweg with that possessed prayerbook far too long."

"If you can get the prayerbook," she tells me, "bring it as soon as you can."

"So you can exorcise it?" I ask.

She looks at me defiantly. "No, so I can use it."

"What?" I'm stunned. "Don't you think your tree-demons have caused enough trouble? The last time you talked to them, the archprince's daughter ended up pregnant and sentinels raided Yan's! You're thinking of trying again?"

Istehar is immovable as a tree. "It's too late for the Sha'an to flee the city. You know it's true! We couldn't all fit on a ship, and anyway, ships might not be safe for us. Who knows whether some captain might heave us overboard? And if Vilya marches us all upstream, Morish soldiers will slaughter us. I have to ask the forest-spirits for help. I have no other choice."

I stare at her, but I don't see an inch of doubt. "Fine," I say. "I'll bring it to you. But don't you leave this house. You're walking target practice for Vilya's malcontents, and I'd prefer not to lose two wives in one day."

She nods, relieved, and goes downstairs.

I rush to my room to put on the anonymous blue tunic and pants I use for housework—I'd be much too conspicuous in Library blacks. I pull a cap down over my forehead, leave the house—no mean feat with all the crowds in the hallways—then sprint over the bridge and into the alleyways of Seven Lanterns, as the sentinels set to surveil our comings and goings watch me go by. I know I'll be followed. But Bastina doesn't have any more cousins to serve as camouflage, so I'll have to manage.

Barely slowing, I vault a neighbor's wall and dart across their garden, then through a low door in their eastern garden wall and into the next neighbor's garden. I open a latched gate and slip back onto the street, where I cross straight into a tiny alley. Running the length of the alley, I turn onto a major thoroughfare, weaving quickly through the crowd and whipping into another tiny alley before anyone who's watching can spot me. This is Keyhole Alley, and there's a dovekeeper's tower here—not the closest or even second-closest one to our house, so it's less likely to be monitored. It's old and ramshackle and I like it—it reminds me of Saisse, the first girl I loved, who kept a dovecote.

From the courtyard, I can hear the endless fluttering and cooing of doves in their high niches. In the house, someone is roasting fish for dinner. I knock at the door, which has a worn spot from the knocks of countless customers. One of the endless pack of children who roam the household comes outside to give me a slip of paper and a wet inkstick. The child waits impatiently, scratching a leg, and then takes my message, which says: "Thalweg—Meet me at the bathhouse and we can work off our demons.—Saisse" Thalweg knows enough about my love life that they will know it's me.

The child races off with my message to attach it to a bird. The bird will fly the note to a dove-tower in the Sand Market, where a young runner will receive it, then discreetly throw stones at a second-floor window at Yan's, and deliver the message to Thalweg—assuming Thalweg isn't in a cell. Now I have to get myself to Drake's Hoard.

I leave the dovekeepers' doorstep and head back into the alleyway, checking behind me to see if anyone's picked up my tail. More dinner smells rise up. The sky darkens as I weave through the back streets of Seven Lanterns. I wonder, not for the first time, where Vasmine is—in the palace with Jalian, or already on her way to some foreign land? Humiliating tears spring to my eyes. When I was nine, the local captain of the canal-ball team recruited me, it turned out, just to get close to my handsome older brother. I deserved to be on that team, but it sure didn't feel that way after I found out what happened. I feel like that now, except also, I can't breathe.

My ruthless inner logic tells me that at the River School, if Vasmine had gone for Istehar or Olloise, that would have been completely implausible. I, on the other hand, was popular enough and wealthy enough to be a believable object for her affections. Once she was in good with me, she could get close to them. That's what happened, my brain tells me. The rest of me doesn't have a good reply.

The idea of being the odd one out in Istehar and Olloise's accident-prone love nest does not make me happy. I can't go back home to my clan; they never want to see me again. I wonder what Thalweg pays for rent; maybe I should ask to be their roommate.

I walk fast over the Long Bridge, leaving behind Seven Lanterns with its layered, steep-pitched roofs and walled gardens in the style of forested Yanuilt. Lamplighters with tall torches are lighting the great branching lamps of the bridge, one after another. Each golden glow fizzes in the water like a firework. On the other side of the bridge, Opal Island greets me with its covered alleys, spires, domes, and lancet windows—a throwback to desert cities of Uluria hundreds of years ago. Moonstone is like being everywhere at once, my sister Julis used to say.

I don't see any marauding mobs, but I do see a few knots of young men—Vilya's partisans—watching everyone, looking to make trouble. I take a left and hurry over the Gilded Bridge, nearly knocking over a cheese-cart in my haste. On the far side of the bridge is the isle of Drake's Hoard. The architecture changes again, this time to the style of far Nordynor—many-sided buildings, roofbeams carved with monsters, porches screened by lacy wooden lattices. Drake's Hoard, center of the district of String of Coins, is my childhood neighborhood—which may be one more reason I dislike its prince. I remember Giya Lutei from when I was a girl at festivals at Madder House—he was an arrogant young man, unsocial and easily irritated. So what if he's secretly supposed to be archprince?

The Drake's Hoard Bath, not far from the bridge, is a six-story octagonal building with porches at every level. Crazily leaning stairs connect the porches to one another. Steam vents from the large circular windows, as if the whole building is an immense multi-spouted teapot. It was built by Nordynori settlers to remind them of the hot springs at home. Everyone in the city comes here sooner or later. The bath is possibly the best place for hide-and-seek ever, and that's just how we used it as children. Of course, if the bath guards caught us, they fined our parents and gave us a good beating. So I learned early that if one goes to the corner of the street and takes the stairs to the second-floor bakery, and swings from the bakery landing to the porch of Madam Xirim's rooming-house, just opposite, it is possible to climb up on the railing and step across to a bathhouse porch just outside the third-floor steam room. And now as an adult with a lot more to lose than I had at ten years old, I do exactly that.

From there, outdoor stairs lead up to an out-of-the-way fourth-floor tea-porch where there is a table laden with plates of cookies and glasses of chilled moon-plum juice. I snatch a towel from the railing and drape it over my shoulder so I look at least somewhat like a client. And there, on a stool, in a pristine white robe, is Thalweg, frosty glass in hand. I look around and don't see anyone else but an elderly couple sharing a cookie. I hope they aren't spies.

"First of all, you're crazy wanting me to take a book to a bathhouse," Thalweg greets me when I sit down. "Do you have any idea what the humidity in here could do to this book?" Thalweg gestures toward the steamed-up windows. "I came out onto the balcony to save it." They reach a hand into the deep pockets of the robe, pull out the little prayerbook, and put it on the table gingerly, as if it is alive and might bite.

"Thalweg, I'm so, so sorry about Moa," I stammer. "I saw the trial but didn't understand how they came to arrest him. Was it because of the book?"

Thalweg shakes their head. Then their tough exterior melts and, putting down their glass of juice, they start to cry.

"At first it was fine," Thalweg says through their tears. "I just prayed and lit lots of candles. A hundred, I think. The book just sat there. I didn't even believe you that it *was* a demon book. But then there were voices..."

"It spoke to you?" I ask, horrified.

"It was more a *they*," Thalweg says. "Different voices, telling me to get out. I had a terrible feeling, so I ran and got Moa and told him about what'd you'd asked me to do, and asked if he thought we should evacuate the bar. He was worried, and he did start to close the bar and send people home. And then *she* came..."

"Ursel Kyze," I prompt.

"The archprincess's tutress, the stuck-up one. She wanted libation wine, without delay. Moa wanted to send her away but he knew Tilgana Mai would be offended if he did, so he rushed to get her the goldenwine she wanted..."

"And she saw him enchant the wine jug," I finish. "She said she went into the cellar because she heard moaning."

"That's a fiendsbegotten lie," Thalweg says, indignant. "Even if she heard me, I was on the third floor, not in the cellar. She'd been snooping around for months, trying to catch him doing magic. I'd been telling him he and his lover should take the next ship out and stay at sea. But he didn't listen. He loved Yan's, and he didn't want to leave!" Thalweg sobs.

"How did you escape?" I ask.

"I almost didn't. The sentinels were right outside; they came racing in when the tutor screamed, and questioned all the boarders. I climbed right out my window, left the book in a bird's nest by the chimney, slid down the wall, and went across the street to my friends the glassblowers. The sentinels arrested a lot of people that night, but not me. By the time I came home, they were gone, looking for bigger fish to fry."

"The book warned you," I say in awe.

Thalweg inspects the thick bandage on my wrist. "You didn't tell me people were after you!"

"I didn't want to get you involved," I mumble.

"You should have been more careful, *Your Vigilance!*"

"You're right," I concede. "I should have. What happened at the Library?"

"I put your demon prayerbook on my repair cart while I was on my mending shift in the Controlled Section, like you asked me. When I got to inspection, the sentinels practically jumped on me. But this little book wasn't what they were expecting, because they sorted through the piles of books I had and then let me go."

"They were looking for something else," I said. "Not this." They of course would have thought I might use a bookmender to try to get hold of the Covenant forgeries—or that someone might. But an old Silvilline prayerbook wouldn't worry them much.

"They were disappointed," Thalweg notes, raising an eyebrow. "I had a good feeling about it. But I've been watching for tails since then. I think some cloaksmen might have followed me here, though if they did, I think I lost them in the plunge baths."

Thalweg is right; I should have been more careful. I put the book in my satchel. "I have Moa's account books at home," I say. "Do you want them?"

"Saints' vertebrae, what are you running over there, a forbidden books exhibit?" Thalweg shakes their head. "This is all to do with that Snowhair girl you married. No, I don't want them. Too dangerous. Maybe later, when this all calms down, you can give them to Fimias." Fimias is Moa's lover and bookkeeper.

"How is he?" I ask.

"He's hiding out at the Leaning Inn in Sorcerer's Kettle. He's heartbroken over Moa. He plans to keep Yan's going." Thalweg smiles. "He's brave. I'm going to keep the place organized till he can come home."

"That's kind, but you'd better make sure you have an escape route in case the sentinels show up again." I get up from my chair. "I'm sorry, Thalweg. Truly."

"Watch your back, Annlynn," Thalweg tells me, touching their huge pink pearl earring. "Just a little advice from a fortune-teller. No charge. Good luck with the demons."

"The demons have already done their worst," I say heavily. "Vasmine left. She'd been spying on us. That was the reason she..." I want to say more but find that I can't.

Thalweg clicks their tongue. "Oh, moon-plum. You two had spice, you really did. This is a fiendsbegotten city, that's all I'll say." Then they look worried for a moment. "Go, Annlynn. Now."

Through the window, I see an edge of garment. Someone's on their way here, and if I jump back to Madam Xirim's balcony, I could be spotted by anyone coming out to the tea-porch. I climb up on the banister and hop over to a fourth-floor balcony outside the massage hall, then shimmy down the pipes to the third-floor pool deck, intending to lose myself in the crowd. I can't get caught. If they find out I was here, they'll never leave Thalweg alone.

On the pool deck, a few colored lanterns cast their glowing hues on the water. A musician is playing a zither in the dark.

I smell bath salts and sweat. All around me are people in various stages of undress, and in front of me is a pool of water I can barely make out because of the steam. I stop to let my eyes adjust. There could be spies here too. If Hoel could hire Vasmine for the entire length of my marriage, he can hire anyone.

Two fully clothed men step onto the pool deck, and I don't need to be a fortuneteller to know this isn't good. I weave through people, duck behind a cart full of carafes and glasses, getting a dirty look from a bartender who reminds me of Moa so much I could weep over it. Then there are other people in street clothes coming up the staircase at the other side of the deck. They'll see me in a moment, so I leave my hiding spot and dart over to a second pool, full of bathgoers and steaming water bubbling up from deep within the rocks of Drake's Hoard. That water, rich with minerals, is also used as part of the unique dyes of the String of Coins district. There's an old legend that a local sorcerer summoned the water up from below, through cracks and crevices in the stone, so String of Coins would draw even more wealth from the surrounding districts and from faraway nations.

A man near the steps of the pool smiles at me, crooks a finger, thinking I might be here for what a whole lot of people in Moonstone come here for. I shake my head impatiently, and he curses me. Heads turn in my direction. I can't wade in and hide underwater, not with the book. The hunters are prowling through the crowd, and some of them are standing at the doors to the inner stairs to make sure no one gets past them. And, in my current state of dress, I'm drawing strange looks from folk who wonder if I'm a pickpocket or a voyeur. If they catch me with this book, I'll be arraigned for stealing from the Library, plus who knows what the angry tree-spirits might do to some unsuspecting cloaksman—or the whole bathhouse?

"This way, stupid," someone murmurs in my ear. I'd slug the speaker and run, except it's a familiar voice: my brother, Farrick, the handsome, toothy redhead who once attracted the captain of the canal-ball team. Now he's in charge of acquisitions for the Library's art collection.

He's bare-chested, wearing bathing clothes, and I can hear his wife Lieta calling him through the crowd, as if he's unexpectedly abandoned her. Still, maybe he's a plant—if Vasmine was, anyone could be. My family hates me; why wouldn't they cooperate with the Council to get rid of me? But I'm desperate enough to follow Farrick through the press of bodies, even if I'm going to get my head bashed in. I've always suspected that unsigned bouquet after the wedding was from him, even if he, like all of my siblings, refused to speak to me after my father forbade it.

He leads me down an outdoor staircase, through a door, and then through a fragrant steam room in which two people, veiled in mist, are having noisy sex. Bathed in sweat, we run out the far door and down another, inner, staircase. After several flights, Farrick opens a door in the haze of the bathhouse and the air clears. I step outside and know exactly where I am, right next to the outdoor broiling pit behind the kitchen.

From here, it's a short sprint over fences and through hedges to my childhood home. Farrick and I tear off like we did all those years ago, me on his heels. It's almost as if none of the rest of my life ever happened.

I look up at the high porches of Wisdom House—our family's mansion for generations, built of stone in the style of our clan to honor our warrior ancestors who roamed the plains of Chaea—with a sudden stab of homesickness. My brother's neat-looking cottage, which my father gifted him a few years ago, is not far from the main house. He leads me there and up the smooth stone steps to his front door. Inside is a cozy little sitting room with couches. My brother gestures me inside, then closes the door and turns to look at me. He's still dripping from the bath—he shakes his head a bit to shed excess water and shrugs on a long shirt from a hook in the hall.

"I hope the laundress made her delivery this morning," he says.

I stare at him in shock, caught completely off guard. "You didn't send me those books! Tommas sent them!"

Farrick looks disgusted. "Come on, Anya, how do you think Tommas got them out of the Library? There was an immediate moratorium on checking them out after the incident with the sorcer—with your wife. The Council got involved. The six forgeries were to be kept in Father's office, along with the other book she was looking at, and no one was allowed to see them. In fact, they'd all been requisitioned to be brought to the Council for safekeeping; some clerk had already been sent to get them. But Father told me how people tried to kill you behind Yan's, and that you'd had a run-in with Prince Giya Lutei the day before. I wanted to know why, so I talked to Tommas, and then I talked to Father, and we all decided that if you needed those books, you'd better have them."

My mouth is no doubt hanging open. "But how did you put off the Council?"

Farrick grins with satisfaction. "Father 'impounded' the books and said the censor had to inspect them and document any irregularities before they left the Library."

"Genius," I say.

Farrick nods, still grinning. "Father said that if Prince Giya, or anyone else, was going to take up arms against his kin, he intended to make sure his kin had the advantage, rules or no rules." He elbows me. "Just make sure you get the books back to Tommas's cousin when she comes for the laundry in the morning, or clan Jissakhar will be at war with all thirteen princes."

I feel like someone has delivered news of a kraken falling out of the sky onto the Library dome.

"Rules or no rules?" I repeat. "That can't be Father, Farrick. It's impossible. He's never been about anything but the rules."

My brother grins. "The rules are, nobody makes a run at the Jissakhar. Even if Father won't mention your name, you're still his daughter. And you know he hates the Lutei."

"It might not *be* the Lutei who are after me. It might be the Mai and the entire Council."

His grin vanishes. “That’s quite a handful, even for you. So will this not be helpful then?”

He goes to a small rolltop desk, takes out a piece of paper, and hands it to me. “It’s the coroner’s report on the death of Prince Symiel Lutei—Prince Giya’s father. It was written by our aunt Jada Jissakhar. She attested he was stabbed to death,” Farrick says. “At night in his office while the family was asleep. The chief interrogator on the case was Prince Hoel Dhagura. He failed to find the killer. The Lutei family forbade the thing to be made public. Father knew about it, of course.”

I fold up the precisely written paper and put it into my satchel. “This *will* be helpful. Thank you, Farrick,” I say awkwardly. It’s hard to accept his help after all the years of silence. But the murder sounds just like what happened to the Mazalls. I appreciate it, what my clan has done for me.

The first thing they’ve done for me in years.

“I’m sorry about the wedding and all that,” Farrick adds uncomfortably. “Father was a fiend about it.”

“No doubt,” I reply. Looking down, I notice I’m still draped in the towel I lifted from the baths.

“Stay for a drink,” my brother offers, and goes to a shelf for a decanter that matches the one I broke this morning.

“All right,” I say. The tears I’ve been fighting back all day gather at the corners of my eyes, and seize the opportunity to fall.

Farrick looks miserable as I cry. “You never cry,” he offers.

“How would you know?” I ask, starting to sob in spite of myself. “None of you have spoken to me in years! You didn’t even come to my wedding! You didn’t have to listen to Father, Farrick! None of you did!”

“You’re right,” Farrick says heavily, handing me the glass and looking as if he’s worried I may throw it. “We didn’t. We were afraid of being expelled from the Sanctum—Father said High Deacon Beldrus threatened to do it. That we had to set a good example for lesser folk.”

“Lesser folk, fiendshit! Father was just worried about his reputation among the stuck-up old guard of the Library,” I counter, and drain my glass. "He disowned me, Farrick! So did all of you. You insulted my wives. You insulted me! If Father has grandchildren from us, he won't even know about it!"

"I'm sorry, Anya," Farrick says, looking at the floor. "I truly, truly am. I thought we had time. For him to get over it. And then time went by, too much of it. And then it felt wrong to reach out, like I didn't deserve it. I've been trying to think of a way." We both sit on a couch, and somehow I don't leave.

"You're still one of us," Farrick says. "Maybe even the best of us."

That makes me laugh. "How are your children?" I ask. I've longed to see them. He points to the bedrooms where his boys are sleeping, tells me a little about them and their escapades. The stories remind me so much of us when we were young.

And by the time Farrick's wife Lieta comes home from the baths, we've laughed a few more times. So that's a start.

CHAPTER 28
Vilya Mai, Crown Prince of Moonstone
Sundial House, Golden Sands
Daemoniday, 9:00 p.m.

Sundial House, in the district of Golden Sands, has round courts set with channels of flowing water and planted with tall tropical flowers painstakingly kept alive by a team of world-class gardeners. The Zuzierres, Sedessan ambassadors-turned-princes, built their family seat to be as magnificent and graceful as the palace of Sedessa's kings, and the Sedessan royal family sometimes visits, now that the blood-feud between the Zuzierres and the ruling family of Sedessa has been resolved. The feud began after Moonstone's secession from the nations that had built the city, but it was known from the beginning that the feud would eventually be resolved. Sedessa, positioned as it is between Uluria and Taradia, is a land where the art of diplomacy is especially cherished.

Through these courts, hung with glass lamps in the shape of starfish, Crown Prince Vilya Mai walks with Princess Talva Zuzierre. He's considering her as a wife, now that her brother Egno's been cast aside by Vilya's sister. Vilya wouldn't have liked to marry into the same family as Kalicent, and always be attending the same holiday gatherings, the same water-blessing balls in spring and Angelsfeasts in winter. Kalicent's presence reminds him that his father the arch-prince hates him. Years ago, Vilya overheard Jalian Mai saying that he never should have married Tilgana of Mor, since she'd produced such a heartless boor of a son, and only one son at that. And he said it to Hoel Dhagura, no less! After that, Vilya spent several hours with his pipe and a mound of powdered dreamcloves.

Dreamcloves shave off the sharp bits of the mind, Vilya likes to say to his friends. He gets his dreamcloves not from the streets of Sorcerer's Kettle but straight from his uncle Griseus of Mor, who first gave him a pipe when he barely had a beard. Folk grow the finest dreamcloves in the marshes near Cypresston, and Vilya's uncle, when he sends a letter, always sends him a packet of the stuff. In the autumn, when Griseus of Mor comes to Moonstone to shoot seabirds, he brings Vilya a whole box, and the two of them smoke it together in the Maze of Fireflies, looking out to sea. Vilya's uncle inspires him—or makes him feel he may never measure up, which amounts to the same thing. Vilya's father has fears that make lines on his face, as if a rooster made of terror has walked on his skin. Vilya remembers once when Jalian Mai received a velvet box, a gift from Hoel Dhagura, and paled. The archprince had the gem inside taken to the treasure-house, and never mentioned it again. But Vilya's uncle is different. He rushes ahead fearlessly, like a thundercloud blown by a storm wind, and he has whole burned forests to his name.

Talva Zuzierre is Abbatine, demure and very wealthy, and would make a good wife for an archprince. If he married her, likely Vilya would be able to finagle a suite at the Sandmaze Hotel, which would please him immensely. If he married her, his mother would, in due course, stop pestering him about producing an heir to the archprincipate. However, he hasn't decided yet. He has women, of course, but he does often find females, particularly those of his own class, to be opaque and not accommodating. The royal barge is anchored in Sandstone Cove, awaiting his return, and if he's dissatisfied with his encounter, he can escape quickly.

Dark, willowy Talva has black curls that are escaping charmingly from the circular braid pinned on her head. She wears a lemon-yellow gown sewn with bands of lavender gauze, and her signature silver pomander hangs from her belt. Her long face has a broad smile, which makes her seem friendly, even though he wonders if she's smiling at him or just at the look of the broad white lotuses floating in the palace ponds under the night sky. Vilya can see just a trace of earth under her fingernails; her herb garden, which she sometimes tends herself, is the envy of chefs and hostesses everywhere. Even the fields and gardens of the Perfumery have nothing so fine.

Talva's described throughout the city as too shy for Moonstone's push-and-pull politics, which is part of her appeal, as far as Vilya is concerned. He observes as she looks out to the east, across the water, all the way to the Lanternhouse on Seven Lanterns, with its hundreds of silver, bronze, and wrought-iron lamps. There's a dark haze over the lamps tonight: the smoke rising from smoldering silk houses.

"The Library must attend to the needs of the people and their government," Vilya says to Talva, putting his arm comfortably through hers. They've been discussing the charges against the Librarians, which Vilya shouldn't be talking about, but he can't help boasting of his plans. "The Library is here to serve us, not the other way around. Librarians who let impious, dangerous texts into the Library are disloyal to their mission. As the son of the archprince, it's my duty to ensure the Library is cleansed of their influence."

"Lord Jissakhar's charged with deciding which texts are dangerous, no?" Talva asks.

"He's supposed to, yes, but he's not doing his job, and his family connections are questionable, to say the least," Vilya complains. "His daughter's an outright traitor! The censor and his ilk would be in Hundred Keys Fortress by now, except the high deacon who issued the warrants against them left them in a drawer in his office and they were stolen! Incompetence on the high deacon's part, but it will all be rectified soon. The Sha'an and their allies won't corrupt our city much longer."

Talva fingers a lush green plant on the shore. "Tea can be made from this plant, Your Eminence, and it's excellent for the digestion. Wanderwisp, it's called. It can only be harvested at this season. Shall I have some picked for you?"

"How thoughtful," he replies drily. He hates tea, but he knows what he's supposed to say. "What an excellent gift. Your knowledge of horticulture is a great resource for our city."

"Eminence," says Talva, "on that subject, I wonder if you'd like to tour the new woodsmoke-heated greenhouse projects in Golden Sands and the Perfumery. Moonstone could be far less dependent on produce from warmer countries if the Council funded more such." Vilya knows Talva is trying to distract him from a subject she finds uncomfortable; her family makes money off the tourist trade, and tourists may find a more fundamentalist regime off-putting. Plus, she's an advocate for the latest horticulture, and as the city gets more and more crowded, better and better means of food production are necessary.

Out on the dark water, Vilya sees Prince Hallan's barge, bedecked with pearlescent ribbons in indescribable hues that glow in the moonlight, on its way from Drake's Hoard—probably the bath, since Hallan is a known libertine. The curtains of its riding-compartment are closed. As Vilya watches and Talva methodically discourses on agriculture, the barge makes its way downriver toward Scattered Pearls, no doubt to dock at the Nethre home palace, City-of-Bridges. Hallan used to be his friend, Vilya thinks. Then, one day, he was suddenly the butt of Hallan's politically dangerous jokes. Vilya aims an invisible crossbow at the barge. Talva titters nervously.

Earlier today, at dinner with his mother in the Forbidden Tower on the southeast corner of the palace, Hoel Dhagura told them both how Prince Hallan's solicitor arrived at the Magistery and voided the arrest of two lacemakers who'd been cited by Dhagura's people for running an illegal inn. "He's intent on making trouble," Hoel Dhagura had grumbled, stroking the points of his beard and stabbing at roasted fowl organ meats with a two-tined fork.

Vilya's mother, uninterested once she realized sorcery was not involved, returned to her usual subject of finding Vilya a sufficiently noble, pious, and modest bride. She pressed the case of her current favorite, Sophesma Wyrex, granddaughter of the High Servitor of Taradia. Sophesma suffered an unknown terror as a child and doesn't speak, which his mother seems to regard as a good thing. When the High Servitrix visited Moonstone last month on her grand year-long world pilgrimage tour, she brought the archprincess a portrait of said Sophesma: a sallow, snub-nosed girl who reminded Vilya of his mother's mother, a woman who barely existed, or so his father liked to say. Like taking tea with a ghost, Jalian Mai would murmur. He said it without rancor, even with gentleness, but it frightened Vilya when he was a child, to think he was the son of the daughter of a ghost. As if he too might not really exist.

"The crown prince is too young to settle down. Wouldn't he prefer a concubine instead? Or in addition?" Hoel asked, and completely shocked the archprincess. Vilya, who finds the public kind of concubine perfectly adequate, wonders what Hoel is up to, since Hoel almost always sides with his mother.

Talva, seeking to lift the silence that has fallen on their conversation, gestures to an alcove with a marble bench, and the two sit down. The bench overlooks the river. Talva casts a glance at the dark haze over Seven Lanterns. Out of his satin coat's pocket, Vilya takes out his long churchwarden-style pipe made of clay dug from a river shore in Little Vex. He also takes out a pouch of oiled silk filled with powdered dreamcloves, and fills the pipe. He tamps the powder down with the edge of his bone knife, a primitive implement from Turtle's Clutch an old girlfriend gifted him long ago. It makes him feel dangerous, owning that knife. Talva gestures to a footman lingering nearby to bring a flame.

"It calms the nerves," Vilya mumbles by way of explanation. At the palace, it's well-known Vilya goes into his well-appointed washroom and smokes his pipe at least once a day. He offers Talva the pipe but she declines.

"Is Your Eminence nervous this evening?" Talya asks warmly, placing her hand on his, a little methodically, in his opinion.

"I'll be archprince soon," Vilya says. He's being more honest with her than he should, for no reason he can name. He supposes he wants to impress her. He falls silent again and blows smoke out on the water to meet the smoke of the silk houses. He does worry about Hoel Dhagura and his secret plottings on Jalian Mai's behalf, but even Hoel Dhagura will have to serve him once his father's gone.

"Is that so?" Talva asks, politely but with a worried glance at Vilya. "I wish the archprince every good health."

Vilya nods, taking Talva's statement as a courtesy if not exactly a statement of support for Vilya's future reign. "Thank you for allowing me to invite myself," Vilya says. "I should be going. My father may need me."

Talva rises and bows. Vilya takes another moment to stare out across the river, to where the Library dome shines under the moon, hovering above the streets of Opal Island as if it is the sky-realm of the saints. In the morning, Vilya will be brave enough to lead the people on the course he and his mother have determined. He'll inspire the common people to rise up against corruption and heresy. He'll be a hero.

Joeve often told him he was a hero. He does think about Joeve. He shouldn't, but he does.

He ambles along the shoreline toward the royal barge, wondering if his valet has shooed away the wench he hired for the night or if she'll still be on the barge when he arrives.

Talva kneels down in the grass and delicately grasps between her fingers the stem of a saptrap plant, just above the roots. It's a local weed, and its sticky leaf-fluids can cause a rash if an unwary passerby brushes against it with bare skin. With a practiced jerk, she pulls it out by the roots and throws it into the river.

CHAPTER 29

Istehar Sha'an, Illuminatrix
Cemetery, Holy Ibis
Sanctiday, 2:00 a.m.

Under cover of darkness, in the small cemetery allotted us Sha'an, we dig Tiarath's grave. The first shovelful of earth is thrown up to the sky, as is the custom. Nizhar Sha'an and I agreed that a public funeral for Tiarath could become the scene of a riot. So we have come like criminals, in the middle of the night. Nearby looms the Sanctum of Holy Ibis, where the patron ancestors of Moonstone are said to dwell. The light of the saints' stone lanterns does not reach us.

There is little room in this archipelago for the dead. In the last few hundred years, most funerals in Moonstone are cremations. Ashes are put into family crypts or scattered out at sea. But we Sha'an, being forest people, do not light cremation fires. When we came here, we leased a small graveyard for burials, one that will revert to the city in time. We will not have our ancestors' bones for long. It was that way in the forest too; graves were swallowed up by roots and underbrush, sometimes within weeks.

The earth is soft and heavy. Its fecund smell rises into my nostrils. My shovel slips and clangs against someone else's. Tiarath's husband, Dozya, wields his shovel more fiercely than the rest of us. I step back to make way for him, finding a place in the circle of mourners that surrounds the grave, adding my voice to the others, finding my place in the Song of Returning to Earth.

Dying the song is born,
on the breath long is borne,
until the thread is shorn,
turning, returning.
Fading the flower blooms.
Rising from seed and womb,
life unwinds to its tomb,
learning, returning.
Falling the leaf unfurls.
Knowing, the spine uncurls,
caught in the seasons' whirl,
burning, returning.
Dying, the song is born.
Birthing, the veil is torn.
Husk that is seed, go on
yearning, returning.

The chant goes on, and soon the hole is deep enough. Men bring the body, wrapped in a moss-silk shroud. The crone Salomir, expert in the art of lamenting, begins to wail. We hardly need her services; we all have tears on our faces. I reach out to Tiarath as they put her in the earth, knowing it is the last time my hands will touch her in this form. After this, I will find her in the soil of her grave, and in the flowers in my garden.

Tiarath and I escaped the forest together. She had my mother's name—*tiarath*, the crown of a tree. When she and I gardened, it was as if my mother was with me. Tia, I called her. Little garland. I watch my people fill in the grave.

You are planting a human, the tree-spirits say from their hiding place. *We want to be planted too. Plant us.*

My hand finds the small book in my pocket. I have not opened it since Annlynn staggered home with it at midnight, dead drunk. *Wait*, I plead. *The Sha'an need your help. We have nowhere else to turn.*

We want earth and water. The voices come to me in the dark like the fluttering of moths.

You gave me a place to grow, the one in my womb chimes in. *You must do the same for them.*

Plant us, the voices say. *We will be more powerful in the earth than in your hands.*

I slip the prayerbook out of my pocket. In the black of night, no one sees as the little book falls into the grave. Dozya's frantic shovelfuls cover it in an instant.

I am left in the dark with the funeral singers. What have I done? I might have summoned a forest-spirit who could strike down Vilya Mai, or change his heart to be more like his father's, or change the city itself. Now, I am helpless. Perhaps the tree-spirits will grow a new forest for some new tribe, after we Sha'an are gone.

Tiarath, watch over these honored ones for us, I charge my old friend. *I will watch over the one I carry.* Tears run down my face. As I step back from the lip of the grave, Olloise, who has been here all along, gropes for my hand.

By now, we wives of Undersong House have all realized that when the laundress comes in the morning and Annlynn returns the three books to her, we will never see them again. The Council will get hold of them, and this time they will be destroyed. Without the other "forgeries," it will be impossible to make a case that the Lutei forgery is the original Moonstone Covenant. Olloise has brought us evidence of the poison in the bones of Karel Lutei, yet if we brought it to the courts, they would object that these events happened hundreds of years ago, and anyone could have used a poison like that. It is hardly enough evidence to overthrow a government. And that means, in a matter of days, Vilya will rule.

Could the Sha'an try to leave Moonstone after all? Maybe the mines of Lower Phantos might take us in, though the work there is hard and the owners are cruel. Can I reconcile myself to such a fate for the Sha'an, for my unborn child? I don't think I can bear it.

We need help, and if I cannot get it from the spirit world, I will need to find it in this world.

When the funeral rites have ended, I retrieve my staff from where it leans against a silversilk tree, wondering if it will ever produce another miracle. I whisper to Olloise and Annlynn that I have someplace I need to be. Olloise nods wearily. Annlynn makes a fuss. I tell her I will take Sha'an warriors with me. She says I am being selfish: fighters are needed to guard the house.

"It won't be dawn for hours," I say. "The mobs are sleeping. We can spare two people."

In the end, Annlynn sends thin-lipped Eyra with me, a Sha'an warrior woman scarred from battling the Mor, and young Hanael the boatman, who has ferried Sha'an folk from Seven Lanterns to Holy Ibis for the burial. "It might be dangerous," I tell Hanael.

"You returned my family's Book of the Tree to me," he says, bowing. "I'm glad to be of service." Slight but muscular, he takes up his pole gracefully, as if he is a dancer. His head is almost shaven (a modern custom his elders must deplore) but I can see the dark fuzz growing in on top. He waves to his large family and a slight but fierce-looking girl who might be a significant other before gesturing that Eyra and I should come with him.

The Sha'an boats all cast off at once and head in different directions, so if spies are tracking us, they won't know whom to follow. When Hanael asks in his soft voice where we are going, I tell him: "Scattered Pearls."

For a while we pole past the edges of Holy Ibis—broad steps down to the water, white cottages and mansions glowing in the moonlight. Eyra stays on guard, and insists I cover my hair with my cloak lest some insomniac householder spot us. There are clumps of reeds where the ibises nest, and we pass one of the holy laundries, where for a fee the laundresses will wash the clothes of ordinary folk together with the tapestries of the Sanctum, as a blessing for the household.

Then we find the current, and shoot downstream past Juniper Island. The bookboats are all covered and the bookmen and bookwives asleep among their books. On the shore, a lone window-knocker stretches up a wooden baton to tap on a window and wake some poor soul who has to get up before dawn. Higher up on the island, the gray towers of Disappearing House, where the reclusive, genius princes of Juniper Island reside, are almost invisible in the mist that always seems to surround them. Some say the house is guarded by Tamirlian glyphmen—sorcerers expert in dueling—though no one would ever admit to that. A light in one of the towers suggests someone cannot sleep, though I'll never know who.

We pass the lamplit late-night gambling circles of the Sand Market, and the Library, where boats are unloading at the docks even at this hour. Hanael goes as fast as he can to spare me the headache and nausea. We veer left with a few jabs of Hanael's pole, and come to the Short Bridge that joins Opal Island to Sorcerer's Kettle.

Even at this hour, the heart of the city is bustling. On piers and boardwalks, there are people already awoken, or likely never gone to bed—folk selling dumplings, fruit ices, salted fish skewers, flower-lanterns, shots of moonwater. Others furtively sell dreamcloves for those who want to forget their cares for a few hours, or oil of spikerose for those who want relief from their magical gifts—I can smell the forbidden scents even out on the water. A circus troupe from Tamirlia juggles oranges, and nearby a Belakkosi procession honors water sprites with a whirling dance in the folk tradition called Ourea, which means "one with the elements."

Poet-calligraphers wander the streets or pole the canals, offering freshly scribed love-poems. The puppet-theaters are just letting out, and crowds mob the snack-carts. The houses of the public concubines are open, their flags flying. There's an inn that tilts out toward the water; they call it the Leaning Inn. It's rigged with all kinds of ropes and weights and carefully cantilevered porches, to keep it balanced. Rumor has it Prince Hallan's new lover keeps an apartment there. On the lowest floor of the inn is a pawnshop, and when Hanael ties up at the dock, Eyra accompanies me to the shop's front door. I know Ngin is often up this early. Some people say Ngin never sleeps.

I knock at the door and gingerly open it. Wild-haired, wrinkled Ngin is on a stool, wrapped in shawls and blankets, surrounded by pearl necklaces on pegs, crazily hung paintings of pearl-divers entwined with sea-drakes, shelves with bowls of ancient coins and stacks of porcelain cups. She seems as old as the city itself. She might be from the slums of Lower Phantos, or a refugee noblewoman from Upper Phantos, or a witch from the sea towns of Tamirlia for that matter. Folk say the shop has been open since the reign of the previous archprince—some whisper, since the founding of the city. There are even people who claim that the fungus that threads through the piles of refuse tucked away in Turtle's Clutch and the Moon's Daughters, rapidly (some whisper, sorcerously) converting the city's garbage into fertilizer, came from a jar in Ngin's shop.

I barely get up the courage to speak.

"Good morning, madam." I bow a little. "Has Vasmine Kinora brought something to sell? A river-drake's eye?"

"Not many of those anymore, since the river-drakes were hunted out of existence," Ngin grouses. "No one's brought me one of those in two decades, not that it's any of your business."

"I'm sorry to waste your time in asking," I say.

"Just as well they haven't," Ngin goes on as if she hasn't heard me. "People say those eyes see like eagles and are mean as feral cats. Many try to use them, but only the pure of heart can prophesy by the river-drake's eye!"

I remember my false prophecy to Kalicent and shiver. "You haven't seen Vasmine?" I press.

Ngin shakes her head. "Not in many years, child. That chit's too wealthy now to need *my* services! If you want, you can check upstairs with my great-grandbaby."

I nod. As I ready to leave, the little jingle-bell attached to the door rings, and someone comes in: a girl in a plain brown dress and bonnet, with pale skin, an elfin chin, little breasts, long dark hair swept up into a bun. I don't know her, but I greet her politely, and when I do, she hisses and puts out her hands to fend me off. I back toward the counter, not sure how to comply with her wish that I go away, without brushing past her toward the door.

"Out, both of you," Ngin commands, making some warding sign from whatever culture she's from, and we both bolt from the pawnshop in terror.

"I don't know you," I insist to the girl on Ngin's doorstep, as she backs away from me. Eyra approaches, concerned, but I gesture her away.

"I know *you*," the girl cries. "When I went up to the Watchers' Heights to jump into the ocean, I heard your voice! 'I see her cold body in the deep,' you said." She shivers. "It frightened me so much I didn't jump! And now I don't know what to do!" She hugs herself and wails. "If I go back to my father, he'll put me in an ancillary and make me pray for the rest of my life!"

Her voice rises. "You should be in jail. You're the sorceress, not me!"

"You're Memmiam Yurenai," I say. "The archdeacon's daughter. You were Prince Egno's lover."

The girl begins to sob. "Egno doesn't want me anymore. Vasmine could have covered for me, but she betrayed me."

"Why did you come to the pawnshop?"

She wordlessly shows me a tiny pearl-and-glass pendant on a silver chain. It might be worth ferry fare, maybe.

I still have Kalicent's coin in my pocket. I want to give it to Memmiam, but I can't. This money is all I have, if I need to get my people out of Moonstone.

But if I did give it to Memmiam, might the merit of that act save us?

"I'll rent you a room," I say desperately. "I'll pay for three nights. Maybe I can think of a way to help you."

She reluctantly nods. Shadowed by Eyra, we climb the outside steps to the second floor, to where Trip, Ngin's great-grandbaby, is drowsing at the innkeeper's desk. Trip speaks a dozen languages and even a few words of Sha'an dialect; I know them because they sometimes ask Vasmine to consult about the handwriting on hotel bills, if some deadbeat needs to be tracked down. I gently wake them up and hand over coin.

"What's the inn gossiping about these days?" Trip asks me, teasing. "Does the desk have any wisdom to share?" But the inn guards its guests' privacy and doesn't whisper much in my mind at all, and furniture is incredibly boring; you'd never want to listen to it. I smile and shake my head.

Trip gives Memmiam a cast-iron key. Memmiam clearly expects to never see me again; she doesn't thank me or bid me farewell before going up the weirdly slanting stairs. I ask Trip if Vasmine has been by, but the answer is no.

Now time is even shorter before Annlynn will expect me back, but there is one more place I need to try. Eyra helps me back into the boat and Hanael pushes us back into the traffic flow. We jet under the Short Bridge at speed. The city pays us no mind.

When we reach Scattered Pearls, the islands are so small and close together that Hanael has to navigate very carefully. The knees of tall cypresses partly block the canals. Willow branches brush my cheeks as we pass. I can hear the trees' sleepy night whispering. Almost every house has a dock, or a balcony that leans out over the water. We pass university islands with dormitories and halls of learning, and students raucously singing in liquor parlors. A young street-singer tosses a rose to Eyra, who snorts and drops it in the river.

We come to the House of Blossoms, with its high white walls and aquamarine-colored slate roofs, and its round door with two haughty goldenberry trees on either side. A flag embroidered with lush flowers hangs from a pole imbedded in the wall facing the river. Balconies on higher stories of the building look out on the water. A few students in bright robes, up far too late, are leaning over one of the balconies, watching the boats go by—girls from concubine lineages, being trained to do what Vasmine once did. One of them plays a quiet, haunting melody on her flute, as if sending a tender message to a lover—or mother—she's left behind.

Below her, the door opens and a man in maroon velvet leaves with a cat-like grin. The door closes behind him. No doubt he's spent hours negotiating a contract for a lovely, graceful woman to come live in his house, entertain him and his guests, bring him to erotic heights, raise his prestige, make no demands on his title, family, or inheritance, and leave whenever he requires it. He can only be pleased with the deal he's made.

We pass the house and pole onward. I know Vasmine isn't there. She resigned that status long ago.

Hanael navigates a small channel and ties up the boat at a dock that serves a little street, a footpath really. On either side of the footpath are two-story buildings, dwellings for multiple families. At the end of the path, there is a little square with stalls for a market, though the stalls are empty in the pre-dawn dark. I see a shuttered bakery, and a dove-tower with dimly lit windows. "Wait here," I say to my companions. I get out and walk softly, as if I am walking in the forest, until I come to the garden apartment of Taurelanthe Kinora. It's impolite to ring the bell at this hour. I ring it insistently.

After a few moments, Madam Kinora answers the door in her ruffled dressing-gown. She is in late middle age, with a silver streak in her auburn hair. She has Vasmine's small stature, graceful bearing, amber eyes, and arresting looks. I have been to her home before, for a very proper, awkward tea after the wedding, and a few other times to visit more informally. Back then, Vasmine's mother seemed disapproving. Now, she looks terrified.

I bow in the fashion of the Moonstone court. "Please, Madam Kinora, I am so sorry to wake you, but is Vasmine here? It's very important."

Madam Kinora stares at me for a moment, her eyes wide. "Why would you be looking for her at this hour?" she asks after a long moment. "Didn't you just ask her to leave your house? I'm sorry, dear, but I don't think I can help you."

"Madam Kinora, I know you must be angry with us," I offer desperately. "We all love Vasmine. We were just surprised by what she told us. We all may need to leave the city, maybe even today, and I don't want to leave without her. I'm afraid I'll never see her again!" And then I start to bawl on the doorstep.

"Come in, come in," she hurriedly gestures, no doubt worried about the neighbors waking. "But she isn't here."

I find myself in Madam Kinora's little parlor, which is overfull with silk screens and silver creamers and figurines and vases. She gestures me to a cozy armchair and hands me a teacup of water and a handkerchief. It's almost like having a mother, I think, which makes me cry harder.

"If she isn't here, she must have gone to the palace," I say between gulps. "Do you know if she went there?"

Madam Kinora pauses and straightens a portrait on the wall—not Vasmine's. Some beautiful woman in antique clothes. Maybe a grandmother? She seems to be considering whether or not to tell me something.

"People think little of concubines," she says then. "But generations ago in the Fenge, we were diplomats and peacemakers. We entertained heads of state and negotiated treaties. We occupied seats by the throne. We were called *firwyverin*: 'peace-wives.'"

Madam Kinora has a famous tendency not to speak directly to the point. "I have the utmost respect for your and Vasmine's former profession," I say, composing myself.

"I understand why she no longer wanted it," Madam Kinora says, fingering a porcelain statuette of a pearl-diver, naked and ready to descend. "The place we have in Moonstone is not the place we once had. It's not easy for us here. But one can't leave behind one's true calling. Not really. She thinks she has done everything she's done solely for herself. But it isn't true." She touches the pearl-diver's cheek. "It isn't true."

"I know," I say. "She's protected us for many years. Just like she protected you by buying your contract from the lord provost."

"And now she is protecting the city," Madam Kinora muses. "She is a *firwyveris*. It is her fate."

I let the silence hang a moment. "Where has she gone, Madam Kinora?" I ask quietly. "I want to help. Truly."

"Always running between princes, that one. When she was sixteen, she promised her father that if he negotiated a good first contract for her, she'd make it worth his while. And she did. He and I were on visiting terms with the noblest houses in the city. When she left Prince Hallan to be with you, she devastated the prince *and* her own father." She shrugs. "I didn't mind. The truth is, I never liked either of them. But I did miss the invitations a bit."

She is not rambling; I know better than that. She is negotiating with me. "I don't know what Vasmine told you about what happened," I say, "but we won't tell anyone about her work with Prince Hoel. Ever. She is our wife. We would never tarnish her reputation. Or yours."

At least not any further than you already have, Madam Kinora's eyes reply to me. She nods, just once and very subtly. "Is she at the palace?" I ask again. "Or"—fear grips my chest—"did she perhaps seek out Prince Hoel?" If she did, I think, then she has gone over to the other side, and there is nothing to be done.

"She did see Prince Hoel yesterday," Madam Kinora says. "He met her in the Sandmaze." My heart sinks. But my hostess continues: "Then she came here. And just now, right before you came, Prince Giya Lutei sent a barge and cloaksmen for her."

"Prince Giya?" I repeat, astonished.

"Yes," she replies. "She said to me, before she left, that common enemies are the fastest way to make a friend."

CHAPTER 30
Vasmine Kinora, Ink-Merchant
Moonstone River
Sanctiday, 4:00 a.m.

During the day, the felze of Prince Giya Lutei's barge is draped in crimson silk with a fringe of hyacinth blue— an eye-catching blaze of color appropriate for the prince of a district famous for dyes. We'd be quite noticeable during the day, but at this hour all the colors look black, and the barge moves like a legendary mist-cat, unseen and unheard. They came to me this morning—last night, really—and knocked on the door, and said the prince had accepted my request to meet him and discuss the situation regarding the Moonstone Covenant.

Between the districts of Scattered Pearls and String of Coins, there's open river. The boatmen doggedly pole upstream in the near-dark. Far ahead of us I can just barely make out the cliffs of Drake's Hoard, with houses of various shapes and sizes piled atop the cliffs and ledges. The colors of the curtains in the windows are so bright I can see them in the pre-dawn haze. Some folk say that the folk on Drake's Hoard worship not the Ancestors or the Pattern or the Great Tree, but color itself.

Hallan went to Giya himself last night, I understand, to express my desire to meet. A message would have been too dangerous. I hope Hallan said flattering things about me. I hope I can convince Prince Giya that our information is worth his protection, because if I can't, I'm going to have to tell the remaining residents of Undersong House that they have to get on Jalian's boat, even if they're not speaking to me.

If Vilya Mai stays in power, it's not safe for any of us here, separately or together—not to mention that Hoel Dhagura isn't going to let it pass that I've defied him and vanished instead of hastening to kill people on his behalf. If this doesn't work, this is my last night in Moonstone.

"Will His Eminence be up at this hour?" I ask the chief boatman, who's just outside the felze. It feels strange to be in full fashion form, with a lavender brocade robe patterned in blossoms, a sash the color of a blue-skinned moon-plum, and a white lace cloak—an outfit borrowed from my mother—at a time of day when I should be in a nightgown or at the very least a house-robe. But in front of the prince of the dyers of Moonstone, I cannot be seen in anything less than royal hues.

"Indeed, madam, he's eager to greet you," the man replies, bowing a little.

I imagine he is, either because he wants to ally with me or because he wants to kill me. I'm taking a huge risk with what I'm doing. It's a good thing I'm taking it alone.

And then a shape is moving toward us out of the mist and the dark, so fast I think it's some kind of ghost. It cuts across our path and then I see it's a fast, sharp-nosed craft—a needle-craft, they're called. They're mostly used for battle. The chief boatman calls to the other three men aboard, quite alarmed. Whoever these folk are, they've picked a good time to attack. I look around for other boats but there's no one nearby to ask for help.

The intruders steer directly toward us and come alongside; they fasten their smaller boat to ours with sharp iron hooks, and within seconds they climb onto our deck. I think of the Morish pirates we learned about in school. Giya's people are armed, and they rush to confront the intruders, but there are more men climbing aboard and the Lutei boatmen are outnumbered.

There's a brief scuffle, during which Giya's people are overpowered or pushed overboard. It all happens so fast it's hard to believe it isn't a dream. The boat jerks to a halt; the boarders must have dropped the anchor. These marauders are either cloaksmen, or unusually talented thieves. I don't dare leave the felze and make myself a target.

The chief boatman is still fending off the invaders with his rapier. I still have a chance. Inside the felze, I crouch down and unsheathe the silver-handled knife I keep under my coat, which my mother and I dedicated to the nameless goddess when I came of age. I kick off my shoes. If the pirates want money, the river-drake's eye is in my pocket and worth a king's ransom, and the pouch of coin from my till is there too. But if they are here to make an end of anyone who knows about the real Covenant, diving into the river might be the best option. The gown I'm wearing is a little too long; best take it off if I plan to swim. I let the cloak fall from my shoulders, untie my magnificent sash, and swiftly shrug off the dress, leaving only the thin shift beneath.

I can see the fighting continuing on deck. If they've found me here, whoever "they" are, I hate to think of what might be happening back at Undersong House. I do wish Olloise would have left well enough alone. Though eventually, Vilya would have been a problem, no matter how quiet and docile we were.

I move toward the opening of the felze. A bulky form moves to block my way. Even in the near-dark, I recognize Hoel Dhagura.

"Sit down," he snaps. A wicked knife is in his hand, much larger than mine, suitable for butchering.

"You're attacking a prince's vessel," I point out. "That's treason."

"Sit down, I said!" Hoel comes toward me, his knife gleaming. I know if I cry out, there will be no one to help.

"I prefer to stand," I reply.

He laughs. "You damned insubordinate bitch. I almost believed you intended to do as you were told this time, until my people saw you step onto this boat."

"If you thought I would kill my family, you weren't paying enough attention these last eight years," I reply, my eyes casting desperately about for something that will help.

"At first your information was good," he growls, moving closer, "but then you were sucked into the airless void of those silly enmeshed girls trying to replace their mothers by climbing on one another. I would have thought you were too smart for that pathetic circus."

"It appears not," I say, wondering how quickly I could cut through Giya's heavy velvet curtains and leap into the water. Probably not quickly enough. I reach within my purse for Olloise's poison vial, the one that Hoel gave me to use on his assassination targets. I'm hoping I can unscrew the lid and throw it at Hoel. But he has thought of the same thing; he knocks the purse out of my hand.

"No one wastes my time," Hoel informs me coldly, shoving the purse away with his foot and watching my eyes dart from side to side. "Particularly not a conniving harlot like you, who had the opportunity to hold an honored position as a spy for the Council, and instead foments sedition and chaos and tries to overthrow the government. The archprince forbade me to put you at the bottom of the river where you belong, but the archprince is nearly dead! His successor doesn't like you nearly as much."

"It's mutual," I snap, "and he isn't the successor!"

Hoel laughs. "Are you stupid enough to think the Council is going to overthrow generations of precedent because of some piece of paper hundreds of years old?" he scoffs. "You're as deluded as the Lutei, coiled in their pipe dreams all these generations. All fools run toward each other!"

"You're putting in power a man for whom hate is a fetish," I reply. "He'll leave the city in ruins. Are we the fools, truly? There is another possibility staring you in the face, and you're too corrupt and hidebound to see it."

He chuckles. "You should be on your knees to me instead of lecturing me! I saved you from a contract marriage anyone could see you hated. I offered you a pile of coin few are ever going to see all in one place. And instead of giving me your loyalty, you give aid and comfort to witches and traitors. And lie to my face, fiends take you."

"I lied to *you*?" I cry. "You told me you had Olloise's parents killed to protect the city. That it would be better if she never learned they had committed treason. All of it was a lie. They were killed for learning your patron should never have been in power to begin with."

"Nidaba Mazall was willing to murder people at my command," Hoel spits into my face. "She had little cause to complain that her fate was the same as theirs."

"I wonder what you had on her," I counter coldly.

He smiles. "Why don't you ask your prophetess? Doesn't she know everything? Except…she doesn't know you're here, does she?"

"If you kill me, the others won't rest," I tell him, trying not to let my voice shake. "They are persistent."

He chuckles. "Little good it will do them. And once they're gone, I'll wager no one else will come poking around talking about dead princes and their covenants."

He steps closer to me. "Olloise was sweet once," he says. "An appealing little girl. I would have been happy for her to never know about any of this. But she couldn't keep from meddling, just like her parents. Now I have no choice but to kill all of you. I regret it but it can't be helped. Yours, my dear, is only the first of the boats I intend to sink today."

In the dark of the tiny enclosure, my knife out, I can practically feel the hairs of Hoel's beard. Our blades almost touch.

One of Hoel's men is squeezing into the felze behind him, grinning. "Maybe don't kill her quite yet," the thug suggests. "The most beautiful woman in Moonstone, don't they say? All that beauty shouldn't go to waste."

"I do like to keep my staff amused," says Hoel, considering. He eyes me as if wanting to witness my fear and fury.

"And she's already done the disrobing for us," the broad-faced thug adds. "How thoughtful."

"It seems like a sign, doesn't it?" Hoel says. "Well, get to it, man! I haven't got all morning!" Hoel steps back from me, daring the thug to come closer. I scoot back against the wall as the villain comes close to me. He grabs my wrist, wrests the knife from my hand, grins a yellowing smile. If I had anything like a harp...

There's a howl out on the river. At first I think it must be a large bird, or one of the boatmen who has been thrown overboard, going down for the last time—but the howl goes on for some time and becomes unnerving. A second one begins, higher-pitched and even more haunting than the first. "River-ghosts," one of the men on deck calls. "Hoist the anchor! Let's get out of here!"

"Fiendsbegotten Moonstone superstition," Hoel complains to his cloaksman. "Get out there and see what it *really* is. I can manage the girl myself. Deal with it!"

His minion leers at me and reluctantly goes back out into the night. The boat lurches. Hoel refocuses on me, his expression business-like. And then there is the sound of metal on metal, and more cries, these far more human. And splashes—several of those.

In seconds, Annlynn comes into the felze, dripping wet and wielding that great sword she seems to love more than any of us. The sword has blood running along the blade; likely the blood of the miscreant who just went out there. I wouldn't confess it to one of my instructors at the River School, but the sight makes me a little sick.

Long before libraries existed, long before Taradia built its empire, subdued the clans of Chaea, and converted them to its own Abbatine faith, long before Chaean warrior librarians trained to keep the peace in the holy city of Taradium, Annlynn's ancient Chaean ancestors were plains warriors. Expert in close combat, they fiercely defended their herds, lands, and kin from raiders and rival clans. I can see them in her at this moment.

Hoel lunges toward me, but Annlynn somehow gets between us and strikes the weapon from his hands with her sword. She hauls him out onto the deck, and slams the hilt of her sword into his hand so that he shrieks and clutches at his fingers. Then she and an older Sha'an woman I don't recognize unceremoniously dump the prince of Seven Lanterns overboard. Annlynn uses an oar to prod him, flailing, away from the barge. I suppose killing him is unwise, given that there'd need to be a trial, but I do wish Annlynn had. After this night, I wouldn't like to run into him again. I bend down to carefully retrieve the vial of poison that has rolled into a corner, and put it back into my purse.

I emerge from the felze in time to see Istehar knock the last of Hoel's cloaksfolk off the deck into the river with her staff. "I hope he can swim," she worries as the current carries the last one downstream. Idiot girl. Moonstone is wasted on her.

"It's a good thing your mother's neighborhood has a dove-tower that answers the door before dawn," Istehar says to me. "Annlynn and Olloise met us north of the Gilded Bridge so we could come find you. I didn't think Prince Hoel would let you defect to the Lutei without a fight."

Well, perhaps I am wrong about Moonstone being wasted on her. Or maybe some tree told her everything.

On the other side of the boat, sturdy Olloise hauls a Lutei boatman out of the river and pounds the water out of him. A Lutei cloaksman gets up from the deck, badly bloodied, and works on the grappling hooks until we are free and the other craft floats, empty, downstream. Out on the water, young Hanael hails us before taking his boat off into the darkness.

"Onward to Madder House?" the head boatman asks me as Istehar fishes another of his colleagues out of the water with her staff. I nod.

"Is that wise?" Olloise asks Annlynn. Apparently she is still not speaking to me. "Do you think we can trust Prince Giya?"

"Well, we can't trust anyone else," Annlynn says. "We may as well try."

She sees what I see. Prince Giya needs us. With the archprince's death looming, Prince Giya is a potential threat to the Mai, the Council, and the way things are. He must make his move now or be knocked from the board. So the information we have gathered is priceless to him. And I find myself willing to throw my weight to his side. I had always thought all my machinations were in order to be left in peace, but as it turns out, I am a meddler after all.

When the boat has been put to rights, the chief boatman calls out, "Bring her about!" and we are moving once more. Annlynn invites me into the felze. We wipe our respective weapons with the felze blankets—it feels like a ceremony of sorts.

"You could have told me," Annlynn says. "About the spying. About Hoel. You could have told me even back then, Mina. Didn't you know that?"

"It would have spoiled everything," I answer. "I couldn't bear to spoil everything."

She thinks about that for a moment. "It could have been just the two of us, you know," she says. "If you hadn't needed to get close to Olloise. If you hadn't been Hoel's spy."

"If I hadn't been Hoel's spy, we wouldn't have met," I point out. "Or else we'd have met at some princess's party years later and had a sordid fling in the washroom. Not nearly as dignified." Annlynn laughs out loud.

"Plus, are you sorry?" I gesture at Olloise, expertly bandaging the hurt boatman, and Istehar, leaning on her staff and staring out into the mist at the faintly lit coastline of Drake's Hoard. "Would you have wanted to leave those two behind?"

"I guess I wouldn't," she replies. She thinks a moment. "No, I'm not sorry for any of it." Then, her eyes narrow. "Are you?"

"I am sorry for so much," I say, stepping in close to her, "but never for being with you."

CHAPTER 31

Annlynn Jissakhar, Vasmine Kinora,
Olloise Mazall, and Istehar Sha'an, Students
River School, Vexmere
Five years ago

In the small room, dim lamplight touches faces and little else. Three of them are on the bed closest to the window, heads bent over the object Vasmine has just plucked from its velvet box. It's red-purple, the size of a plum, with depths like river-water.

"A river-drake's eye! Perfectly fossilized! Is it from your prince?" Olloise asks. Her dark eyes are fixated on the treasure; they all know she wants to take the eye to the makeshift laboratory she keeps in a box in the corner, to find out what it's made of.

Vasmine nods and cradles the orb in her hand. "Hallan expects me to set it for jewelry," she says, lifting it to her cheek to feel its smooth chill. "So other men can admire it. And me." She laughs. "I wonder what he'd do if I put it up for auction?"

Istehar sits cross-legged in her shift, her face solemn, her odd white hair glowing in the darkness. Olloise often jokes that they don't need a lamp with Istehar around. "I think it means he's watching you," she says. "It's not just a present. It's a threat, Mina, isn't it?"

Vasmine shrugs. "What if it is?"

"You might be in danger," Istehar points out.

"I can handle it, elf-child, don't you worry."

Istehar persists. "Maybe you're not safe with him, Mina."

Vasmine puts the orb back into its box, gracefully rises, and goes to sit on the other bed next to Annlynn. She sets the drake's eye in its box on her tiny night-table and fishes a comb out of a chipped lacquer bowl. "Istya, don't you know that in my business, you keep a prince's threats to yourself?" She undoes her topknot and begins to work her dark tangle into a smooth waterfall. "It's not your fault, poor girl. You're not from here; you were raised inside a tree or something. But trust me. Everything is fine." She pushes the comb through the strands that fall around her shoulders, delicately, as if she's playing the harp. Her satin robe is too opulent for the bare little room.

"He's found out, then." Annlynn half-glances at the sword hanging on the wall near her head. "He's angry at you for being with me. With us." Annlynn's face remains still, as always, but by now they all know how to detect the traces of rage beneath. "You know I could do something about him, Mina."

"Not without getting killed, you couldn't." Vasmine pulls the teeth of the comb through her hair and says nothing further.

Olloise snorts. "You bring the city's elite to salons at his house. You wine and dine his supporters. Not to mention offering him paradise on a pillow every night you're home. He should be thanking you, not threatening you. What does he care if you have affairs with a few fellow students? What's going on, Vasmine? Is Istehar right? Are you in some kind of trouble?"

"Leave it alone, all of you." Vasmine drops the comb back into the bowl and turns onto her stomach. "I only have to see him on weekends, now that I'm at school." She turns again and faces Annlynn. "Let's do something fun. This conversation is boring."

"I could buy out your contract," says Olloise. Istehar draws a sharp breath.

Vasmine lets out a bitter laugh and turns her face back into the bed. "Don't be ridiculous, little orphan. I'm the most beautiful woman in Moonstone. You couldn't afford my contract."

Olloise sits up, suddenly fierce. "I may not be a prince, but the Council sold my parents' townhouse after they were murdered. I have money. Annlynn has money too."

"He has to take the money, if you ask him to," Annlynn says. "It's the law."

Still face-down, Vasmine names a sum. There is silence. Even the sale of the river-drake's eye—which would surely offend the prince—wouldn't cover a sum like that.

Annlynn shrugs as if it's of no consequence. "Well, we can save up. I'll have a good salary at the Library soon. Though I'll have living expenses. My family's paid quite enough for my rearing and education, or so my mother tells me. It's time for me to work for a living. Or get a husband."

"Indeed you should get a husband." Vasmine rears up and punches Annlynn in the arm. "Reproduce that aristocratic blood of yours." Annlynn glowers at her.

Istehar says quietly: "I don't have money. But I have a house."

Vasmine shakes her head. "That's not your house, dearling. You only live there because you're the illuminatrix, whatever that is, for that Sha'an rabble. The house belongs to them."

"My family is allowed to live there with me," Istehar says calmly and stubbornly. "The Sha'an have said so."

Annlynn and Olloise look at each other. "Technically speaking, Istya, you don't have any family," Annlynn says carefully. Istehar and the people of the Sha'an forest arrived in Moonstone as refugees several years ago. Her parents, who were once leaders of the Sha'an, are dead; her brother's whereabouts are unknown but he is presumed cut down by Morish soldiers or burned in the fires. The Council, they all know, sent her here to the River School to keep an eye on her.

"You could be my family." The same calm and stubborn tone. Like when she tells them what the trees in the school's orchard have been saying. The tone that makes them wonder sometimes if she's entirely sane.

"Are you proposing to us?" asks Olloise, a little playfully. "I thought at least you'd propose to me first."

"I *will* marry you first," Istehar replies. "The Sha'an will be happy to have a healer around. We can marry Annlynn and Vasmine later. Once my people get used to the idea."

"You're talking about a group marriage," Annlynn interjects. "Like the radical Errantines have, or the Bo people from Gengrassia."

Istehar nods. "The Sha'an call it a braided marriage. We had them more often long ago."

"Mostly artists and public concubines have marriages like that," Annlynn says doubtfully. "But it's legal here. Even princes do it now and then." Annlynn goes off into one of her thought-trances, reading some law-book in her mind. "It's perfectly legal. My family will hold their noses. But that's a selling point." She chuckles to herself. "That's not boring at all, Mina, is it?" She touches Vasmine's shoulder but there's no response.

"If we didn't have to buy a house, we might have enough from the sale of my parents' townhouse to buy Vasmine's contract," Olloise calculates. "I have the apparatus from my father's workshop; I can build a practice, and sell salves and potions to hospitals. Annlynn will have her salary from the Library; they're bound to hire her as soon as she graduates. We can manage."

"And we'll live in Undersong House," Istehar crows triumphantly. She leaps up and nearly knocks over the spiky little plant she's been tending in a clay pot on her desk. The rest of them shush her, glancing at the door. The rectoress will wake up. So will half the school, at this rate.

And then, on the far bed, the painted face cracks. In thirty months, the other three have never seen as much as a single tear in Vasmine's eyes. They are stunned speechless as she begins to sob. She sweeps the drake's eye and its box onto the floor, where the eye rolls into a corner. Then she curls around herself, weeping quietly. The other three slowly gather around her as if around a hearthfire.

"Well, that settles it," Annlynn mutters.

CHAPTER 32
The Wives
Madder House
Sanctiday, 6:00 a.m.

Madder House looms above the sea-facing cove, its bulk set apart from the crazily piled houses that crowd the shore. Four-story tapestries fall from the mansard roof to the foundation, all along the façade of the house. Tall, narrow, canopied, balconied windows squeeze between these tapestries, peering out like hooded eyes. The morning is bright but cool; Olloise shivers a little in her long sweater. She imagines her parents arriving to this same view.

The boatman makes a quick report to the dockmaster and arranges care for the wounded. Liveried staff sweep the four wives up the switchback stairs, past the household cloaksmen, and up to the front doors, massive and elaborately carved with looms, wheels, and spindles. The halls within are lined with tapestries and banners in rich, gorgeous colors.

The sub-archipelago of String of Coins, which includes the islands of Drake's Hoard, Wyrm's Vestry, Giant's Purse, Hermit's Tryst, Trollswimple, Hueshaven, and Summercrown, is home to a variety of brightly colored plants and flowers that can be made into vibrant dyes, due to rare minerals in the soil. Long ago, the Lutei of Nordynor settled here, and became expert in the making of such dyes, as well as in the spinning and weaving of fabrics—particularly wool from the local riverweed-grazing sheep. String of Coins is named for the wealth the clan has acquired from this industry.

"Maybe that's why Karel Lutei was chosen as the first arch-prince," Annlynn comments under her breath as they proceed through the tapestried halls. "The Lutei had all the money." Vasmine, her arm through Annlynn's, nods in agreement as she notes the ceilings painted with river-drakes, sea-drakes, snow-sirens, and leviathans.

Istehar grips her staff as if she needs it in order to walk. She is very quiet. Maybe, Olloise, thinks, the house is speaking to her. Or maybe there are too many books in Giya Lutei's personal library for Istehar to manage.

A butler shows them all into a second-floor loggia open to the formal garden below. The river spreads out before them—they can see almost to Vasmine's mother's house. The lean and elegant Prince Giya Lutei, in a sapphire-blue suit kings could not dream of, bows in a grand gesture of welcome. They bow in return. As trays of chilled moonwater and plumcakes circulate, he waves them to seats, and sinks back into his thickly cushioned armchair. Annlynn devours a plumcake in seconds.

"So you did, indeed, have a reason for your interest in the Moonstone Covenant," the prince says to Annlynn, archly, as if he's settling a debt.

"It was an urgent state matter," Annlynn responds. Lutei almost smiles.

"It's not funny," says Olloise angrily. "My parents died because of the secret we're here to discuss."

"You are right, Madam Mazall," says Lutei. "More than right. I'm very glad Madam Kinora has inspired you all to come here. It gives me the opportunity to correct a few wrongs, or at least acknowledge them." He bows from his chair.

"You haven't offered to side with us up to this point," says Annlynn warily.

"I thought you were working for Prince Hoel and the Council," Lutei explains, gesturing with his beringed right hand. "That was why I thought you confiscated the true Covenant from me a few days ago in the Library—in order to protect their interests. But let me begin at the beginning.

Madam Mazall, you may suspect me of killing your parents, but I assure you I did my best to be their protector."

"You hired my parents?" Olloise asks. The prince nods.

"Why?" she asks, and anger and sorrow comes through in her voice.

"If you're here, you must know the answer," he replies. "And, given that Hoel Dhagura is out to kill you, it is in your interest to cultivate me as an ally. So there need be no secrets between us. Let me state it plainly: I hired the Mazalls to prove my claim to the archprincipate."

"What claim were you pursuing?" Vasmine asks when Olloise is silent, taking in the enormity of this confirmation. "Just to be clear."

The prince nods again. "I will tell you the story, though it may be of little comfort to Madam Mazall. It was known in our family that Karel Lutei was chosen as the first archprince. Karel had told his wife and son so, and they were awaiting the formal announcement of his new rank when they learned that he had been poisoned." Giya Lutei sips his drink. "At the time, they did not protest overmuch. Truth be told, they were not sorry he was dead; as you may know, he was a terrible man. And they did not want to be assassinated themselves, or accused of being murderers. So, on the advice of his family, young Erius Lutei signed the Covenant that named the Mai family as archprinces in perpetuity. But as the generations went on and the Mai amassed wealth and power, my clan began to realize what we had lost. We began to search for the first Covenant."

"To enforce it?" Vasmine asks, as Olloise looks at the ground, thinking.

Lutei grins bleakly. "Or at the very least to blackmail someone over it. Such a historical anomaly ought to be worth something, no?"

"Why didn't the Council just burn it?" Annlynn asks.

"They wanted to keep the Mai in line," Vasmine suggests when Prince Giya hesitates. "If the Mai ever really crossed them, the other princes could reveal the document and have them deposed."

"A four-hundred-year standoff," Lutei agrees. "Well spotted, Madam Kinora. If you had been at the Founding, no doubt things would have gone more smoothly."

"If I had been at the Founding," Vasmine says, "we would certainly be having a different conversation."

Giya Lutei leans back in his chair, with his drink in his hand, and looks at Vasmine speculatively. "I expect Praxinia Lutei would have liked you."

"Your ancestor," says Annlynn, who has been drilled in genealogy. She glances at a nearby painting of a severe-looking woman in a magnificent crimson dress. Olloise is still looking down, saying nothing.

Lutei nods. "About three hundred years after the Founding, Lutei spies discovered the document still existed in the Library undercellar and, in a feat of brilliant daring, stole it. Praxinia Lutei, my ancestor, as you say, presented the authentic Covenant to the Council, but unbeknownst to her, the Council had discovered the theft and made five other copies, each with a different family named to the archprincipate. They circulated the rumor that there were six forgeries, created as a party prank. The other princes colluded—all of them agreed it had been a joke, and that the Lutei had been taken for fools. Praxinia was humiliated; she never left the grounds of Madder House again."

"I saw a scribe writing one of those duplicates by night," Istehar says quietly.

Prince Giya looks startled. Then, with a flourish, he takes a monocle from his pocket and peers at Istehar. "Ah, yes, the visionary. Fascinating." Istehar stares back.

"So it wasn't out of sheer arrogance that you kept checking the so-called forgery out of the Library," Annlynn says.

"I suppose that depends on how you define arrogance," the prince responds, chuckling. "I have been determined to follow my father's example. You see, after Praxinia, my clan set aside all hope of regaining our rightful place. But my father, Symiel Lutei, once he had learned the old tale, couldn't put it aside. He paid scholars to comb the Library for evidence, and one such scholar found *The Poisoner's Guide to Moonstone*. Your Vigilance asked about it at the Long Bridge, so I believe you know it?" He turns to Annlynn.

"I gave it to Olloise as a birthday present," Istehar says. Lutei looks at her oddly.

"We know it, Your Eminence," adds Annlynn, clarifying.

Lutei nods. "It contained a confession by my ancestor's murderer. The book was printed not long after the city's founding, but the Library, I've learned, at the Council's orders, bought and destroyed almost all of the copies. Apparently a few survived, and centuries later, some little printing press reprinted the item, thinking it an interesting fiction. It is a copy from this edition that the scholar brought my father."

"The same edition as the one I found on the bookboat," Istehar exclaims.

Lutei nods. "When my father saw the text, he realized it was evidence that Karel Lutei was murdered not by a jealous family member but by the Council. He sought more evidence, planning to demand that the Lutei be reinstated as rulers of Moonstone. At the very least, he hoped to receive a considerable bribe for his silence. But one of his researchers betrayed him to the Council, and his wife, my stepmother, found him stabbed to death in his study."

"Just like my father," Olloise blurts out. "And you wanted justice." Olloise's voice is shaking. Annlynn is nodding; she has seen the cause-of-death documents for Symiel Lutei, and this account fits with the facts.

"But you carried on your father's plans," Vasmine notes. "That was brave, under the circumstances. Or power-hungry, perhaps."

Giya Lutei looks out to sea. "Like Erius Lutei long ago, I was very young when I ascended to my principate. But I always intended to avenge my father. He was a good father, and my only real companion in life, since my mother died when I was small, and my brother was younger."

"I understand that," Olloise says with intense feeling in her voice. "I truly do."

Lutei pauses. "I imagine you do. Like you, Madam Mazall, I was left alone in the world. Since my younger brother died in a boat race a number of years ago, and my... predilections do not lean toward marriage, I am the only heir to String of Coins. The family legacy is mine to exalt or throw away." He pauses. "I didn't and don't want to be archprince. Yet the idea that the Mai are lounging in the Palace of Innumerable Pearls, counting their gold, throwing their grand tantrums, and murdering their enemies without consequence, enrages me. Even as a young man, I knew your father and mother, Madam Mazall, through their work with the Council. I knew they had the skills to bring the truth to light. I offered them a considerable sum to gather evidence that would force the Council's hand."

"But why would they work with you?" Annlynn asks. "It would be judged treason, if they were caught."

"Ah." Lutei nods. "They had reason. As you know, the sainted Madam Mazall was an assassin for the Council. I was aware that Prince Hoel Dhagura coerced her into becoming a spy when she was a young orphan, by threatening that if she did not work for him, he would close down the orphanage where she lived, and drive her fellow residents—her siblings, essentially—into the street. Over the years, he demanded a variety of political murders, mostly overseas but sometimes here in the city. Prince Hoel and the Council also forced her husband, that is, your father Zevid, to corrupt his forensic work—by manufacturing evidence, and the like. I imagined the two of them wanted to escape their situation, and I turned out to be correct. I promised them a place in my household and protection from the Council. A new life, of sorts. For themselves, and their daughter."

Tears roll down Olloise's cheeks. "I didn't know any of this," she murmurs. Istehar takes her hand.

"They were quite successful in their investigation," Lutei muses. "They disinterred a bone from Karel Lutei's tomb on Vexmere and determined that the poison described in the *Poisoner's Guide* was a match. Madam Mazall convinced the Librarians to let her check out the Covenant forgeries. But I suspect one of those Librarians was in the pay of the Council. The night your parents were killed, they were comparing the various forgeries to discern differences in the ink." Olloise's tears are flowing faster now.

"There are such differences, Your Eminence," Vasmine affirms, when it becomes clear Olloise is too overcome to respond. "I can testify to it as an ink-merchant. At the time they were all written, it might not have been possible to tell, but now it is clear: the Lutei document is older than the rest."

Lutei nods. "Alas, the Mazalls never made that report to me. That morning, a river-drake's eye arrived at my door in a velvet box. Then I heard both husband and wife were dead. When my people inquired, neither the bone nor the books could be found at the scene of death." Giya nods to a box on the mantel at the back of the room. Vasmine raises an eyebrow and goes to look. A magnificent river-drake's eye lies within the velvet case.

Lutei gestures to a servant, who offers Olloise a handkerchief. She methodically dabs her eyes with it. "I inquired after your safety, Madam Mazall, but you had been taken into Prince Hoel's home. I later learned you had been sent to the River School. I could not, of course, reveal anything, without risking your life and my own. Prince Hoel's gift had made that very clear. I am sorry about that—that I left you to be raised by your parents' killer. Your parents surely would blame me for that. But it seemed the best way to save you."

Olloise stares at him. "Why didn't the Council and Prince Jalian kill you?" Annlynn demands of the prince suspiciously. "Prince Hoel must have been acting on their orders."

"I have no spouse or heir, Your Vigilance," Lutei says. "If they kill me, my line ends. That would solve their legitimacy problem, but then there would be a vicious fight for who would control the wealth of String of Coins. Power in the city would be out of balance, and the city would be destabilized. The Council doesn't want that, at least not at this time. So they let me live, in hopes I will marry and produce offspring, and keep the balance of power unchanged."

Prince Giya sips his drink. 'They know that without evidence, I can do nothing. I would sound insane if I tried to make any of this public. Perhaps I even sound so to you. But I haven't given up. The day you confiscated my overdue book, Your Vigilance, I was searching for rare maps, maps Karel Lutei had drawn up, that might show Drake's Hoard to be the original capital of Moonstone. I confess that at the time, as I said, I thought you might be an agent of the Council."

Annlynn, Vasmine, and Istehar all look at Olloise. Olloise composes herself and leans forward. She seems to have made a decision.

"What if I told you we had all the evidence my parents collected and more?" Olloise asks. "And that we have every reason to wish the Mai deposed?"

"That very possibility is the reason I was willing to invite you here," Lutei says. "Though I didn't expect all of you to come at once."

"You are a prince of Moonstone," Vasmine points out. "A member of the Council. A very wealthy man. The status quo doesn't appeal?"

Lutei laughs loudly. "It perhaps might. But the young Prince Vilya is much less likely than his predecessor to be worried about destabilizing the city. He, I suspect, will have no trouble ordering my assassination. So it is wise for me to make my move now, while I still can. And...I still have not avenged my father." Olloise nods.

"You said you didn't want to be archprince," Vasmine observes.

"I don't," Lutei agrees fervently. "But is that not one of my qualifications for the job?" He smiles mirthlessly.

"I'm not at all sure we have enough evidence to convince anyone," Annlynn says doubtfully. "The different inks and the bones and the poison are all interesting, maybe even compelling, but is the city really going to rise up because of it? People will claim we invented the whole thing, and the Council will have us executed for treason."

"We might be able to strengthen our position," offers Vasmine. "If the Council kept documents to blackmail the Mai, then the Mai might have kept documents to blackmail the Council. And I know where they will be."

"I don't want you going back to the palace," Annlynn warns. "It's not safe. Especially now they surely know you've been here."

"At this point, dearling, we are well beyond the territory of 'safe,'" Vasmine tells her. "Eyra Sha'an is waiting for us downstairs. She can escort me."

"With regret, I shall not provide you a gondola, Madam Kinora," Lutei says. "So that if you are detained, you can say I attempted to recruit you, and you were fleeing my house." Vasmine nods.

Annlynn looks distressed. "I told Bastina to give the Covenants to the laundress to bring back to my father," she says. "If we're going through with this, we need those books as evidence. We can't let the Council get hold of them. I've got to get to the Library!"

"I have an employee, a cloakswoman, who I understand knows you," Lutei says. "She will accompany you through the streets, for safety. Vilya's partisans are out in force, I'm told. It's best to be cautious."

Big Chessa steps out of the shadows of the loggia. She is grinning widely. On her back is sheathed the huge two-handed sword she favored the last year they were in school together.

Annlynn laughs. "Saints' toenails, Chessa! You always did like doing the right thing."

CHAPTER 33

Olloise Mazall, Apothecary
Gilded Bridge
Sanctiday, 8:00 a.m.

As we were crossing the Gilded Bridge, Annlynn bade us farewell, touched the pole at the end of the bridge for good luck, and turned quickly toward Festival Square and the Library. Istehar stayed with me. When Annlynn was out of sight, she turned to me and said: "I'm going to have a baby."

It was not as much of a shock as learning Vasmine had wormed her way into our lives in order to spy on us, nor was it as much of a shock as discovering that my foster-father was the one who ordered my parents assassinated. It was certainly not as much of a shock as finding my parents dead when I awoke one morning. But it was still a shock, and I didn't like it.

I stopped dead at the edge of the bridge, blocking traffic. People scowled at us as they went by. "At a time like this, you tell me you have yet another lover?"

"I don't."

"Istya, please. The way of the world is the way of the world, even for you."

Istehar shook her head. "The forest wanted an offering from me, and I gave it. The tree-spirit that was in Kalicent Mai is in me now. It wants to be born as a child."

She really is mad, I thought. It was just all too much, the constant blows to my sense of what was real. I walked away from her, into the crowded, covered streets of Opal Island. She called after me, but I knew she wouldn't follow me; she had to get back to the Sha'an at Undersong House. Her people.

My people, I suppose.

Now I'm walking along the slanting, spiraling streets of Opal Island, passing a store that sells candles of all shapes and sizes, a notions shop that offers thread, ribbons, and mother-of-pearl buttons, and an Abbatine school where children are chanting texts from ancient Taradia and Uluria, the rival empires that once burned one another's Libraries and tried to send one another back to pre-civilization. In the window of a jewelry store, I see a flag with a stylized image: a tree on fire. Looking around, I see another such flag in the arched window of a spice emporium. Minutes later, a motley group of young, proud-looking men struts down the street, bearing a banner with the same image. I shiver as I realize what the icon must mean: the tree on fire refers to the ascendancy of Prince Vilya, heir to Moonstone, scion of Mor, enemy of the Sha'an. I pull my coat around me, hunch into my hood, and walk faster.

In Carpenter's Row, I run into a procession of young men and women in blue and gold livery, bearing a palanquin with open windows. Within rides my old classmate, Vilya Mai. Clad in armor, he raises his fist to the folk crowding on the street, trying to get a glimpse of him. People cheer and shout his name. Carpenters gleefully bang on their window-frames with hammers in celebration. An old woman throws flowers from a balcony.

"Drive out them fiends!" someone yells. "Stop them witches!"

"Straightaway!" he calls back lustily. "I'll chase the sorcerers out of Moonstone, and drown them in the sea!" The crowd shouts his words back to him, enthralled.

Someone else dares to call out: "Long live our future archprince!" I press myself against the wall.

As the palanquin passes, I take a quick glance inside. He's paring his fingernails with a rustic-looking bone knife. Though he is older and more polished, Vilya looks the same to me as he did years ago at school: barely containing his rage, pride, and shame. I remember how he mercilessly cast aside sullen Joeve the day he graduated; she was no longer enough for him. Now, only the murderous roar of a crowd fulfills his need.

I don't need to be a prophet to know that he will not stop after he exiles the Sha'an. Othe Azhuin said it—Vilya will accuse the Zhinj and eradicate the remnant of the first peoples of these islands. Then he'll purge the city of anyone with a hint of magic. He'll arrest the Librarians who dare to stand up to his lies. Eventually, he'll attack all Silvillines, even the "civilized" ones like me, the ones Moonstone aristocracy has valued until now. When there are no more of us, he'll decide the Errantines are traitors. His sigil tells truth: like a forest fire, he will burn anything he can reach.

Bastard, I mouth. I can't help myself.

And then I see my contemptuous glance has drawn his attention, and he's watching me. He might even have seen the word my lips have formed.

He beckons to one of his young lions, says a few words, and points at me. He likely recognizes me from the River School, or maybe he just wants to make an example of me. Three youths break away from the procession and walk quickly toward me, batons in their hands.

I flee back the way I have come. The youths follow, joking with one another but quite serious in their pursuit of me.

"Madam witch," one calls to me casually, "we'd like a moment of your time. Just to talk to you, please, about Prince Vilya's policies." Another of the boys sniggers. The carpenters' shops offer no shelter.

"Why don't you stop and talk to us?" another boy tries, while people in the crowd glance over and smile cruelly. "Maybe we can come to a meeting of the minds!"

"About your leaving the city," the sniggering one adds. "Feet-first."

One of them starts to smack his baton into his hand. More people are staring, or rushing past while trying not to stare. The street is so full of people it's hard to keep ahead of my pursuers. The jewelry-store owner has come outside and stands with arms folded across her chest, under her burning tree banner. There are no sentinels to be seen. In a moment, the crowd may turn on me, and I'll become one more victim of the city's unrest.

The spice emporium is ahead of me. Large cloth sacks of cinnamon and starwort, black pepper and moss-balm, mountain mint and cumin seed, line the edge of the sidewalk. I remember dipping my fingers in them when I was a child, looking at the colored stains they made on the whorls of my fingerprints. My father used to cook those spices when he was making medicine. Sometimes, to tease me, he'd throw them in the air and make me sneeze, and Mother would scold us and tell me to sweep up...

I grab the edge of the sack of black pepper and knock it onto the sidewalk, take handfuls of it and throw it at the passersby. I knock over the cumin seed for good measure. People sneeze, blink, and curse at me. The shopkeeper rushes for the sidewalk, furious. Someone who's been sneezed on curses loudly—the city's slums are full of disease and foul humors; no one here likes being sneezed on. I saw fist-fights when I was a child because of an ill-timed sneeze.

And then, as I'd hoped, there's an argument in the street and the crowd stops moving entirely. I throw a few more handfuls of pepper, then run before the store owner or anyone else can lay hands on me. The crowd of sneezing, yelling people grows behind me, and Vilya's young henchmen are trapped in the mass of people. I slip across the street, run past the sour jewelry-store owner, and dart down an impossibly narrow alley I know leads to the Short Bridge.

The noise fades behind me, but when I come out the other side of the alley, the crowds are still thick and there's an ugly mood, as if everyone is angry at everyone else. I rush through the streets, farther and farther away from Undersong House. Where am I going? What I am doing is irresponsible; my patients need me back at home and time is of the essence. Vasmine, Annlynn, and Istehar are all making themselves useful; I am wandering the streets like a madwoman. I've nearly been beaten to death, I've vandalized a store, and I still could be kidnapped, or pushed into a canal like poor Tiarath.

I reach the high-arched Short Bridge to Sorcerer's Kettle. I watch the hurrying rabble come and go across its cobbles of black stone. I remember stopping on the bridge with my mother to watch the boats go under. And then I realize what I am doing. What I have been doing since I left Istehar at the Gilded Bridge. I am going home.

My parents owned a townhouse overlooking the Boil: the broad canal that flows between the island of Sorcerer's Kettle and the subsidiary island known as the Lid. They bought it because it wasn't far from the orphanage where my mother had grown up, and she was sentimental about the neighborhood. The Council sold that townhouse after their death, to provide me with living expenses when I was young and to give me an allowance to live on later. I haven't been back to the neighborhood, not since I gathered my things and packed up my father's laboratory.

But I feel compelled somehow to cross the bridge, fight the crowds of folk milling past narrow, looming houses, heading to work at sewing shops, lacemakers, bakeries, theaters, joiners, printing presses, hotels, brothels, glassblowers, and metalsmiths. I pass the Errantine chapel with its stained-glass windows in spiral patterns—many folk here are Errantines, and freethinkers, though they may not admit that to their workplaces in case their employers are prejudiced. I pass an Abbatine deaconess with her charity basket, bringing bread to the poor to earn the favor of the saints. She sniffs in disapproval as she passes the spiral windows.

Then I make the familiar left turn at the puppet-makers'. A tall, thin house, one of a row of joined houses with sharply angled roofs, comes into view. I almost expect my little doll-carriage—which I used for potion storage—to still be near the stairs.

I have no idea who lives here now, or how they might feel about my knocking on their door. I've long since taken away everything that matters to me. Yet I linger near the doorstep. There's something to find here; I don't know what. I wonder for a moment what Istehar would do.

Then I remember the dream. The nightmare that has come to me so often, the one in which my mother stands in her nightgown on the balcony, my father's corpse at her feet, holding out to me a bloodstained letter.

But he was killed in the study, and she was killed in the bedroom. Why does the dream always begin on the balcony?

If Istehar were here, she would tell me to trust the dream.

It's worth a try. I edge around the end house in the row and make my way down the wide footpath between the houses and the canal until I come to the rear of my childhood home. Out on the water, barges, sailboats, and gondolas float by. A few pedestrians pass me as well: a boy running while bouncing a red ball, a Zhinj-looking woman walking a fistful of leashed Ulurian desert hounds.

The first-floor balcony, where my father told me stories, is about the height of an average person, just over my head. I look upward, carefully scanning the cracks in the wood. Then I dare to reach up and search with my hands, feeling into the cracks. Any moment someone will pass and think I am a thief or a madwoman, and call the sentinels.

There's nothing in the cracks, nothing I can see or feel. Disappointed, I pull my fingers out, now covered in flecks of dark wood. I try again, willing something to happen, but can't feel anything. But next to one of the cracks, a piece of wood is loose. I wiggle it until it comes out.

There's a hole now in the wood. I feel eagerly into it, but there's nothing in it. But it is weirdly smooth at the back of the hole. I stretch up on my tiptoes and put my eye to the hole, and jump in shock as I see an eye looking back at me.

I take a breath. It's not a ghost. It's just a mirror. Someone in a velvet snood passes by and glances at me; I pretend to be clearing away bird's nests.

A mirror. There's a mirror in the hole. I look again, and see the dim image of my eye, and also see a bit of ground reflected in the mirror.

I kneel down and feel into the dark soil. There's a little wooden lid buried just below the surface, and when I pry it loose, there's a cylinder underneath. Inside the cylinder is a leather envelope, and inside the envelope is a letter.

No one thought to look in the ground under the balcony, not even Prince Hoel.

I stuff the envelope into my pocket and walk away. I have nothing like Vasmine's misdirecting grace, but I try not to attract attention. As I move away from the house, I can't resist looking back. A man comes out onto the balcony, carrying a plate with crumbs. He whistles. A little gray bird perched on the roofbeam whistles back. I hear him set the plate on the rail of the balcony. I continue down the path and don't look back again.

Not far down the path is the public garden of the hospital, where I often went to have lunch with my father. There are patients sunning themselves here, tourists resting their feet, children playing, and poor folk who have no other place to sit. There's a merry-go-round with carved sea-creatures: drakes, krakens, leviathans, and wide-winged seabirds. It costs a few pennies to ride. Tinkling music rises from a cranked music box. I remember riding on that merry-go-round, while my father smiled and waved. Nearby, a young broad-shouldered zealot stands displaying Vilya's banner, calling the people to march to the Library to protest the Librarians' heresy and the Sha'an presence in the city. A lump rises to my throat as I search for a bench to sit down on. I brush the dust off the envelope, open it, and take out the paper inside.

To my beloved Zevid, my dearest Olloise, or whoever may find this,

I am ashamed to write down these things, but in the event that I am no longer alive, I hope these words will stand witness to what I have seen and done. I do not intend to let the Council benefit from my ill deeds and then remove me like ash from a fireplace after the wood is burnt up. I wish to offer my Zevid who has accompanied me through everything, and my Olloise, my greatest joy, my words of apology for these acts, should I not be able to offer those words in person.

I testify with this letter that I, Nidaba Mazall, served as an assassin in the employ of Prince Hoel Dhagura of Seven Lanterns, and at his direction carried out a variety of murders in the name of the Council of Moonstone. An orphan-keeper identified me to him as a talented girl, hardworking and unusually bright, good at navigating the city, and he recruited me and blackmailed me into serving him…

My mother then lists names—foreign officials she has eliminated, then a few Moonstone citizens—a judge, a physician, the last archdeacon, even a princess of Sorcerer's Kettle. I weep as I read her description of how she—sensitive soul that she was—carried out these crimes with dedication, believing she was protecting the city, and knowing her family would be harmed if she did not.

I read of my mother's misery as she realized the Council's deceit and corruption, and then of her joy when she received the miraculous offer of a second chance from Prince Giya Lutei. The letter documents the evidence she and my father gathered that the Lutei line were the true heirs to the archprincipate—and tells of her hopes that her life might be different under a new dynasty. Then my mother relates how Prince Hoel became suspicious of her and threatened her, demanding she reveal what work she was doing for Prince Giya.

And then I raise my eyes. As if, like a demon, his name has summoned him, Hoel Dhagura is sitting on a bench across the garden from me. He must have changed his clothes since falling in the river; he looks quite dry and like an ordinary wealthy old man, though one of his hands is bandaged. His kindly eyes are on me, as they often were when I walked in his gardens in Seven Lanterns during the summers I spent in his household. A shiver goes through me as I realize I am in immediate danger of dying. My tears feel cold on my cheeks. He crooks a finger on his good hand, beckoning me to approach.

His cloaksmen must be all around; they must have been following me since I left Istehar on the bridge. And who knows if she made it home, pregnant, alone? I bitterly consider my options. I wish I could write my confession next to my mother's—my crimes too are mounting. I should have told someone where I was going.

I see people in the garden subtly shifting toward me, as if I'm in a dream and horror is intruding on an ordinary scene. I cling to my mother's letter as if it can save me. I don't want to die like my mother and father, stabbed in the back, so in the end I fold the letter, rise, and start walking toward my former guardian—the man I thought had rescued me from being alone.

I'm shaking so fiercely I'm not sure I'm going to make it there. He looks at me with a mix of compassion, pity, wariness, and eager anticipation. The subtle watchers in the garden are beginning to move toward me. One of them will come up behind me and stab me with a hairpin or dab me with an undetectable poison. Very well. If they're going to kill me, let them do it in front of everyone, with Prince Hoel right next to me. I keep walking toward him, and he keeps watching me come. The music of the merry-go-round provides a strange undersong for a murder.

"How grown-up you've become," says Prince Hoel as I get close enough for him to speak. "That was very brave, Olloise. You should be proud."

I can hear the footsteps behind me.

Then, from the corner of my eye, I notice that the woman with the pack of leashed hounds is in the park. She has dropped the leashes and is exclaiming in distress as the dogs run pell-mell through the garden. The presence behind me yells, and when I turn, I see one of the dogs has bitten a nondescript man and is dragging him through the park. Other dogs are biting other people. Folk are screaming for the sentinels. Children and adults run from the garden, or wheel themselves toward the hospital doors.

Prince Hoel rises and moves toward me, reaching for my arm. "We'd better go," he says. "It's not safe here. We should talk elsewhere. Come, Loli." I want to pull away, but I'm paralyzed with terror, and I just look at him.

One of the smaller dogs, barking and snapping, approaches me and grabs the edge of my sweater. Startled, I cry out as the dog pulls me toward the south side of the garden. A puppy has leaped into Prince Hoel's arms and has knocked him back onto the bench, and is licking him, or biting him, I'm not sure which.

The hounds' owner approaches and grips my arm. "Get home now," she hisses at me, and points to a narrow, walled side road. I rush to where she's pointing and hurry up winding stone stairs to a high street that looks over the canal. When I glance down at the hospital garden, Prince Hoel seems to be dozing on his bench, his head slumped a little onto his shoulder. The dogs have run out of the garden, and the hound-walker is nowhere to be found. The man who cranks the music box for the merry-go-round is putting a thin long object, a straw maybe, into his pocket. The music tinkles on.

CHAPTER 34
Sajine Chei, Princess of Sorcerer's Kettle
Phantosia House, Sorcerer's Kettle
Sanctiday, 9:00 a.m.

Half an hour later, Princess Sajine of Sorcerer's Kettle is settling in for tea with her wife on a high balcony set in a conical roof overlooking the public garden. A tall woman smelling of hounds has just left the room. An Errantine labyrinthette, a tiny model of a labyrinth, beautifully shaped from bronze, stands on a shelf in the corner, signifying the arduousness of life's journey.

"As you know, Hoel Dhagura had my grandmother murdered," Sajine muses, setting her cup carefully on the saucer. "I've wanted revenge for that for many years. Plus he keeps raiding my orphanages for spies and assassins, and killing random folk, even chambermaids who he felt threatened him somehow. It was high time to get rid of him. His visit to the public garden provided the perfect opportunity. I've had someone in place at the carousel for just this sort of eventuality."

"Indeed," replies her wife, Onyxe, admiring the tea set, which is fine painted porcelain from Yanuilt, painted with the twelve fairies of the months: Mistmantle, Lightlinger, Sickleswipe, and so forth. "How fortunate that you were able to seize such a rare chance. How did it come about?"

"Cloaksfolk of Prince Giya's came swarming into the district," Sajine remarks. "They made quite a racket, so of course our people noticed. When my cloakswoman Darda'a—the one with the hounds—stopped one of them and demanded to know why they were in Sorcerer's Kettle, they claimed they weren't here to fight us but had come to protect the Mazall girl from Hoel Dhagura, who was after her to kill her."

"What's their interest in her?" Onyxe asks, pouring more tea for herself and Sajine.

"I'm not sure—one would think she'd be on Dhagura's side, since he raised her. But in any case, we now knew Hoel Dhagura was here, on our home ground, making mischief as always, and that we had an opportunity to be rid of him. We had people in place already because of the riots, the streets were chaotic, and even if we were accused, we'd be able to blame it on the Lutei. It was the perfect moment to strike."

"And there'll be no repercussions?" Onyxe asks, biting into a forkful of delicate white cake flecked with lavender. Onyxe has run clandestine operations herself and knows the importance of avoiding the authorities.

Sajine nods. "My bet is there won't. Jalian's dying and everyone's focused on that. Plus, the murder is unlikely to be investigated by the chief interrogator, seeing that Hoel has now vacated the position and won't be here to advise his successor." She chuckles. "The mobs running about Opal Island will muddy the waters a good bit if anyone does try to investigate."

"You'd think the chief interrogator would have been better protected," Onyxe muses. She glances out the curtained window at the view of Kettlehandle Bridge, which connects the two islands of Sorcerer's Kettle and the Lid. Agitated crowds are streaming southward over the bridge on their way to the city center.

Sajine sips her tea. "Arrogant fool. He wasn't paying attention to the web I wove around him. He's been trying to spy on me for decades and learn my secrets, but he has no notion how to go about it." She nods at a velvet box on her shelf. "He even tried to spy on the archprince with one of those. Stupid. He ought to know by now that those river-drake's eyes only show you their surroundings if it pleases them to do it. For a miscreant like him, they're dead as skulls in the cemetery."

"And the Mazall girl?" Onyxe asks delicately.

Sajine shrugs. "I could have taken the opportunity to revenge myself on that assassin Nidaba Mazall, who carried out my grandmother's murder, by killing her daughter. But the girl hasn't done me any harm. Plus she has three wives." Sajine smiles. "I rather like her nerve."

Onyxe smiles back at Sajine and refills her cup once more. Their husband is at the seashore with the children. If they can stave off the mob, they have the whole day together.

CHAPTER 35

Annlynn Jissakhar, Warrior Librarian
The Library
Sanctiday, 9:00 a.m.

The laundress will have delivered the books to Tommas hours ago; we might well be too late. The glowing marble walls, with sunlight coming through them, look like flesh to me, as if we're in the belly of a massive beast. Familiar smells of silk, leather, paper, and dust fill my nostrils. Chessa matches my stride in the crowded red-lit halls. "I intend to watch your back in here," she says to me cheerfully. "Easy to meet with an accident in the dark."

"It's not that dark," I protest. But there are lots of corners to peer around, and I find myself nervous in a place that has been a second home since I was a child. The roar of the crowds outside can be heard even in here.

We navigate the labyrinth of passages and make our way toward the Lord Censor's Office. I get a few dirty looks from folk who likely count themselves Vilya's people. I also get anxious questions about the mob outside, which Chessa and I managed to pass through only by displaying our weapons. "What do they want?" a sentinel asks me. "For us to burn all the Silvilline books," an underlibrarian grumbles. "The books of magic, too. All the heretical books. The archdeacon was just out there egging them on!"

When we reach the marble doorframe of the office, I see my father bending his head over his desk. Tommas is next to him. The Covenants—saints be praised—are in front of them, their covers glinting with moonstones. They haven't been sent to the Council. All six forgeries are there—I should say, all five forgeries, and the real Covenant.

"Father," I interrupt, then correct myself: "Your Vigilance."

"Annlynn," he exclaims, startled. He rises. "Your Vigilance." We stare at each other. He's done a lot for me in the last day, but it doesn't quite make up for the last several years.

"My colleague Chessa Hellbed, from school," I say, gesturing to Chessa. "Cloakswoman to Prince Giya Lutei."

My father and Tommas nod formally. "I'll wait outside," Chessa tells me, and stands on guard at the door, clearly annoying the bookwardens already stationed there.

"The books arrived back this morning but with no note," Tommas says once Chessa has left. "We were worried. It's good to know you're all right."

"I've been in battle, actually," I say. "Among other things. Long story. What's happened here?"

"We've been examining the three books we sent you," Tommas replies. "And the others as well. It seems one of the six *is* older."

"Someone should have noticed it long ago," I say. "Karel Lutei wasn't assassinated by his family. He was elected and installed by the Council, and then poisoned so a new Covenant could be written and Surian Mai could take the throne. We know what kind of poison they used—the Council hired a man who called himself the Deacon to brew it. Traces of the poison are still in Karel Lutei's bones. It wasn't lordsbane."

"Even if it's true, that was hundreds of years ago," my father protests. "Who cares?"

"Oh, someone does," I say. "Prince Hoel had Olloise's parents murdered to keep this information from becoming public. He's likely behind the attack on me in the alleyway, and he tried to kill Vasmine this morning. Clearly he believes Giya Lutei has a chance at becoming archprince based on this evidence. Prince Giya believes it too; it's been a long-standing hope of his family."

My father nods slowly. He looks tired. "Council politics

will sink Moonstone," he observes. I heard him say it often when I was a child, but never with such resignation.

"Better for the Council to sink it than for Vilya to burn it," I say. "At least most of us have boats." My father smiles a grim smile. I haven't seen him smile in years.

"We kept the books back from the Council," Tommas explains, closing the book he's been examining. "Clerks have been here twice already this morning to take charge of them, and we've put them off. They've become increasingly ugly about it. If the mob gets in, I'm sure cloaksmen will infiltrate this office and make off with them."

"They'll destroy those books," I say. "Prince Vilya will want to protect his throne. He'll remove any evidence that he's not the rightful archprince."

"No one is destroying books on my watch," my father asserts firmly. "Mob or no mob."

"You always were about the books," I say, with more of an edge than is perhaps wise in this moment.

"Tommas," my father says, "would you leave us for a moment?"

Tommas rises and goes out to talk to Chessa, and my father and I stand alone in his office.

"Thank you for your help with the Covenants," I say coldly.

"Thank you for doing your duty to this city," he replies in a similar tone. "The truth is the truth."

"It doesn't change the fact that you haven't spoken to me in years and didn't come to my wedding," I say to him, my voice starting to rise. "You may have helped me today, but you're still a hypocrite. You have a wife and a mistress, for saints' sake, but you disinherited me for being with women!"

"A great many women," he huffs.

"Three is hardly a great many, and no more than you've had over the years of your marriage," I snap. "And I don't forget that you tried to arrest one of them. She would have been killed, Father!"

"I apologize to Madam Sha'an," he replies stiffly. "I do understand now what she was trying to do. That she was trying to help you."

"So she's not a charlatan?" I retort.

He pauses. "She is...unfamiliar."

I stare at him. It's not exactly an admission of prejudice, but it's close.

My father sighs. "I was wrong. Forgive the way I am, Annlynn," he says. "You're always trying to rebel. Tradition means a great deal to me."

"It means more to you than me, I gather," I say bitterly.

"No," he says, and there's something in his voice that makes me break open. "Not more than you, Anya. Not more than you."

We both have tears in our eyes. Which means I have cried way too many times this week. I reach out to touch his hand.

"Father," I say with sorrow. "We've lost so much time."

He spreads his hands to indicate the Library, smiles a little in a bitter way. "We're Librarians, Anya. This place is timeless."

"Annlynn," Chessa calls from the hall. "Get out here!"

Startled, Father and I come to the door, to an awful sight. Yelling, flailing people are coming up from a hole in the floor down the hall.

"The mob's gotten into the understory!" I shout to Tommas. The network of book cart channels beneath the Library floors connects to the docks below. The mob must have found a way up from the docks—or some sympathizer let them in. I see torches—torches! In the Library! Sacrilege. Four hundred years of Librarians are rolling in their graves.

"Give us the keys to the Library," some disheveled woman demands. "They belong to Prince Vilya!"

Some imbecile bearded youth knocks half a shelf of books onto the floor and sets it ablaze. "Burn the heresies!" he cries. Well, all right then. I unsheathe my sword.

Chessa follows suit and unsheathes hers. My father steps back into his office and comes back with his well-honed rapier. I can hear warrior librarians rallying in departments all around us. Tommas unsheathes his blade reluctantly, with a puzzled look on his face, as if he never thought it could come to this.

"This is why warrior librarians wear weapons, isn't it?" I say to Tommas. "For when the hordes descend?"

"I thought it was more of a meaningless tradition," Tommas mutters.

"More fool you," my father retorts. Seconds later, a tide of bodies collides with us. Some of the vandals, encountering our blades, retreat and flee back into the cart channels under the floor. Others, armed with knives, hammers, and spears engage us. My father spits one on his rapier. Tommas reluctantly but capably battles a fighter I recognize from the attack on me near Hourglass Alley. I take the opportunity to slice the man's calves.

Leaving Tommas to engage some other idiot, I squeeze through the melee to where the fire is blazing, climb a teetering bookcase, and pull a cork out of the pipe just under the ceiling. A spray of water jets out and soaks everything in the immediate vicinity. A few books will be ruined but at least the fire will be out. My sister Julis is in charge of the water pipes that run through the Library. She showed me how to uncork them, years ago when she was still speaking to me. Julis and her water brigade better be on their way.

I wave my arm at some terrified interns huddling behind a bookcase. "Pull corks, you fiends! Save the damned books!" A spray of blood hits the side of my face. Chessa has done something gruesome to someone trying to hack my head off with an axe. I try not to look, but it almost doesn't matter; in the red light of the Library everything seems covered in blood.

Not far from me, a wild-eyed young man with a ponytail and spectacles plunges a carving knife into the assistant recordkeeper for foreign-language manuscripts. The red tide spills onto an open book lying on the floor, marking its pages with a final notation. The murderer turns to flee and I cut him down; he falls against an ancient bookcase and books tumble to the floor. His spectacles slip and shatter.

My ancestors have protected this place for four hundred years. I'm not going to let that archfool Prince Vilya and his rabble burn it down and kill my colleagues. Doesn't anyone realize this city will sink back into the river without the Library?

On the floor, a thick old tome burns with an awful stench. Tommas is stifling the fire with his bare hands. Tears glisten in his eyes. Who knows how old and rare that volume might be? My father is standing over Tommas, holding off the mob with wicked slices of his rapier. I lose sight of them as Chessa and I fight, sometimes side by side and sometimes back to back, using the flats of our swords when we can, driving the invaders toward the outer halls. My brother Farrick comes from a side hallway with reinforcements from the Art Division. And Julis does come, with folk in oilcloth cloaks bearing grappling tools to pull the corks on the pipes.

The mob is still running amok among the shelves. Farrick runs into a side room where the Library keeps items donated by estate sales, and comes back pushing a chest. He calls to Galter Heyn, from the Maps Division, to help him open it. Inside are several crossbows someone was desperate to give away. I pull one out and Farrick tosses me a handful of arrows. I place my foot in the stirrup, cock the bowstring, and load the arrow. Then I move to where I can see the center of the hallway, which is full of rioters touching their torches to piles of books. I aim high, for the chandelier hanging in the hallway intersection, the one that gets lowered every night so its lamps can be refilled with oil. I've always been worried it will fall and kill people. I guess now is the time. I fire, and miss. People start to notice what I'm doing, and some of them turn to run. I load another arrow, aim again, and this time the arrow severs the thick rope that keeps the chandelier aloft. The star-shape of metal and glass crashes down on the mob, pinning folk and breaking bones. The oil lamps make several small explosions, and people scream. The tide of our enemies begins to reverse its flow, heading toward the outer doors. A lucky thing Julis can rain water down on the books—and the people—before the whole place catches.

But the vandals still leave damage in their wake. Chessa has taken another crossbow and is finishing off the most determined of the invaders. My gray-bearded aide, Oskin, arrives on the scene with a group of folk accustomed to checking out volumes and collecting fines. With shocked faces, they look around at the wounded and dead sprawling in ones and twos from the cart channels to the front door.

"They rushed the Librarian-in-Chief onto a boat; he's out in the harbor, for safety," Oskin tells me. Coward. Kirin Spong, the Librarian-in-Chief, is a cousin of mine on my mother's side; he doesn't share the Jissakhar spirit, to put it mildly. My heart sinks when I see the Library doors wide-open and more crowds pressing in from the outside. I see Renice from the Catalogue Hall lying half in, half out of a knocked-down bookshelf, her throat cut, her face cold and quiet. I lean down to close her eyes.

The crossbow's no good to me in such close quarters, and I hand it to Oskin. Chessa and I draw swords and rush forward to meet the crowd, which wields bottles, clubs, torches, and knives. I shove a portly deacon backward so that his head clunks on the marble floor. A washerwoman with a wen on her nose strikes Chessa in the chest with a large wooden bucket and Chessa staggers into a wall before knocking the woman down with the hilt of her sword. And then I have bigger problems: ahead of me is one of the thugs from the alley behind Yan's. It must have been Hoel who sent them then, and he's sent them here as well, to aid Vilya's overthrow of civilization. The wiry young assassin, who's only just barely passing as a religious fanatic, looks thrilled to get another chance at me. He draws a curved Tamirlian dagger that seems even more dangerous than the rapier he wielded yesterday.

I close with him. The wound in my arm from the fight behind Yan's is sore now, and I'm slower than I should be; I only just barely deflect the dagger that's aimed for my heart. Chessa's now fending off a beefy hooligan who looks as if he woke up on the floor of a liquor-parlor this morning and suddenly found religion. My enemy and I cross blades, my grip slips, and my opponent cries out in triumph as he pushes his way through my guard. Around us, the zealous mob howls gleefully to see my predicament.

But Tommas is there suddenly, his burned hands still wielding a sword. He comes between us, and sends the startled young bravo to the underworld. For a moment, Tommas stands looking shocked, as if he cannot at all believe what he has done. I clap him on the shoulder, check to make sure Chessa's hooligan has slunk away, and head toward the brightness of the open doorway.

My father stands in the wide hall, opposite the door, his rapier ready. "Let Prince Vilya come!" he barks at the crowd. "That coward sent you to do his dirty, ignorant work, with his father not even dead yet. Let *him* claim the keys to the Library! I'll make short work of him."

The mob falls silent at my father's challenge. Then, to my horror, Galter Heyn from the Maps Division turns his sword against my father. My father, utterly taken by surprise, falls. I see blood pooling on the marble. The rabble howls in triumph and streams inward. Oskin takes several of them down with the crossbow.

Farrick, screaming, closes with the traitor. I run to my father's side. His Librarian blacks are soaked with blood. I undo his jacket and shirt to see how bad the damage is. My sister Julis kneels at his other side. Chessa emerges from the crowd, gathers others to form a circle to protect us from the violent crush.

"Observe, children." My father enunciates the words with effort, and reaches out to clasp my hand. "This is how a Jissakhar dies."

"Guard wisdom," Julis whispers fiercely. Behind her, with a frenzied shriek, Farrick cuts down Galter Heyn. Tommas comes to the door and stares in sickened horror at the scene, at the broken bodies and the blood on the steps.

My father catches my eye and shapes a last grim smile. "Protect the books," he rasps. His eyelids close. My sister Julis and I, who haven't spoken to one another in years, stare at one another through tears. I wish I'd hugged my father, during our conversation only a few minutes ago. But there was no time. And there's no time now, to grieve.

"The prince is coming!" the mob is chanting. "Give him the keys!" Where in all the fiends' hells are the city sentinels?

Olloise emerges from the maelstrom and pushes up the steps to where I kneel by my father's body. How she got here I have no idea. She kneels beside me; feels my father's wrist for a pulse.

"I can help," she insists, searching among the vials in her pockets.

But it is far, far too late for that.

CHAPTER 36
Istehar Sha'an, Illuminatrix
Undersong House
Sanctiday, 10:00 a.m.

The noise of whatever is happening in Festival Square can be heard all the way here, a dull thundering groan like a tidal wave about to crash.

"This is our time," Nizhar Sha'an tells me. The pit at the center of the Chamber of Elders is crowded with the staffs of the Sha'an leaders present, as is our custom. We have hurriedly finished the chanting necessary when the elders convene, and the Book of the Tree lies open nearby to witness our conversation. Nizhar's staff leans against mine as if trying to heave it out of the pit. "While no one is paying attention, we should boat to the Narrow Forest, hike upstream, and take back our forest!"

"The Mor will be waiting for us," I point out.

"If they are, we will climb up into the Stone Waves and disappear," Nizhar says. "We'll wage a guerilla war on them!"

"Nothing grows in the Stone Waves," I say. "What will we eat?"

"We are Sha'an. We will find what we need," he replies. Many of the elders murmur in agreement with Nizhar's words.

"Our enemies in Moonstone are distracted now, but when they finish whatever foul business they have at the Library, they're going to come here," worries Ketiya Sha'an, the head of our budding school. "This is our chance, maybe our last chance, to save ourselves and our children!"

"If you flee now, you'll convince our fellow citizens we are criminals," I say. "I believe we should stay. I have just asked the

Book of the Tree what we should do, and all it shows me is the day we entered this place!"

"Because that was the day we went wrong!" Nizhar Sha'an raises his hands in frustration. "You want to stay here because of your foreign wives. Not because it is good for the Sha'an!"

"Many of us understand it was wise for you to marry folk close to the heart of the city's power," says Mereb Sha'an, Hanael's father. "We have not blamed you for that. But whatever protection that gave us is at an end. We must go now, while there is still time!"

I shake my head and rise. "You all do what you must. I am going to the Library. I am an illuminatrix; it is my duty to bring wisdom where there is none."

"If you go to the Library, you won't return," Nizhar admonishes me. "The Library is death for you. We all know it. And even if you survive the evil of the place, that mob will tear you to pieces."

"Nevertheless." I move toward the door, to general consternation. The crone Salomir lets out a wail.

"I will go with you to the Library," says Dozya. I turn to him, astonished. I would have expected Tiarath's widower to be the first to want to leave this city.

"I'll go too," says young Hanael. Maliki, whose boat half-burned near our dock, silently rises. I remember how Annlynn and Olloise threw buckets of water on the flames.

"You are Sha'an," Ketiya protests. "We can't go without you."

"We will catch up," Hanael tells her gently. And before there can be further protest, I close the Book of the Tree, take my staff from the sacred staff-pit at the center of the room, bow to the elders, and leave, with my small tribe around me. A tribe of fools, no doubt. But I do take the time to take off my moss-silk vest, put on one of Olloise's coats, and pull the hood up over my white hair. A fool doesn't have to be stupid. The men similarly disguise themselves.

The streets of Seven Lanterns are eerily empty, but the opposite is true when we cross the Long Bridge and come to Opal Island. The narrow covered alleys are packed with scowling people, some with torches, and banners with images of burning trees hang from many windows. As we move closer to Festival Square, I see a small Errantine chapel with its round windows broken, and a Zhinj ropemaker's shop where I've bought clothesline has its goods strewn on the sidewalk. The mob isn't confining its rage to the Sha'an, apparently. Everywhere I see the subtle signs of people, some with children in hand, who are quietly trying to rush home and get behind locked doors. A few hunched elders, some with canes, are gathered on the sidewalk outside an elders' hostel, looking around in bewilderment as if their city, which they have known all their lives, has become a strange place. There's a knot of fine ladies on a balcony, watching and whispering to one another as if this is some form of entertainment.

Peering from under my hood, I keep looking for Olloise but of course I don't see her; I have no idea where she went after she walked away from me at the Gilded Bridge. I should have waited to tell her about the baby until we got home. Now who knows what kind of trouble she may have run into? There are so many Abbatines here, eager to riot, fired up by their leaders—and miscreants glad to use the general unrest as cover for their heartless activities.

I worry what the Sha'an are doing back at Undersong House, the place we named in our language *Firn Udili'il*, the house of the song that lies beneath all things. Are they debating? Packing? Loading the boats for the trek upriver? If my companions and I are fortunate enough to return home again, will there be no one there?

Hanael turns ashen-faced from a girl with ringlets, who trots past us bearing one of Vilya's banners and a mop handle. "I courted that girl for a while," he confides to me in a whisper. "She was always after me to become an Abbatine, and finally we broke it off. Now look—she's here to do mischief!"

"You're best off without her," says Dozya. But Hanael's eyes have a great hurt in them.

The closer we get to the Library, the noisier the buzzing of the great hive becomes. The crowds roar, but I can barely hear them, because the books are up in arms. Angry and frightened, they cry out in their myriad strange voices—half-tree, half-human. Some of them are burning, and their wails rise to the skies. The dizzying headache that has only partly receded since the last time I came here returns with a vengeance. I feel nauseous—I hope my baby is all right. If it *is* a baby. I close my eyes and, overcome by pain, allow Dozya to lead me.

We make our way over the Long Bridge and through the streets of Opal Island, and bit by terrifying bit, we push our way into the hateful noise of Festival Square. The Library dome looms above us. The rageful shrieks of the people merge with the squeals of the thousand thousand books. Ahead of us is a palanquin, carried by folk in gold livery, bobbing through the vast river of people. The crowd parts, cheering lustily. "Give Prince Vilya the keys!" the mob chants.

In Moonstone, the keys to the Library hold all power. When Vilya has them, he will rule even if his father is not yet dead, and he will waste no time in purging the Library of half the wisdom it has collected these many centuries. He will appoint Abbatine censors who throw away any book not of their faith, the histories of the Sha'an and Zhinj people will be erased, and all the records on sorcery will be destroyed.

On the steps I see Annlynn standing with people—her family, I realize. With them is Olloise. Thugs from the crowd surround them, threatening them with hammers and blades, looking toward the approaching palanquin as if for orders. At any moment, the whole crowd could move for the Library and trample its defenders—or recognize me and my companions for who we are.

Dozya puts his arm around my shoulders as if I am his old grandmother. Hanael and Maliki press close. Faces in the crowd glance at us suspiciously, but are distracted as the palanquin comes to the bottom of the stairs.

Out of the palanquin steps a woman in a magnificent red-and-gold gown with a train so long it has to be arranged and carried by four handmaidens. Her braided hair is woven with jewels; her gold silk hood billows out around her like the bloom of a snapdragon. The crowd gasps in surprise.

"Kalicent," I breathe.

The princess climbs the steps. Two of her handmaidens unroll a paper scroll in front of her. Another of her servitors hands her a cone of stiffened silk, and she daintily raises it to her lips. "My brother has sent me to beg for your respect for our father, who lies dying at this very hour," she proclaims, her voice carrying across the square. "This paper I am holding, signed by my father and the Council, announces that Prince Vilya indeed will rule our noble and beloved Library at the moment of Archprince Jalian's death. At that time, Vilya will receive the keys."

"That paper is blank or I'm a river-toad," Dozya mutters. I would laugh except that pain from the overwhelmed books seizes my brain.

"Until then," the princess pleads, "go to your homes and pray for my father as he enters the realm of the saints. Pray for my mother and me as well at this time, for we sorely need your prayers. Pray for Prince Vilya who is about to assume the crown of our dear city and the throne of our Council."

Kalicent's voice trembles and tears roll down her cheeks. A handmaiden rushes to dab at her face with a handkerchief. A deacon mounts the steps and begin to sing a hymn. People in the crowd sob and fall on their knees. The hymn is one I know: Bastina sings it when she does the laundry.

O saints that bore us, and went before us, and labored for us, how bright your auras!

Now you implore us from heaven's chorus: our dear descendants, o now remember us!

Hanael tugs at my sleeve and gestures to where another palanquin, simpler and more martial, is mired in the crowd. "Make way for Prince Vilya," the liveried young folk around the palanquin cry. But they have no cones to amplify their voices, and the moment is lost. By the time Vilya arrives on the steps with his sister, the mood of the crowd has shifted. He waves and accepts the cheers and well-wishes, trying not to scowl.

As the crush of bodies loosens, we work our way through the milling people until we are close to the stairs. Terrified, I sing the hymn loudly as camouflage, as we proceed closer to Annlynn and Olloise. Vilya still has enough sentinels here to conduct a few executions, though the audience won't be what it was a few moments ago.

Kalicent turns and thanks the rioters on the Library steps effusively, making it clear they are to depart now. "Remove your father's remains from this place," she sternly orders Annlynn and her sister and brothers, all of whom now surround what I see is the body of Sterven Jissakhar, Lord Censor of the Library. "Let no Abbatine chapel receive him, since he raised his hand against Prince Vilya's emissaries." The mob jeers and edges away.

"Bring him this way," someone I know with a pink pearl earring calls to Annlynn from the crowd. "We'll lay him out at Yan's. He liked it there well enough."

"Right you are, Thalweg," Annlynn agrees, in a more subdued voice than I've ever heard her use. "All together: one, two, three, lift." I reach to touch her arm as she bears her father down the stairs. I'm not sure she feels it.

"We'll honor the mourning period," Prince Vilya snaps at the Jissakhar clan, finally thinking of something to say. "But once my father passes, you'll be held accountable for your crimes against the people of this city!"

The prince gives another royal wave at the crowd, smiles thinly, and hisses quietly to his sister, "I'll deal with you at the palace. I hear you're grief-stricken enough over our father to retire to an ancillary in the cliffs of Turtle's Clutch, and never be seen in public again."

Princess Kalicent makes a graceful obeisance as if he's complimented her. Prince Vilya grimaces and descends the steps, followed by his minions, who perhaps are confused about whether they have achieved a victory or suffered a defeat.

Then Olloise is by my side. We embrace fiercely. "I thought you might be dead," I admit.

"I thought *you* might be dead," Olloise replies. "I'm so sorry I left you, Istya." We cry on each other, unremarkable among the weeping folk in the doorway. "There are many wounded in the building," she tells me. "Can the Sha'an healers help?"

"The Sha'an healers may no longer be in the city." I quickly explain what transpired in the Chamber of Elders. "But I have three men here who can carry people to hospitals." I gesture to Hanael, Dozya, and Maliki, who nod vigorously. "And I can help."

"Not you." A vehement voice interrupts us. I turn, shocked, to see Princess Kalicent, no longer smiling and waving, but gazing directly at me. "I have a task for you, Istehar Sha'an."

I bow deeply. "I am at your service, Your Eminence." Princess Kalicent is as capricious as the rest of her family, but she saved lives with her theater on these steps. And, it occurs to me, Kalicent Mai is the only other person alive who has borne what I am bearing in my belly now. We are kin, of a kind.

"Attend me," she commands, and descends the steps trailing cloth-of-gold.

"Go on," Olloise whispers when I linger. "Be careful."

I follow the princess, who does not enter her palanquin but rather, surrounded by her retinue, approaches a different grand doorway in the Library complex. A banner of Moonstone—a sky-blue circle surrounded by twelve smaller pale blue circles, on a sea-blue background—hangs on either side of the portal. Sentinels open the doors for the princess and salute as she passes. One of them brusquely gestures me in. I slip off the hood of the coat I am wearing and shake my hair free. Everyone knows who I am; there is no point in hiding now.

The Council of Moonstone meets in the Library, not the Palace of Innumerable Pearls, because it is the Library that is at the heart of Moonstone's duty. Even now that the thirteen lands that founded this city no longer rule it, Moonstone is still the world's archive, the place where everyone comes to seek knowledge. Nations do not war against this place. The risk of destroying the world's wisdom is too great. There is the printing press now, and it is not as hard as it was for countries and cities to amass books, yet the treasures here in the Library are irreplaceable. So Annlynn tells me. But by the Tree, I wish they weren't so noisy.

The Council Chamber is at the heart of the Library, directly beneath the main dome. I have been here once before, when the Council questioned me and sent me to the River School. It made me beyond ill, standing there at the center of a circle of bullying royals, flooded by an ocean of book-voices. I had a headache and fever for days afterward; the healers thought I might not survive. But I have no choice now, as I had none then. My heart pounds as I follow Kalicent Mai and her people into the arched passage.

One foot in front of the other down the long hall that leads not to the shelves and shelves of books but rather to a round chamber. I hear the echoes as my staff taps against the polished stone floor. At the end of the hall, people cluster to greet the princess. The voices of the books are all around, choking me, like smoke from a forest fire.

I move into the wide space past the corridor's end. A vast dome above lets light in through intricate patterns carved into the stone. The walls, patterned in white and blue marble, are hung with the banners of the thirteen districts. Set in a half-circle are twelve lavish seats with violet velvet cushions. Opposite the half-circle stands a silver throne ornamented with moonstones and opals. It glows irresistibly in the light, as if inviting me to sit there.

Princess Kalicent seems equally transfixed. Yet she moves not toward the throne, but toward the low round table at the center of the hall. On this table is a book—a book with a moonstone-studded violet silk cover I have now come to know well. She beckons me, and I reluctantly approach.

"Open it," Kalicent orders. "I want to know what you see."

In Moonstone, treespeaking is sorcery and a crime. I could be executed. The implacable eyes of this daughter of the Mai rest on me impatiently. I can barely think through my pain and nausea. I grip the staff my ancestors held, and put my other hand to the book.

Eleven princes and one princess meet in the dark of night. They are writing in this very book. I see their hands: some smooth, some gnarled. The princess hides the book in a satchel and brings it to this chamber.

A prince with a cruel smile sits on a throne—the one in this room. The princes sitting in the half-circle of lower thrones hate him—I can feel it. They all rise, one by one, to sign a book on a round table—not this book, but one like it. This one remains in the satchel, waiting. The new archprince leaves the room.

A herald arrives with news and a grieving-bell. A different prince rises, graceful as a hunter. The princes bow. The princess opens the satchel and takes this book to the chamber's center. She puts the other one in the satchel and takes it away. The princes all breathe a sigh of relief. The one with the cruel smile does not return.

Unmoored in time, unsure if the room around me is past or present, I hear a voice speaking that I realize must be my own, telling what I saw. "So," Kalicent Mai says, breaking my trance so that I sink to the floor dizzied, "now I know. The book that all princes of Moonstone swear their oaths on is a forgery. My brother is a usurper, and our father, and his before him. My spies have whispered it to me. But now I believe it."

"It is not good news for you, Your Eminence," I say.

She shrugs. "Nor for you, since it changes nothing. But when Vilya exiles me, I will know he is a fraud, and so will he. The truth will eat him from within."

A herald enters the room, wearing black and carrying a grieving-bell. At first I think he is from the past and no one else can see him, but Kalicent gives a little scream. "Father!" she cries.

She is wrong. "Prince Hoel Dhagura of the district of Seven Lanterns is dead," the herald cries. "May the saints receive him." The herald takes a black cloth and covers the book on which I have just laid my hand.

Kalicent Mai leaves the chamber quickly, her shocked retinue behind her. She gives no order regarding me. I do not know whether I am to be arrested or not. My head pounds. My heart races. I lean on my staff, exhausted. The staff does nothing unusual. But the tree-spirit within my womb is singing to me of leaves and air and soil. That singing guides me out of the chamber, down the long passage, and out into the light.

CHAPTER 37

Vasmine Kinora, Ink-Merchant
Palace of Innumerable Pearls
Sanctiday, 10:00 a.m.

Everything depends on him having kept the harp.

It's never difficult getting into the palace. There's always someone who wants you to owe them a favor. In this case, the guards know Jalian's standing orders and let me past the boathouse. There's a door at the base of a thick tower, not far from the mosaicked halls of the palace steam baths, generally used by the simpering lady-in-waiting Zelibet Fosca as she departs for her umpteenth morning attempt to paint the river-pavilions of the Maze of Fireflies. Zelibet no doubt has heard there's a warrant for my arrest, and she won't be happy to see me. I wait behind a colonnade-pillar and let her pass. The sweating attendant carrying the lady's easel, canvas, brushes, and paints nods to me and leaves the door a crack open.

But getting a private audience with a dying archprince is not so easy.

Especially when you have an enemy you didn't consider. As I make a turn up the wide spiral staircase in the northeast corner of the palace, Fausten Yurenai, archdeacon of Moonstone, meets me on the landing. He wears his full regalia—blue-and-silver robes and a silver mitre that marks him as high prelate of the Abbatine rite and the archprince's confessor. Not that Jalian is likely to tell him anything.

"Where do you imagine you're off to, harlot?" he hisses at me. "Do you think I'll let you beg mercy from the archprince, after you dishonored my daughter?"

"Your tide is ebbing, fool," I snap at him. "Get out of my way."

"You think you're still Jalian's favorite?" He laughs and waves a folded paper. "Jalian repudiated you and signed a warrant for your arrest."

"*Another* warrant?" I sigh. "Let me see this repudiation."

He hands it to me. I scan it. It's close to Jalian's handwriting, but not close enough. I can tell it's the archdeacon's hand.

Then I see the trap. If I accept the document as real, they'll arrest me. And if I say it's a forgery, it'll be proof of my sorcerous gifts as a graptomancer, and they'll arrest me anyway.

"I know where your daughter is," I tell him.

"You and the Sha'an sorceress told Princess Kalicent that Memmiam leaped to her death," he replies, his voice full of smoldering rage. "Don't you stand by your prophecy?"

"We both know Memmiam isn't dead," I point out.

"The girl who used to be my daughter is in the Ancillary of the Blessed Initiatrix," he says. "And if she isn't, river take her." But I see sorrow in his eyes.

"Not long from now," I say, "Vilya will become archprince. He will want to control the Abbatine faith as well as the Library. And his mother has always preferred High Deacon Beldrus to you. You're in the way, and you're from the wrong sect. How long do you think they'll let you live?"

I can see from Yurenai's sour face that my arrow has found its mark. The archdeacon has been Jalian's advisor since he took the throne; he is a great power in the city. But Fausten Yurenai is of the Ulurian Abbatines and Beldrus Leathe, chief cleric of the Sanctum, is of the Taradian Abbatines. The rivalry between the two sects can be bitter in some decades, and while Jalian favors the Ulurians, his wife and son are of a Taradian bent. Given Vilya's intolerant mood, a purge of Yurenai and his allies is not at all unlikely.

"Not to mention that your daughter has a better chance of happiness in another city rather than in an ancillary," I add. "She's not the praying kind."

I take Jalian's ring from my finger and dangle it before

the archdeacon. "The *Windswift* is at harbor in Hundred Quays. Her captain will recognize this and take you and Memmiam anywhere you want to go. My gift to you." After all, if I am successful in what I came here to do, I won't be needing a ship. "But you'll have to collect Memmiam from the Leaning Inn and go quickly, before the archprince dies, or who knows if the captain will honor the agreement?"

The archdeacon glares at me with his hawk eyes. He imperceptibly glances at the deacons who flank him, as if embarrassed by what he is about to do. Then he snatches the ring and abandons his escort where they stand, striding down the corridor.

Ignoring the men who remain, I fold up the forged warrant, put it in my purse, and continue up the stairs. I know what to do. I think I've known for days now.

In the east wing of the palace, about three floors up and open to the sky, is the palace's Bridal Garden. From the shadows of the colonnade, I peer into a floral fantasy: low chairs and tables painstakingly shaped from hornbeam and magnolia roots; dainty trees with white blossoms casting their glow like lamps; intensely colored songbirds perched on the edge of a gently burbling fountain.

At the center of this lavish, whimsical garden, the archprince lies in a four-poster bed with bedposts formed from thickly spiraling wisteria vines, topped with a canopy of wisteria flowers and fragrant jasmine, and a mattress of velvety moss replanted from the Sha'an forest. His coverlets are woven from the soft leaves of silversilk trees. Most folk would envy him such a charming place to die.

Anxious-looking sentinels guard the archprince. His wife Tilgana sits near him, muttering prayers and working at her embroidery, her tutress Ursel at her side and a few court ladies to attend her. She doesn't look upset, of course; she never loved her husband, and her son is far more likely to share power with her than Jalian ever was. As I watch, she glances for a moment at the water glass by Jalian's bedside and smiles to herself. I think now that I might know who poisoned Jalian. But that's not why I'm here.

A flock of black-garbed folk sweeps into the garden, squawking and wanting the still-lucid archprince's attention. With the flock comes the crown prince, red-faced and enraged. The archprince wearily raises his head as some officious nurse props him up on pillows. He has deteriorated rapidly since I saw him yesterday morning.

I come out of the shadows, tie back my sleeves, and sit down at the harp, gazing down at my instrument as if I belong where I am. A lady-in-waiting glances at me as I put my fingers to the strings and pluck a note. Then another. Then a gentle melody. Notes wander through the garden like soap-bubbles, bursting where they will. One by one the clerks and heralds surrounding the archprince yawn and wander away. The ladies-in-waiting droop on one another's shoulders. Tilgana dozes over her embroidery, and Ursel lies down in the grass, her lace-wrapped bun coming undone. Vilya kneels down beside his mother and falls asleep, his head in her lap. Only the archprince is awake, and his eyes are on me.

I make my usual deepest bow, and sit near him under the wisteria canopy.

"Vasmine," he whispers.

"Jalian," I whisper back.

He smiles faintly. "My courtiers finally pay attention to their dying archprince, and you come and chase them away."

So he knows about my sorceries. Maybe he has always known. "Are you angry with me?" I ask.

"I have little time to be angry with ink-merchants. Or sorceresses. The city is falling apart."

I can see he is in pain. "Your Eminence once spoke of sinking ships. But a sinking ship need not take down the whole fleet."

He looks away. "The city is in Vilya's hands."

"Not by right. You know the Lutei forgery is not a forgery."

He almost laughs. "What of it? Hundreds of years ago. Proof or no proof, the people will never accept another clan to rule them." He braces himself and sits up a little straighter. "Come, girl, you know better. Sheep do not question the sheepdog's pedigree. Your friends are clever, I admit that. But an uprising in favor of the Lutei will fail."

"Perhaps." I pause. "There will be blood in the canals before the outcome becomes clear. Many in this city do not want to be ruled by your son."

He raises an eyebrow. "Many would rather be ruled by my son than descend into chaos."

I nod. "There is another possibility."

He sighs and casts a glance at the sleeping ladies-in-waiting. "My hours are few. Explain."

I look into his eyes. "Make Kalicent your heir. Let her marry Giya Lutei. The Mai will continue to rule, and the Lutei will gain the fatherline. It is just, and no one ever has to know why."

"Kalicent?" He looks astonished; he perhaps remembers some little girl with pigtails, putting on rouge.

"Moonstone has had two archprincesses. History would be better off if there were a third."

"The Council will never ratify it," he hedges.

"They will if it means avoiding a scandal about the city's founding, or a civil war. They are no doubt having second thoughts about your son's fitness for the throne."

"Vilya's people will rise up!"

"If the crown prince is nowhere to be found, any uprising won't last. Send Vilya away. The crowds will adjust themselves to Kalicent soon enough."

"Exile my son?" Jalian looks both shocked and intrigued.

"Today, he half-burned the Library. Tomorrow, the city. Likely he is an accomplice in your untimely death."

He snorts. "And how is a dying man supposed to compel a crown prince to flee a city he is about to take by storm?"

"Tell him if he does not, you will expose his ancestor as a murderer and he will be forced to step down in favor of Giya Lutei. I think he likely will prefer to plot in exile."

He coughs. "You are elegant, as always. But I will have

you know, my ancestor was justified. Karel Lutei had to die."

"Because he was cruel?"

"He was cruel, as men go, but that is not what I mean." Jalian coughs again. "Karel Lutei was a hydromancer. The River-Drake, they called him. He could speak to water, the way your Sha'an woman can speak to trees. He kept it a secret from most, but he could raise tides and abate floods. Some say he raised some of these islands from the river. Others say he would take lovers one day, and the next day drown them for his enjoyment."

"So the other princes were afraid of Karel Lutei?" I ask. "That's why they elected him?"

"When it came time to write the Covenant, the Lutei threatened to flood every district in Moonstone if he was not made archprince. So the other twelve princes acquiesced to his demand, while in secret, they plotted his murder. They hired the best poisoner in the city to do it, and then spread false rumors about what happened, to throw everyone off the scent. I can tell you they regretted nothing."

The archprince coughs again and takes a sip from a cordial at his bedside. "That was why the city forbade sorcery, so as not to have another arise like Karel Lutei."

"How do you know this?" I ask.

"I have a letter from the first Council in my possession. It has been passed down through generations of archprinces of Moonstone. Vilya would be given it upon my death if he were to succeed me." He laughs softly. "It is in the base of the harp, with other secret documents. Do you think you are the only reason the instrument accompanies me everywhere?"

I laugh too, with relief as much as surprise. "Your Eminence, give the harp to Kalicent instead. She will make better use of it."

One of the snoring ladies-in-waiting begins to stir. I reach into my purse, take out the vial of poison, and press it into his fingers. "This is for you, in case the end comes too slowly. Do you understand?"

"Yes," he whispers. He sees the act of generosity for what it is: gratitude for the years of poems, music, enchantment. "Thank you."

I turn to go. "Vasmine," Jalian says urgently, "it was not I who ordered the deaths of the Mazalls. I did not know. Not until later. Hoel was...zealous on my account."

I bow. "I am grateful to know it, Your Eminence."

He has told me this because he wants me to remember him kindly. I reach out to put my hand on his. "Farewell, Jalian." There need be no more honorifics now, between us.

He nods and closes his eyes.

There is no more time. I step quietly out of the enchanted garden and into the shelter of the colonnade as Tilgana's eyelids flutter. Vilya, sprawled on her lap, awakens and leaps up, embarrassed. Ursel grabs at her loose hair and pins it back up. Councilors, heralds, and clerks wander back from various spots in the garden. I pause in the shadows and look back.

"Send for my daughter," Jalian Mai commands hoarsely.

Vilya's petulant mouth curves upward into a smile. He is thinking his sister is about to be punished. "Gladly, Father," he says.

CHAPTER 38

The Wives

Magistery, Opal Island

Four years ago

"Just let me do the talking," says Annlynn.

They're on the steps of the Magistery, the poor cousin of the elegant Council Offices. The Magistery is old and drafty and its marble steps are uneven after years of wear. A statue of a saint with a candle stands on one side of the steps. On the other side stands a statue of a fiend with a gaping sack, ready to snap up the unwary.

"Which side are we on?" Istehar asks, looking at the statues.

"A vexing question," Vasmine muses. They enter the building, which is quickly filling up with petitioners and document-filers, and are met by a white-gloved, gray-haired greeter who asks their business.

"We need the Marriage Records Office," Annlynn replies in a business-like way.

"Which of the four of you are the happy couple?" the pleasant-looking lady asks.

"All of us," Vasmine smiles when Annlynn hesitates.

The flustered clerk smiles insincerely and points up the stairs and to the left. Olloise glances back and sees her whispering to a sentinel.

"Are they going to arrest us?" asks Istehar anxiously.

"We're not doing anything illegal. Let's just hope we don't end up in a gossip column," says Annlynn.

They arrive in the hall adjacent to the Marriage Records Office. There is a line of couples, mostly gentlemen with ladies, and a few of what look like other sorts of couples. Seeing this diversity, Istehar breathes a sigh of relief. “Now and then,” Vasmine notes, “the city does know how to mind its own business.”

The line winds its way into the office, where a jowly clerk in a red robe and a tall red hat is writing things down in a massive leather-bound book. He loudly interrogates each couple and writes down their personal names, their parents’ names, their clan names, their genders, their addresses and home districts, and their religions.

“Sha’an weddings are better,” Istehar says. “We have dancing instead of documents.”

“We know,” Annlynn replies. “We were there with you, remember?”

Finally, it is their turn at the counter. “Well, step up,” the clerk booms at them. “Who’s getting married?”

“We are all getting married, sir.” Annlynn bows a little and hands him a carefully inked paper.

“Really?” The clerk’s voice seems to carry through the whole office. “I can’t think why anyone would want to make marriage any more complicated than it already is!”

Everyone is staring at them now. The clerk opens a massive volume on the table before him. “Clan names?” he barks.

Annlynn lists their names, in alphabetical order.

The room begins to buzz. Istehar’s name was in the penny journals when she and the Sha’an came down the river and healed the archprince. The other three aren’t exactly anonymous either: the Jissakhar are well-known, and Vasmine appears often in the society pages. Olloise, of course, was once a cute child caught up in a murder investigation. The city’s journalism industry is in its infancy, but gossip-writers have been around for a long time.

The clerk takes down a volume from a shelf. “Now, hold on a minute,” he says, checking a few pages. “I believe you’re a special case.”

After checking yet another tome, this one on a higher shelf that requires a stepladder to reach it, he grumbles:

"Definitely a special case."

"Stop holding up the line," someone calls from the back of the room.

"A wedding shouldn't have to take all day; I don't care how many people is in it," someone else grumbles.

"I'll have to hand you off to my assistant," the clerk informs the four women, and rings a bell. Annlynn nods. She expected this.

From a door in the side of the office emerges a lanky, mischievous-looking man with black ruler-straight hair. It's Pirrip, whom they knew at the River School. Since graduation, he's been the underclerk in charge of genealogy at the Magistery. He too is in red, the color of Moonstone's civil service.

His eyes twinkle as he gestures them into his office, which is crowded with rows of cabinets. "I guess you didn't become the Junior Secretary for the Recovery of Books that Fell into Canals and Floated Out to Sea," he says to Annlynn, grinning.

"Not exactly," she retorts. "But close. What's this all about?"

"In order to marry in Moonstone, you've all got to be legal adults," he tells them.

"We all are legal adults," Olloise replies testily. "Obviously."

Pirrip cordially shakes his head. "Not yet. You, Madam Mazall, have been a ward of the Council since your parents' death. Normally we'd need your guardian to emancipate you, but since you're of age and getting married we can just have you sign an affidavit." He produces a piece of paper from a drawer, dips a quill in ink, and hands it to her. "Once you sign this, the Council will no longer be responsible for you, and you can conduct your own affairs."

"Very good." Olloise signs her illegible signature to the document. "Now can we proceed?"

"Almost." Pirrip places the signed document on an easel to dry and goes to another drawer. "To form a plural marriage in Moonstone, one has to be a citizen. An ordinary marriage can be contracted even by foreigners, but certain kinds of marriages require citizenship. I suppose the Council didn't want polygamous folk flocking here in crowds to wed."

"But I'm not a citizen," says Istehar. "I'm a refugee. A resident alien."

"Right. So we need to fix that. If you were a more recent resident we'd have a problem, but you've been here plenty long enough for citizenship. I might get in trouble for this, but I'm making an executive decision. Please place your hand on the book."

Pirrip sets down a large yellowish pamphlet, a printed version of the Moonstone Covenant. Istehar puts her hand on it and immediately pulls it away, wincing. "It's loud!" she complains. "How many people have touched this?" Encouraged by Pirrip, she puts her hand back on the paper cover.

"Repeat after me: I, Istehar Sha'an, vow loyalty to the free city of Moonstone, its laws, and its duly installed governors. So may the ancestors guide me to fulfill my promise."

Istehar repeats the vow nervously, pulls her hand away from the pamphlet, and signs the paper he gives her. "Am I not a woman of the Sha'an anymore?" she asks, upset, as he places the paper on the easel next to the first one.

"The Sha'an are an ancient people, madam. I feel certain such administrative matters have little relevance to your core identity," Pirrip responds, smiling.

"Can we file the paperwork now?" Vasmine asks testily from her place near the door. "It's getting noisier outside. Someone's probably called a columnist."

"Before we can do that, you, Madam Kinora the younger, need to terminate your status as a concubine," Pirrip explains. "Concubines have certain legal privileges; for example, their contracted partners cannot claim any of their income or put any sort of lien on their possessions, nor do they need a divorce to terminate a liaison. However, they cannot marry. If you wed today, your special status will be terminated, and any daughters you bear will not inherit this lineage. They will be ordinary citizens, as will you. Do you understand this?"

"Yes, I do," Vasmine says. Her voice shakes a little. She didn't invite her mother to be here; they all now understand that this is why. Pirrip gives her a paper to sign. Vasmine signs it resolutely and steps back. Onto the easel it goes.

"As some good citizen said, we're holding up the line," Annlynn points out. "Are we finished, sir?"

"You would think so, but no. There is still the matter of Sanctum law. You, Madam Jissakhar, are an Abbatine. These women are not. Technically, your marrying them converts them."

"No," Istehar, Olloise, and Vasmine all say together.

Pirrip shrugs. "Marriages contracted with Abbatine citizens are Abbatine marriages. That is the law. You'd need a dispensation from Abbatine clergy to waive the conversions. You can get one and come back at a later time."

"I have a waiver right here," Annlynn informs them all quietly.

"You do?" Vasmine turns to her in shock. "Impressive."

"Who could possibly have written it?" Olloise asks.

"Abigella Shorn, the recently retired rectoress of the River School, is an ordained deaconess," Annlynn says. She produces a letter folded in an envelope. Pirrip opens it, reads it, nods, and goes to file it.

"The rectoress?" Istehar turns to Annlynn. "She hated us!"

"Maybe not as much as we thought," Annlynn says.

"Clan name?" Pirrip asks, and begins to fill out the marriage form.

"Each to keep their own," says Annlynn. "Any children born of each mother to do the same."

"I could receive a doctorate for this one," Pirrip mutters to himself as he writes.

"Why all this?" Istehar asks Annlynn quietly. "What does the city care if people marry or not?"

"It's Moonstone," replies Annlynn. "Words create worlds."

When Pirrip finishes, he takes all of the filled-out forms and ushers them back into the front room. He hands the forms to the chief clerk, who inserts them into the leather-bound registry. The couple at the counter, who have been rudely interrupted, glare at the quartet. Finally, the clerk asks the four wives to sign the registry, which they eagerly do.

"Congratulations," the chief clerk announces dramatically, as if performing in a play. "Enjoy your wedded bliss!"

They all bow to the chief clerk and to Pirrip, and then they back toward the door. "Perverts," someone mutters as they leave the room, but they are too relieved to care. A columnist has come from a penny press and is scribbling frantically, but the four of them refuse to answer questions.

They hurry out of the building. As they exit between the statues of the saint and the fiend, Vasmine pinches the righteous-looking saint's cheek. Annlynn kicks the fiend. It's an old superstition; Annlynn learned it from her siblings.

When they get to Undersong House, Annlynn lights a fire in the hearth, muttering the names of all their known ancestors, which takes some time. Olloise brings out a wedding feast. Vasmine pours wine for everyone. When they have all drunk, she collects the glasses and hurls them into the fire, an old custom of the Fenge. Laughing, they all cover their faces to avoid shards.

Later, after the meal, Istehar shows the Book of the Tree she has worked on for a year. Its moss-silk cover has roots woven into it for texture; flowers and syssyrup bark and willow leaves are pressed into its pages. Alternately solemn and giggling, they all put their palms to the first page, the way Sha'an folk do. When they take away their hands, which have left no perceptible imprint, a silence settles over the room.

Annlynn puts aside her glass of hard cider. "I think our wedding night should begin," she announces.

"Annlynn's room has the biggest bed," Olloise points out. Vasmine giggles. Istehar shyly covers her face with her hands.

Annlynn flashes a self-deprecating smile as if to say: *Are any of us ready for this?*

CHAPTER 39

The Wives

Library Docks

Initium, 10:00 a.m.

The day after the attack on the Library, the city is quiet. The wives get into Hanael's gondola and go to the Library loading dock, where they have been invited to attend the private, quiet funeral of Sterven Jissakhar.

The crematory of the local Errantine chapel, which is not under orders to deny Lord Jissakhar a funeral, has already done its work. The Jissakhar clan gathers at the edge of the dock to scatter ashes in the bay, exactly where their patriarch would have wanted to be.

Annlynn, Vasmine, Olloise, and Istehar stand at a formal distance, until Farrick comes over with the urn and asks Annlynn to scatter the first ashes. Her siblings all nod eagerly, except for her eldest brother Valenten, who stares resolutely out at the water and will not look at her.

"We need you now," says Annlynn's younger brother Dunekin. "Especially now, Anya." So Annlynn takes the urn, scatters a handful of ash, and hands the urn to her sister Julis, who sobs as she takes her handful. Soon all six children have made their offering to the river, and Annlynn's mother comes to make hers.

The wives hold their collective breath. They know how deeply Annlynn regrets the years she lost with her father, with her whole family. They know how much pain it causes her that her reconciliation with her father was pitifully brief. They know she doesn't want to lose any more precious minutes. And they also know how incandescently angry she's been for so long.

After the last of the ashes is in the river, Annlynn speaks to her mother for the first time in years.

"I saw you at the Sanctum," Annlynn says to her mother awkwardly.

"I saw you too," Annlynn's mother replies, and then embraces her and weeps. Annlynn doesn't say much, but she does return the embrace. Tommas, who is also in attendance, comes forward to invite Madam Jissakhar to meet Istehar, Olloise, and Vasmine. Thalweg—who is acting proprietor of Yan's—offers drinks. Healing will take a while, but at least now there is something to begin from.

Later that day, at the Library, the family joins in as the Librarians all help carry water-damaged books out onto the dock to dry in the sun. Lerreg and the other bookboaters come around the curve of Opal Island in a long procession—they've come to help, and they know all about how to deal with wet books. The Librarians nod to them cordially. Nobody makes any jokes about floating junk.

"Erm…Reverence?" Lerreg edges over to Istehar, who is bravely tolerating a headache from the noise of the Library's tomes. "We took up a collection. Not coin, I mean. We don't have much of that. Books."

"What sort of books?" Istehar asks, blanching at the thought of more voices in her head.

Lerreg waves at a few of his companions with their heavy eyeglasses and thick robes against the river chill. These are some of the members of the Bookboaters' Council, which, ragtag organization though it is, holds considerable sway in Moonstone. They are holding Books of the Tree, Sha'an hymnals, and other books Istehar recognizes as confiscated by customs officials years ago.

"We found these," Lerreg explains. "In the inventory." He waves vaguely at the dozens of bookboats docked haphazardly by the pier. "Maybe you could bring them to their original owners?"

Istehar's tears begin to fall. "I will," she says with emotion. "Of course I will. So much gratitude to you!"

The booksellers nod and doff their caps. Istehar bows and rushes off joyfully to reunite several Sha'an families with their most precious possessions. Not far away, Tommas slips Annlynn a certain controversial moonstone-studded book for safekeeping, since the powers that be have a significant motive to destroy it.

Meanwhile, Vasmine, wearing a sober gown, quietly enters Hanael's gondola and goes off to take tea with the grieving Kalicent Mai (and bring her Othe Azhuin's notebook, just for added clarity). Later, she plans to visit with Giya Lutei. There are negotiations that must occur, and Vasmine intends to oversee them herself. She wants everything to go well.

Olloise goes off as well, on foot, back to Seven Lanterns to tend to her patients at Undersong House. Some of them need beds at hospitals, and some of them she can send home. The Sha'an need a hospital of their own, she thinks.

The day after that, Annlynn makes a decision, and goes to pay a condolence call on her father's mistress in her cottage in Turtle's Clutch. She notices how quiet the streets and waterways are. The new ruler of Moonstone has not yet been announced. The Council is meeting in closed session.

Istehar is at home, writing new Books of the Tree for the silk houses that burned, pressing ashes into the pages. Those silkworkers who are well enough are rebuilding the burned silk houses. The Sha'an are staying, for now. The elders have decided to cast their lot with the city a while longer.

Prince Vilya is nowhere to be found, though his supporters gather in front of the palace to implore that he appear. That evening after dark, Vasmine arrives home and reports that sentinels have arrested not only the heads of Vilya's bands of thugs, but the instigators of the mob that rampaged through the silk houses as well. The warrants against the Librarians and the Sha'an—and against Vasmine—have been canceled. The new archprincess is starting to make her presence felt.

In gratitude for this news, Olloise makes Vasmine a plum-and-chestnut tart with cream, of a quality rarely seen in the city. The four of them finally unroll all the birthday scrolls baked into pastries for Olloise's birthday. One of them says: *May unexpected blessings abound.* Afterward, they go up to the balcony of Olloise's room, at the top of the house, to look as far as they can over the city. Istehar brings the great Book of the Tree from the silvirium, in order to inscribe its pages with the sight.

Also that evening, a note arrives at Undersong House for Istehar.

I refused my father's offer to leave the city, the note says. *I'm still here at the hotel, and the room is only paid up through tomorrow morning.—Moxi*

"Moxi?" Vasmine asks. "Is that her name now? The archdeacon's daughter?"

"I'd better go," Istehar says.

"I'll go with you," says Vasmine.

They put on cloaks and pull up hoods; it is drizzling a chilly spring rain. They have their own boatman now—Hanael is on retainer, since Vasmine will be going back and forth to the palace often, and wants to avoid spying gondoliers. As they pass under the Gilded Bridge, Vasmine points out the Skyboat, with Captain Cattiette Salbera at the helm, coming the other way—in open water, not hiding in the tiny channels of the Moon's Daughters. The people aboard are not drowsing or staring into space; they are laughing and talking.

"The city feels different," Istehar exclaims. Vasmine just smiles.

"I thought we were going to support Prince Giya's claim," Istehar ventures. "That was what we agreed on."

"We did agree on that," says Vasmine. "And we did support his claim. We just did it without causing a civil war. If he had publicly claimed to be the archprince, he wouldn't have won in the end, and we'd have been killed. This way, he gets some of what he wants, Kalicent gets some of what she wants, and the ruling family of Moonstone has us to thank."

"You could have discussed it with us," Istehar points out.

"Moonstone is my area of expertise, dearling. And there wasn't time." Vasmine smiles. "It's not like you discussed with me what you were planning to do with that tree-spirit!" She glances significantly at Istehar's lower half. Istehar nods and pats her belly.

Hanael lets them off at a well-worn dock and they edge around the street urchins playing a particularly vicious game of canal-ball. At the Leaning Inn, they stop at the desk and rent a room. Trip, the innkeeper, smiles and hands them a heavy iron key. On their way up the crazily crooked stairs, they stop at Memmiam's—that is, Moxi's—door, and hang on the doorknob a purse with a good portion of the coin Kalicent gave Istehar. They knock, and then quickly vanish, ascending the steps to their own room. They hear the door open and close behind them.

"Maybe she'll train as a concubine," Vasmine speculates.

"Maybe she'll go to the River School," Istehar counters.

"Or both," they say together, laughing. Vasmine puts the key in the door. The room is a little love nest with robin's-egg window seats and sky-blue couches with pillows, and a bed canopied in golden gauze. Istehar runs to the window seat to see the view of the Short Bridge, high-arched and lit with lanterns. Vasmine joins her there. Istehar takes Vasmine's hand and squeezes it, then leans into her, sighing. Vasmine's perfume surrounds them both, like a fine lace veil.

"Well, elf-child? Why did you never want to do this before?" Vasmine asks Istehar.

"I was scared," Istehar says.

"Of my famous beauty? Or of my prowess as a spy?"

Istehar solemnly shakes her head. "Of your magic."

"Ah," Vasmine nods. "So my magic is terrifying even to a great sorceress like yourself?"

Istehar blushes. "Your magic is beautiful."

"Oh?" Vasmine grins. "Should I have brought my harp?"

Istehar smiles. It is a new kind of smile, for her. "You don't need it."

"Hmmm. Well, if you say so. I wonder what else we don't need." Vasmine reaches, and begins to undo the buttons of Istehar's dress.

"*Ehar*," Istehar says, interlacing her fingers. The interweaving of bodies. Of things and events.

In the morning, the archprince dies. Bells ring throughout the city. Istehar and Vasmine, behind shuttered windows, tucked into the canopied bed, do not hear them for quite some time.

CHAPTER 40

The Wives

Cemetery, Holy Ibis

Two Weeks Later: Initium, 6:00 a.m.

At dawn, in the cemetery on Holy Ibis, the Council gathers for the sounding of the bells. Archprincess Tilgana rings for her dead husband, Jalian Mai, now buried in the royal plot near the Sanctum. Princess Angelissa rings with her young son in memory of Prince Hoel, whose murder has still not been solved. Elibet Jissakhar, surrounded by her six children, rings for Lord Censor Sterven Jissakhar, slain on the Library steps, posthumously reinstated in honor.

There are others to remember: the assistant record-keeper for foreign-language manuscripts, and the others slain in the Library. Moa Nhakbir, whom the new chief interrogatrix, Princess Sajine Chei, has determined was unjustly executed. The citizenry crowds around on balconies, on bridges, on rafts and boats, mourning the dead. The Librarians are gathered, Tommas among them. Bastina stands by the steps of the Sanctum, ringing for her mother.

Prince Vilya Mai is nowhere to be found. The official story is that, driven by a mystic vision, he abdicated and set sail for parts unknown. Rumor has it that his father disinherited him for sacrilege against the Library and he fled in shame. Madam Taurelanthe Kinora, who entertains princesses in her small apartment, has been instrumental in spreading this rumor; indeed, some say she started it. Vilya's followers, however, say that the time was not ripe for the cleansing of Moonstone—the saints have hidden the hero away in a secret place for when he will be needed to save the city.

Archprincess Kalicent is resplendent in a circlet of moonstones. Her betrothed, Prince Giya Lutei, soberly escorts her through the crowds. Vasmine, now a lady-in-waiting, helps to carry Kalicent's train.

Various princes come to pay their respects: Prince Hallan Nethre of Scattered Pearls. Princess Sajine Chei of Sorcerer's Kettle. Prince Egno Zuzierre of Golden Sands. Kalicent is particularly careful to snub Egno Zuzierre. In a few days, the new archprincess will be crowned in the Council Chamber. Breaking with custom, Kalicent has insisted her bridegroom be crowned along with her.

Some distance away, Olloise and Istehar and the rest of the Sha'an scatter petals on the river for their own dead: Tiarath Sha'an. Yilshik, the silk house supervisor, who never regained consciousness, and Lufriki and Eferel, the husband and wife silkworkers who died in one another's arms. Olloise's parents, and Istehar's. They sing the Song of Returning to Earth:

Falling the leaf unfurls.
Knowing, the spine uncurls,
caught in the seasons' whirl,
burning, returning.
Dying, the song is born.
Birthing, the veil is torn.
Husk that is seed, go on
yearning, returning.

Nearby is Tiarath's grave, where Istehar buried the spirits of the forest. Dozya Sha'an sits there, quietly singing to his wife. Istehar hears no voices, but very small sprouts are beginning to arise in the soil of the grave. Istehar silently makes a promise to the tree-spirits, and to the child inside her. She will inscribe a Book of the Tree for the city of Moonstone. She is sure the city needs one, and it is her city, after all. She will begin today.

Istehar's swollen belly hurts her as she bends down to float a few flowers on the water. She wonders what kind of babe is dreaming within her. Nizhar Sha'an watches Istehar, smiling. Since he found out she was pregnant, he's been somewhat more cordial to Istehar's spouses. To him, her belly is not a worry; it is a relief. A new child will be born to bear the tribe's burdens, and he can retire to his garden.

Nearby, Istehar's staff leans against a tree. Istehar remembers the night Prince Vilya broke it. Now she knows why, that night, she saw seeds of light scattered on her dormitory floor. Vilya's offspring will scatter; they will never rule Moonstone. She wonders what the ex-prince will do now. She hears he is in Mor, among his mother's people. She wonders if she will meet him again one day, in the fields that were once the Sha'an forest.

Not far away, a crowd of Zhinj people gathers on the beach to greet the ibises that carry messages to their ancestors. The archprincess has given them license to perform this ritual, once forbidden. She has stopped the executions in the Sandmaze. There has even been some talk of giving the Zhinj the principate of Drake's Hoard now that Prince Giya is otherwise occupied as the archprince-consort. The Council will never ratify this notion, Othe Azhuin says to Olloise. But even the thought is a start.

When relieved of their courtly duties, Vasmine and Annlynn make their way to the river shore and reunite with Olloise and Istehar. Vasmine reaches into the hidden pocket of her emerald satin dress and pulls out the river-drake's eye. It would make a fine wedding present for the archprincess. Or a birth-gift for the baby. But Vasmine holds the eye over the muddy waters.

"When one receives a gift, one must offer a gift in return," she reminds them, half-solemnly, half-mischievously. "I think it's time for an offering, don't you?"

"Let me do it," demands Olloise.

"We all have to do it," says Annlynn.

"Maybe we should wait…" Istehar wavers.

But Vasmine is too quick for them. She hurls the eye into the river. They all laugh at the plunk.

When the others have wandered off, Istehar gets the book she has made out of her bag. Then she sits down on a protruding root, empty book in hand, to take in the light on the water: silver-blue-green, sparkling, and ever-so-slightly shifted by the jewel sinking in its depths.

EPILOGUE
Tia Sha'an
Undersong House
Five years later

The child has bronze ringlets the color of the leaves of the syssyrup tree. Her eyes are pale gray-brown like syssyrup bark. Her belly is round like a burl. Her feet are like roots: immovable, when she wants to be.

Tia loves to swim, to run, to hop from rock to rock, to devour fruit from the little orchard. She likes the cool marble floors of the Library, and the ink-castle on Ma Anya's desk, but she does not care about books, not even books without words. She likes to touch her mama's staff, Ma Loli's potion bottles, Ma Mina's dresses, lily pads, stones from the shore of the river. All these things have voices: soft ones, shrill ones, smooth ones. They don't say words to her, or even pictures—they are like wordless songs, making her feel happy or sad or excited or scared. She begs Uncle Dozya, who guards Undersong House and lives with Aunt Bastina, to take her to the moss-silk workshops a few streets away, where she plays with the soft furry silk. It has the best voice of all, like a furry harp.

She knows about harps. Sometimes Ma Mina takes her to visit Nonna, who lives in an apartment stuffed with pillows and porcelain. Nonna is teaching Tia to play the harp, even though Tia's little fingers tangle like twigs when she tries. Nonna is a little strict. She tells Tia stories of palaces and sanctums, and whispers that Tia comes from a long line of keepers of the peace. Tia doesn't like that much. She doesn't want to keep the peace. She likes to fight.

And very soon, she will have someone to fight with, because there is going to be another baby. Ma Anya is pregnant. No one will explain to Tia exactly how this happened, but it has something to do with Uncle Tommas who visits sometimes. Ma Anya says there have to be more people to protect the books. Ma Anya has a big family and often takes Tia to visit the cluster of houses near the bathhouse, where the relatives live. The relatives all wear black and are a little scary, but there are many cousins who let her run through the bathhouse and splash in the pools.

Once in a while, the mothers put her in a long dress, and Hanael poles them all to a place where there are lovely little buildings standing in the river, all linked by bridges, with tiny lanterns hanging all around. There is an archprincess there, a very pretty one, though she fights with her husband—Tia has seen it happen. The archprincess has bronze skin and jet-black hair braided with moonstones. The other princes and princesses are all scared of her.

Which is why they do not complain when the archprincess takes Tia to the round room with the thrones, and shows her the purple book studded with moonstones that is the Covenant for the city. Then the princess lifts up that book and shows Tia what is under it: the Book of the Tree that her mama made for the city of Moonstone. It has a blue-green silk cover sprinkled with bronzed leaves from thirteen kinds of trees. When Tia asks if the book is magic, the archprincess smiles and asks: "What do you think?"

Magic used to be against the law, but it isn't anymore, if one has a license. People are even pretending to have magic who don't have it at all, Mama says. Ma Anya says the Magistery is making a fortune selling magic licenses. Tia isn't sure what that means, but she wants a magic license. It seems like it would be a wonderful thing to have, and might give her an edge over the new baby.

There is a grove of trees on the island of Holy Ibis that belongs to the Sha'an. It has grown far more than it should, Ma Loli says. It has shady hideaways, and roots that climb over one another. Another Tia, a friend of Mama's, is buried there. When Tia goes to the grove, she hears the song of the trees. This song does have words, or at least it has one word.

Upriver.

She doesn't know where that is, but it pulls her like the current.

APPENDICES

THE WAR OF THE LIBRARIES AND THE FOUNDING OF MOONSTONE

Four hundred and fifty years ago, the empires of Uluria and Taradia battled one another. During the reign of Queen Genjet, Taradian infiltrators burned the Temple of Scrolls, the magical Library of Uluria located in its capital city of Jirin, in order to take revenge for the assassination of the High Servitor of Taradia. Uluria reciprocated by burning the sacred Library of the city of Taradium. Taradium shuttled its books to Sedessa, which resulted in the burning of the Sedessan library, and a world war ensued in which many seats of knowledge were destroyed.

As a result of this terrible loss of knowledge, the Ulurian and Taradian empires broke up. The resulting thirteen nations agreed to sign the Treaty of Wisdom and to find a neutral city to house a single Great Library. The treaty nations founded a city with thirteen districts in the north of the continent of Copalan, in an area that was home to the Zhinj tribes. Thus, Moonstone was born.

About thirty years after its founding, the thirteen nations fell to fighting again, and directed their districts to sabotage one another. The rulers of Moonstone rejected their former nations, and appointed the governors of each district as hereditary princes. With little violence, Moonstone declared itself as an independent city.

THE DISTRICTS OF MOONSTONE AND THEIR QUALITIES

Golden Sands was founded by the land of Sedessa and is ruled by the clan of Zuzierre. It is a relaxation spot for tourists because of its hotels and beaches. It is known for the Sandmaze, an ancient Zhinj holy site. Sundial House is the Zuzierre clan palace, currently inhabited by Egno Zuzierre, his sister Talva, and their parents. The district produces sandstone, glass, ceramics, ores, and metal oxides; farmers grow fruit, nuts, wheat, and oatgrass. Bakeries in Golden Sands supply the city and outgoing ships.

Holy Ibis was founded by the land of Taradia, and was the first island settled by the consortium of thirteen nations when they arrived. Ruled by the conservative clan of Quareen, the district is famous for the Sanctum of the Holy Ibis, and is also the site of most of the graveyards in Moonstone. Its main industries are pottery, dairy, metalwork, carpentry, and clothing. The people here are known as especially pious and a little arrogant because they live on the holy isle, and there are many ancillaries here. The beaches here are sacred to the Zhinj people because of the gatherings of ibises that take place here.

Hundred Quays was founded by the island of Belakkos. Merchant ships dock at the massive docks. Fish, meat, and fruit are dried here and sold to sailors, and paper and wood are local industries, as is banking and currency exchange.

Businesses based here build large voyaging ships and the city's fleet of paddlewheel boats. The prince of Hundred Quays, Didias Xilphis, is a shipping magnate who speaks many languages and suffers from seizures, and lives with his wife Ning in a massive cliffside dwelling called the Balcony (his concubines live elsewhere).

Juniper Island, founded by the secretive magic-loving nation of Tamirlia, is known for its bookmarkets and is a printing, bookselling, and bookmaking center of Moonstone. The princely family of Juniper Island are the Kest (who took over from the Mingre two hundred years ago) and the family seat is called Disappearing House because mists from the river often shroud it. The Kest are known for their intellectual prowess, and the current prince, Judovic, who specializes in water science, is one of twins—his brother Pendric is deaf and has embarked on the standardization of Moonstone's sign language. Juniper Island also has a liquor district and produces moonwater and other spirits of the region. People say that a visit to Juniper Island can either expand your knowledge or cause you to forget it completely.

Moon's Daughters was founded by the people of Gengrassia, and also contains many communities of the Zhinj. The capital of the area is the island-town of Bilha'a and the ruling family of Berduin is a matrilineal clan in the Gengrassian tradition; Sylte Berduin is the reigning princess and has more spouses than she lets on. The people often grow plants in water—they cultivate rice, rice-paper trees, riverweed, and mulberry shrubs, and wax and honey from beekeeping. The district is known for having more than the usual dollop of sorcery.

Opal Island is Moonstone's seat of government—the site of the Library, the Palace of Innumerable Pearls, and the Magistery. Founded by Uluria, it is ruled by the Mai clan, and inundated by a constant flow of merchants, tourists, and diplomats. There are districts for glassblowing, pearls, moonstones, carpentry, fashion, moneylending, produce, fowl, fish, flowers, and silk. The Sand Market, the largest market in the city, can be found here. The neighborhoods of Opal Island are: Festival Square, Palace Row, Cousinsgate, Little Uluria, Foresquare, Sand Market, and Bridgemarket.

The Perfumery was founded by the nation of Chaea and is ruled over by the farmer-warrior clan of Girgorra, who live in Dunekin House. This peninsula district has the most arable land on Moonstone and produces vegetables, berries, flowers, fruit, spices, oils, medicines, and herbs for the city. The prince of this district, Samwin Girgorra, is aged and has three daughters; he's planning to pass the district to a grandson though his daughters may have something to say about it. There is a healing school here as well as a school for midwifery. There is a significant Zhinj population living here, and a number of Sha'an have moved here too due to their expertise with orchards and gardens.

Scattered Pearls is a sub-archipelago of many islands, the largest of which is called Diver's Strand. This area was settled by the Fenge, and the ruling family are the Nethre. Their palace is City-of-Bridges, built by Princess Violette Nethre a few generations after the Founding, and famous for its graceful architecture. In this district is the Pearls of Wisdom University, and also the House of Blossoms that trains concubines. This is also a fashion district, and there is a long tradition here of pearl-diving; whole lineages have devoted themselves to this practice.

Seven Lanterns is a large island settled by the Yanuilt people, who brought their expertise with farming, shepherding, and orchard management. The island is ruled by the clan of Dhagura, from their seat known as the Lanternhouse. There are micro-orchards here, and the Sha'an people have settled here, bringing with them the industry of moss-silk (which is cultivated among the orchards). The central canal is known as the Lanterners' Canal. The two islands known as the Lanternelles, where sea-sheep are raised, are also considered part of this district.

Sorcerer's Kettle is ruled by the clever and unorthodox clan of Chei and Sorcerer's Kettle was founded by revolutionaries from Lower Phantos. The district palace, Phantosia House, was named after the capital city of Lower Phantos. Currently, the district is the major entertainment district of Moonstone, and contains theaters, taverns, puppet-theaters, and the houses of public concubines (which constitute a legal red light district). There is also an industry of illegal substances including dreamcloves (which cause visions) and spikerose (which suppresses magic). Journalists, lacemakers, leatherworkers, healers, and shoemakers work here, and the pipe-laying factory makes pipe for the city's water system.

String of Coins is a sub-archipelago settled by the Lutei clan of Nordynor. The Lutei rule this island from their seat known as Madder House. The island's main industries are weaving and dyeing, and the land and sea produce rare plants that create expensive dyes. The industry of raising messenger doves is also centered here. The largest island is known as Drake's Hoard; the others are Wyrm's Vestry, Giant's Purse, Hermit's Tryst, Trollswimple, Hueshaven, and Summercrown. There are famous baths here, a significant tourist attraction.

Turtle's Clutch, a collection of four islands and several micro-islands, was founded by people from Upper Phantos, and is known for its conservative attitudes. There is a fortress here called the Shell where sentinels are trained and berthed. The main industries here are fishing, boatmaking, herding, pearl diving, shepherding, and the harvesting of sea plants. Many sentinels' and sailors' families live here. The ruling family is called Phorya; the current prince of the district is ill and it is widely rumored that his wife is in charge. The four large islands are Bellbillow, Sesserina, Kestrelery, and Saintsfish.

Vexriver is the farthest upriver of all the districts. It is composed of three islands: Vexriver, Vexmere, and Little Vex. The district was originally settled by Mor, and has a high population of Zhinj. The district is ruled by Prince Leo Lent, and the clan seat on Little Vex is called Cumulonimbus House. The tall pillar-like rock formations of Vexriver are shot through with tunnels and chambers, and these chambers and tunnels constitute a functioning fortress that guards the city from any attack from upstream. The island of Vexmere houses the River School which trains public professionals, including warriors, diplomats, scholars, scientists, engineers, healers, and magistrates. Little Vex is a logging, fishing, agricultural, and merchanting community that provides Moonstone with peat and wood via work in the Narrow Forests and the marshes upstream. The main urban area of Little Vex is called Vexenden and contains the Zaggery, a famous house of public concubines.

ETHNICITY IN MOONSTONE

Most of the people in Moonstone come from one or more of the thirteen founding nations (each of which is associated with a princely line and a district of the city). Of course, after four hundred years there is significant ethnic mixing. Some of the city's residents are Zhinj—of the original people of the area—and some are Sha'an—from the forests north of Moonstone. A small portion of the population come from lands to the south or north of the thirteen nations.

Belakkos (*Hundred Quays*) is an island nation not far from Moonstone, known for silverwork, metalwork, woodcarving, and artistry in general. They are also known for their seagoing merchants—and pirates. Belakkos is a nominally Abbatine nation but has a strong tradition of Ourea, land religion, which includes nixies, fairies, and other land spirits. Each town is governed by a council of selectmen (also known as selectfolk) and the island is ruled by a hereditary prince.

Chaea (*The Perfumery*) is on the eastern side of the continent of Broceland. The nation is mainly flat steppe and grows much of the grain for the region, and also herds cattle. It has been conquered multiple times by Taradia to the north and by Nordynor to the south. It is a strictly Abbatine nation governed by a system of clans and war chiefs, and is ruled by a steward appointed by the war chiefs. The Jissakhar clan of warrior librarians was originally Chaean; they trained in Taradium to protect the library of Taradia, then the one in Moonstone.

The Fenge (*Scattered Pearls*) is a peninsula on the southwest of the continent of Seile. The Fenge once worshipped a goddess and were ruled by kings and *firwyverin* or priestesses of diplomacy and relationship. Today they are governed by a suzerain elected by a senate, and mostly Errantines (with some Abbatines and some followers of the old nameless religion, known in Moonstone as the "concubines' religion"). They are known for their trade, their fishing industry, their art, theater, and music.

Gengrassia (*Moon's Daughters*) is an island to the west of Taradia and Yanuilt. Once a protectorate of Taradia, Gengrassia is fiercely independent and uses diplomacy as well as a strong tradition of martial arts to remain free of conquerors. Gengrassia is a matriarchal tribal society known for its elaborate manners and organized similarly to the Zhinj, and in Moonstone the two peoples have a strong bond. The people were converted to Abbatine religion during the protectorate period but maintain their own spiritual tradition known as Bo.

Lower Phantos (*Sorcerer's Kettle*) is located in the south of the continent of Seile. It was once governed by noble landowners, and was part of the single nation of Phantos. There was a revolution, and the two realms of Phantos split into Lower and Upper Phantos. Now Lower Phantos is governed by an elected body. Lower Phantos is known for its mines and industry and is home to Phantosia, the largest city in the world. The Errantine religion originated in Lower Phantos, and most of its people are Errantines.

Mor (*Vexriver*) is to the south of Moonstone and on the same island continent of Copalan. An Abbatine nation, it was settled centuries ago by Taradians. It is a low-lying country of swamps and flooding is a problem. Mor provides wood and fuel (peat) to the region. Mor is ruled by Griseus of Mor, a hereditary lord from a family that traces its line back to coastal pirates. Mor has always coveted the Sha'an Forest as potential farmland and recently chased out the Sha'an tribes in order to burn parts of the forest and use them for crops and cattle.

Nordynor (*String of Coins*), also known as Far Nordynor, is an island continent to the east of Moonstone. The island is forested and has a strong woodcarving tradition, and is also known for its tradition of hot springs and public baths. The people are Abbatines and Errantines but there is little civil conflict over this. Nordynor has five provinces that are virtually independent of one another, and elects representatives to a national council that has a precentor. Nordynori particularly dislike the Mor, after generations of Morish piracy.

Sedessa (*Golden Sands*) is an island of gentle beaches right between Uluria and Taradia. It has been conquered by both at different times and eventually gained its independence. Sedessa is expert at diplomacy and brokered the Treaty of Wisdom after the War of the Libraries. It is said to have been settled centuries ago by unknown lands to the north and holds unique scholarly and magical traditions; it is ruled by a king or queen. The ruling family in Sedessa has close ties with the ruling family in Golden Sands; this is not usual among the other nations.

Tamirlia (*Juniper Island*) is a mountainous island ruled by a circle of wizard lords, to the west of Upper and Lower Phantos. The island exports dreamcloves and spikerose, as well as books. Sorcery is legal and common here and people with magical powers sometimes move here for safety. A number of traveling circus troupes come from Tamirlia and are said to be spies for the secretive island. Tamirlia is technically politically neutral but has strong ties with Uluria—sorcerers of the two lands correspond often.

Taradia (*Holy Ibis*) is a large nation, spanning the whole northeastern continent of Taradia. This nation founded the Abbatine religion and once held an empire that included Chaea, Yanuilt, Sedessa, Gengrassia, and Mor. Taradia began the War of the Libraries and was one of the first parties to the Treaty to Preserve Wisdom. Eventually, the empire collapsed due to rioting after a volcanic eruption. Today, Taradia is still an Abbatine theocracy and persecutes magic-users. It is ruled by the High Servitor and his wife the High Servitrix. Its central river is known as the Esla.

Upper Phantos (*Turtle's Clutch*) is the central nation on the northwestern continent of Seile. It and Lower Phantos were once one nation, but they split after a revolution. Upper Phantos is provincial and conservative and ruled by wealthy landowners, most of whom are Abbatines and some of whom are Errantines. Its land is fertile and it grows much produce. Upper Phantos has kept its independence from Uluria by allying with Taradia.

Uluria (*Opal Island*), part desert and part steppe, is the northernmost nation of the continent of Seile. Jirin is its main city. It is an Abbatine country but its Abbatinism, often known as Ulurian Abbatinism, focuses less on the saints and more on the first human ancestors (called initiator and initiatrix). Uluria is famous for sorcerers, scholars, and inventors. Uluria was once an empire and is today a network of alliances, spanning Phantos, Fenge, Tamirlia, and Sedessa.

Yanuilt (*Seven Lanterns*) is a thickly forested kingdom with beautiful lakes, in the west of the continent of Broceland. Yanuilt was conquered by Taradia but was always difficult to control because of the wild nature of the forest, and is now independent. The Taradians converted Yanuilt to the Abbatine religion but the Yanuilt still strongly believe in forest spirits.

The Zhinj are the Indigenous people of the Copalanj, or moonstones—the islands in the river of Moonstone. They originally made agreements with the settlers who arrived to claim Moonstone as the site of their Great Library, but those agreements were broken. This event is known by Zhinj as the Betrayal. The Zhinj are a matrilineal tribe. Today, many of them live on Little Vex, in the Perfumery, or in the Moon's Daughters. The Sandmaze, now in the district of Golden Sands, is the most sacred site of the Zhinj.

The Sha'an are a forest people native to the Sha'an forests north of Moonstone. They worship the Great Tree, and are governed by their religious leaders, who are titled "illuminatrix." They have the secret of spinning silk from moss-silk plants. Some of the Sha'an can speak to trees. Generations ago, some Sha'an left the forests and went to Moonstone—their religion became known as the "Silvilline" religion. When Mor invaded the Sha'an forest, many of the remaining Sha'an people fled to Moonstone, where most of them live in the district of Seven Lanterns.

RELIGION IN MOONSTONE

The Abbatine religion was founded by the empire Taradia, which evangelized aggressively during its time as an empire. The Abbatine religion honors the virtuous ancestors (saints) and understands them as spiritual beings guiding the lives of the living. There is a hierarchical clergy of archdeacons, high deacons, deacons, and deaconesses, as well as ancillas and ancillans, who are monk-like semi-clergy devoted to prayer. Moonstone is part of the Abbatine Communion.

The primary houses of worship in Moonstone are the Sanctum of Holy Ibis, the Chapel of the Initiatrix in Festival Square on Opal Island, the Chapel of the Ancestors in Saintsfish, the Shrine of

Bells on Drake's Hoard, the Chapel of the First Spark on Seven Lanterns, and the Chapel of the Descendants in Hundred Quays. There are other chapels throughout the city. There are ancillaries (monasteries) in the cliffs above Turtle's Clutch and Hundred Quays and in other places as well.

Taradian and **Ulurian** are two sects of Abbatinism. The majority of Moonstone's citizens are Taradian Abbatine; however, the Chapel of the Initiatrix is an Ulurian chapel and also houses an Ulurian ancillary. In Ulurian practice, the original creator/ancestor, the Initiatrix, is revered as Mother of Saints.

The Errantine religion is also a major force in Moonstone. The Errantine religion was originally a heresy from the Abbatine religion and began in Lower Phantos. The Errantines believe in the Pattern, a cosmic ordering of energy that gives rise to life, determines individual fates, and will determine the end of history.

The Silvilline religion arose in the Sha'an forest and is practiced by Sha'an folk and descendants of that region, and some converts. The core of Silvilline religion is belief in the Tree of Life, an energy that unites all beings. Silvillines believe all things are alive, including the stones and the earth, and have a particular reverence for trees as their allies. Their clergy are called illuminatrix (or, sometimes illuminator, though their clergy are mostly female) and are channels for the messages of trees and the memories of the tribe.

The Zhinj practice their Indigenous religion, which honors their ancestors and the more-than-human world, and have a strong connection to water as a sacred substance. They honor the Moonstone River as a living entity. Some other Moonstone folk, particularly on the islands of the Moon's Daughters, have chosen to practice the Zhinj tradition.

The "concubines' religion" is an ancient tradition practiced by descendants of the *firwyverin* of the Fenge. This tradition worships an ancient nameless goddess and addresses the elemental powers through ritual. This religion is also sometimes practiced by others, particularly those from Tamirlia and the Fenge.

Bo is a meditative tradition from Gengrassia.

Ourea is an earth-based tradition from Belakkos.

TIME IN MOONSTONE

Moonstone has alternating six-day and seven-day weeks. The names of the six "common days" of the week are:

Progeniday
Deceday
Anteceday
Ancilliday
Daemoniday
Sanctiday

The seventh day, which occurs only every two weeks, is called Initium. In a second week, the days of the week look like this:

Progeniday
Deceday
Anteceday
Ancilliday
Daemoniday
Sanctiday
Initium

The origins of these days is in Abbatine religion: Progeniday honors those who will be born, Deceday honors the dying and recent dead, Anteceday honors the ancestors as a whole, Ancilliday honors the angels, Daemoniday is a day for fighting demons, and is treated as a day off for many because it is bad luck. Sanctiday is a day honoring the saints and the shrine and is a day of worship. Some Abbatines go to worship on both Daemoniday and Sanctiday. Initium, which occurs only once every two weeks, is a market day and sometimes a day for public festivals and gatherings. City offices are open four days a week, from Progeniday to Ancilliday, on six-day weeks—and five days a week, including Initium, on seven-day weeks.

Initium is a sacred day for the Errantines, who are often agitating not to have to work on that day. Silvillines hold their sacred gatherings on the new moon and the full moon.

There are twelve months in the year, each having thirty days. Originally these months had Abbatine names, but about three hundred years ago, the city culture (as well as surrounding nations) became enamored of the twelve fairies of time in Yanuilt myth, and so the current calendar uses the names of the fairies as the month names.

Spring
Mistmantle
Greengirdle
Brideblossom
Summer
Lightlinger
Ripenrind
Sickleswipe
Autumn
Windwend
Leafleap
Darkdelve
Winter
Winterwife
Frostflower
Branchblood

Angelsfeast (a single-day month that is considered New Year's Day)

Moonstone counts its years in reference to the founding of the city, though it also uses the calendar of Taradia, which dates itself to the first saint, several thousand years ago.

LANGUAGE IN MOONSTONE

The language spoken in the city is a version of Taradian that contains Ulurian and Zhinj words and phrases, as well as a smattering of Phantosi, Sha'an dialect, and much more. The complex legal system in the city, reminiscent of the Ulurian empire, retains concepts from a variety of cultures. Most Moonstone folk speak more than one language, due to the high volume of foreign merchants and tourists in the city. The people of Mor speak the same language as the people of Moonstone. The Sha'an and Zhinj peoples speak their own tribal languages as well as the common language.

INSTITUTIONS OF LEARNING IN MOONSTONE

There are four systems of public schools for children in Moonstone, run by the Abbatine sanctum, by the Errantines, by the Sha'an, and by the Zhinj. There is also an international school for foreign children. General standards of education are set by the Council.

There are also institutions of higher learning:

The River School, on the island of Vexmere, has four sub-schools and trains warriors (Sword), scholars and Librarians (Book), public health workers such as physicians and scientists (Candle), and bankers and merchants (Coin). Those who will be in government or public service are expected to attend here.

The Western School, in Saintsfish (Kestrelery, Turtle's Clutch) is a famous school for captains, navigators, seafarers, etc. and also trains balloon pilots. It is not far from the Ancillary of the Blessed Ancestors.

The Eastern School, an institute for midwives, nurses, and physicians, is found within the Ancillary of the Blessed Descendants, nestled in the cliffs above Hundred Quays.

The Colleges for the Arts and Masteries, in the district of Scattered Pearls, focus on arts, literature, architecture, etc., and have many small sub-schools on different islands. There is also a school on Scattered Pearls that trains concubines, known as the House of Blossoms.

The School of Landcraft, in the district of the Perfumery, teaches farming and other skills related to agriculture and animal husbandry.

The Glassmakers' School and the **Carpenters' School** are among a number of guild schools on Opal Island.

The Abecedary School, also on Opal Island, is a school for languages.

An archaeological school is located in the district of Golden Sands, near the Sandmaze.

The Sanctum of Holy Ibis trains Abbatine theologians and clerics.

The Freethinkers' School in Sorcerer's

Kettle trains Errantine philosophers and clergy.

While there is currently no official magical school in Moonstone, there are a number of people, particularly in the Moon's Daughters, who teach sorcery privately.

TRAVEL IN MOONSTONE

Those in Moonstone who can afford it have their own boats, or travel by hailing a barge, rowboat, or gondola. There are also large city-run ferryboats that travel on a schedule from one island to another.

There are four north-south ferry lines:

The western Amethyst Line goes from Saintsfish in Turtle's Clutch to Niniane's Spear in the west of Scattered Pearls, then stops at Madder Cove on Drake's Hoard in the String of Coins district, then West Lanternelle (part of Seven Lanterns district), then at Forefinger Point (the tip of the Perfumery) and finally at Vexenden in Little Vex.

The middle Opal Line goes from Merchants' Square in Turtle's Clutch to Riverthrone in Scattered Pearls, to Palace Cove and Long Bridge Dock (both on Opal Island), then to the Lanterners' Canal on Seven Lanterns, to the isle of Generosity in the Moon's Daughters, then to Vexriver Fortress.

The eastern Tourmaline Line begins at Hundred Keys (a fortress on the east side of the river, facing the ocean), stops at the Main Dock at Hundred Quays, then at Lid End on the Lid (part of the district of Sorcerer's Kettle), then at New Phantos in Sorcerer's Kettle proper, then at the Library Docks, then at the bookmarket on Juniper Island, then at the Beak and the Sanctum (both on Holy Ibis), then at Bilha'a in the Moon's Daughters, at Vexmere, and then at Vexriver Fortress.

Garnet Line, on the far west, connects points in Golden Sands and the Perfumery, beginning at Idyll's Gate and ending at Pulpit Rock.

Crossriver ferries run:

From Main Dock in Hundred Quays to Merchant's Square and Saintsfish (both in Turtle's Clutch) to Watchers' Heights in the Narrow Forest.

From Last Quay in Hundred Quays to West End in Sorcerer's Kettle to Palace Cove on Opal Island, to Drakestooth Bridge in String of Coins to Sandstone Cove in Golden Sands.

From the bookmarket in Juniper Island to the Sand Market on Opal Island to Drakesmouth on Drake's Hoard to the Sandmaze in Golden Sands.

From the Sanctum on Holy Ibis to the Lanternhouse Pier on Seven Lanterns to East Lanternelle to Nubae in the Perfumery.

From the River School at Vexmere to the Vexriver Fortress to Vexenden in Little Vex to Upriver Port in the Perfumery.

There is also some air travel. The Council military/police force, known as the sentinels, also maintains a hot-air balloon outpost at Vexriver Fortress, and can send out balloons for reconnaissance. They are not, mostly, used for civilian travel.

BRIDGES IN MOONSTONE

Some of the major bridges include:

The Long Bridge between Opal Island and Seven Lanterns

The Short Bridge between Opal Island and Sorcerer's Kettle

The Gilded Bridge between Opal Island and Drake's Hoard

Kettlehandle Bridge between Sorcerer's Kettle and the Lid

The Lanternelles Bridge between West Lanternelle and East Lanternelle

The Stony Bridge between Vexriver and Little Vex

Every year at the Gilded Bridge in late spring, the archprince or archprincess conducts a blessing of the waters. This blessing ceremony is said to restore the vitality of the river and renew the life-force of the city and its people.

There are many minor bridges connecting smaller islands and crossing canals, in areas like Scattered Pearls and the Moon's Daughters. Bridges are generally built high enough for gondolas to pass under.

PRONUNCIATION OF SOME IMPORTANT NAMES

Annlynn *an' lin* *a* as in and, *y* as in lynx

Bastina *bah-stee'-nah* *a* as in ark, *i* pronounced like *ee* as in queen, *a* as in ark

Dhagura *da'-goo-ra* *a* as in ark, *u* pronounced like *oo* as in cool, *a* as in ark

Griseus *grih-say'-us* *i* as in if, *e* pronounced like *ay* as in bay, *u* as in up

Hanael *hah'-nah-el* *a* as in ark, *a* as in ark, *e* as in bell

Hoel *Ho'-el* *o* as in mole, *e* as in bell

Istehar *is'-teh-har* *i* as in is, *e* as in bell, *a* as in ark

Jalian *jahl'-ee-an* *a* as in ark, *i* pronounced like *ee* as in queen, *a* as in ark

Jissakhar *jih'-sa-khar* *i* as in if, both *a*'s as in ark, *kh* like *ch* as in the German achtung or the Hebrew Chanukah

Joeve *jo-ehv'* *o* as in bone, *e* as in bell

Kalicent *kahl'-i-sent* *a* as in ark, *i* as in is, *e* as in bell

Kinora *kee'-nohr-ah* *i* sounded like *ee* as in queen, *o* as in or, *a* as in ark

Lutei *loo'-tay* *u* as in mule, *ei* like *ay* as in clay

Mai *my* *ai* like *y* as in sky

Mazall *mah-zahl'* both *a*'s as in ark, with the accent on the second syllable

Nizhar *neez'-hahr* *i* sounded like *ee* as in queen, *a* as in ark

Olloise *ol'-oh-eez* first *o* as in Oscar, second *o* as in roll, *i* sounded like *ee* as in queen, final *e* is silent

Othe *oath'* *o* as in mole, *e* is silent

Sha'an *shah'-ahn* both *a*'s as in ark, with the accent on the first syllable

Taurelanthe *tor-eh-lan'-thee* *au* like Maud, *e* like bell, *a* like an, *e* sounded like *ee* as in queen

Tommas *tohm'-as* *o* as in dot, *a* as in ark

Vasmine *vahz-meen'* *a* as in ark, *i* sounded like *ee* as in queen, final *e* is silent

Vilya *vihl'-ya* *i* as in is, *a* as in ark

ACKNOWLEDGMENTS

I wish to thank Rabbi Dr. Julia Watts Belser for her comments on the original manuscript and for her wise publishing advice, Kohenet Liviah Wessely for her edits of the manuscript and her enthusiastic approval of the story, and Joy Rosenberg for being the first person to read this novel and tell me it was ready for the reading public. I am also grateful to Mai Bar for publication research and to Kohenet Ketzirah Lesser for her encouragement and advice, and to Penina Eilberg-Schwartz for being the first to edit the Moonstone narrative.

The deepest thank you to Ayin Press: Eden Pearlstein, Penina Eilberg-Schwartz, Tom Haviv, Joanna Steinhardt, Carly Lewis, Cem Eskinazi, and the entire staff, for believing in this vision and for all their work to make this project happen in the best way possible. Many thanks to Jonathan Oliver for his thoughtful edits. Profoundest appreciation to Federico Parolo for the amazing cover artwork, and to Melina Sonia Monteagudo for the map of Moonstone—both of which brought the book to life. So much gratitude goes to Arthur Fried for his unfailing support of this book. Thank you to Manda Scott for her wise comments and interest in this manuscript, and to Jonathan Vatner and Ellen Frankel for their appreciative words. And deep thanks to Dr. Rabbi Jay Michaelson for being a co-traveler on parallel literary journeys.

Most of all, many thanks to my daughter Raya Leela Jedwab-Hammer for her love, for her unfailing support of this novel, and for her plot, character, and fashion advice. And much gratitude goes to my wife Shoshana Jedwab for all of her love and partnership and for her thoughts on this manuscript when I truly needed them. Moonstone has been so blessed by you both.

I'm so grateful to all the fantasy authors who have inspired me in my work and given me much wonder and joy as a reader. It has been a great dream of my life to practice the craft of writing fantasy. Thank you to the readers who will join me in the world of Moonstone!

Jill Hammer is a celebrated author, scholar, rabbi, ritualist, poet, and dreamworker. *The Moonstone Covenant* is her first published work of fantasy fiction, but she has been reading and writing fantasy since she was young. Like some of her characters, she has a deep love of books, trees, enchanted castles, and mysterious alleyways. She is the author of eight other books, including works of fiction, poetry, and feminist theological scholarship. She lives with her family in Manhattan, where she spends a great deal of time in Central Park.

Ayin Press is an artist-run publishing platform and production studio rooted in Jewish culture and emanating outward.

Both online and in print, we seek to celebrate artists and thinkers at the margins and explore the growing edges of collective consciousness through a diverse range of mediums and genres.

Ayin was founded on a deep belief in the power of culture and creativity to heal, transform, and uplift the world we share and build together. We are committed to amplifying a polyphony of voices from within and beyond the Jewish world.

For more information about our current or upcoming projects and titles, reach out to us at *info@ayinpress.org*.

To make a tax-deductible contribution to our work, visit our website at *www.ayinpress.org/donate*.